I0653498

THE ARIZONA STARSEED

PHOENIX BARR

All rights reserved under International and Pan-American Copyright Conventions.

Published/Manufactured in the United States of America

Cover design by John Cameron

Edited by Natalie June Reilly

No part of this publication may be reproduced or transmitted in any form or by any means, electronic or mechanical, including photocopy, recording or any information storage and retrieval system, without express written permission of author(s).

Copyright © 2021 Phoenix Barr
All rights reserved.
ISBN: 978-0-578-98167-3

This book is dedicated to Bryson, Dylan, Heaven, Cass, Aden and Jardin.
Everything I accomplish in my life is with you in mind—first.
Thank you God, Universe and all that I can't see, but know are there to
help get me through my life and keep me on track.
I am grateful.
Thank you, Jeff Hayes, for helping me find a wonderful editor named
Natalie. She brought everything to life with every page.
And to my late grandmother, Mary Francis Daily,
when no one else wanted me or believed in me, you truly cared, and you
always loved my writing. You were the only real mother I experienced in
my life, and I thank you for being there when you were.
Rest in Peace, Grandma. I love you.

Lastly, I dedicate this book to domestic violence survivors everywhere.

"He made the bear, Orion, and the Pleiades,
and the constellations of the southern zodiac."
—*Job 9:9*

CHAPTER ONE
Apache Junction, Arizona

The alarm went off right at 7 a.m. Twenty-nine-year-old River Anderson jumped out of bed wearing her favorite sporty, white Vegan-logo tank top with dainty, nude, barely-there panties. Bouncy, spiral curls, cut perfectly about her neck, flowed with her energy, enhancing her naturally-tan facial features. Throwing on a pair of Nike sport leggings, she hurried into the bathroom. This was her new Sunday morning regime. River was Type A personality when it came to her health and fitness, especially after becoming a vegan two years earlier. Something inside of her screamed for change, and she eventually manifested habits that enabled her to do just that.

Every Sunday morning started off with a ten-mile run from her mountainside home to the local recreational center. Once inside, she went straight into a morning yoga class. From there, she did a little weight training, mostly legs, before a visit to the local health food store where she would pick up a smoothie. And then it was the long run home, in the direction of the Superstition Mountains. Later in the day, River would do some gardening or find some familiar tasks to keep her busy around her small stucco, brick cottage-style home.

That morning was different. Upon reaching the recreational center, River was disheartened to find that her usual yoga class had been canceled. That upset sent her thoughts into a wild frenzy, as she bolted back down the highway on foot toward home. She kept thinking about her ex-boyfriend, Coty, who made her life miserable. He almost killed her a few years earlier—fracturing a few bones and bruising her spleen. After that horrible incident, she took her registered nursing license and moved as far away from Ohio as she could get. Struggling with anxiety, she would often overcompensate by filling up her days off with exercise, sewing her own clothes and whatever newly-obsessive task required her attention around the house. Most people throw themselves into their career, but not River. Nursing was not a relaxing occupation. So, she worked the necessary hours at the therapy center each week and left it at that.

As she reached home, River stopped in her beautiful front yard to sit between an enormous saguaro cactus and a dilapidated mesquite tree to stretch her short, petite legs. She didn't feel much like hanging at home, so she jumped into her 2013 gray Jeep Wrangler and headed back into town. *I should be more social; put myself out there a little more*, she thought. She wasn't necessarily ready to date, but rather get out just enough to feel a little less like an introvert.

Stopping off at an outdoor farmers market, River browsed organic vegetables, while listening to a local folk band jam nearby. As dusk settled in, she decided it was time to get home. Throwing her purchases in the front passenger seat, River put the key in the ignition and tried turning the engine. The Jeep wouldn't start.

"Shit! Not again," she exclaimed.

It was getting dark. She never ran in the dark, too many hit and runs this side of Arizona. However, it was looking like her only option. Calling her best friend, Amy, was out of the question since she was at her cousin's wedding.

"Screw it," she whispered under her breath, shoving her produce into a backpack. "I'm running home."

At the entrance to the long and winding uphill road, she stopped. There was at least another fifteen minutes ahead in nothing but full-fledged darkness.

I can do it this, she thought.

Using the flashlight from her cell phone, she kept her eyes on the path, as best she could. The desert moon was exceptionally beautiful and abundant with the sultry, mystical vampire-movie view. Crystal-clear, twinkling stars blanketed the sky, making this the most beautiful run home she's ever had.

Startled by a noise, River looked over her right shoulder without stopping. The wildlife in Arizona proved to be quite busy and noisy this time of evening. Picking up her pace, she ran to the left of a pile of rocks, jumping a large unforeseen hole in the ground. Every once in a while, she would scan her world, being extra aware of her senses, which were now extremely heightened.

A loud crackling noise followed by a snap sounded in the nearby brush, startling her again … only this time she missed her footing and slipped into a long, downhill skid to the side of the road and landing next to a large set of boulders.

"Owww! That's going to hurt tomorrow," she groaned.

Moving her body was a struggle, as she slid further down the ravine. Her cell phone was her priority. She reached for it while on her knees. Suddenly, the hairs stood straight up on her arms, a rattling noise slowing her to a halt. She froze. The noise became louder. River looked at her phone, which was face up with the flashlight still on. That's when she realized the rattlesnake was coiled up next to her, disguised by the dirt.

3

Her stomach clenched. In fear and desperation, she stared into the snake's eyes. River's breathing became deep and shallow, as the snake rose into a striking position. Something else moved in the brush beside her. She stood motionless. Wishing she had called for an Uber or for Amy to pick her up after the wedding wasn't going to do her any good, nor was the regret pounding in her head.

This was a matter of life or death, and she knew the dire consequences if she was bitten by this snake. With no regard for what could happen next, River decided to get out of the way. She slowly folded her knee into position. Defensively, the snake backed its head, ready to strike at any moment. Its rattle warning her.

"I am dead for sure … going to get bit," she breathed.

The snake jumped at her. River let out a deafening scream. Suddenly, a large animal jumped in between her and the snake, knocking her backwards. The animal growled fiercely, grabbing the snake by the throat and throwing it to the ground. The snake hissed, quickly making its way back through the rocks and down the hill.

River quickly grabbed her cell phone and, like a lightning bolt, ran up the hill until she was safely back on the highway. Adjusting the light, she looked to see what kind of animal grabbed the snake. As it came into focus, it appeared to be the largest coyote she had ever seen in her life. The coyote tilted its head, sitting on its hind end. River breathed a slight sigh of relief. She would take a coyote in place of a rattlesnake any day of the week.

"Good little guy," she whispered. "Thank you."

Backing away slowly, she started for home with an air of caution before picking up speed. Upon reaching her front porch steps, she turned around, but didn't see the coyote. Bending forward, she never felt so much relief, as she did when going through the whole scene again in her mind. It was like a western movie, and she almost died. River limped into her house, holding her extra-bloody scraped knee. She managed to hobble to her kitchen sink for a cold glass of water. Pushing through a hot shower, she threw on her tee shirt and some clean underwear—thankful to be alive.

Climbing under her overpriced, high-thread count, beige sheets, and Navajo blanket, she listened to the calming noise of her white, floor fan while gazing at her draped, string lights that decorated her bedroom walls with a beautiful light flow. River felt the excitement of the whole day start to calm down, until she heard a large howl pierce through the night. Jumping out of bed, she peered through her windowpane. She saw the large coyote, the same one that rescued her, pacing back and forth along her desert drive. River quickly opened the window, staring curiously at the animal. He stood up on his hind legs, releasing another howl before jetting off into the desert canyon. *What the fuck is going on?* she wondered, as she slipped back into her bed. Feeling oddly safe, she drifted off to sleep.

CHAPTER TWO
The Price for Peace

The work week proved to be chaotic for River. Elderly, winter vacationers, commonly referred to as "snowbirds" were filling up the therapy rehabs and hospitals rather quickly. Her shift was more hectic than usual, adding more to her frustration. All day she thought about the large coyote that saved her life. Her dreams became more vivid, lasting longer than usual since the incident. Sometimes the dreams were more like visions, increasingly realistic and other times they were just a repeat from the night before. Mostly, the dreams started off with her fighting, using her hands like swords and martial arts techniques, stuff she had never even practiced before. The dream she had the night before involved her being pushed off a cliff, and as she fell, she looked right into the coyote's eyes before hitting the ground. River quickly awoke, strangely concerned for the animal.

"I can't explain it," River told Amy, her closest friend, after yoga class. "It's just all so weird … the whole event. I mean, seriously, Amy. That coyote saved me from a rattlesnake!"

Amy looked at her friend with a humorous expression.

"Well, maybe it's your guardian Angel or something, a sign from God above," Amy said, cranking her head back, raising her dark, perfectly manicured eyebrows. "There are some who say many angels come in the form of animals to help people. I read these stories on social media all the time."

River watched her best friend speak, while admiring Amy's beautiful soft brown eyes and flawless Mexican-American complexion. Sitting back in her chair, River thought about it for a minute. She decided Amy's idea was a little too strange and shook it off.

"Have you heard anything about your ex getting out of prison yet?" Amy asked.

"No, but the prosecuting attorney told me she would let me know at least a month before he gets out," River replied, uneasily.

"Be careful girl. Get a gun or something. You've got a crazy ex after you ... and now coyotes and rattlesnakes, too." Amy laughed, trying to lighten the mood.

River didn't find it funny. In fact, her stomach started to tighten when she thought about Coty and the fact that he tried to kill her.

Later that night, she sat on her front porch, listening to music while sipping herbal tea. Her mind held fast to things that happened in her past, including the man she thought she once loved and, who she thought, loved her. He almost killed her and not many people in her life seemed to care. No one in her family reached out or wanted to help her. That was probably the worst revelation. No one ever truly loved her.

She was still dealing with the trauma, steadily trying to heal. It was proving difficult. The gnawing, raw emotions still existed, even though the actual physical pain had left her body. Moving almost 2,000 miles away to ensure her peace, sanity and safety was considered brave by most, but she still missed home, that little Midwest town in Ohio. River missed the change of seasons, the familiarity, the Amish surroundings, and the excitement of events the town inspired ... just not enough to die for it. While summer in the Arizona desert could be miserable, the winters were beautiful, and it almost made up for everything that she left behind.

Being single for almost three years helped her adjust to her new life. River was lonely, but she wasn't ready for another relationship.

"Just take things slow," she would tell herself.

One day at a time.

After listening to the night birds, she decided to go inside and go to bed. A sudden chill ran down her spine. She felt something, or someone watching her. Turning around, she saw a coyote staring at her from a short distance. This was not the same coyote that had rescued her. This one was smaller … a female. River set down her vintage teacup, so she could shoo the coyote away.

"Go on … shoo!"

The coyote did not move. In fact, five more coyotes walked out from behind the shed to join the small one. River became fearful, unsure what they were planning to do to her. Why were they there in the first place? Backing up slowly, until her back rubbed against the screen door, she felt for the doorknob. She turned the knob and went inside.

A low-pitched howl rang through her house, and within an instant the large coyote appeared. It was the same coyote that had saved her life. He stood in front of the pack, walking closer to the porch. He sat down. River thought they might be hungry, but she was warned once, by an animal activist at a vegan protest for animal rights, never to feed wild animals, lest they trust the wrong person and get themselves killed.

"Thank you for helping me little guy," River said, from behind the protection of her screen door. To her amazement, the coyote seemed to nod in her direction. Surely, it was just her over reactive imagination. After a long gaze, River closed the door and locked it behind her. River tried to call Amy, but there was no answer. Watching from the window, she sat on her overstuffed denim sofa to ponder the intention of these wild coyotes.

After about an hour, the coyotes left, and every room River entered, she looked for them through her windows, wondering if they would come back. Finally, Amy called her back. River eagerly told her about the coyotes.

"Listen, I know this shaman from a reservation. I visit him frequently," Amy said. "Maybe I can ask him about all this and get some answers for you."

"Sure, um ...whatever you can find out," River replied, as she finished washing up the last of the dishes.

That night, before bed, she could hear the coyotes barking outside, playing with one another. Oddly, River felt comfortable with it now, almost like she was being protected while she eased into sleep.

CHAPTER THREE
Back into the Woods

River and Amy were on their way to Sedona, Arizona—a beautiful scenic road trip that took almost two hours. The only thing River could think about was, *WHAT DID SHE ALLOW AMY TO GET HER INTO NOW?*

Knowing she was going to an Ayahuasca ceremony made her even more nervous, especially after researching it online for the last two weeks. She had changed her mind several times. Amy quickly booked their tickets as a gift, making her feel pressured about the two-hundred dollars. When was it ever a good idea to purposely go back through past traumatic events in your mind while hallucinating on DMT? Having lived an unusually terrible life, River wasn't expecting a sweet hallucinogenic experience.

"But you haven't truly found closure for all those bad things that happened in your life River," Amy persuaded. "If you had, maybe you wouldn't be so afraid to move on right now. You know, date somebody."

There they were, heading to a well-known shaman, in a private ceremony for spirit seeking individuals that need insight to other unforeseen worlds or their own lives. Will taking DMT be the remedy she was waiting for? River just hoped she wouldn't embarrass herself or her friend, if she fell frail into a psychotic break by rehashing the past.

Arriving at their destination, River's nerves lit on fire as she tried to back out. Amy pushed her forward with excitement. They were introduced to a Peruvian shaman who was scantily clad in animal skin shorts, as well as a Navajo shaman who humbly wore blue jeans & a tie-dye tee shirt. Both women sat comfortably upon recycled cork mats amongst a handful of other nervous people. There were a few women dressed all in white who were appointed as "guides" to help them through their spiritual journey.

The guides passed out wooden shot glasses of Ayahuasca. Burning sage and ceremonial tobacco being feathered off large seashells by the women began to fill the atmosphere. After listening to a speech given by both shamans, River started to feel the raw side effects of the Ayahuasca tea. River looked at Amy, who gave her a comforting wink, before she lay back on her own mat.

The Navajo shaman began to beat lightly on a tribal drum made of animal skin with sinew. River closed her eyes and suddenly felt very heavy and tired. She wanted to fall asleep at first. The drums soulfully burst through her ears, drums holding her attention while some type of flute reverberated in her body. The music started to carry her away, as she kept telling herself, "TRY TO RELAX," or was that someone else telling her to relax?

Within minutes, images intensified, as her mind reeled with projections of her life flashing before her eyes. The emotions of her childhood roared, like flashback movie images and, at times, she was filled with feelings of fear or sadness. The next set of images took her through a large dark hallway, until she was in a forest of trees. The roots of the trees started moving, as if they were responding or talking to her. She could feel the earth loved her. The earth started to pulsate rapidly beneath her feet. Soon, she realized her soul was on fire. She never felt so alive.

"Help me," River managed to whisper weakly, as she started to cry. "Someone … please help me."

Was she saying this out loud? Did anyone in the ceremony actually hear her? Did they know she existed? These were the questions River asked repeatedly during her Ayahuasca journey.

River's soul kept walking among the trees with the endless chatter of voices, echoes, and her many thoughts. If only she could quiet her mind a little—just get some rest.

"Relax," a woman's voice commanded her. At this moment, River opened her eyes. No one was next to her, not even Amy. Wondering where that woman's voice came from, she lay back down closing her eyes. Instantly, River was back in her kitchen in Ohio—two years earlier. Her ex, Coty, violently punched her in the face. River flew back into the wall. Coty grabbed her again, but she saw another man in the room with them. He was dressed in a blue uniform with a strange crest on the right upper pocket. That mystery man was shouting for her attention, but she couldn't make out what he was saying to her.

Suddenly, Coty punched her again, jolting her body to the floor. He sat on top of her, choking her and calling her names, like he usually did. Turning her head, she saw the man in the blue uniform watching her calling her, "Amariah!" He told her to get up, but she couldn't. Coty was too strong for her.

Coty grabbed her by the hair, sitting her upright, as she cried. River felt the tears, the pain, and the horror of it all. It was as if she were going through it all over again. She used the kitchen chair to help herself climb to her feet. Coty yanked her up, still holding on to her hair. The man in the blue uniform was angry as he watched, aggravated with the events unfolding in the kitchen. He kept calling to her, "Amariah!"

River was very confused. She felt helpless. Coty let go of her hair, just long enough for River to make a run for the front door. Then, it happened, the dreaded she was forced to experience once more. It was a thrust kick to her lower back. River found herself lying on the floor face down, unable to get back up. She was broken and afraid he would finish her off. Coty laughed at her, called her some more vicious names while finishing his chicken dinner. The man in blue, whom she never saw before, was now bent over her holding up a shield of light around her body. He was protecting her somehow. She felt him.

The protection of light covered her body for a moment, before absorbing into her, filling her with a shimmering elation that tickled her spirit with enlightenment. In another instant, River's body was quickly pulled through a whirlpool vortex of light, leaving her feeling warm and loved. A pronounced presence of security enabled her to wrap her arms around this man in blue, as he carried her away from her Ohio kitchen, the same one she used to share with her Coty.

Would she die now? She wondered, as her body traveled through a sea of colors with this beautiful, strong man holding her in his arms. Their bodies landed in a field of wildflowers and grass. The man pulled her into his body closer, kissing her forehead lightly.

"I found you, Amariah, I missed you."

"You did?" River asked, quietly. "Who are you?"

The man nestled her, his energy pulsing through her body.

"Now that I found you, I will never leave you, River," he whispered in her ear. "Time to wake up."

River's soul fell into another vortex of color, as her mind raced back to the present. The Ayahuasca ceremony was loud, and Amy was now moaning on her own journey beside her. River shot straight up, trembling from her experience. A woman guide came to her quickly, consoling her telling her to relax. Another wooden shot glass of ceremonial tea was offered to her. River drank from it. Closing her eyes, she was back in the forest again with Coty running after her at full speed. He was holding a knife. River began to run, as a pack of coyotes fell in step with her. The large coyote, the same one that rescued her from the snake, was now beside her. Coty reached for her, but the large coyote bit at him until he released the knife. River shot back into reality again, this time ready to vomit in the present. A female guide brought over a steel bowl for her to puke in.

"It's okay, sweetie," the woman said, kindly. "Let all that negativity out—purge away."

River cried and puked all at once, unable to reason with her hallucinogenic visions and thoughts. A shaman sat down beside her, releasing the sound of the drums that had once lifted her spiritually and euphorically. She was finally able to calm down. Another woman sat beside her.

"You are a messenger set upon Mother Earth to heal with your amazing energy," the woman said, gently. "You have gifts, and soon God will show you how to use them."

River looked at the woman. Her heart was beating slowly to the rhythm of the drums. She was forever changed. There was no turning back. She declined the second Ayahuasca ceremony that was to follow the next day. Amy didn't argue.

The next morning, River dropped Amy off, so that she could experience DMT once again. She took Amy's car and explored Sedona, wandering through gift shops. She tried to eat a salad, but flashbacks of her experience the day before left her feeling uneasy. If she never did Ayahuasca again, that would be fine with her. A beautiful copper coyote wind chime caught her eye at a tourist shop, and that became her final purchase for the day. From there, she went back to the hotel to sleep.

The next afternoon, they drove home with Amy prattling on about her Ayahuasca experience. River sat silently, trying to take everything in. She struggled to embed the conversation into the deepest grasps of her mind. All she really wanted to do was get home and rest some more. Her body ached. Her heart was breaking, and she wanted to forget what Coty had done to her.

Once River was home, she hung her wind chime on the front porch and sat a large bowl of water and food out for the large coyote. She waited for him to appear, but he never did. River finally slept.

The next morning, she quickly checked outside. She expected the food to be gone, but it hadn't been touched. Combing her hand through her hair, she bent over with a sigh of disappointment. The sun was already bright at 6 a.m. She needed to get to work. Just then, her cell rang. It was an Ohio area code.

"Hello?"

"Hi, River! This is Gwen. I worked on the domestic case concerning you and Coty. I was your advocate with the prosecuting attorney's office ... not sure if you remember me."

River's heart dropped into her stomach.

"Um ... yes. I remember you. How are you?"

"I'm fine, River," she replied. "I'm sorry. I hope I didn't wake you. I know there is a time difference. I just wanted to let you know that Coty will be getting out of prison next month."

"No, it's okay," River said. "I was on my way to work anyway. Thank you for letting me know."

"Are you in a safe location, River?"

"Uh ... yes, I don't think he will find me here."

"Good," Gwen sighed. "I wish you well. If you have any problems with him, call the police. Okay?"

"Yes. Thanks. I doubt he'll even care about me once he's out. I'll be okay."

"Alright, hon. Have a good day."

River put her cell in her purse and jumped in the Jeep. The whole conversation left her rattled, but she had to get to work. Pulling out of the driveway, she saw the large coyote sitting on a rock, not far off. He was watching her. Pausing for a moment, before putting her sunglasses on, she stared at him. Then, punching the Jeep into reverse, she roared out of the driveway.

CHAPTER FOUR
Squaring Up

"Alright, River and Jason … you're up," Sensei Pete, River's Kenpo Karate instructor, shouted in the small dojo gym at the recreational center. "Remember what we practiced! Keep that check hand up, opposite your strike hand! Let's go!"

River squared up with Jason on the mat. She watched his movements carefully, as they bounced around a little—neither one eager to throw a strike.

"Come on! Kick! Punch! Do something!" Sensei hollered.

Everyone in class stood around the mat, watching in anticipation. Jason threw a right punch at River's head, but she swiftly blocked it. He tried throwing a left hook. River ducked, moving out of the way. She returned with a punch. Jason blocked it, and suddenly the punches started to fly. In a heated moment, River thrust a roundhouse kick that had enough force to successfully put Jason down on the mat. He stood up fiercely and went angrily for River. He threw punches at high speed, forcing her to block, duck and move out of the way. In response, she finally jumped into a high-wheel kick that knocked him to the other side of the mat.

"GOOD JOB!" Sensei praised. "You are a little surprise, River! With those moves, they won't see you coming!"

River and Jason faced each other, bowing. She took off her sweaty helmet and stretched her neck roll from side to side. It was time to watch the other classmates square off. When practice was over, she ran out of the gym in a rush, hoping to beat the traffic leaving the parking lot.

River kept herself busy at the rec with Kenpo karate, yoga, and dance class. It was a high-traffic area, and she wasn't the only person in Apache Junction who spent a lot of time there.

A month had passed since the Ayahuasca ceremony. River decided to make herself busier than usual. The less she thought about that day, the better. Every once in a while, she would catch a glimpse of the coyotes around her home. They always seemed to be passing through. They never ate any of the food she left for them.

River reached her Jeep as her cell started ringing. It was Amy.

"Hey! What's up?" River asked, breathlessly, as she continued to clamor into the vehicle. Sweat poured down her face.

"We are going out tonight!" Amy shouted, exuberantly into the phone. "There's a band playing at a tavern down the road from my house. I'm dating the lead singer. The place is a hole in the wall, but always packed with hot guys."

"You mean you and this guy are going out tonight?" River said unable to back the Jeep out.

"No! You and I are going out tonight, River."

"Nope. Not me … sorry. I don't do bars." River said, annoyed as she put the phone on speaker and tried backing out of her parking space.

"Oh, God. STOP," Amy huffed. "You need to get out for once in your life!"

"No, Amy. I'm not going. My answer is the same every time you ask, so stop asking me. I. Don't. Do. Bars."

"Please, River. I need you to come with me. Please, please,

please …" Amy pleaded, sounding like a child.

"Ugh. Alright. ALRIGHT! I will do it but just this time."

"YAHOO! YES! Girl, we are going to have so much fun! I will text you the address. It's just down the road from my house. Meet me there at about eight o'clock tonight."

"Fine, whatever." River said, ending the call. She backed up her vehicle, almost ramming into an oncoming car.

"OH, COME ON! Move!" she shouted, hitting the steering wheel.

Once home, River took her time getting ready, and decided to put more make-up on than usual. It would be the first time she stepped into a bar since her relationship with her Coty. Picking up the pace, she threw on a pair of tattered jeans, open-toed heels, and a crop top. Taking one last look in the floor length mirror, she pulled up the waist of her jeans a bit and said to herself, "You can do this because you are really a bad ass."

Once inside the old Tavern known as Nelson's, River ignored turning heads from tables. Men gawked at her, and women sneered, but that didn't matter to her. She was used to those types of reactions when she entered bar-like establishments. Amy was already drowning herself in shots when River spotted her from across the room.

"He's cute right," Amy said, pointing to the band and her new man. "They are still warming up."

He was dressed in 90's grunge with choppy, punk hair and piercings covering his face. River cringed. He wasn't cute at all, but she nodded in agreement to her friend.

"What's his name?" River asked.

"Tyler." Amy answered loudly, as she pointed to the bartender to pour her another drink. "You ready to get wasted?"

"No. I'm not drinking. Just an observer … supporting you tonight.

Anyways, I drove."

"No. You need to let loose and have fun with me," Amy begged. "Tyler's not drinking, so we can take you home later."

River thought about it for a second and then agreed.

"Fine—one or two shots. That's it!"

River downed a couple of shots rather quickly and turned towards the band. They weren't too bad, and the guitarist turned out to be exceptional. A tall, built young man wearing a polo shirt sat down beside her. He showed interest in River, but she ignored him. She declined his offer to buy her a drink, over and over, but he wouldn't leave her alone.

"No thanks. I've had enough," she assured him.

"Want to dance?" he asked with an innocent grin.

"To this? I can't dance to this kind of music."

"How about a game of pool," he offered.

River hesitated before giving in, "Okay …sure. Why not?"

Leaving Amy at the bar, she headed over to the billiards section to play her lousiest game of pool ever. Another man made his way to her, asking to buy her a drink, to which she quickly declined. River was still feeling the last two shots. She listened to the band a little longer then went to the restroom. When she came back, the young man she played pool with was waiting for her with two drinks in his hands.

"Okay, so what is this?" she asked with a grin.

"Just take one shot with me. That's all I ask. And if you want, I won't bother you the rest of the night."

River nodded, took the shot out of his hand and said, "What the hell!"

Downing it quickly, she handed him the empty glass. Ten minutes later, she started to feel nauseous and dizzy. River made her way back to Amy.

"Hey, I'm going to step outside for some air," River said, as she took out her Jeep keys.

"Okay, but don't go anywhere. We can take you home."

"No, I'm not. It's the whiskey. I think," River said, pushing herself out the tavern door.

Her legs felt like they weren't moving like they should, and suddenly she was very tired. Struggling through the parking lot, she found her Jeep. She tried unlocking the door. Her vision was becoming severely impaired. She needed to lay down in the front seat.

"Hey! Hey! Little woman … where are you going?" a man asked, *the* man who wouldn't leave her alone all night. He pushed his body into hers, trying to hold her up straight.

"I'm just trying to get into my car, so I can rest for a few minutes. I'm not feeling well," River said, hoping he would go away and leave her alone. Her head felt like it was going to split in two, as she doubled over feeling severe nausea.

"Come into my truck. You can put the seats all the way back and relax," he replied, grabbing her arm. River fell back, hitting the ground.

"No. Please … I just want to sit in *my* car." She said, her vision doubled and her joints stiffening.

"Come on, short stuff," the man said, picking her up like a baby. "Up you go. We are going to my truck."

River was too weak to protest. Her head wobbled back. She had no control over it, as she tried to look at the man's face. Everything was spinning, blurring, moving too fast.

"Hey! Is everything alright?" a bar employee asked, on his way to throw trash in the dumpster.

"Oh, yeah! My wife never could handle a few too many shots."

The bar employee waved his hand and walked through the side door. Not able to stop him, she was suddenly put into this strange man's truck. Quickly, he pushed her over to the passenger side and shoved the keys into the ignition.

"You and I are going to have fun tonight," He grinned.

River tried to move her head and talk, but the only thing that came out of her mouth was drool. A mile down the road, a large, dark figure of a man walked in front of the truck, causing the vehicle to swerve right and back to center.

"WHAT THE FUCK WAS THAT SHIT?!" River's captor shouted. He sped up, grabbing River's arm as her slumped body slid to the floorboard of the vehicle. Further down the road, a large coyote ran out in front of the truck—coming to a complete stand still. The man slammed on the brakes. The back tires screeched, leaving tread on the highway. River's head hit the dash. The driver's side door opened abruptly.

"WHO IN THE FUCK ARE YOU?!" the captor screamed.

In an instant, he was yanked out of the vehicle and thrown hard against the bed of the truck. River heard a lot of rambunctious movement and a scuffle, but she still could not move. There were roaring sounds, but she couldn't make out if it was coming from a human or an animal. A group of coyotes started making high pitch barking sounds, until a large coyote stopped to release a large howl. The captor took a few powerful blows to the head and stomach before being thrown high into the air. His body soared, then fell into a patch of Agave cactus off the side of the road. River tried to move her head again. Her breathing became shallow with a loud pulsating in her neck. Her mouth was now drooling heavily, long strands of saliva stringing from her mouth.

The passenger side door opened, and she panicked. River's body was carefully picked up and removed from her captor's truck. Her head rolled back, and all she could do was close her eyes. The hope in her heart was that it was a rescue attempt from Amy and her boyfriend.

Strong, tight, warm muscular arms held her close. She sensed whoever was carrying her was walking. She wondered why they weren't in a car, driving already. A mouthful of froth spat up, as she choked on her own spit. She rolled her head toward the man's chest. The man carrying her said nothing. He only held her close to him as he walked.

River opened her eyes. She saw the coyotes she had heard earlier. They were walking beside them. The large one, the coyote that had saved her once, made a low whimpering noise when she focused on him. Her vision was slowly returning. Looking down, she noticed the man carrying her was wearing ripped jeans. He was barefoot.

"What is going on?" River managed to whisper.

"You are safe now, River," the stranger replied.

"Oh, you know me. Thank you." River whispered, as she silently passed out in his arms.

The next morning River could barely move. She woke up in her bed, suffering a hangover. Willing her body to move, she rushed to her bedroom window to see if the Jeep was in the drive. She sighed relief when she saw it was there. She sat back down on the bed, trying to piece the night before together in her mind.

She couldn't. Everything was a scramble, and she had no idea what happened or how she made it home. Her head throbbed, as she slathered on Noxzema and tried to scrub her face. River was never able to handle hard liquor. She deserved this for even trying.

"Never again," she whispered to herself.

Later that day, she found her cell in the back pocket of her jeans. She had noticed seven missed calls from Amy. Ignoring her phone, she pulled on a clean set of clothes and headed out her back door. Turning on the sprinklers, she watered her garden as the cabbage, kale and wildflowers sucked it up. Looking towards the mountain scape, she took a deep breath and sat on a wooden Adirondack chair. Her head pounded as her cell phone started to ring. River was annoyed, but answered, knowing it was Amy.

"What the hell is wrong with you?!" Amy roared. "I was about to call the police!"

"What? Why? I just woke up," River replied. "I'm sorry. Calm down, Amy. I'm hungover today."

"How? You only had three shots last night. I've been worried to death about you. That guy you were hanging out with last night came back to the bar all beat up. He said some guy took you out of his truck."

"What? That never happened. I wasn't with anybody last night Only you. That guy wasn't my type."

River was silent, bits of her memory coming into focus.

"I thought that guy was lying. Your car was gone before that guy even came back to the bar. His name is Keith by the way," Amy said, sounding calmer. "I'm glad you are okay. That guy was probably on drugs or something and made the whole story up in his mind."

"I don't know, Amy. I guess I just got sick and came home." River added, suddenly uneasy because she wasn't at all sure what had happened the night before. Something wasn't right.

"Keith was beat up really bad. You should've seen him."

River started to remember someone carrying her down the highway, and there might have been coyotes. "Amy I'm fine ... really. Now, I've got to go. I'm not feeling so well."

"Okay. Will I see you at yoga or dance class later this week?"

"Yes," I assured. "I will see you then. Bye."

Relentless questions were running through her mind. Who carried her? How did her Jeep get home? How did she get in bed with most of her clothes off, except for her bra and panties? The coyotes? The man? Were those his pets? River hurriedly turned off the sprinklers, locked herself in her house and fell asleep with her pepper spray in hand.

CHAPTER FIVE
No Going Back

"**N**o Elaine, I cannot give you any more pain medication," River said sternly to the impatient, elderly patient blocking her nursing cart with her wheelchair.

"Why not?!" the woman screamed, as she edged her wheelchair closer to the cart.

"I'm sorry, Elaine," River replied, adjusting her gray headband while searching for another patient's medication. "But you just took your prescription an hour ago. It's too soon. Every four hours is the doctor's order ... remember?"

"I'm going to report you," Elaine snarled. "I'm calling my doctor to tell him how you treat me!"

"Okay. That's fine. Please ... do whatever you have to do to make yourself happy. I'm kind of busy here."

River was exhausted from picking up extra hours on top of her regular shifts. It was all she could do to take her mind off the incident at the bar last weekend.

"I'm going to sue you, bitch!" Elaine screamed, turning her wheelchair around. River watched Elaine with exasperation, as she rolled away. She often wondered if she was truly getting paid enough for this job. A shift change was approaching. *Finally*, she thought. She waited for someone to relieve her.

Suddenly, from down the hall, there came a loud THUD! Followed by a CRASH! Running toward the sound, River found one of her patient's lying on the floor in a small pool of blood. She was calling out for help.

Shit! I'm not getting out of here anytime soon, River thought. Just then a tall, tan man in gray scrubs entered the room. She couldn't help but notice the wild tattoo sleeves covering his arm, not to mention the fact that he was good-looking.

"How can I help?" he asked, bending down to assess the patient.

"Are you the new relief nurse?" River asked, noticing his athletic build and neatly cut, almost shaven to the scalp, head.

"Yes. I am," he replied with a perfect smile. "You must be River."

"I am, and I need your help," River said, purposefully.

She noticed another male nursing assistant walking down the hall. He looked as exhausted as she did, but she needed him—now!

"I need a full set of vitals on this patient, please!" she shouted.

The nursing assistant stopped in his tracks. He rolled his eyes and took off down the hall in search of a vital machine. After assessing the patient for swelling and broken bones, River and "Sleeves" lifted the patient into a wheelchair. That is to say, she tried to help in the lifting, but the new male nurse, whose name she would later learn was Alex, did all the heavy lifting.

River quickly sat down with Alex and gave him a daily report on all her patients. She noticed he was staring at her, instead of his paper. It made her uncomfortable, and as she quickly stood up to leave, the contents of her backpack fell out of a large, unzipped pocket. Without hesitation, Alex bent over to help her pick up what she had dropped.

"I'm having a rough day," River said, forcing a smile. "I hope it's not so bad for you tonight. Thank you for your help."

She scurried to the elevator and got the hell out of there.

"Okay, so I can't twerk." River giggled. "Stop laughing at me!"

"It's funny how a man and an elderly woman can twerk better than you can," Amy joked, tears of pleasure coming from her eyes as she made fun of her best friend.

"I have buns of steel, Amy."

The two fell into a fit of laughter, having just finished their hip-hop class together at the rec center. Amy sat with River on a bench outside. There was intermittent laughter mixed with moments of silence as they watched two doves fight over a nest tucked inside of a Saguaro cactus. The weather was nice. A slightly cool breeze washed over them, as River began to rock gently back and forth while hugging her knees.

"He's getting out," River whispered.

"What?" Amy asked in surprise.

"Well, he is probably out by now. I got a call from the prosecutor's office."

"He's such a dickhead for what he did to you—scum of the earth," Amy retorted, angrily.

"Yeah, well I'm over it," River said, looking off into the mountains. "I tried to make it work with him. I tried to help him, and he just raged, staying drunk all the time."

She didn't want to feel this anymore.

"River, some people don't deserve your help, and he sure as hell didn't deserve you!"

Amy leaned forward to look into River's eyes. "I just don't understand how someone could have hurt you like that or why you would put up with it for so long. He almost killed you."

River sighed. These were questions she didn't know how to answer without sounding like a weak enabler.

"He just liked to drink too much. He had to be in charge of everything I did. I can't explain why I even stayed or why I put up with it. I just really thought I could help him."

"Promise me you won't ever do that to yourself again. You have to stop trying to help everybody," Amy begged. "Stop going out of your way all the time."

"I know, but I love to help people. You know that. It's not in my nature to stop," River said, matter of fact.

"You are a bleeding, fucking heart!" Amy exclaimed, pretending to pull River's heart from her chest.

River smiled. She wanted to tell Amy about the weird events that happened at the bar over the weekend, but she resisted. River didn't want her worrying about her or burdened with her constant problems. She, on the other hand, was used to this rough lifestyle. Her mother never wanted her, and at the age of eleven, she lived with her maternal grandparents, whom both had thriving medical careers.

There was a lot of pressure being a bi-racial teenager, growing up on a small farm, living with the Caucasian side of her family. She never got to know her biological father's family. She battled her way through an all-white school, often having to defend herself from certain students and teachers. That's where her compassion started to set in her soul. Anything or anyone who was treated like she was (or worse) became her personal project. Wounded birds, stray animals and, later on in life, broken people.

Her heart couldn't stand to see anyone, or anything suffer. River's nature-loving spirit expanded to her going vegan, growing plants, nurturing everything she came in contact with. Her empathy was deep, so deep, in fact, she was unusually intuitive. There was definitely a fiercely strong spirit within her, now more than ever. She was a force to be reckoned with. She stood up for everything she believed in, and she no longer was able to back down from a fight. That is where her obsession for Kenpo karate and self-defense came in. River had no intention of letting any man beat her, like a rag doll. While she was kind, she wasn't naïve, nor was she going to allow anyone to take advantage of her compassion again. Standing at 5'2, 117 pounds, she could hold her own, and she was proud of that.

"I am here for you," Amy said. "If you need anything, just get a hold of me. Okay?"

Amy could see that her friend was in deep thought about her life and her past. She reached out and gave River a big hug. River nodded inside of Amy's embrace. It was deep and it comforted her.

After saying their goodbyes, River took off in her Jeep toward the Superstition Mountains. The evening was brisk, as she parked her vehicle, so to get a good look at the moon. Taking an old horse blanket out of the back, she spread it across the hood and sat on it, leaning her back against the windshield. She listened to the radio, as the stars peered through the night sky. She missed Ohio, but she would not be so foolish as to throw away her new life in Apache Junction.

There were certain things River had never experienced before, like the unconditional love of a parent and a real, true-love type of relationship, complete with respect and balance. She loved too much, and she had never in her life experienced that kind of love in return. Coty never loved her, not the way she deserved to be loved. He hit her, kicked her, spit on her, called her names and no matter what she did for him, it was never enough.

Every melt down Coty had, he would grab River by the hair or the throat and violently throw her into a wall. When he was really on a rampage or a bender, he would kick her, or try to suffocate her, or destroy her things. Sometimes she would ask God, "Why am I even alive?"

A nervous wreck, she would walk around the house before he'd get home, hoping he wouldn't hurt her. There were times she tried to leave, but he would hunt her down and beg her to come back. He was manipulative, controlling her every move, even her ability to drive. The man would remove parts from her car or take her car keys.

That night, River looked toward the night sky and declared, "NO. I WON'T GO BACK."

After an hour or so of stargazing and reminiscing, she decided to head home. She jumped into the Jeep with Jimi Hendrix blaring on the stereo. A soft coyote call was heard from a nearby boulder. River pierced her eyes through the window, as it echoed through the canyon. There he sat, watching her. It was "Little Guy," the same large coyote that had saved her life. She knew it because of his unusual size. A smaller coyote peered around the corner and walked up the stone to sit next to him. River's mind reeled. She couldn't imagine why they were so interested in her. River rolled down her window and stared at them for a moment, then punched the Jeep into reverse and reeled out on to the dirt road.

CHAPTER SIX

The Ring

Over the next few weeks River became very close with the new nurse Alex. She loved his sense of humor and how he purposely would make her laugh. They seemed to be so in tune with each other, both similar in personality. They enjoyed the same things in life. It didn't matter that they had completely different upbringings, they were strangely in sync.

Alex was very attractive. River tried not to let that distract her, but it proved to be hard sometimes. When he stood next to her, she would get a tingly feeling along her arms and throughout her body. When that happened, she wanted more of that odd feeling and would purposely seek him out to see if it happened again.

One week he was a normal new guy, someone she wasn't sure about. And then, suddenly, he was more to her. It was definitely a surprise that they were so compatible, and it sometimes scared her. The last thing she needed was to put herself in a bad relationship again, trapped like a defenseless animal in a cage. She convinced herself that all she needed at the time, perhaps forever, was a friend in Alex.

Nothing more.

River tried avoiding Alex as best she could, but he kept coming to her with his shaven head, dark complexion, and deep, dark eyes that melted her knees. At 6'4, he was so tall, and she was so short in comparison.

"Do you want to go on a motorcycle ride with me?" he asked, oblivious to her wanting him near her.

Save me! her insides would scream, even though she knew it was ridiculous.

"Wow ... really? You have a bike?"

"Yes. I do, and I have an extra helmet," he said. "I thought we could take a little ride, maybe go out for dinner or a drink afterward."

"Um ... sure," River replied, momentarily looking at her phone in response to a strange text notification. "I would like that. When do you want to ride?"

"How about this weekend?" he asked. Alex noticed she was suddenly uneasy. It had something to do with her phone.

"Everything okay?"

River turned her cell over onto the nurse's cart and lied to Alex.

"Yes," she said. "I'll text you my address in a bit."

"Awesome," Alex said, winking at her as he backed away. "I will be waiting for your text."

River dared not look at her cell. She hurriedly gave a report to the relief nurse, then grabbed her bag and took off down the elevator in a flash. She took out her cell and looked at the text. Her heart pounded in disbelief. The elevator doors opened and River, in a hurry, ran into her charge nurse supervisor.

"Hey, River! How are you? Is everything okay? You look like you've seen a ghost."

River took off toward the time clock to punch out. She yelled out, "I'm fine, Danielle. All is good. I will talk to you later. I have to be somewhere."

Finally, behind the steering wheel, she looked at the text again.

Hey babe, I'm out. I know you are mad at me. I love you no matter what's happened. I would like to see you, but I'm not sure exactly where you live or where you are. Let the past stay in the past and let's move on. I love you, pretty girl. Can't wait to kiss your sweet loving lips again. Love, Coty

River couldn't believe what she was reading. Her stomach clenched tighter with every word. She didn't ever want to forget what he had done to her or just let the past be the past, not when it came to him. She was angry, tired, sad and completely exhausted. Leaning back in the driver's seat, she allowed herself to let the hot, uncontrollable tears fall down her face. The one thing Coty didn't say was, "I'm sorry for almost killing you, then mocking you while I sat down and ate my dinner. I'm sorry I left you laying there when you couldn't get back up—wounded and alone."

Wiping tears from her face, she put the key in the ignition and sped away. Driving in an emotional upset, she pulled off to the side of the road, put her face in her hands and cried. All her fear, deep feelings, and anxiety hit the surface—manifesting pent-up tears. She wondered, *Why do I feel guilty? Why do I feel guilty for leaving while he was in prison and guilty for having the nerve to feel guilty?* After twenty minutes of deep sobbing, she looked into the rearview mirror at her sad, red, wet eyes and, with her trembling hands, she got back on the highway.

Saturday morning couldn't come fast enough. River was both excited and nervous about going on a motorcycle ride with Alex. After making sure the house was impeccable, she sat and waited anxiously for Alex. Her outfit was simple as always—jeans and an off-one-shoulder tee shirt ensemble. Only this time, she wore worn-out brown boots and turquoise dangling earrings with very little make-up, since (in her mind) this was *not* a date. It was just two friends on a motorcycle ride.

Looking out the window, she noticed a little box with a note sitting on her front porch. Quickly opening the door, she rushed outside to pick it up, thinking maybe Alex had backed out. The note attached was carelessly handwritten, almost eligible. It read: *"I WILL ALWAYS WATCH OVER YOU, RIVER. WEAR ME, SO I CAN PROTECT YOU."*

River read the note a few times, going over it in her mind. She was not sure if she should even open the box. Setting the box down on the coffee table, she stared at it for a moment before finally deciding to open it. Inside the small box was a smaller box, delicately wrapped with thin tissue paper. After tearing off the paper, she flipped off the lid. Inside was a beautiful, handmade gold and gemstone ring, in the shape of the solar system. It was delicate, and very strange to look at.

Trying it on, she was astounded that it fit perfectly on her small tan finger. Chills instantly went through her body, as she held the ring up to the sun spilling through the window. The jewels were pure and robust with colors containing indigo-blue, emerald-green, ruby-red, and a stone with many flashes of color. All the gems were raised up just enough to create a pattern River could only describe as astronomical.

River nervously jumped to her feet, as the thundering of a motorcycle roared into her driveway. She took one final look in the mirror and opened the front door. Just as River was about to jump on the bike with Alex, she noticed her coyote, "Little Guy," staring at her from a distance. Alex handed River a helmet and backed up the bike, turning it around.

"Hold on to me tight," Alex commanded. River put on the helmet and did as she was told. She grabbed him around his muscular, taut waist. They drove off under the dreamiest of skies and into the most beautiful desert landscapes. Cacti blanketed the open areas of deserted land along the brush overgrowth, until they were out of Pinal County.

River took in the fresh-blowing air, as her invisible spirit was set free. She felt happy. Alex could see her reveling in the ride in his rearview. It revealed a huge grin of his own.

"Are you okay?" he asked, every once in a while.

River nodded in return.

The ride seemed to peel away a month's worth of stress. She was suddenly thankful for Alex, more than words could say. They purred around canyon corners that were traced with decorative mesquite trees and along rugged mountain sides. The path led them to evergreen trees and greener landscapes, as they entered Show Low, Arizona.

Parking outside of a local bar and grill, River suddenly felt a tightening in her chest, as she recalled her last visit to a bar.

"A bar?" River asked, pulling the helmet off her head.

"Well, kind of," Alex shrugged with his perfect smile. "It's more of a family diner. You can eat and drink or drink and not eat. What's your pleasure?"

"Well, let's check it out," River replied, withdrawing from the question of "pleasure."

After a quick trip to the restroom, River went to grab the ladies' room door handle when she noticed the mysteriously gifted ring on her finger light up. An enchanting trilogy flared briefly from the gemstones, just long enough for River to see it. An unexpected bolt of energy shot through her back, sending a quiver of electricity throughout her body. In a panic, River tried to remove the ring from her finger—to no avail. Moving abruptly to the sink, she used soap and water to try and squeeze the ring off. It still wouldn't budge.

"What the hell," she whispered, as a large, busty, redhead threw open the restroom door. River dried her hands and returned to the table with Alex.

"Good news for you," he said, poking fun at her. "They have veggie burgers and fries. You can have fries, right?"

"Yes. Fries are potatoes, Alex."

River trailed off, looking out of the huge glass window and into the burrows of the nearby trees.

"Hey! You okay?" Alex asked, as he gently touched her hand. "Everything alright?"

When his skin touched the ring, it made River flinch as a spark of electricity bit into her.

"I'm fine," she said, moving her hand back. "A lot of stuff going through my head right now is all."

River allowed Alex to order her a whiskey and Coke. He tried touching her hand again. This time she let him. She forced a smile, trying her hardest to pay attention to everything he was saying, but she couldn't take her eyes or her mind off the ring. She wasn't sure if she actually saw the ring light up, or if she made it up in her head.

The long ride back to Apache Junction was not as wonderful and exciting. In fact, River was relieved when Alex parked the bike in her drive and helped her off. He rubbed her lower back as she walked up the porch steps. The whiskey was wearing off, leaving her in a bit of a stupor.

River jumped, as a large lizard ran across her boot. She landed in Alex's arms, but she was not ready for that and quickly corrected, pushing away from him.

"Would you like to come in?" she asked, secretly believing, if not hoping he would say no and be on his way. "All I have to drink is tea and water … I think."

"SURE!"

Surprised, River began rummaging through her kitchen cupboards, hoping to find something to take the edge off. Scrambling through boxes of herbal teas, protein powders, mineral and vitamin elixirs, she found something that might do the job. There was a bottle of tequila in her hand and a big smile on her face. Putting on a bit of bravado, she turned to Alex and said, "Do you want to do some shots?"

Of course, Alex was game. Grabbing two cobalt blue shot glasses, they headed toward her couch. Alex grabbed River by her waist and sat her square onto his lap.

"I talked your ear off all night long, but you didn't say very much. Talk to me," he gently coaxed. "I want to get to know you."

"Not much to say really," River lied.

"You're *that* mysterious, keep-it-to-yourself type, aren't you? I like that; it keeps me wondering about you."

Cupping River's chin with his strong fingers, he planted a soft kiss on the tip of her nose, and then two more—one for each cheek. He wasn't satisfied until he met her soft lips with his. Cradling her, his tongue reached for her more deeply, as she relaxed back into his arms. River found herself wanting him, craving him as she wrapped her fingers around the back of his neck pulling him in. Alex groaned. He was hard and ready to take her.

"I want you so bad tonight," he whispered, looking into her eyes. She felt the same way, as lust's fire burned inside her. Nevertheless, she still wasn't sure she should be doing this. The gnawing feeling to wait was there, but she ignored it. Nodding, she said, "Take me upstairs."

Alex didn't hesitate. He picked her up and carried her petite figure up the steps. Just then, there was an ominous knock at the front door— startling them both. Alex looked to River for a sign, wondering what he should do. He had no problem ignoring whoever was at the door.

"I need to get that," River said, her face flushed.

Alex put her down, and River quickly moved to the window to peer outside.

"I don't see anyone there," she said.

Alex went to the door and opened it to see for himself. No one was there. He walked down the porch steps, moving further into the drive and looking around. Not a person in sight. He came back with his hands held up and said, "Nobody."

Without warning a large pack of coyotes started to howl and yip, as if establishing territory. The sound became so deafening, River put her hands over both ears. The ring on her finger lit up in a strange pattern, but River couldn't rip her hands away from her ears long enough to pay attention to it. Alex looked puzzled. He couldn't understand what she was experiencing or what was going on with her. Alex called out to her, rushing to her side, but River couldn't hear him. She could only hear the coyotes yipping and howling. Her eyes were filled with fear, as the pain of the calling from the animals brought her to her knees. Just as suddenly as it all began, it quickly stopped.

"River, what happened?" Alex begged, as he helped her up. "Come on, let's get you inside."

Alex got River back in the house. "You are shaking," he said. "Tell me what happened."

River refused to explain, mainly because it was inexplicable, and it seemed to be the story of her life lately.

"I think I'm sick ... a headache. I can't handle tequila," she said. It was another lie. She was getting good at that. Alex stood up and took a deep, concerned breath.

"Don't leave me, Alex," she whispered. "Please ..."

"I'm not going anywhere tonight. I will be right here when you wake up. You need some rest."

River grabbed his hand, holding onto it with conviction, as she shivered, to the point her teeth had started to chatter. Alex grabbed her heavy Navajo blanket off a nearby chair. He covered her with it.

"Th ... th ... thanks," she managed. River closed her eyes, as Alex gently caressed her forehead until she fell asleep.

CHAPTER SEVEN
The Coyote

When River awoke the next morning, she felt groggy. She stumbled around Alex, who was asleep on the floor, so that she could make coffee and brush her teeth. Alex murmured in his sleep, but he didn't wake up. He just rolled over on the carpet with a slight cough, as his breathing turned into a snore.

Toothpaste dribbled down River's shirt, as she spat into the sink. Rinsing her mouth out with water, she took a brief look at the ring on her finger. That ring was obviously from another time or era. It was not anything she had ever seen before. Again, she wondered where it came from. Who would have given it to her?

Pulling her hair back, she made her way downstairs. She found Alex sitting on her couch, putting on his sneakers.

"Uh ... hey!" He said, softly.

"Hey! Want some coffee?" River asked, as if nothing had happened the night before. She was getting good at that, too.

"No ... no coffee," he said, standing up and pulling River close to him. "I need to get home and let the dog out. If I don't, he chews up everything in sight and ruins my carpet."

River sighed, almost disappointed.

"You weren't feeling well last night. Are you feeling better now?" Alex asked.

"I'm fine. I just had this really sudden earache with a simultaneous migraine. I'm sorry."

Alex pulled her in for a quick hug.

"We can do coffee and small talk another time. I would like to take you on as many motorcycle rides as possible," Alex winked, and then walked out the front door.

River was kind of relieved she and Alex didn't have sex. It was too soon. She didn't need any more drama or unnecessary distractions. She made a mental note to make that point clear to Alex the next time she saw him.

River took her cup of coffee outside and pondered the strange and supernatural things that had been taking place, whether it was in her mind or in reality. Gazing into the Arizona sunrise, she took slow sips of coffee while listening to the bees that were clearly enjoying her flowers. Laying her head back on the rough-edged, wooden porch planks, she climbed her bare feet up onto the side of the wood rails. She quietly ached inside. It was fear, the fear of an abusive ex, the fear of committing herself to another man, and the fear of dying without ever having experienced what so many others have—true love.

Alex made her feel good. She really enjoyed him, but suddenly, she felt as though he couldn't be the one for her. He was not the one she needed. The night before she was flying high on tequila, but this morning her feet were heavy on the ground, and her reality was cut and dry. Alex was her friend. He needed to stay that way.

Gazing into the ring on her finger, River rotated her hand under the sun, inviting the warm light to shine through the gems. A chakra of light summoned around her hand. It moved her. Covering her eyes with her palms, she was brought to tears. She wasn't even sure why she was crying.

Before she knew what was happening, there was a loud whimper and then a long tongue licking at her hands and face. She moved her hands away from her wet eyes and was surprised to see "Little Guy," that large, wild, albeit friendly, coyote, trying to comfort her.

River looked into his soulful golden-brown eyes, as she slowly, very, very, slowly reached out to touch him. He bowed his head, nudging at her neck and then her hand with his pointed muzzle. She petted him, as tears rolled down her cheeks. Finally, she put her face into his fur, hugging him. He placed his paw onto her shoulder. The coyote sat with her for a while, the two of them looking out into the desert together.

"What should I call you?" River asked, as she smoothed her hand over the back of his neck. "Do you have a name?"

Suddenly, the coyote jumped the porch, racing wildly into the desert. He disappeared so quickly, she wondered if it had even happened at all. *I must be losing my mind,* she thought. First there was the coyote who protected and befriended her. Then there was the unknown man who rescued her from date rape in the middle of nowhere, carrying her no less than ten miles home—barefoot *and* delivering her Jeep. On top of which, there was the magical ring, claiming to protect her.

No. This wasn't weird at all.

I am definitely keeping all of this to myself, she thought.

CHAPTER EIGHT

Peace in the Storm

The day started off overcast, dark clouds looming above in the gray skies. River, along with many other Apache Junction residents, were praying for rain. After a few weeks of coaxing, she was able to get "Little Guy" to take certain treats from her hand. Every now and then, the other coyote, the smaller female, would show up for a treat, too.

Worrying about the possibility of a storm sweeping through and her new coyote friends not getting enough to eat, she left a big bowl of food inside the shed, just in case they needed to take shelter. Superstition Mountain was known for its severe flooding. Fortunately, her home had never been impacted. She narrowly escaped a few such catastrophes.

River's ring lit up a dozen times, bedazzling her with chakra colors that bloomed inside invisible prisms. Every time it happened, she prepared herself for the little jolt of electricity. Sometimes she would have to hold on to something to steady herself. The good news was that no one seemed to notice, but her. The ring lit up like a Christmas tree in public, and yet not a single soul took note. Obviously, they couldn't see what she saw. When Amy didn't see the ring spectacle after yoga class, River knew it was for her eyes only. The only thing she didn't know …was why? And how? These were questions she wanted answers to but had no way of getting that information. The internet was no help—whatsoever.

River went through the motions of her Kenpo karate class with very little motivation. The knife techniques were usually her favorite, but her body was drained. It probably had to do with the weather.

"The rain is pouring down like crazy," Sensei Pete shrieked, as the scenery outside of the gym was nothing but a blur of wind gusts and hurling water.

"Let's finish up! I don't want to drive in this!" he shouted. Everyone scurried around, quickly putting away the gym mats, head gear, and boxing gloves. River hurriedly zipped up her gym bag, throwing it over her shoulder and quickly saying goodbye to everyone. Bowing to Sensei, she headed out the door to her Jeep. The rec center parking lot was flooded up to her ankles as she ran. Just within reach of her Jeep she turned and slid into a puddle of water around her tires.

"Crap!" River exclaimed, as rain and wind pasted her hair to her face. Out of nowhere, a man ran toward her.

"Hey, are you okay?" he asked.

He had blonde hair. His wet curls framed his blue eyes and fair complexion. She allowed him to help her up. It was the least she could do—since she was busy slipping and sliding. She tried not to stare at this man's "football player" shoulders, as he grabbed her gym bag.

"Thank you," she said, embarrassed. "Thank you! Thank you!"

She realized she probably thanked him one too many times. All she wanted to do was bolt out of there.

"Here, allow me," the man said, taking her keys and swiftly opening her Jeep door. River stepped up onto the siderail and almost slid again, but he kept her from falling.

"I've seen you before in karate class. You are pretty good," he said with a slight smile, rain rushing down his chiseled cheeks.

"Uh yeah," River replied. "I take a few classes a week."

There was no way he thought she was "pretty good" at karate, but it was kind of him to say.

"What's your name?" he asked.

"River," she answered, wanting to shut the door, but he was standing in the way. She couldn't help but notice he was trying hard to talk to her.

"River," he nodded, taking a step back. "I like that."

She smiled shyly.

"I hope to see you around, River."

"Shoulders" shut the door, the rain showing no signs of letting up. River rolled down the window, as he turned away.

"Wait!" she shouted. "What's your name?"

"Erik," he replied, winking as he turned to walk away.

River watched him strut through the rain before turning the ignition of her Jeep and pulling out of the lot. She saw Erik get into a classic white Chevy truck and a coyote, *her* coyote, standing next to him. Squinting her eyes, she looked closer, but in a flash the coyote was gone.

"Weird right?" River posed, in between gulps of guac and chips. She and Amy were at their favorite Mexican restaurant eating their usual chips and dip, only this time they both indulged in Margaritas.

"I know you... you... you ...you are trying to take this whole coyote thing somewhere it shouldn't be taken," Amy muttered, indulging in a double dipped chip.

"Amy that's gross," River snapped. "STOP DOUBLE DIPPING!"

Amy laughed, knowing it irritated her.

"I just think it's kind of strange. I swear, that coyote was standing right next to him, and they acknowledged each other," River continued, suddenly gushing. "AND … Erik winked at me."

"Erik?" Amy replied, shaking her head whilst rolling her eyes. "Do not do this to yourself, River! He sounds like a cowboy or worse, a cowboy wannabe."

Amy leaned forward into the guacamole, pretending she was going to lick the contents in the bowl.

"Stop, Amy!" River giggled.

"Was he fuckable?" Amy asked, launching her leg up on the seat, revealing her perfectly strong calves.

"Stop." River protested.

"Come on! Was he?" Amy pried. "Would I do him?"

"No," River replied, matter of fact. "Not enough tats or piercings for you."

"Oh, okay," Amy shrugged, biting into another chip. Her large hoop earrings swung against her neck, as she smacked the table hard. "YOU HAVE TO GET LAID!" she shouted. Several elderly diners looked astonishingly in their direction.

"Stop! Oh my God, Amy," River whispered. "Shhh…" Slightly buzzed, they fell into each other in a fit of laughter.

CHAPTER NINE
Nowhere to Run

The morning alarm sounded. River slept right through it. Half asleep, she reached over and hit the snooze button— again and then again. "Why did I drink so much with Amy last night?" she moaned, throwing the alarm clock off her rustic, chipped, blue nightstand. Burying her head back into the pillow, her secondary cell phone alarm sounded.

"Noooooo…" she cried, shutting it off and pulling back the covers. She wondered if her morning run was really *that* important.

"No! I'm not going," she huffed, throwing herself back into bed and under the covers. She was back to sleep in no time flat.

Two hours later, the constant ringing and vibration of her cell woke her up. Looking at the phone on her nightstand, she saw it was Coty calling. Sitting up abruptly in bed, her poor heart pounded in her ears. She stared at the number scrolling across the screen, as she hugged her knees and waited for the phone to stop ringing. This time she was sure to block his number from her phone. Pulling herself out of bed, weighed down with anxiety, she raced downstairs to make sure her doors were locked. Fanatically, she made sure all the windows were buttoned up and locked. She was afraid of him stalking her. It was his way of getting control over her again. The pain he caused. The broken bones. The bruises. The black, swollen-shut eyes and head wounds. The cuts and scratches on top of her fear of him was too much. She had to stop this somehow.

"Pull it together, girl!" she said, coaching herself.

Deciding a run would do her good, River ran the trails near the mountain, pushing herself into a hard sprint every so often to stay sharp. As the sun started to beat down, she walked back toward her Jeep and sat in the air conditioning, long enough to cool off.

She still had energy to burn, so she took off on foot again, sprinting straight up the mountain this time. A white truck drove by, slowing as it passed her. Looking over, she recognized the driver. He stopped, so she stopped, even though she wasn't happy about being hot, sweaty and breathless.

"Erik, right?"

"Yep. You been running all day?" he asked her while lowering the volume of his stereo.

"No. Well … maybe. What time is it?"

"It's five o'clock," he replied.

River realized she had been running for hours.

"I guess I have been running all day. Stress relief, you know," she laughed, suddenly starting to feel dizzy. She grabbed a hold of the side of his truck and puked beside his front tire. Erik threw the truck in park and raced to her side.

"Hey! You're sick. It's the heat. You know today was one of the hottest days on record for this time of year."

River puked some more.

"Are you drinking water?" he asked.

"I'm fine," River moaned, holding her stomach. "I'm not fantastic, but I'm fine."

"Where's your Jeep?" He asked, genuinely concerned.

"Around the wash … over that way … not far," River whispered, pointing. She was feeling the urge to spew again.

"Let me give you a ride."

River shook her head. She wasn't sure about this guy. He could be a serial killer, and with the way her life was going lately, she wasn't taking any chances.

"I'm fine. Too much sun." River said, letting go of his truck and heading toward her Jeep.

"River, I won't hurt you. I promise. Let me, at least, park my truck and walk you back to your Jeep."

Erik's jeans were dirty—a sexy kind of dirty. He wore those jeans well, and there she was out in the middle of the desert with him—sweaty, pukey, and smelly. River looked up at Erik ... all 6'1 of him. She wagged her hand and said, "Okay. Fine."

He (and his shoulders) came in handy. The sun pierced her eyes, as he held her up.

"You are an overachiever," he teased. "I've seen you at the gym a lot. You are very active. It's admirable."

River was afraid to say too much. She let him do all the talking. Her stomach was stirring, making embarrassing noises.

"I've been wanting to talk to you for a while," he grinned. "I don't think I live too far from you. I see you on the road a lot when I'm on the horses."

River looked up a little surprised.

"I train horses, and I give lessons for those who want to ride. I'm a 30-year-old still trying to find his way through life."

"Atler's Ranch?" River asked.

"Yes. I'm not an Atler, but I've been hired on for the next couple of seasons ... maybe more. They gave me a cabin next to the horse barn for the time being."

"Oh," River tried to force a smile, but she really felt too ill to live in that moment. "Well, there's my Jeep. I can make it from here. Thanks."

"Are you sure," he replied, not wanting to leave her side just yet. River could feel his concern for her, and that made her feel uncomfortable. She left his side, hobbling down some rugged rocks and bolting to the Jeep. Before she could open the door, Erik was by her side, helping her into the vehicle. Once again, he shut the door behind her.

"Will you be okay to drive home?" he asked.

"I will. Thank you for coming to my rescue … again. I'm usually not so needy," she muttered, glancing in his direction. "I'm embarrassed."

Erik gave her an odd look, almost like he didn't believe her.

"Turn the air conditioner on high, and when you get home start pounding the water. You need it."

"Okay," River nodded, slowly backing out, heading up the rocks and out of the wash. Erik ran back to his truck. He jumped in, spun it around, and punched the gas … following her home. When she parked in her drive, his truck roared past with a couple of honks.

River stumbled up her porch steps, unlocked her door and plopped in front of her couch floor fans. Later on, after a long shower, she sat on her bed with a blue towel wrapped around her head. She tried to rest with the fans blowing cool air. There was a knock at the door, sending her to the bedroom window. She was startled to see Erik's white truck parked next to the Jeep. Struggling over whether or not to answer, she scrambled around her room searching for her bra.

"Screw it," she said, opening her bedroom window. "Yes, Erik?"

Erik jumped off her porch backwards, looking very handsome, rugged and clean. "Yeah, sorry, I'm probably freaking you out right now. I just wanted to make sure you were okay."

"I'm still a little sick," River answered.

"Look, I know you don't know me, but I'm really not this weird— usually. I just brought you some electrolyte tablets—potassium with magnesium. They might help."

Erik stared up at her. She stared down at him, still undecided. "I can set them by your door, and you can get them once I leave … if you want."

River exhaled. Giving in to his touching gesture, she went downstairs to meet him, forgetting the blue towel wrapped around her hair. Opening the door, she smiled as he handed her the pill bottle.

"Thanks."

"That shade of blue," he whispered, gesturing his cleft chin in the direction of her head. "It's a nice color on you."

River reached up touching the towel, feeling somewhat unspectacular.

"Yeah, I just took a shower."

His eyes were so startling blue, they almost seemed majestic. After an awkward moment of silence, Erik smiled and said, "Okay, I'm also here to ask if you would like to go horseback riding with me this week."

"Huh?" River's eyes lit up.

"Yeah … you know, I can show you some trails and maybe we can do something after."

Erik was searching River's face for an answer. River scanned his muscular physique and put herself on pause for a moment.

"I would love to go with you. I haven't ridden since I was a teenager. I grew up on a farm with my grandparents…" she suddenly felt foolish for talking for some reason.

"What's your number?" he asked. "We can text … arrange a time."

River gave him her cell number and waited as he dialed her digits into his phone.

"There it is," she smiled, sounding a little too excited. "It's ringing in my bedroom."

"Okay," he grinned. "I will get a hold of you soon."

"Okay."

Erik drove off, while River inhaled a big whiff of the wild scents of her flowers and mesquite trees before walking back into the house.

CHAPTER TEN
Shift Happens

River's medication pass on her unit was absolutely horrendous. Getting through it in a timely manner was not going to happen. One patient couldn't breathe because his oxygen saturation was decreasing for no apparent reason, while another patient decided to walk on her own, against doctor's orders, and fell. And that was just the beginning. The nightmare continued with patient and family member complaints pouring in. Doctors were calling for her left and right, and her CNA (certified nursing assistant) was looking more fragile and worn out than she was.

Not only was River attending to her job, but she was also helping her CNA with her duties, like lifting patients, helping them to the bathroom and answering call lights. This is what separated River from the majority of RNs in this type of facility. It made her stand out. It also proved to be exhausting, even with Alex popping in from time to time to lend a hand.

"Are you sending her out to the hospital?" Alex asked, leaning into River's medication cart.

"Who?"

"The patient who fell," he replied.

"Oh … no. She's fine," River breathed. "Just some skin tears, no major injuries."

"Do you need some help?"

"No. Thanks. I'm fine."

"Would you like to go out this week on another motorcycle adventure?" Alex smiled, jokingly moving his hips back and forth.

"No," she said, almost bothered by the timing of this conversation. "I can't. I'm busy this week. I have a lot to do, and I'm going horseback riding with a friend."

This was River's attempt at putting distance between her and Alex. It was the right thing to do, since they almost had sex, and she wasn't ready for that.

"Horseback riding," Alex replied, jerking his chin. "That's cool. Maybe next week. I've been wanting to take a ride up to Flagstaff."

An elderly man with an aggressive cane shuffled toward them.

"Where's my wife's pain pill?! She asked for it over an hour ago," the man growled.

"I have it ready, sir. I'm sorry. I was caught up with the doctor on the phone," River explained, sort of snubbing Alex.

"Let me know if you are interested in a Flagstaff trip," he said, backing away from the cart. As he walked away, River felt sort of guilty for blowing him off.

"My wife is not staying here if she can't get her medication on time! This is ridiculous," the elderly man shouted, waving his cane around.

River looked at the old man, her disheveled hair falling into her warm, brown, tired eyes. "I know, sir. I'm sorry. It's coming now."

She locked her medicine cart, along with her charting screen and hurried into the patient's room with her medication, the woman's husband tagging along behind.

At the end of her 12hr shift, River stepped into her Jeep relieved it was over. The gemstone ring on her finger lit up sending a slight bolt of electricity throughout her body. It took her by surprise every time it happened.

"Damn it," she whispered, recovering from the jolt. She needed to get this crazy ring off her finger, but she didn't know how.

"I. Can't. Get. It. Off. WOW!" Amy shrieked, struggling with the butter-lubed, gemstone ring bonded to River's finger. "What in the almighty fuck! How did you even get that damn ring on your finger anyway?"

"I don't know; it's weird. It just slipped on, then it molded to my finger," River said, hunching over the rusty old bar stool in Amy's kitchen.

"Damn! You need to cut it off with a jewel saw or something," Amy suggested, washing the fatty substance from her fingers.

The last thing River wanted to do was damage the ring. She just wanted it off her hand to avoid any more spasms or electric jolts.

That's all she wanted.

"Anyway, so tell me about this Erik guy," Amy continued, pouring them both a glass of white wine and slipping onto her expensive, overstuffed, lavish, white sofa.

"I don't know. Nothing to tell … yet. I just thought I should give him a chance. He is very beautiful to look at, but I'm still not interested in anything more than friendship."

"Well, give him a chance, River. You never know; he could be the man who was sent to sweep you off your feet," Amy grinned before taking another sip of wine.

River sighed, looking around Amy's living room. Amy's taste was exquisitely tailored and impeccable. It made River always worried she was going to spill something when she came over. River took a careful sip and said, "Thank you for being my bestie."

"Aww! I love you, too, my little, strange coyote-loving weirdo." Amy reached over and gave River a hug.

CHAPTER ELEVEN
The Cleansing

"When somebody attacks you with a knife, you run if you can. If you can't run, you fight for your life," Sensei Pete explained, as attentive students circled around him. "John and I will demonstrate the four techniques we will be practicing today against knife attacks."

River watched her sensei move fluidly through the techniques, like a Bruce Lee movie. He was quite amazing at his craft.

"Now, everyone grab a knife and a partner and let's practice until you get these moves automated in your system."

River started to practice, boldly taking her partner down and even dragging him across the gym floor.

"Very nice, River," Sensei Pete complimented before moving on to another student. All of a sudden, River's ring lit up, and she felt her heartbeat roar like thunder in her ear drums. Was her heart actually slowing down? It was uncomfortable.

"Are you okay?" her partner asked, but she couldn't answer him. With every loud beat of her heart, a rhythmic drumbeat sounded with it. Something (or someone!) was staring at her. She could feel it, watching from outside. The sound of the tribal drums resounded so loudly throughout her body, it dropped her to her knees. Turning slowly, she saw "it" staring at her through the gym window. It was a strange figure, not quite human in form. It was tall with long arms that dangled passed the knees—pale-skinned with large, dark oval eyes, two holes for a nose and long, white hair. Its eyes pierced hers with a still, deafening silence that could never be explained, except to say that time stood still for a brief moment.

River was tranquilized suddenly, unable to move. A tree was moving alongside her … or was it him? River couldn't tell the gender of this "thing." Concentrating on its movements, it lifted its arm in a wave-like motion toward her before moving in the direction of the Superstition mountains. Finally, her heartbeat returned to a normal rhythm, and she could finally exhale. Beads of sweat dotted her forehead.

"Come on, River! Jump back in and join us," Sensei Pete shouted. River snapped back into reality, taking one last look out the window and finding nothing there.

"River! You alright? Come on over here and join us," He encouraged.

"Yeah, okay," River replied, standing and catching up with the group. River kept glancing out the window to see if anything was there, but there was still nothing.

After class, River stopped by the grocery store to pick up ingredients for her routine quarterly juice cleansing. She leisurely browsed the lemons, cabbage, kale, watercress, ginger and apples. Putting some of each in the grocery cart, along with cashews, mushrooms and lettuce, she made her way over to the tofu. Eating cleaner changed her life, and she couldn't help but think about it with every trip to the grocery store. While examining the tofu, a gruff, deep voice said, "It's you."

She jumped.

"What?" River asked, as the man moved in on her until he was looking into her eyes.

"You … from the bar that night," the man snorted. "Your fucking boyfriend broke my damn nose! Where is he … huh?"

The man looked around, nervously scanning the produce aisles.

"Where's your pretty little boyfriend now? He can't save you today," he grimaced, turning River's stomach.

"I think you have me confused with someone else," River said, picking up a pineapple as a possible weapon to throw at his face.

"Oh, no you don't," he snarled, pointing his finger in her face. "I've had nothing but trouble with my back ever since that motherfucker threw me in that ditch of rocks and cactus!"

"I really don't know what you're talking about," River glowered at him, ready to do whatever it took to defend herself.

"Let me refresh your memory. You went to the bar with your friend … umm … Amy. You were going home with me that night. Remember that? Yeah, you were a fucking tease. Your boyfriend was a nut job who ran my truck off the road, then sucker punched me and tossed me into some rocks. He uses steroids, doesn't he?"

River was confused, she became angry as flashbacks from that night hit.

"YOU DRUGGED ME," River shrieked, as surrounding shoppers stared. "You were going to RAPE ME!"

"No way! Not on your life. You wanted me, honey! Can't rape the willing." The man, who was more like a monster, started to back away from her as she tossed the pineapple between both of her hands. River took a good look at him—young, burly, preppy, mama's boy.

"You tell your boyfriend I am coming for him," he warned before walking away.

River was shaken. Abandoning the cart of groceries, she bolted to her Jeep. Jumping in, she locked the door and sped away, but she couldn't escape the memories from that night, no matter how fast she drove. Pulling into her drive, the large coyote was waiting for her on the porch, as if he knew she needed him. River got out of the Jeep, and no sooner did the coyote jump from the porch and run away.

CHAPTER TWELVE
Dream Date

The next morning, River had a run. She kept it short because of the heat—just up the road and back. Later on, in the garden, she worked tirelessly. While brushing hair from her eyes, she smudged her cheeks with dirt. Taking a feverish beating from the sun, she pulled out the weeds and crab grass that were choking out her vegetables. A large shadow hovered over her. It was Erik.

"Are you ready?" he asked grinning with his sparkling blue eyes.

"What?" she asked. "Today?"

She was so embarrassed for him to see (and smell!) her like this.

"I forgot. I'm sorry. I can't. I'm a mess," Feeling guilty, she futilely brushed at the dirt on her filthy jeans.

"You look fine. It's horseback riding, not the opera," he said, as he pointed at his torn jeans. "Do I look dressed up to you?"

He smiled even bigger, and that made River feel at ease.

"You look beautiful," he added. "I bet you don't even know how beautiful you are, even with dirt all over your face."

River stood up, suddenly feeling shy. "Okay, just give me a few seconds to get ready. I will hurry. I promise."

She threw down her garden tool and ran into her house for a change of clothes and a quick face wash.

Locking her front door, River stepped off the porch. Erik stood staring, as if mesmerized by her. He caught himself and shook it off.

"Come here," he motioned toward two of the most enchanting horses she had ever seen. "You will be riding Sun Drop."

Erik hoisted River onto the large painted animal.

"This is a special horse for a special rider, like you. He knows to take extra special care of you."

River petted the horse's mane, wondering if this animal was as special as he claimed. Walking over to a large satchel connected to his black horse, he pulled out two cowboy hats.

"You will want this. The sun is bright today," he said, handing River a faded, gray hat and dusting off his own hat. Erik jumped onto the back of his horse and made a crackling sound in the direction of River's horse. They were off with Sun drop obediently following alongside.

River watched Erik. She wondered why he was still single and even bothering with her. He looked like he was straight out of a magazine ad for a very expensive bottle of cologne. His abs rippled through his tank top, and the fact that he loved these mountainous trails and knew them well made River's heart melt.

Erik urged her horse, Sun Drop, to get closer to him as they trotted side by side up the road. She liked getting lost with him on the mountain. After an hour of riding, they saw their fill of lizards, quail, rabbits and slithering snakes. Coming to a stop on a large boulder platform, they sat and talked awhile, taking in the majestic scenery they were now a part of. Erik helped her off her horse and led her to a shaded area of the rock. There, they talked about everything from River's work to her karate class, and some parts of her past, but nothing too serious.

"You are really funny," Erik laughed. "A sense of humor is a very good quality in a female."

River smiled, looking away, she scooped up some loose gravel and juggled it in her hand.

"What about you? Have you been here all your life?" River asked.

"No … just a few years," Erik smiled. He talked about training horses, giving lessons and even working on automobiles. "I've done some construction, but I'm more of an engineer."

River got the sense he didn't seem to want to go into more detail. "So, you are from Ohio, and I am from Wisconsin," Erik said looking into her eyes. "And we both ended up here in the desert."

He stood up and kicked around his boots.

"You know, we are very similar people, River—a lot more alike than you know."

"Yeah, maybe," she replied, doubtfully. Hugging her knees, she felt insecure about her past and having to keep it a secret from everyone all the time.

"We better head back before it gets too late," Erik suggested, helping her to her feet and getting her back up on the horse. "Sun Drop likes you. He was a wild horse before I rescued him from slaughter. He was rounded up and sold at auction. I bought him, but he was too wild for anybody to ride."

"Really?"

"Yes," Erik continued. "In fact, no one but me has been able to ride him until today … until you."

"What? So, you didn't know if …" she began, trailing off.

"Don't worry. I knew he wouldn't hurt you."

Back on the trail of desert shrubs, trees, and blooming cactus,

River felt nothing but peace on the inside. It was the first time since the motorcycle ride with Alex.

"I want you to know that if you ever need me for anything, do not hesitate to call me," Erik insisted, walking River to her door. "Please. I don't care if it's a broken faucet. Anything."

River nodded, as he leaned in for a kiss.

"I need to go to bed early tonight. Work in the morning," she replied nervously, stepping back and turning away.

"Okay," Erik smiled.

"Thank you. I really had the best time. It was the perfect day."

Once inside the house, River leaned back into the hard wood door—breathless. She wasn't ready for this but holding back was killing her. On the opposite side, Erik put his hand to the door. He was concerned for her. With a deep breath, he turned and walked away. Grabbing Sun Drop's reign and hopping onto his horse, he headed back to Atler's ranch.

River ambled up the stairs, preparing to settle down for the night. A shower, a salad and a cup of hot herbal tea was at the top of her list. The house was quiet, as she thumbed through a recipe book. Canning pickles was her goal that season, as her cucumber vines had taken off. Lying in bed, she looked up at the ceiling. Thoughts of the day consumed her. Erik. He was so different. There was something about him.

River drifted off into a dream. She was dancing with Alex. They were laughing, moving, joking around with others dancing in a crowded room. Soon, they were alone, just the two of them, dancing close. Alex whispered into her ear, "I will protect you."

River suddenly found herself in another room with Erik. He was sitting on a large chair, and he pulled her onto his lap. Everything felt so real, as if they were visiting another dimension or stage of reality.

"Erik, I have to get off your lap," River said fearfully, jumping off. She looked around for Coty.

"Why?" he asked.

"I'm at the dance with Alex, but Coty might be here. I'm scared, Erik."

"Do not fear, River. I'm here. I will protect you from Coty," Erik said, pulling her closer to him. "Who is Alex?"

River resisted.

"You are mine. Forget Coty," he said, pulling her into his lap. River was afraid and shook her head in fear.

"I can't, Erik. He will kill us both."

"Wake up, River. You are having a nightmare. Wake up with me," Erik breathed.

Suddenly, River woke from a deep sleep. Sitting straight up in bed, she saw that it was four o'clock in the morning. She laid back down, wondering if that was a dream or something else. It seemed so real. Not able to go back to sleep, she started her day by walking downstairs to make coffee. While passing her bay window, she saw "Little Guy" watching her. They looked at one another and, simultaneously, walked away … out of sight.

CHAPTER THIRTEEN
Orion's Belt

A few long, boring weeks droned by. River never did hear from Erik, not since their horseback road together. She wanted to connect with him, and was even tempted to call or text him, but she wrangled her emotions and resisted. She figured she had probably messed it up by not kissing him that day. She tried to push it out of her mind—all of it. At the same time, she reminded herself of all the reasons why she shouldn't pursue this man. She trudged through her daily routine with higher anxiety than normal. Ever since the dream she had featuring Erik and Alex, her heart became less sure of what to do about either one of them. Since childhood, River had always had vivid dreams, and sometimes they came true. However, this dream changed her perception of them both. It was actually kind of driving her crazy, making her feel all romantic and ready for love or an intimate relationship in some form or another.

"Just reach out to him, maybe he thinks you need some time, or he needs reassurance you are into him." Amy said, after dance class.

"I want to, but I'm afraid."

"Afraid of what?" Amy asked, wiping the sweat from her brows with a small hand towel.

"I don't know. I want to avoid purposely inviting anyone into my life who could be bad," River said, taking a quick swig of water and stretching her legs along the wooden bench.

"River, you need to live your life. You can't keep rejecting people or you will end up alone."

"You are right," River said, letting out a slight sigh.

"Right about what?'

A deep, sexy voice chimed in from behind, startling both River and Amy. They turned to find Erik standing over them, flashing that easy grin of his. Amy looked at River confused, suddenly realizing this must be the man of the hour—*the* one they were talking about. River's face gave it away immediately.

"Hi," River said shyly.

Erik winked at River, just before giving her an intense look. Amy cleared her throat, so as to get her friend's attention.

"Oh, sorry. Erik this is my friend Amy. Amy this is Erik." River said, introducing the two.

"Hi. I'm her very best friend actually, and your full name is?" Amy asked, offering a handshake.

"Erik Scott," he replied. "I was just upstairs in the weight room. I thought I saw your Jeep here earlier."

"Of course! You lift weights! Look at your body," Amy interjected. "You can definitely tell you work out."

Erik leaned into the wrought iron bench, looking super intently into River's eyes, "Hey! Do you have a minute?"

"Hey! Don't mind me. I need to get going anyway," Amy said, grabbing her bag and taking off in a hurry. "Call me, River."

"Can we walk?" Erik asked.

"Sure."

"I wanted to tell you that I'm sorry for trying to kiss you," Erik said, genuinely nervous. "I was out of line. I don't want you to think that's the only thing I was trying to do that day. You know, sleep with you."

River was touched.

"No. It's ok. It's just that I haven't dated anyone in a really long time. My last relationship ended a few years ago. It was not a good one," River replied, noticeably uneasy.

Walking toward her Jeep, Erik moved in closer. River could feel an energetic surge of electric energy flow up through her arm, warming her entire body. This was a serious attraction. She knew immediately that she couldn't and wouldn't be able to fight this.

"I would like to see you again. We can take this slow if you want. I have no problems with that," Erik said.

"Yes. I would like that. Do you have time now? Do you want to get a drink or something?" River asked, surprising herself.

"Oooh! Alcohol after a workout?" Erik laughed. "I'm just joking. Your Jeep or my truck?"

"Actually, maybe we should meet up later, if that's okay."

WHAT ARE YOU DOING? HE WANTS YOU! TAKE HIM! River thought to herself.

"Sounds good! I will pick you up in an hour," he replied.

"Okay."

River wanted to back out of the deal, but her heart wouldn't let her. She watched him jump into his truck and follow her down the road. He honked his horn as she pulled into her drive.

Almost an hour later, River waited on her front porch for Erik. She fidgeted with her clothes, twirled her spiral curls—in other words, she was restless. Erik finally pulled into the drive, and it seemed as though they both were feeling excited about seeing each other again.

"Are you ready?" he asked.

"Yes," River replied.

His smile was infectious, and she couldn't help noticing the way he looked at her, as if she was his prize. He opened the passenger door and helped her in.

"You are so tiny. I feel like a giant compared to you," He laughed. River noticed how clean the interior of his vintage truck was, southwest printed seat covers and all. "So, where are we going?"

"Honestly," River admitted. "I'm not that familiar with good drinking holes around here."

"Okay," Erik countered, taking a moment before starting the engine. "I have an idea."

Off they went with the windows rolled down and a warm, desert breeze flowing through her hair. Erik pulled into the nearest gas station. He jumped out of the truck and ran in, returning a few minutes later with a six pack of locally-brewed beer. Within another couple of minutes, they were headed back toward Superstition Mountain, taking the curves gently while a sweet melody purred from the stereo.

"I know the park rangers. We'll be all right to do what we please. As long as we don't start any fires," Erik smiled, as he turned into a cozy nook near a wash below the mountain. River sat quietly, enjoying the ride.

"Hold on," he said, jumping out of the cab of the truck, beer and blanket in hand. River watched as Erik spread the southwest-print overlay across the hood. He helped her out of the truck and then gave her a boost up onto the warm hood, climbing up beside her. The sun was showing signs of retiring and they had front row seats. Offering her a beer, Erik smiled. The two clinked bottlenecks, and she took a sip, shivering as the temperature started to drop.

"I should've worn my sweater," she said, rubbing her arms, almost feeling stupid and immediately hoping he wouldn't take what she said the wrong way.

"We can use the blanket to cover up," Erik offered.

"No, it's okay."

"You sure?"

"I'm fine," River insisted, her bottom lip trembling.

Erik jumped off the hood, grabbed his flannel out of the truck.

"It's not clean, but it's yours, if you want it."

River took it into her hands, pressing the flannel to her nose. She got a big, earthy whiff of cedar and sandalwood. It had to be cologne. No man could naturally smell that good—could he? She melted, as she put it on her body. Erik rejoined her, sitting closer this time.

"Do you see that cluster of stars?" Erik asked, pointing off into the distance a darkening sky. "That's the star Alnitak. There is Alnilam and Mintaka. They say all the pyramids are aligned with Orion's belt."

"Really?"

She was somewhat astonished he knew his way around the stars. Erik went on to explain the phenomena of Orion's belt and a galaxy she knew very little about.

"You know a lot about astronomy and astrology," she replied, amazed at his brilliant mind.

"Yes," he said, looking into his beer before taking a drink. "I've done a lot of research in that area."

"It sounds like a passion," she said. "I understand that. I get that way about being vegan … and wildflowers. Flowers should just grow everywhere, all the time—thousands of them."

Erik smiled. He gazed into her eyes. River looked away—force of habit.

"You have a very kind and passionate demeanor. I find it very attractive," Erik whispered.

River looked off into the night, fiddling with her beer cap. Just then they both heard truck tires kick up gravel on the road behind them. Erik and River turned in unison, squinting at the disappearing headlights.

"Do you believe in life on other planets?" River asked, changing the subject. Erik jumped off the hood of the truck.

"I don't know, maybe," he shrugged.

Erik offered his arm to help River down.

"You are cold. I want to get you home."

"I'm fine … really," she lied through shivering lips.

"Nope. I don't want you sick."

Sitting in her front drive, Erik turned up a beautiful song on the stereo. They sat quietly together, listening. River waited like a coy teenager for him to make a move, but he didn't. Erik opened her door, helped her out and walked her to the front door. He resisted reaching in for a kiss. Partially unlocking the door, she asked, "Would you like to come in?"

"Not tonight. I've got to get back. I have a few new students tomorrow. Besides, aren't we taking this slow," he smiled, almost teasing her. Erik stepped in closer, the vibe between them getting real, making her nervous. He gently touched her face. River thought for sure he would kiss her, but he turned away.

"Let's do something this week," he said.

"Uh ... okay," River agreed.

"Lock your doors," he said, just before taking off.

"I will," she said, as he drove away. Looking into the night sky at the cluster of stars, River whispered these words to herself, "Orion's Belt."

CHAPTER FOURTEEN
Burst at the Seams

"**D**o you have anything for me?" a patient named Evelyn asked River as she walked into the room.

"Of course, I do. Here is your Xanax, Percodan, and your nasal spray," River smiled, assisting Evelyn with all of her medications, except for the nasal spray. Evelyn could manage that herself.

"Are you married?" Evelyn asked between raspy breaths, as River checked her oxygen tubing.

"No. I'm not."

"Why not?"

"I don't think I'm the marrying kind."

"You've just got to find the right man, honey. He's out there waiting for you."

"I see," River smiled. "Well, then hopefully he finds me."

"As beautiful as you are, I'm sure he will come along at just the right time," Evelyn assured. Amused, River walked out of Evelyn's room and bumped into Alex. He was waiting for her at her nurse's cart.

"Okay," Alex began. "Flagstaff. This weekend. You and me. What do you say?"

"I don't think so Alex. I've got a lot to do."

"Come on! It's the bike ride of the season," he coaxed.

"I don't know, maybe."

"I am going to ask you again tomorrow," he laughed.

"Okay." River agreed.

After work, and still in her scrubs, River went straight to tending her garden. It was extra hot and dry, and it was wreaking havoc on her vegetables. Turning on the hose, she watered down every growing thing she had. Almost instantly, the garden hose burst wide open, splattering water all over River. As she hurried into the house to change her clothes, her cell rang. It was Erik.

"Hey."

"Hey. What's wrong?" he asked.

"Oh, it's my garden hose. It busted. It got too hot and burst open, and now I'm soaked," River sat back in a sofa chair and sighed.

"How about I come over and set up a sprinkler system for you? We can cover the hoses in the dirt, so they don't get too hot."

"I don't want you to go to any trouble. I have a little sprinkler set up, but it is ghetto," she laughed, drying herself with a towel.

"It's no trouble at all. In fact, it will be easy. I'm coming over," Erik said, hanging up before she had time to respond.

Running upstairs to change, River barely had time to throw on dry clothes before Erik showed up. She took one last look at her hair, and then ran down to meet him outside. Erik pulled two garden hoses and two rotating sprinkler heads out of his truck bed and said, "I've got adaptors for these, and I can make some wooden platforms for them, if you want."

"Thank you so much," she said.

"I know how important your garden is to you. Anyways, I needed an excuse to see you again," he said, gently squeezing her shoulder.

Erik's eyes lit up around her, especially when River smiled at him. *This* smile was the first genuine smile that she had offered him. Erik melted. She lit up his soul.

"Come inside, Erik, I have air conditioning."

Offering him her homemade lavender lemonade, straight from her own flower garden, she and Erik sat down at the reclaimed wood kitchen table and talked for over an hour. It was nice to finally feel okay about getting to know him. River casually brought up Alex's invitation to take a motorcycle ride to Flagstaff. Erik's expression became stern.

"Are you going?" he inquired.

"Well, I haven't said no. He is a good friend, and I do like to ride."

River looked down at the rustic wood, tracing her finger over the natural design.

"It is good to have some quality down time. Just be careful. Maybe I should go with you. I have a bike," Erik said, chuckling.

River giggled.

"No. I wouldn't impose," he said. "I'm just kidding with you."

River thought about it for a minute. It wasn't a bad idea. It would keep the space she wanted between her and Alex.

"I could invite Amy," she added. "We could all ride together, the four of us."

"Are you serious?" Erik asked. "Would he mind if I tag along?"

"Well, let me call him and see what he thinks."

"Let me know. I'm down," Erik said, walking to the back door and giving her a wink. "I need to get going, a horse is waiting on some shoes before sundown."

River called Amy, begging her to join the motorcycle adventure.

"What are you thinking?" Amy asked. "It seems like Erik could be something more, and you are trying to bring him on a trip with Alex. Think about it. Alex wants you too."

River reflected for a split second, but she didn't waver.

"I want Alex to know that he and I are *just* friends. Please come with me. You will enjoy the ride," River pleaded.

"Have you even asked Alex?"

"No, but I will tomorrow. If he doesn't want to do it, I won't go."

"Okay," Amy said, taking a deep breath and exhaling into the phone. "I don't think it's a great idea. I have a bad feeling about it, but for you … I will do it. Don't expect me to be attracted to Alex though."

"Okay. Deal!"

CHAPTER FIFTEEN

Collision

The next day, River caught up with Alex during her routine medication pass. She casually mentioned including a couple of riders into the motorcycle adventure mix. Alex was stoked that River wanted to go, and he had no problem adding two extra travelers.

"Are they a couple?" he asked.

"No," River exhaled. "Erik is a friend of mine, a neighbor."

River grabbed albuterol for one of Alex's patients.

"I will give this to her for you."

So as to avoid certain "details," River hastily walked into the patient's room and administered the medication. Alex could tell something was up. River forced a smile and said, "Just four nice people going on a motorcycle ride together.

"Okay," he nodded, looking at her curiously. He felt a little wounded because he knew what she was really trying to say, but he let it go. "Let's do it … 6 a.m. sharp on Saturday—your house. Anyone late gets left behind."

"OH, THANK YOU, ALEX!" River exclaimed, sincerely relieved for his going along with the unsolicited invite, if not for his discretion.

Alex pursed his lips into a smile, shrugged and walked away.

Amy sat with River on her front porch that Saturday morning. They waited nervously for the men to show up. Alex was the first to arrive, on an exquisite sport bike, different from the one he rode before. River introduced him to Amy, who in return, was awestruck by Alex. It was obvious she found him very attractive. River watched Amy shamelessly flirt with him and felt a slight pang of jealousy when Alex flirted back.

"Can I use your bathroom?" Alex asked.

"Sure, I haven't locked up yet. There is one downstairs, first right off the kitchen."

A few minutes later, Erik showed up on a black Kawasaki. He unfastened his helmet, greeting River and Amy with tousled hair and perfect teeth.

"Wow! That bike looks fast," Amy squealed.

"Yeah," Erik replied, curling his bicep and scrunching his nose. Within moments, Alex walked out the front door. Almost instantly, both men exchanged a series of complicated expressions, followed by a deafening silence. River attempted to break the tension with introductions.

"Alex … this is Erik. Erik this is …"

"We know each other," Alex said, cutting her off.

"What?" River replied.

Amy gave River an uneasy glance.

"Yes," Erik said, calm and cool. "How are you, Alex?"

"I'm good, Erik."

Both men continued an exchange of furious, weird expressions making River very nervous.

"A little far from home, Alex?"

"Funny," Alex huffed. "I could ask the same of you."

"Wait," Amy interrupted. "How do you two know each other?"

"We go way back," Erik said, his chest puffed.

"Well, this isn't weird at all," Amy added, sarcastically.

"*How* do you two know each other?" River asked, regretting the idea of this foursome.

"We should get going," Alex said, blatantly ignoring her question.

"I need a bike with a big seat—big butt, big seat, so I guess I'm riding with you, Alex." Amy interjected.

River let out a grateful sigh. Alex was not happy about it, but he refused to challenge who his riding companion would be.

"Okay, then let's get started," Alex said, handing Amy a helmet. Amy looked at River and mouthed the words, *You're welcome.*

River put on a helmet. She was more confused than ever, but happy they could walk away from the weird facial takedowns.

"Erik, what was that all about?" River asked, hopping on the back of his bike.

"Put your arms around me!" he shouted., ignoring her.

River did as she was told, and soon both bikes were backing out of the drive and racing toward the highway. Passing through the desert, vying upward on winding roads, they reached large mountains with snow-top views and fruitful vegetation. There was the occasional elk and coyote spotting, as they zipped around the pine forests thick with mystery. Erik felt River shiver from the cooler temperatures and the wind, so he lifted up his t-shirt and jacket, placing River's hands underneath so to keep her warm. His attention to such little details melted her. She felt his abs pulsate with every turn he made on the bike. They stopped in Black Canyon for a quick break. River and Amy took off for the gas station restrooms, leaving the men to themselves.

"What are you doing, Erik?" Alex demanded.

"You know why I'm here, Alex," Erik said, matched with an intense look. "The real question is, why are you here?"

As the girls came out of the restroom, they saw the men engaging in a not-so-nice conversation. Amy grabbed River's arm pulling her back and asked, "What in the hell is going on with these two? It's weird."

"I will find out," River insisted.

Back on the highway, Erik swerved around a brave coyote eating something in the middle of the road. River cringed at the smell of the carcass, as it wafted straight up her nose. They were now passing creeks and rivers, riding along fascinating canyons that led to more mountains filled with evergreens. He squeezed her hand every now and then, while River remained fascinated at the landscapes. At every stop sign and traffic light, Erik turned and asked River if she was okay. By the minute, River was finding herself more and more attracted to Erik, and it didn't bother her at all. Alex tried not to notice. He was tail spinning into a darker mood just thinking about it. Amy was doing her best to talk to Alex, but he wasn't interested. Amy was not his type—River was.

Alex kept pace with Erik's bike as they rode side-by-side. Even though he knew he could show him up a thousand times over, Alex chose not to. More than his manhood, his deepest concern was River. This didn't need to be a wicked sports competition, and no one needed to be put in danger out of ego. Alex knew if Erik were to get in the way, there would be a lot at stake. This had nothing to do with a motorcycle ride.

Erik saluted Alex, telling River to hold on tight, as he kicked his bike into high gear. Amy rolled her eyes, as she watched Erik and River speed off. The testosterone was heavy in the air, and her butt was hurting. Alex picked up speed, sticking close to Erik.

Erik suddenly slowed down. Alex shot him a look, shamelessly shaking his head at a stop light. *What was that?* River wondered. She planned to ask Erik about it later. Finally, in Flagstaff, they stopped off to eat and have a drink.

"Brunch! My fucking favorite," Amy gushed, in between sips of mimosa. Erik and Alex ate in silence. Apparently, there was not much to say to each other or to anyone else at the table. Alex finished off his beer and excused himself, so to check on his bike. Erik hit the restroom, leaving the two women alone to their drinks. Amy whispered, "I hope you know; this whole situation is uncomfortable and bazaar. You owe me, girl."

"I'm sorry. I didn't expect them to know each other."

The foursome reunited back at the bikes. Erik suggested they go on a hike. Amy refused her helmet, even though Alex insisted she wear it.

"Are you sure?" Alex asked.

"I'm fine. No more helmet," she said, shaking her hair.

Erik began the hike by leading them to a nice starting place, a clearing in the woods. Amy swatted at bugs, bitching about the insect situation as they walked deeper into the woods. Feeling something in her hair, she screamed, "GET IT OUT! GET IT OUT!"

Alex assisted in ridding the small spider from Amy's strands. He then took the lead, while Erik and River lagged behind. Erik interlocked his fingers into River's. He noticed Alex looking back and grumbling.

"Pick it up! You're slowing us down back there," Alex muttered.

River quickly let go of Erik's hand, picking up the pace, so to catch up with Alex. The foursome arrived at a large swimming hole, to which Amy wasted no time throwing off her clothes, except for her under garments, and moving to the edge of a large cliff.

"Amy, wait!" River shrieked, as her friend jumped into the water .

"Your friend can't handle her mimosas," Alex said, stopping

abruptly. River ambled down to the creek bed, rolled up her jeans and waded into the water. Erik did the same. They watched Amy swim and draw the attention to herself. When Amy finally decided to come out of the water to sun herself on a large boulder, River joined her. Rather than breathe in the surrounding beauty, they were both witness to yet another heated conversation between Erik and Alex.

"What are the odds that they would know each other? I mean, I want the actual fucking odds of these two men, the same two you are finally attracted to, actually knowing each other in fucking Arizona. Nobody is really from Arizona. It's creepy," Amy ranted. "Only you could make this weird connection happen."

"What do you mean?" River asked, somewhat annoyed.

"Haven't you noticed how wild your life is yet? Honey, your experiences are one in a million. Not many people have a life as complicated, horrific or as weird as yours."

"Wow, Amy! Thanks a lot. Tell me how you really feel."

"I'm always going to," Amy said, putting her arm around River. "You are my hero, for all you've been through and all that you continue to go through. When it comes to a man, just remember ... don't settle."

River laughed. Amy had sucked down a few too many mimosas at brunch and it was showing.

As they walked back to the bikes, Amy hitched a ride on Alex's back. After thirty minutes of riding back toward Apache Junction, a storm rolled in. It quickly went from a light mist drizzle to an uprise of rain. Erik motioned for Alex to pull over.

"It's really starting to come down hard!" he shouted.

"No shit! What do you want to do?" Alex asked.

"Let's pull over at the nearest place once we get into town." They still had a journey ahead. The rain was becoming fierce and the roads slick. Alex had experience with this kind of riding, but he was concerned with Erik and River, as they slowed almost to a stop to round a tight curve.

Thunder carried on, as a monsoon cell burst of water suddenly dropped its weight from the clouds. Erik stopped his bike, not able to go any further. Alex parked for a moment behind him.

"We are stopping for a minute!" Erik shouted, as the large valley along the cliffs started to fill up with water.

"What?!" River shouted.

She couldn't hear everything he was saying, as the sky roared. River buried her head deeper into Erik's back. They were both soaked, nowhere to go.

"It's too dangerous!" Erik shouted out to Alex.

"If we don't get out of this area, we are going to encounter flash flooding from the mountain!" Alex hollered back. Watching the water fill the valley below, Erik agreed to keep moving, albeit cautiously. Erik set the pace, as they slowly rounded corners.

The rain paused, and Erik and Alex were able to pick up more speed. Just as they were feeling more confident with road conditions, a car came up from behind, carelessly passing them all at a high rate of speed. The car clipped Alex's bike, throwing it to the side. The car circled off to the side of the road, as Alex's bike was flung against a steel guard rail.

River's eyes filled with fear, as she watched Amy fly off the motorcycle and into a large rock wall opposite Alex's bike.

"NO!" River screamed.

Alex became pinned under his bike, while Amy lay lifeless along the wet road. Erik punched the break, suddenly jumping off his bike. Scared teenagers in the car watched Erik and River run in the direction of

Amy and Alex. One teenager was crying, while he frantically made a call on his cell phone. Another got out of the car and ran to River's side, but she didn't even notice him. She was too busy breathing life back into her best friend.

"AMY! OH MY GOD! SOMEONE CALL 911."

She performed CPR like she had never performed it before. Erik helped Alex get out from under his bike.

"Are you okay?" he asked.

Except for road rash and a limp, Alex seemed to be fine. The rain started to fall again, only harder this time. River paid no mind, as she stopped long enough to check for a pulse.

Grabbing Amy's wrist, she waited and then went right back into chest compressions. Erik rushed to River's side.

"What can I do?" he asked, as the sound of sirens could be heard in the distance. River ignored him, as she continued to perform CPR.

"COME ON AMY!"

Tears, mixed in with rain, fell down River's cheeks. Erik jumped up and ran to Alex.

"What do you want to do?" Erik asked.

"We do nothing. We aren't to interfere with them, remember," Alex said, remaining sullen and somber. Erik became enraged.

"It's her best friend!" Erik shouted.

Alex turned to him and said, "No, Erik. Leave it alone. You've got yourself into enough shit as it is!"

Erik looked at him in shock, as if the reality of the situation had taken root. He ran back to River's side, moving her out of the way, so to takeover compressions. River cried with her face pointed up at the sky, not even bothered by the small pebbles carving into her knees.

First responders rolled up on scene. River shouted, "BRING THE AED! HELP PLEASE! MY FRIEND!"

Erik pulled River out of the way, so the medics could work on Amy. River fought like hell to get out of his grasp, but she was powerless to him. Erik tried to hold her arms down without causing more of a scene.

While the highway patrol had the teenagers distracted, Alex crept up on River, touching the back of her neck and instantly sending an electromagnetic impulse through her. It put her to sleep in Erik's arms. Exasperated, Erik looked at Alex.

"I thought we weren't intervening," he said, lifting River up and cradling her in his arms.

"You know, as well as I do, she is the one exception."

Erik and Alex watched as the chaos to bring Amy back to life ensued. She was carefully put onto a gurney and lifted into the ambulance. The doors closed, and the ambulance shot off to a nearby hospital—sirens screaming. Highway patrolman made their way over to the two men, asking questions concerning the crash. There seemed to be some concern for River, as she appeared lifeless in Erik's arms.

"Is she okay?"

"Yes," Alex assured. "This is Amy's best friend. She fainted."

Another set of medics ran to River, as Erik set her down for them to examine. The medics insisted on taking River in for a thorough exam and observation because her vitals were that of a person in shock.

"Go with her. I will meet you there," Alex said, nodding at Erik.

Erik remained at River's side, remaining supportive while she cried at the news of her friend's death. Erik got used to the delicate balance between holding her and giving her space, as needed.

"I can't believe she's gone," River repeated over and over again, until she fell completely silent. When Alex showed up to pick them up from the hospital, River ran to him, holding on for dear life. Looking up at him, she cried, "Alex, this doesn't feel real."

"I know, baby," he said, holding her tight. "I'm sorry."

"She was my only family—all I had," she sobbed.

"I'm your family, baby, and umm … Erik, too. We will get you through this."

Alex helped her into the backseat of the car. River laid down, cradling herself until she fell asleep.

"They gave her valium," Erik whispered.

"Good. We are in it deep, my dear brother," Alex replied.

"I think so."

"We can work together on this," Alex continued.

"Why did you try to have sex with her?" Erik asked.

"Oh, that was you," Alex glowered. "Knocking on the door? What did you do to her?"

"Doesn't matter. Don't try it again."

"Be careful, little brother," Alex warned. "You forget too much."

"She's mine."

"Really?"

"She's always been mine," Erik breathed.

"Let's focus on getting her back home in one piece," Alex exhaled.

"Exactly what I want," Erik agreed. "To see her home safe.

"You shall eat the good of the land, but if you refuse and rebel,
you shall be devoured by the sword."

-Isaiah 1:19

CHAPTER SIXTEEN
Food for the Soul

Three weeks passed. Amy was gone. Her funeral was the only thing motivating River to get out of bed and get dressed. Every other day was the same—laying around, barely breathing. She was thankful for her PTO time during this terrible tragedy. Sitting at great lengths in the shower, physically and emotionally naked, helped soothe her anxiety and grief.

Erik and Alex called her cell, endlessly texting when she failed to answer. River didn't have it in her to respond. When Erik showed up at the funeral, it surprised her. Still, she barely spoke to him, even though he held her hand during the service. Who would she lean on now? Who would push her to take risks? Amy was her "ride or die," and now she was gone.

Never coming back.

One afternoon, River woke up to the sound of sprinklers splashing against the side of her house.

"What the …" she mumbled, hopping out of bed and running down the steps in a flash. Throwing open the front door, she noticed more flowers planted along her flagstone walkway. Rounding the corner, she saw Erik watching the rotation of the water sprinklers.

"Hi," River whispered.

"Hey!" Erik said, with a compassionate grin.

"Thank you. I haven't watered in a while."

"I know," he nodded.

"I guess I'm freaking out," River said, shifting her feet, using her hand to block the sun from her eyes.

"I know," Erik replied, turning back toward the water sprinklers.

River had visibly lost weight. Erik realized she hadn't only neglected the garden, but herself, as well. Her lips were cracked. She had dark circles under her eyes, and her cheek bones appeared more prominent with her thinning face.

"You're barefoot," Erik said, grinning. "I can't get over how tiny your feet are."

"What can I say? I have weird DNA," River shrugged.

Erik's smile vanished. That statement was so true, and she had no idea.

"You look really hungry. What do you want to eat?" he asked.

Erik already knew everything about her—her likes, her dislikes and her habits. She didn't have a clue.

"I'm not hungry."

"You are, too," He insisted, coming off a bit irritated. "You need to eat."

"Don't go to any trouble. I will throw something together later."

"I am getting you something to eat. Don't worry. It will be a vegan meal."

Before she could protest, Erik put up his hand to stop her. He jumped in his truck and was gone. River walked back into the house. She decided to get dressed, even though she didn't want to. She brushed the knots out of her hair and then lay on the couch in front of the television, flipping through the channels. Erik returned with a tofu spring salad and tempura vegetables from the local Japanese restaurant in town—her favorite.

"How did you know I eat this? I order these two meals together all the time," she said, sitting up and giving him a confused look.

"I mentioned your name to the woman who runs the place, and she said this was your usual."

He lied.

Erik knew what she ordered because he WATCHED her order it often.

"Oh," River replied, scooching to the edge of the sofa, picking at her food. She wasn't that hungry, but she appreciated the gesture, so she gave it her best effort. River looked at Erik, stoic and sullen and said, "I was in a very abusive relationship with my ex. I was always trying to please him, but he was never happy with anything I did."

River took a deep breath, then continued, "He was a walking timebomb, always blowing up. He would beat me up over little things."

River looked down at her food, pushing it around with her fork. Erik tensed up. He knew he had to hear this. More importantly, he knew she needed to talk about it.

"He broke my nose a couple of times. I had bruises on my face, black swollen eyes—a lot. It got to the point I felt no one cared about me and that sooner or later he would eventually kill me."

Erik's breathing became shallow, his face hot.

"One time he kicked me over the hood of our car. I don't remember why. It's weird. You think I would remember why he did that, but I don't," River whispered. "He hated when I talked out of turn or spoke my mind about anything. He would beat me because of it."

"River ..." Erik said softly.

"He almost killed me once," she continued, unable to believe the words were falling from her mouth. "He fractured my back in a few places ... bruised my spleen. That was after two days' worth of beatings and dumping trash on me."

Erik put his hand on her shoulder, squeezing.

"I do remember the reason for that beating. It was because I didn't want to eat. I was so depressed because of everything he was doing to me, I stopped eating. That day, he bought me a chicken dinner. I refused it. So, he tried to kill me. When he saw me on the floor, unable to get up, he sat down and ate his dinner. Then he just left me there out there … in the middle of the country."

River choked back tears.

"Someone eventually showed up," she said. "It was his mother and her friend. His mother did nothing to help me. It was her friend who called an ambulance. I was sent to a trauma unit. That's when I knew I had to get out of Ohio. If I didn't, he never would have left me alone."

She took a much-needed breath.

"I got on a plane, and I landed here. I was alone until I met Amy. I got a job working at a local restaurant. I worked there until my nursing license was turned over to Arizona. Amy owned the joint. We became best friends … like sisters. She listened to my endless frustration with my ex—Coty. Amy helped me heal," River cried, stopping herself. "I'm sorry, Erik, I'm talking too much."

River leaned back into the sofa, feeling a little relieved, looking as though she had just unloaded the weight of the world from her shoulders.

"No," he encouraged, leaning back next to her. "Keep talking. You need this."

Erik was doing his level best to be supportive, but what he really wanted to do was go find this asshole and kill him. River looked up at him with a soft, weak look. The warmth of him sitting next to her motivated her to sit up and take a big bite of her tofu salad.

"Oh, this is *so* good," she said, inhaling. "Thank you."

It was more than the tofu. Everything in that moment felt good.

It was sustenance for her soul.

"You are welcome," Erik replied, rubbing her back and shoulders. He could feel the pent-up stress and tension loosening. He wanted to massage her more, but he also didn't want to overstep his bounds. "You know I'm here for you … right?"

"Yes," she muttered, meekly. She loved the feel of his hands on her. It was nothing like what she had experienced in the past with Coty— not even close.

"Alex is here for you, too." Erik added, almost reluctantly.

"Oh, now you two are getting along," River teased. "What was going on with the two of you anyway?"

"It's a long story—ancient history. We are over it now."

Erik stood up, stretching tall. River hated that he stopped touching her. She needed it. She found him very comforting.

"Oh, good," she smiled, sleepily. "Erik?"

"Yes?"

"Are you busy today?"

"No."

"Can you hold me," River began. "Until I fall asleep?"

"It's only two o'clock."

"Please," she yawned. "I'm so tired."

Erik wanted her to eat first, but after hearing her story and looking into her eyes, he simply smiled.

"Of course," he said. "I will hold you. Come here."

He helped River to her feet before carefully throwing her over his shoulder and taking her upstairs to her room. It made her giggle a little out loud, and that made him feel good, if not hopeful that she would come out of this in one piece.

Pulling back her linen duvet comforter, Erik gently plopped her down and then leaned in to kiss her on her forehead. He knelt down next to her bed, strumming his fingers through her tangle of curls.

"I want you in bed next to me," she said, her eyes becoming heavy.

"Are you sure?"

"Yes."

Erik climbed into bed next to her, holding her close to him. He could feel her heart beating in sync with his, as he got swept into her brown almond-shaped eyes. Tears fell down her face, as she looked at him with deep longing. It was a test of wills, as they each tried to resist the other. The energy between them was just too strong, growing more urgent and intense with every passing second.

River leaned in, kissing Erik gently on the lips. Unable to hold back any longer, he responded with a ravenous, passionate kiss in return. He was immediately on top of her, kissing her lips, neck, ears, and whatever his hungry, eager mouth could manage. He wanted her so badly, but he knew the consequences if they were to become one. He knew, in good conscience, he couldn't take her, as much as he wanted to.

Erik tried to break free of her hold, but she pulled him in and rolled over on top of him. River kissed him some more, feeling the arousal overtake her.

"I need you," she said.

"I want you too," he whispered, his hands clutching at her shirt. Grabbing her, he rolled over top of her, holding her down. Erik took a deep, ragged, (regrettable) breath and sighed, "No. This isn't the right time."

"What?"

"Not right now," he said. "We can't"

"Why," she begged. "I want you."

"You are vulnerable, and besides, we have plenty of time. I'm not going anywhere."

River pushed him off of her. She leaned back, frustrated and confused. She could feel him. He was as hard as a rock.

"I'm going to hold you all night," he promised, rolling onto his back, leaving a warm nook with her name on it between his strong arms and his chest. River slid down into him, relenting to his ridiculous reason and his resistance, even thought it was killing her. Nevertheless, his sense of duty to her was refreshing, and with that, she soon fell asleep.

Erik thought about how close he came to disrupting her life. For that, he felt a pang of guilt. He knew that he loved her, that he'd always loved her, but River didn't remember him—yet.

Erik watched River sleep for a while before stepping outside barefoot. A large coyote came to him. He bent down to greet it with a warm tussle on the animal's scruff.

"Good job," he whispered. The coyote sat on its haunches, as Erik radiated a light into the distance. The light landed on a female coyote standing on a boulder. Empathically, Erik emanated the command, "Protect River."

The large coyote placed his paw in Erik's hand before running to the female coyote. Erik walked back upstairs and sat in the overstuffed chair in the corner of River's room. He continued to watch her sleep.

Before she woke the next morning, he kissed her cheek and left her a note. It read: You should go to your karate class tonight. Blow off some steam. I will see you there. ~Erik

CHAPTER SEVENTEEN
Her Guardian

When River woke up, she read the note and decided she would go to her karate class just to see Erik again. Her first instinct, as she got dressed, was to call Amy. She reached for her cell, and it suddenly occurred to her that she couldn't call Amy anymore. There would be no answer or sarcastic remark about her and Erik's first kiss.

There would be no more Amy.

Looking at her phone, she pulled up Amy's last text message. It read: `"I will be there in 20 minutes. This guy better not be an asshole! Love you! Get up! ha ha!"`

"I love you too, Amy," River said, tears streaking down her cheek.

"River, focus! You are overthinking the technique," Sensei Pete scolded.

Pete knew of Amy's death. He tried to remain compassionate and understanding toward River, but her mistakes weren't making sense. The technique she was using should have been routine—muscle memory. River took a deep breath, nodding and fighting back tears.

Positioning himself into a neutral bow fighting stance, Ryan, a black belt student and River's sparring partner, took her down with a sweeping kick. Her legs flew out from under her. Landing on her back, she laid still on the mat for a moment, ignoring sensei.

When class was over, the students bowed and went about their day. River walked over to Erik, who had been watching over her with a proud smile on his face.

"You're alive," he joked, as they walked to the parking lot together. He put his arm around her, pulling her in close to him. River inhaled his intoxicating scent, musk mixed with sandalwood. It made her want him all over again.

"How are you with guns?" he asked, as they walked to her Jeep.

"Not so experienced," she answered.

"Want to be?"

"Maybe," River replied, feeling a little uneasy about it. "Amy was a gun lover. She used to go to a firing range somewhere around here."

"I bet. She looked like a tough woman," Erik smiled. "What do you say we go fire off some of my rifles."

"Seriously?'

"Yeah. It's good to know how to properly use a gun. I can teach you."

"Where will we go?" River asked, intrigued.

"The desert … I'm thinking Florence."

"Should I follow you then?"

"No," Erik replied. "Put your bag in the Jeep and come with me."

Once again, River found herself in Erik's truck, feeling a little bit nervous. He reached out and squeezed her hand. It sent little vibrations throughout her whole body. Florence was a twenty-three-mile drive east of Apache Junction, not known for much more than a prison system. Erik pulled onto a gravel road, and the two of them traveled around a small mountainous area.

"Wow! This is off the grid," River whispered.

"Don't worry. No one is out here, and I have a special place with targets already set up to practice."

"Oh," River sighed, as she watched a hawk dive down at a large cactus and then swoop back up into the air.

"We should've brought your Jeep!" Erik exclaimed, carefully maneuvering the rough terrain.

Arriving at their destination, River jumped out of the truck. She looked around, amazed at the utter silence of the deep wilderness.

"I have rifles *and* a handgun," Erik said, carrying a bag and a small metal ammo box to a spot set up with targets in the distance. River followed closely behind, rabbits darting every which way.

She watched and listened intently to Erik's instructions concerning gun safety, until they both agreed she was ready. River put on a pair of safety glasses, along with ear plugs. Wielding a firearm, she suddenly felt like a badass.

"Shooting a rifle is easy," he said. "Just aim and shoot. It's much easier than a handgun."

River positioned herself, pointing the rifle in the direction of the targets. She could feel Erik sidle up behind her, sculpting her into position with his hands.

"Okay," he said. "Hold this hand here, watch your stance."

Damn, this is sexy, she thought. She wanted to turn around and kiss Erik so badly.

"When you feel ready, pull the trigger," he breathed into her ear.

Oh, *I'm ready*, she thought.

Erik stepped off to the side, giving her room to operate. River concentrated on her target, pulling the trigger. The rifle fired. Her shoulder and body budged back a little. It was an exhilarating feeling. Her insides were screaming.

"Okay," Erik chuckled. "Now do it again. There's plenty of ammo."

River adjusted and pulled the trigger again and again and again. Her heart pounded with excitement, and a smile lit up her face.

"This is kind of fun!" she announced, feeling empowered.

"Yes, it can be. Now it's my turn," Erik said, taking out the small handgun. She watched as he loaded the firearm.

"Stand back, he said.

Erik shot off every round in the magazine, straight through the center point of the target. He blew it wide open.

"Wow!" River shouted in astonishment.

She liked shooting. They practiced until the sun went down.

"Thank you, Erik," River smiled. He could feel both elation and strength rising inside of her. He could feel everything about her, and it drove him wild. He turned toward her beautiful face and stared into her eyes for a moment. River swallowed hard, as Erik grabbed her and sat her up onto the hood of his truck. He kissed her, tasted her and teased her with his tongue. River pulled him in close, wildly wrapping her legs around him. They couldn't get enough of each other. It was a fire that burned between them.

Erik picked her up, opened the passenger door and sat her down on the seat. He had to will himself away from her. River grasped for him, but he resisted, shutting the door behind him.

"When it happens, and it will happen, I want it to be the right time," he said, jumping into the driver's seat. River sank into her seat.

The two drove back to Apache Junction, listening to the low melody on the stereo.

"You know," River said, breaking the silence. "I could've used a gun a little while ago."

"Really? Why?"

"Some guy at the grocery store …" she continued. "It's a weird story, but he went crazy on me about something that happened, or maybe it didn't happen. I don't know."

"I'm sorry, but what are you talking about?" Erik asked, concerned.

River explained the events as she remembered them—Amy, the bar, the creepy guy, the truck, the coyotes, the rescue.

"The lasts thing I remember was a man carrying me away."

Erik got quiet, focusing intently on the road. He avoided looking at her until they pulled into her drive. River reached for the door handle. Erik stretched across her, putting his hand on top of hers.

"There's something you need to know," he breathed, stopping her.

He regretted saying it, just as soon as the words fell out of his mouth. He couldn't tell her, not yet.

"What? Are you okay?" she asked, feeling like she shouldn't have told him so much. Her life was complicated. It was too much, even for her.

"I … I don't want you to hesitate if that guy shows up again. Call me, okay?"

"I will," she replied.

"Promise me."

"I promise."

Erik walked River to the door. He kissed her. It took everything he had to pull himself away from her.

"Lock it," he said, as he trekked back to his truck, suddenly in a hurry to get to Nelson's Old Time Tavern.

Erik ordered a beer. He walked around the crowded bar while a drunk, loose, makeup-smeared woman belted out karaoke. Local barflies drunkenly cheered her on, even though she was hardly carrying a tune. Erik scanned the room with his extra-sensory vision, but he didn't pick up on anything. His eyes had the capacity to detect blood type and DNA—human, creature or hybrid—within a two-mile radius. So, he always knew what he was dealing with.

The sound of pool balls clacking caught his attention. There he was, Keith, the animal who drugged and attacked River, put her through a night of fear and hell. Erik watched him from a distance while the man put his hands all over a drunken blonde who seemed to be a willing participant.

Erik watched as Keith slipped something into the blonde's drink when she wasn't looking. When Erik saw that, he just about lost it. His fists tightened. His aggression was about to get the better of him. He wanted to kill Keith, right then and there, but he knew better. The blonde woman was oblivious as she downed her drink. She laughed hysterically, as they headed out to the parking lot. Erik followed them out.

The blonde tripped over herself, falling to her knees and breaking a heel. Keith jerked her to her feet, scanning the lot to see if anyone was around. He thrust the woman onto the passenger seat of his dirty truck, climbing in quickly and shutting the door behind him. Keith, sweaty and smelling of whiskey and cigarettes, landed on top of the blonde, pawing her while pulling down his pants. Erik watched, as the woman had a sudden change of heart. She tried to fight him off, but she couldn't. She tried to scream, but he was too heavy and strong, and she suddenly didn't feel well.

Erik closed his eyes, took a deep breath and telekinetically ripped the truck doors off the hinges, leaving Keith's hairy ass exposed. The truck doors were thrown onto the roadside.

"What the fuck!" Keith shouted.

Erik moved swiftly toward him, pulling him out by the scruff of the neck. Keith tried to fight him, but he couldn't out power Erik's superhuman strength.

"Remember me?" Erik grumbled. "I heard you were looking for me."

Keith scrambled, trying to throw kicks and punches, but Erik set him down quickly, pummeling him with less force than he deserved, so as not to kill him. Keith lay on the ground unconscious. Erik grabbed him by a boot and dragged him back into the bar.

"What's going on?" a large bouncer asked, quickly intervening.

"This man is giving a date rape drug to females, and he's got a blonde victim in his truck right now."

Erik let go of Keith, as a crowd of people started to gather. They were too drunk to care about some loser laying passed out on the floor, as they quickly went back to what they were doing.

"I'm calling the police," a hefty female bartender shouted, as she picked up the phone to dial 911. "Winston, go get that woman out of Keith's truck."

The bartender moved toward Erik, phone in her hand. "We've been trying to catch this guy for a while now. We had a lot of reports, but the women weren't ever able to describe him."

Dazed, Keith lifted his head. The hefty bartender kicked his face with her boot, knocking him out again.

"Thank you. He was bad for business," she said. "Tie him up, Billy, till the cops get here."

Erik watched as Billy the bouncer restrained Keith with a fat roll of duct tape. He saw Winston walk in the front door, practically carrying Keith's latest victim. It was time for him to leave ... before the cops showed up. Erik nodded and quickly took off. He knew that they would have questions he wasn't willing or able to answer. So, he hit the road.

Erik wasn't the violent sort, but humans were some of the worst monsters in the universe. He was a protector, and while he didn't believe in killing or destroying any living thing, he did believe in safeguarding everything he loved, and he loved River.

CHAPTER EIGHTEEN
Between Brothers

"We are to uphold customer service and keep that pleasant standard with all patients, no matter the circumstances," the nursing director spouted off during the mandatory in-service meeting. River checked her cell, wondering how much longer this meeting was going to take. Considering she was already late in delivering patients their medications, customer service couldn't have been *that* important.

"We need more nurses, nursing assistants and staff willing to go the extra mile to make this therapy rehabilitation center the best," the nursing director continued. River intently watched the clock, adjusting the stethoscope that hung around her neck.

"Are there any questions?"

NO QUESTIONS. NO QUESTIONS, River thought to herself.

Too late! In came the questions from other staff.

"I can't always get coffee for a patient during a med pass and the CNAs are busy enough as it is," a tall, pretty, black woman complained.

"Make it happen. Make time. It's those small efforts that give us great feedback on this facility," the nursing director replied, emphatically.

Alex looked over at River, rolling his eyes. She smiled, albeit sarcastically. This was the third meeting on the topic of customer service in one year, and while they were wasting time in yet another meeting focused on "making the therapy rehabilitation center *the* best," there were patients probably screaming for pain medication and coffee as they spoke. After the meeting, Alex caught up with River.

"Now, make sure you are upholding customer service with a smile today," he teased.

"Does that mean smiling while abusive patients are beating us up," River half-heartedly joked.

"Right," Alex agreed. "Good one! You should've brought that up."

They both laughed.

"So, what are your plans for tonight?" Alex asked.

"I'm probably going to hang out with Erik," River replied, suddenly wishing she hadn't said it.

Alex inhaled, shifting his weight.

"So, are you telling me that you are dating my brother?"

"What are you talking about?" she laughed, looking at Alex sideways. "You are messing with me, right? Erik is not your brother! You two don't even look alike."

"How are we different?" Alex asked, enjoying rocking the boat.

"Well, I mean, you are so exotic looking. You could be bi-racial or Spanish ... maybe. And he's so ..." she trailed off, feeling like an idiot.

"He's so white?" Alex said with an enormous laugh. "River, Erik is my brother. We are fraternal twins."

"What? No!"

"Yes, I am his brother, and he is mine. Ask him."

Alex walked away, leaving River at her nurse's cart before she could ask any more questions. She was super confused, wanting to know more about these "brothers." Grabbing a fax left at her station, she went back to her medication pass. All she could think about was why neither one of them told her this unexpected news a lot sooner. Her shift couldn't end quick enough. When it did, she flew out to her car, trying to reach Erik by phone. He wasn't answering.

Heading home, River hastily passed her house to look for Erik at the Atler's ranch. As she pulled into the long drive, she couldn't help but admire the million-dollar adobe estate. It was huge! Spotting Erik, she parked the Jeep and jumped out. He was instructing a beautiful, thin blonde on horseback. When Erik saw her pull up, he quickly ran over to her because she had never shown up at the ranch before.

"Is everything okay?" he asked.

"Yes," she assured. "I just wanted to talk to you, so I thought I would seek you out this time."

"Sure. I'm in the middle of a lesson, but we're almost done. Can you hang tight?"

"Okay," she agreed, trying to stay focused on the task at hand, but he had that damned easy, melt-you-like-wax smile.

River watched Erik and his student from a rustic, wooden fence. As soon as the lesson was over, he jogged to her, jumping the fence and reaching for her hand.

"You look great in a nursing uniform," he grinned.

"We call them scrubs, and I doubt that," she smiled, putting her sunglasses over her eyes. "Erik, is Alex your brother?"

Erik's face fell.

"He told you?"

"Yes, he did. Today at work."

It was true. She could see it in his face. River was suddenly reeling on the inside.

"Yes. Alex is my brother. We are fraternal twins"

"Why wouldn't you tell me that? When were you planning on telling me?" River asked, annoyed and almost frantic at the same time. She never wanted to come between two brothers.

"Because it's a long, drawn-out story, and I can't explain everything to you right now. You'll have questions that I won't be able to answer," he replied rather bluntly.

"Did you know he lived here in Arizona?"

"No. *That* I didn't know. I was surprised to see him the day of the motorcycle ride."

"Did Alex know you were here?" River asked, staring up at him.

"That would be a question for Alex. I don't know."

"Oh," River exhaled.

"Listen … don't worry about this. I will explain our situation to you soon," Erik said, looking down at her, hoping she would let it go. "Can I come over later?"

"Sure," she said, tapping her leg nervously with her fingers. "We can hang out."

She walked away from Erik, less sure of everything.

When River got home, she cleaned her kitchen, watered the garden, and then turned up the music in her bedroom while she took a hot shower. Her cell rang over and over while she washed her hair. She wondered if it was urgent. Throwing a towel around her, River jumped out of the shower to try and catch the call. It was too late. She missed it, and since she did not recognize the number, she checked her voicemail. Her stomach clenched tight. A wave of nausea washed over her. It was Coty: "RIVER, COME ON! I KNOW YOU THINK YOU HATE ME RIGHT NOW. WELL, YOU WANT TO HATE ME, BUT WE LOVE EACH OTHER, RIVER. WE NEED TO BE TOGETHER! I NEED TO SEE YOU. I'VE CHANGED. DON'T BLOCK THIS NUMBER. I HAVE IT WRITTEN DOWN, AND I WILL JUST KEEP CALLING YOU FROM WHATEVER PHONE I CAN FIND. I LOVE YOU, BABY, CALL ME BACK."

River felt sick. How far was he going to take this? Why wasn't he moving on from her? Feeling light-headed, she grabbed hold of the bathroom counter to steady herself. After a moment, she made her way into the bedroom. The thought of him being in her life again disturbed her, and she was suddenly coming to grips with the reality that he was going to be a problem.

There was a knock at the front door. It startled her, causing the phone to hit the floor. She thought it might be Coty. Her paranoia ran wild. Could he be the one at her house? She quickly threw on clothes, racing to the window and breathing a sigh of relief. It was Erik's truck in the drive. River ran downstairs, flung open the door and threw herself in to his arms.

"Whoa! What's wrong? You are trembling," he said, grabbing her by the waist and holding onto her. "What's going on?"

"Nothing, I just spooked myself earlier. I watched this silly horror movie the other night, and I scared myself today while in the shower."

Erik smiled and said, "I can stay with you until you fall asleep again, if you want."

River smiled, nodding and holding onto Erik for dear life.

Somewhere around midnight, while watching television, River fell asleep on Erik's chest. He caressed her hair, thinking about her and how he could protect her from the Archon and their fallen army. Archon was the reason he was there, the reason why he risked everything, including his reputation. Eventually, he would have to tell River about the Archon, but he couldn't—not yet. She wouldn't understand.

Erik heard the coyote scratching at the front door, whimpering. He carefully stood up, so as not to disturb River. He quietly opened the front door and stepped outside. Bending down, he held the coyote's face and looked him in the eyes.

"Do you have any information about the Archon?" he asked.

"No, sir," The coyote replied.

"Keep an eye out. Something doesn't feel right. River was spooked today and wouldn't tell me the truth."

"Yes, sir."

Erik walked back inside and locked the door. He woke River and helped her up to bed. She restlessly stirred a little, reaching out for Erik to lay down beside her. He crawled into bed next to her, and he waited patiently until she fell into a deep sleep. Then ... and only then did he leave, so to head back to the ranch.

CHAPTER NINETEEN
Ancient History

"River," a woman's voice said in a serious tone.

"Yes," River replied, looking all around, as she drifted in space, suspended among the stars.

"Do you know where you are, River?" the woman asked.

"Yes. I am above Saturn."

"Could you explain that to me … please?"

"I'm sorry, but no," River said. "I've been sworn to secrecy."

"Very good, River," the woman continued. "I am here to better explain your position. You are planted on Earth for a reason … during this time of spiritual disruption. Please understand that as a light bearer, you're not to allow anything to get in the way of your purpose. Do you understand?"

"Yes," River responded, as if in a trance.

She looked around at the surrounding stars. She saw Earth in the far-off distance. How beautiful it was. Looking down, she noticed she was wearing a long, flowy, white dress—her bare feet dangling in space. When she turned her head, she noticed her hair was longer, past her shoulders. It appeared to be lighter in color. Suddenly, she heard an alarm. Where was it coming from? *I need to find that alarm,* she thought.

Waking up suddenly, River realized it was her cell alarm going off. *Just another weird dream*, she thought. It was time to get to work.

River took a few extra minutes on her lunch break, scrolling through her social media account. She noticed the natural disasters were getting worse—at a global level. She tried not to pay attention to the earthquakes, sink holes, sonic booms, melting Arctic, and polar bears dying of starvation, but those things always seemed to matter to her. Since she was a small child, River had a strange sense that something serious would happen concerning Earth, and for some reason she always felt she was prepared for it.

Putting her cell phone in her pocket, she headed back to her unit to finish her patient charting. Alex was waiting at her desk.

"What's going on these days River?" he asked, theatrically.

River smiled at him as she sat down.

"Not much beyond work."

"How's my brother doing?" he asked.

"He's good," River said, plotting an idea. "Why don't you come over this weekend. We can have a vegan cook out."

"Just us?" Alex asked, surprised.

"No. Erik, too."

River paid close attention to Alex's reaction.

"I don't know. My brother and I can barely stand one another for longer than an hour."

"So, come over for an hour," she said.

Alex grinned slyly and replied, "Count me in."

He tapped her desk with his pointer finger and walked away. River shook her head and went back to charting. When finished, she shot

Erik a text about the barbecue. She was sure to include that Alex would be coming.

                    Erik
            Was this Alex's idea?

                    River
        No. It was mine. I figured, he is your brother,
    and he's become one of my best friends. Is it cool?

                    Erik
    It's okay. He's just a pain in the ass sometimes.

The last few hours of work ran River ragged. Finally, she was on the highway headed home, wishing she had chosen another profession. Turning in to her drive, the mystery ring lit up, this time shuddering her insides with magnetic fire. Her foot missed the break, as she slammed into a large cactus. The fifty-foot cactus shook, then fell over. River let out a loud scream, as the cactus narrowly missed falling on her Jeep.

Erik, standing just around the corner of her house, heard the noise and came running to the front. When he saw the cactus falling, he telekinetically moved the cactus, so it wouldn't fall on her vehicle. The cactus slammed to the ground, breaking into large pieces.

"What happened?" Erik asked, opening her door. "Why did you hit the cactus?"

"Did you see that," she replied, in a panic. "That cactus almost fell on me! It could've squashed the Jeep!"

"You must be tired. Why didn't you see the cactus?" he asked helping her out of the Jeep.

"It's this damn ring! It gives me these horrible spasms!"

"What?" Erik asked, looking at the ring on her finger.

"I tried to take it off, but I can't."

Erik examined the ring, scanning it with his special eyes. It was ancient … beyond thousands of years.

"Where did you get this ring?" he asked.

"It was a gift. I found it in a box on my doorstep."

"Did you show anyone?" Erik asked.

"Just Amy, and now you."

Erik was confused. Why had he never noticed the ring on her finger.

"Can you help me get it off my finger?" River asked.

"I can try. That is if you don't mind me cutting it off. Maybe Alex and I can do it tomorrow when he comes over."

"It definitely can't stay on my finger. What if this would've happened while I was on the freeway?"

Erik shuddered at the thought. He took a picture of the ring and sent it via text to Alex.

Alex

I've never seen this before on her finger." Alex text back.

Erik

Me neither. Why is that?

Erik walked outside and called Alex, while River took a shower.

"What do you make of this?" Erik asked.

"Looks like trouble to me," Alex replied.

"Yea, but what kind?"

"Well, it's old, and we couldn't see it, and we see everything. She can't get it off her finger, and you said it was an anonymous gift left at her door?"

"Yeah," Erik sighed.

"Okay, that's trouble. It's no ordinary ring. That's for certain."

"What are you saying?"

"With all that information stored in that brain of yours, and all your wisdom, you don't know what that ring is?" Alex asked.

"No. Just tell me!" Erik exclaimed.

"I'm just messing with you, bro," Alex chuckled. "I don't know what that ring is either."

Erik hung up the phone. He didn't have time for such nonsense. He watched over River and her mysterious ring the rest of the evening, until she collapsed on the couch in a pair of yoga pants and fell asleep. Erik held her hand, examining the ring. He researched it on his cell. It was genuine and raw with an unmarked 24K gold band. The gemstones were grade A, top-quality material. He tried loosening its bond from River's finger, but he had no power over it. He knew whoever gave it to her was an ancient like him and could be more powerful than him. Whomever left this at her door, had a slim chance of being human. That he knew for sure.

CHAPTER TWENTY
Good Stuff

The next day, River busied herself, preparing vegetables with tofu skewers for the barbecue—party of three. Alex was due to arrive any minute. He texted her, offering to pick up beer from a nearby gas station. River had high hopes for providing peace and reconciliation between the brothers. She would settle for them just getting along over the course of dinner.

River realized she knew very little about their past, and they knew very little of hers. She thought it odd that she had been attracted to both brothers at different times.

"Well, if it isn't my favorite lady," Alex said, giving her a strong hug and holding up a twelve pack. "I brought beer."

"Great, thank you."

Alex leaned over, whispering into her ear, "I told you. I wouldn't miss this for the world."

He smirked, placing the beer in a cooler filled with ice.

"Behave yourself, Alex," River smiled.

"No. I bet you wouldn't miss this, Alex," Erik said, surprising them both from behind.

"Nope!" Alex agreed.

River gave Erik a quick hug and then held up a tray of tofu skewers with flavored seitan and vegetables.

"It looks delicious," Alex said, stealing a sliced bell pepper.

River hustled inside to get more marinade. Alex quickly turned to Erik and whispered, "So, I asked a Blue last night about the ring she's wearing."

"Yeah ... and?"

"It's ancient," Alex said, helping himself to a beer.

"We already know that."

"Yeah, well, did you know it's BEFORE CHRIST ancient?" Alex mumbled.

"What?"

"Apparently, it's a perfect match for one of our rings. You know, from when the last global shift happened? Protection rings went to certain individuals, only this one doesn't belong to us."

"Okay. Interesting ... tell me more," Erik said, grabbing a handful of chips out of the bowl.

"Are you ready for this? It's a prototype of planet X among other planets. When the planet is about to shift, the Ruby gemstone lights up, so the individual can take cover or at least have a heads up."

"This could be a myth," Erik sighed.

"Aren't we also a myth, brother?" Alex asked, looking at him sideways.

"Whatever it is, it's causing her body to spasm. I don't think it was meant for her to wear. We need to get it off her finger before she gets in a car accident or something," Erik demanded.

"We could always take a trip home and find out," Alex said, already anticipating Erik's response.

"No. That won't be necessary."

"Hmm ..." Alex hummed.

River came out of the house with more skewers.

"Okay. Someone fire up the grill for me," she said, excitedly. "Alex hand me a beer, I'm ready!"

She sensed seriousness, too much seriousness for a barbeque.

"You guys seem like you are in a deep conversation, is everything okay?"

"Yes. It is," Alex reassured, lightheartedly. He lifted up her hand. "Nice ring, River. How is it I never noticed this before?"

He scanned the ring with his superpowered eyes.

"Well, I don't know, but it's pretty. I just want it off though."

The skewers smelled like they were done.

"Let's go eat," she said, popping the grilled vegetables on the tray.

The threesome took a seat at the kitchen table, as River poured everyone a dish for dipping.

"I was just telling my brother that he should return home with me for a visit," Alex said, instigating trouble.

"Knock it off Alex," Erik snapped.

"Really? You both would go home together? That sounds nice."

River was happy that her plan to reunite these two brothers was working.

"No. I have no desire to go home right now," Erik insisted.

"Why?" River asked.

"Yes, Erik. Tell us why?" Alex inquired.

Erik glowered at Alex, and River could suddenly feel the tension.

"How are the skewers?" she asked, changing the subject.

"I can't speak for Erik, but it's probably the best meal I've had in a long time," Alex replied, excitedly rubbing his belly.

"I'm going to get the sun tea I made, Hibiscus flower lemonade."

River jumped up and headed outside. Erik kicked Alex hard

underneath the table.

"Owww! DAMN!"

"Don't bring that shit up again," Erik warned.

Alex chuckled. He was loving every bit of this, and it clearly showed.

"Are you worried about the repercussions from our famous parents?" Alex added.

"No. I'm worried about her. Honestly, you should be worried about her, too."

"Yeah … whatever. Let's just find out what's happening with this ring," Alex said, becoming serious.

"For once we agree." Erik agreed.

River brought the large, glass tea jug inside and poured a pick-me-up for both of them. They each took a drink. Their eyes watered, as they tried not to show how horrible it tasted. River smiled as they both swallowed with a hard gulp.

"Good stuff," River said, running back outside to grab something, Alex quickly jumped up, grabbing his and Erik's glass of tea and dumping both down the sink. River's face was overjoyed when she walked back into the kitchen and saw the empty glasses.

"Do you want some more tea?" she asked, ready to pour them another tall glass.

"No. No," both uttered, kindly refusing in unison.

The brothers exchanged a hard look that screamed, *Oh, hell no!*

CHAPTER TWENTY-ONE
Only in Dreams

Joshua Path stretched his long legs out on a large boulder at Saguaro Lake. He watched as some friends dove off cliffs, laughing at their stupid jokes. Laying back in the warm sun, he admired a bald eagle, as it flew above him. Donning his ragged cut off shorts, his Native American skin blended in with the color of the light, tan rocks. Joshua's dark black hair, spiky and jagged, gave him a rocker, bad-boy edge, which was not done on purpose.

Joshua was drying off quickly, so he figured it was time to dive back in the water. His muscular body kept the females close by, but he never gave them much attention. He was only nineteen in human years, and his whole mind and body projected that. He knew he was chosen. He knew he belonged, and he knew this was not an ordinary life.

Violet walked over to Joshua and sat down next to him in her bright aqua stripe bikini top and orange low-rise bottom. Her beautiful black hair hung low to the middle of her waist, flowing down her back effortlessly as she hugged her knees.

"We've got to get back, Joshua," she said.

"I know."

"We aren't supposed to leave her house unprotected for this long. Those were strict orders."

"Uh huh," Joshua muttered, annoyed.

"I'm not trying to make you angry, but ..." Violet started.

"Shh …" Joshua interrupted.

"What?" Violet whispered.

"Smell that?" Joshua asked.

Violet took a deep breath … smiling.

"Ducks," she said.

"Should we?"

"No. It's too early. We will bring too much attention to ourselves," she sighed. "Let's wait till tonight."

"Right. We better get going Violet."

Joshua stood to his feet, shouting goodbye to his friends splashing in the lake below. Violet mocked one of them, who, in turn, whistled back at her.

"Hey! How are you guy's getting home," one of their friends yelled from the water.

"We've got a ride!" Joshua shouted.

Joshua and Violet made their way into a thicket of trees and bushes, reappearing in their new earth form as Coyotes. The two jumped over a fallen mesquite tree, running through the desert landscapes as fast as they could. They passed wild horses in the Salt River, drinking from the lake. They hurdled a fence in the wild, kicking up rocks behind them. Violet looked at Joshua, as they stopped a short distance from River's home and laid down in the sun. They both caught a glimpse of her and watched her through the living room window.

Wouldn't it be funny if she started dancing in her underwear again? Joshua conveyed through thought to Violet.

You would like it if she did. You have a crush on her, Violet reflected, smiling.

Joshua lay his snout upon a large rock, ignoring Violet's ridiculous claim. He did think River was very beautiful, and he wasn't the only man in his right mind who had a crush on her. Violet quickly turned to face the right. She was picking up a smell, a jack rabbit … perhaps.

I'm so hungry, Joshua, Violet conveyed.

Me too, Joshua replied.

There's probably a dead animal on the road somewhere or a little cat or dog someone dumped in the desert, Violet yawned, letting out a coyote sigh.

They both perked up when they heard a car coming up the road. It drove past them and parked near River's home.

Do you want to check it out? Violet asked.

No, he thought, laying down his head and closing his eyes.

Joshua felt lazy and didn't think it was anything suspicious. It was probably someone stopping off to take photos of the mountain. Elderly snowbirds were known for it. Violet laid down next to Joshua to lick her paws aggressively. Something was biting into her skin.

So much hair goes in my stomach, but I can't stop licking. It brings me so much satisfaction, Violet thought.

What's that? Joshua conveyed, jumping on top of a boulder with his eyes focused intently on River's home. A large man with short brown hair staggered up River's drive, creeping toward her window. River had no idea he was there, as she lay comfortably on the couch, channel surfing.

We need to do something, Violet panicked, sitting upright, snout searching for a scent.

Who is that guy? Joshua wondered, his ultra-large, supernatural eyes glowering, scanning the man.

We should go after him, Violet snarled.

Calm down, Violet! Do you want a coyote witch hunt on our ass?

That's what humans do, Joshua warned.

Yeah. You're right, Violet concluded. *They are assholes.*

We need a closer look, Joshua contemplated.

He moved lightly within proximity of the man and River's home, laying low in a large sage bush. Violet followed, putting her snout to the ground along with Joshua.

He smells funny, Violet noted.

He's drunk, Joshua broached.

We should contact Erik, Violet yelped, almost blowing their cover.

Calm down, Violet. We can handle this.

Joshua watched the man peer into River's window and smile. River was clueless, as she laughed out loud at a comedy show on the television.

He's too close, Joshua. Remember what Erik said about being "too close."

Violet sat up and started pacing anxiously behind the bushes.

I ... we need to know what this guy wants, so we can get to the bottom of it before we go spouting off to Erik, Joshua reasoned.

It's obvious to me! He's a peeping Tom or a stalker, Violet yipped, as she continued to pace. Joshua sat on his hind end to further observe. The man moved toward the other living room window and pulled something out of his pocket. Violet wasn't waiting any longer. Jumping over the bushes, she darted up onto River's porch as fast as she could. The man saw Violet land on the porch, and in a sudden panic, he lost his footing and fell sideways into a small cholla cactus.

"OWWW! MOTHER FUCKER!" the man shouted in pain.

Hearing the commotion, River turned off the television and peered out the window. The man flung folded papers from his hand into

into the air, as he tried to stand with cactus needles burrowed throughout his body. His face took the majority of the damage.

Violet, Joshua thought.

Violet rounded the corner of the house, standing bravely in front of the man. She growled fiercely, as. the man kicked at her.

"Get away from here, you mutt!"

The man kicked at her again. Just then, Joshua leapt through the air, knocking the creeper back into the porch. Something deep within River told her not to open the door. She made sure her doors were locked, grabbed her cell and ran upstairs.

"AWW … FUCK!" the man shouted.

Hearing the man shout, River dialed Erik's cell and before he could say hello, she started yelling into the phone.

"SOMEONE'S HERE! IN MY YARD! HE'S CURSING," she said, grabbing a baseball bat out of her hall closet and waiting.

"I'm on my way," Erik assured, dropping what he was doing.

Erik jumped into his truck and took off down the road.

"I've called the police!" River shouted to the man outside.

The large man covered in cactus needles flinched at the sound of her voice, hobbling to his car as quickly as he could. Cursing the pain, he sat down behind the wheel, turned the engine, punched the gas and took off. Violet and Joshua looked at each other, relieved the man was gone.

Erik's coming, Joshua transmitted to Violet.

Both coyotes waited as Erik pulled in the drive at high speed, barely stopping his vehicle before slamming it into park. River raced outside to meet him on the porch, giving him a huge, clingy hug as he scanned the property with his hyper cell eyes. River would not let the baseball bat go. Erik practically had to pry it from her fingers.

"I know someone was out here," River cried.

Erik could smell it. He believed her and needed no more persuasion than the scared look in her eyes. Besides that, the man left an echo of energy trails marking the route he took back to his car.

"Go inside. Sit down while I look around the property," Erik said.

He knew the human male was gone, but he wanted to make River feel better about it, and he wanted to search for clues. After a little while, River poked her head out the window, worried about Erik.

"Erik, what if someone is still out there? You need a weapon."

River was hysterical, but Erik had to hold in his laughter. He had no reason to fear nor did she with him there. She just didn't realize that.

"River, I'm fine. I have my gun. Don't worry," he reassured her, lifting his shirt and showing the holstered weapon.

She watched Erik closely, no less concerned. Erik scanned the porch, the garden, the Jeep, the front yard, the side yard, and around back by the large boulder where he met up with the two coyotes.

It was a human man, Violet transmitted.

A very large man, a drunk. Violet scared him off, Joshua added.

"What was he doing here?" Erik asked empathically.

We don't know. He was peering through the windows and trying to do something with his hand in his pocket, Violet added.

Maybe he was getting ready to jack-off, Joshua retorted.

"Next time you do not handle this on your own. You contact me right away," Erik said, sternly. "Good job though. I appreciate what you are doing for me … for River."

Erik knelt down and gave them both a rub along the scruff of their necks. Violet wagged her tail, craving more.

"Both of you get on this man's trail for me. Let's find out who he is and what he wants," Erik commanded.

Both coyotes nodded, as Erik turned and returned to the house.

Don't act like a dog, Violet. It's embarrassing. Joshua snapped.

But we are dogs, Joshua—kind of.

We are coyotes, Violet, Joshua transmitted, irritated.

Same thing, she thought.

In the distance, they heard a high-pitched cackle of coyotes, announcing a fresh kill. It excited them.

Come on! Food, Joshua yelped.

I'm starving, Violet howled.

The two young coyotes took off toward the sound of hungry coyotes.

"We need to get you a home security system," Erik grumbled. "You need a gun and more protection when I can't be here."

River sat down on a chair, interrupting Erik.

"I wonder if I'm going crazy," she whispered.

"What? Why?"

"I keep seeing weird things, hearing weird things," she said, trying to take the ring off her finger. "And this ring on my finger keeps doing crazy shit."

Erik knew she wasn't crazy. He also knew she was more special than she realized. He just couldn't explain it to her. Instead, he opted to comfort her. He touched her shoulders gently, bringing her closer to him.

"You are fine, and nothing is wrong with you. It's brave of you to live all by yourself, out in the desert, miles away from your closest neighbor. It's normal to get spooked sometimes, you are a brave woman. More than you know."

Erik kissed her lips. They were soft and sweet.

"No more baseball bat," he added. "You need a gun."

"The bat was all I had until you got here," she smiled. "Can you stay with me tonight?"

"I was planning on it," he grinned, kissing her neck, as she lay back on the couch. He wrapped his arms tight around her, pulling her so close to his arousal that she gasped. Chills shot through her body.

Erik tuned into her senses, listening to her heartbeat as if it were a soft melody of drums. Telepathically and with a simple caress to her neck, he calmed her circadian rhythm, helping her relax until she fell asleep. Almost immediately, River began to dream of Erik. He knew she would.

In her dream, she and Erik made love so passionately and for so long that it took her breath away.

(Erik smiled when she softly panted in her sleep.)

She slowly tore away from him when she saw two coyotes playing with one another in the desert. As she focused in on them, Amy walked through the door.

"Amy," River said, catching her breath.

Standing in a beautiful, flowing, white gown, Amy began to walk toward her. River was about to run at Amy with arms wide open when Erik called her back to him. Amy slowly stopped, held out her hand and waved goodbye. From out of nowhere a car screeched and collided into Amy, flinging her body through the air.

"AMY! NO! NO, AMY!" River screamed, trying to run toward her friend, but her feet were stuck in quicksand. She was unable to move, unable to get to Amy.

"River wake up," Erik called out, shaking her. "It's just a dream … a bad dream."

He soothed her as she sat straight up, crying into the palms of her hands. Erik rocked her softly.

"It was just a crazy dream. It's not real."

"I can't believe she's gone," River sobbed, choking on heavy tears.

Erik held her tight, until she fell back to sleep. He didn't mean for the dream to go in that direction, but River was stronger than he realized. He just wanted to make love to her, and he figured there was no harm in doing it in her dreams. He was astonished that he didn't have much control over what happened to her when she fell asleep. His kind was often very good in that area of the subconscious. Erik decided to forego that tactic, giving himself permission to do nothing more for her that night, but fall asleep beside her. So, that's exactly what he did.

CHAPTER TWENTY-TWO
Ancient Protection

"The etchings of the ring are just fascinating!" the professor exclaimed. "I would love to see it in person. I did a lot of archaeology work in Egypt, and I found similar markings as these. The placement and genuineness of the stone clarity is truly high quality."

The stout, elderly professor, an archeologist and historian sporting a long, graying beard and eyeglasses studied photographs of River's ring intently.

"We would like for you to examine it in person, professor, but we have one small problem," Alex disclosed.

"What is the problem?" the professor inquired curiously.

Alex grinned, "We can't get it off her finger."

The professor gave a peculiar expression, asking the obvious question, "Soap and water not working?"

"No," Erik said, jumping into the conversation. "What my brother is trying to say is that something or some power is attached to the ring, keeping it locked on her finger."

"Does she understand what's happening?" the professor asked.

"No," both Alex and Erik replied in unison.

The portly professor looked up at Alex with pursed lips and sighed, "So, I suppose this is another one of your weird, 'top-secret' cases?"

"Yes," Alex nodded. "She is waiting in the car."

The professor lowered his gaze, his eyeglasses slipping down the length of his nose. Pushing them back to the bridge with his forefinger, he thoughtfully considered the prospect.

"If you do this, can you keep the whole 'supernatural thing' on the down low?" Alex pleaded. "We would appreciate it."

"I see," the professor said, clearing his throat. "Bring her in. Tell her I'm a jewelry appraiser."

Alex nodded. As he turned to leave, the professor probed, "Alex, are you healing okay since the accident? Did the crystal phosphorus work?"

"Um … yes, Professor Michaels. Thank you! I am feeling like my old self again," Alex replied before quickly vanishing around the corner to retrieve River.

While Professor Michaels studied the ring under a large microscope, River looked around at the built-in bookshelves along the walls and the myriad of National Geographic magazines piled high on the floor. The professor's name was Peter Michaels, and according to Erik and Alex, he was some kind of historian who owned a jewelry store outside of Apache Junction. River never questioned the appointment. She just wanted to get the ring off her finger.

"Can you twist the ring around your finger?" the professor asked.

"Yes, a little." River replied.

The professor spun the ring around her finger and gasped.

"Remarkable etchings on the band. It is ancient Sanskrit. I would have to take a picture of it in order to find out what it says."

For a "jewelry appraiser," he seemed awfully intrigued and knowledgeable on the subject. Professor Michaels continued. "I have a friend who can do that, but it will take some time. I noticed the gemstones are set in a pattern. My guess is that it is a star system … a galaxy. These are very rare gemstones, two of which are not well known."

He held the ring up to his magnifying eyepiece, stopping only to take notes.

"Hmmm … impressive," He hummed.

"So, it's an antique?" River asked.

"Yes. It is ancient."

He scooched the rolling chair to his desk, so to type on his laptop.

"Okay," the professor said, jumping up and climbing a ladder up a tall wall of books. Reaching for the dead sea scrolls, he skimmed through its pages rather quickly.

"You think my ring is *that* old?" River asked, surprised.

Alex walked over to her, giving her shoulder a light squeeze.

"Erik would like to speak with you," he whispered.

River stood up and headed out of Professor Michael's office, moving briskly down the long sculpturesque hallway. River saw Erik studying a glass figurine. She began tip-toeing, so as to creep up behind him. Erik turned abruptly, grabbing her by her tiny waist and picking her up very quickly. He growled in her ear, startling her as they both melted against each other with a light giggle.

"Alex said you wanted to see me."

"Yes," he smiled. "Are you interested in riding quads through the desert tonight?"

"I don't know … another cycling adventure?"

River's expression fell. She instantly thought about Amy and the motorcycle accident that killed her.

"You can have your own quad and move at your own pace, even if it's only five miles per hour. It's just for fun," Erik reassured, pulling her in close and giving her a soft kiss.

"Okay. That sounds fair," she smiled. "So, this Peter … I mean Professor Michaels, he's a jeweler, right? Can't he just cut this ring off?"

"Not until we know what it's worth. I don't want you to regret it later, should we damage it," Erik fibbed, knowing the ring's power would likely not allow anyone to remove it. There was no tool that could match such ancient power, not even a modern-day jewelry saw.

"Oh," she sighed. "So, when will we know?"

"Soon. He's very good, and he will tell us all we need to know."

Alex and Professor Michaels joined them in the hallway. Alex shook the professor's hand, thanking him. He appeared anxious and overwrought as he stared into River's eyes. She physically felt Alex's energy in that moment, making it a long, quiet ride back to his house. The look he gave her was deep and urgent with emotion. She wondered if it was because he was uncomfortable with her relationship with Erik. It must have been. The three of them were silent, until they landed on his property in Queen Creek. Alex had a modular home with a full, wrap-around deck and a two-car garage on a large plot of land.

"You own all this?" River asked, surprised.

"No," he replied. "I'm leasing it. I'm not sure yet if I want to live in Arizona for life."

River understood. She felt the same way sometimes. The three climbed out of Alex's car. Erik and River followed Alex to the garage.

"Riding here is safe. So, no worries. It's all flat land, no surprise holes. Let's just enjoy the ride," Alex said, lifting the garage door. River gasped at all the boy toys, including two beautiful motorcycles, a couple of paddle boats, a jet ski, four colorful quads, and a canoe strewn among a plethora of organized tools.

"Wow! So, *this* is where the adventure starts," she laughed.

"Yes," Alex agreed, winking at her. "And with me, the adventure never ends."

"Don't you mean ... with you the drama never ends," Erik replied, rolling his eyes.

Alex ignored Erik's comment and continued, "I have plenty of helmets, so take your pick, River."

He loved how her eyes lit up, as she climbed onto *the* most wicked-looking ATV.

"Okay. I'm ready. Let's do this," she said, eagerly.

"So, you know how to ride?' Alex asked.

"Are you kidding me? I grew up on a farm near an Amish community. There's nothing to this."

"Okay, then I guess we're ready," Erik said, putting on his helmet.

All three started up the ATVs and took off. River raced Erik and Alex to the end of the property. She quickly turned off onto a dirt path, kicking up rocks in their direction. Alex swerved, narrowly missing a large cactus, so as to avoid an enormous rattlesnake slithering across his path. Erik was suddenly inspired by his brother's daredevil moves and began competing against Alex. The three of them stopped at the bottom of a crick bed. It was full of river rock with a six-foot deep trench.

"What's around that crick?' Erik asked.

"Nothing really!" Alex shouted. "It's not that long. If we cross here, we could come back around without having to jump it again."

"You two wait here. I'm going to jump the crossing." Erik replied.

"What?! Are you crazy?! Why would you jump it?!" River shouted. "You can just go around it!"

Erik gave Alex a menacing look and shouted, "I'M DOING IT!"

He revved the ATV in hopes of impressing River.

"Go ahead, bro, I've done it. It's no big deal," Alex said, giving him a thumbs up.

"ERIK … DON'T!" River shouted, as she watched him turn around, using a distant fence line as a starting point.

River's stomach tightened into a knot. She closed her eyes.

"It's okay, girl! Relax. He and I do crazy shit like this all the time," Alex reassured.

Only it didn't reassure her. River pursed her lips, as Erik's quad pushed full speed towards the crick edge. He jumped at full force, crossing safely to the other side … to River's surprise. Her face lit up in relief at the rough landing. Erik sped off around the trench to meet up with them. Pulling up to River, Alex gently touched her shoulder.

"You okay?" he asked.

"I'm fine."

"Relax, girl. We got this. I told you. We've done crazier shit than this."

After more than an hour, the threesome got thirsty. They landed back at the house. Sitting on the deck and drinking beer, Alex lit a fire in a custom-built fire ring. Nightfall invited the stars to light up the sky. Erik wrapped an Aztec-print blanket around River's shoulders. They sat and talked about anything and everything, avoiding the topic of the ring on her finger. River was starting to feel the effects of the alcohol. She moved closer to the fire, even though she was feeling pretty warm on the inside. The brothers kept close watch over her. At the same time, with roving eyes, they scanned the property for any uninvited guests. Erik turned to Alex asking, "What exactly did Professor Michaels say about the ring?"

Alex pulled a folded piece of paper out of his pocket, reading from it.

"It's an ancient, protection ring. The markings are Sanskrit, or Coptic. The gemstones are in the shape of a protective, star system or galaxy. Twenty-four karat gold … likely never coming off her finger, not without express permission from whoever or whatever gave it to her."

"Right," Erik sighed. "We've got to get it off her finger and maybe get it to our …"

Alex instinctively interrupted, "Wait! Are you suggesting we go back home over a ring?"

"No. Not me—*you*."

Alex squinted his eyes.

"Nope. Sorry, bro! You are stuck with me, and you aren't getting rid of me that easily. Besides, you need me around right now. Whoever gave her that ring is powerful, and they are putting some type of claim over her. I'm not going anywhere right now, so forget it."

Alex picked up a rock, throwing it angrily into the night. Erik could appreciate his brother's conviction, not to mention his devotion. He knew there would be no dissuading him. River stood up, swaying away from the fire sparks popping out from the flames.

"I think she's had too much to drink," Erik said, rushing to her side. "Easy now. You almost fell into the fire."

"Yeah," she smiled. "Being vegan effects how I handle alcohol."

"Are you ready to go home?" Erik whispered.

"I am. I am ready," River smiled, feeling severely buzzed.

Alex drove them home to River's place. He parked by the fallen Saguaro cactus in River's drive.

"I will miss that cactus. It was my sweet, planted friend," she said, drunk.

Alex and Erik exchanged a funny glance, as they both went to help her inside.

"Alex, you have been so nice to me. I'm so grateful for you. I really, really, *really* love you."

"I love you too, River."

Erik was beginning to look annoyed. The brothers both helped her up the porch steps, one on either side of her.

"Erik, you are just so … OH MY GOSH!"

River shrieked, startling them both. Looking past Erik, toward the edge of her porch, she stared intently, trying to adjust her eyes.

"What is it?" Erik asked.

"My Dahlia flowers are blooming! They are *SO* precious. Aren't they?"

"You need a nap, honey," Erik nodded.

River broke free of the brothers, running inside and up the stairs to the bathroom.

"Are you good from here?" Alex asked, turning to Erik.

"Yeah," he grinned. "I'm fine."

Alex turned to leave.

"Hey, Alex?" Erik breathed.

"Yeah?" Alex replied, turning back.

"Thanks for being there, man. I appreciate your help lately," Erik said, digging both hands deep into the pockets of his worn-out jeans.

"No problem. You're my brother. We've been through hell and back," Alex said, breaking off—reluctant to elaborate.

The corner of Erik's lip curled up into a smile. He knew what Alex wanted to say but couldn't. He could read it on his face.

"Take it easy," Alex said, waving. " I will talk at you later."

Erik nodded, looking up to the sky and whispering, "I see you."

CHAPTER TWENTY-THREE
Striking Distance

"Hit him harder! He can take it. Come on, River! Use some muscle," Sensei Pete yelled, as River fell back onto the mat. She hurriedly bounced back, putting herself into a good fighting stance. Ryan, her sparring partner, quickly advanced, using an offensive martial arts technique. River grabbed his arm, but once again was strongarmed to the mat. Sensei walked over to her, moving Ryan out of the way.

"I'm your attacker," he said. "I'm going to throw a left straight punch. I want you to grab my arm, throw it to the side and punch at my throat or face with your other hand."

River nodded, acknowledging his instructions, even though she was quietly, frustrated inside of her head gear. Sensei threw a hard punch. River grabbed his arm, but instead of throwing it, as instructed, she merely pushed it out of the way. Sensei, growing frustrated, himself, whacked her helmet and threw her off balance.

"You never lose control or contact! When you do, you leave yourself wide open for me to hurt you."

River nodded, feeling nauseated and overheated.

"You need to grab the arm, yank me forward, step in and punch at my face," Sensei shouted.

Again, River nodded, this time giving up and allowing the next guy in line to take her spot. Sometimes, fighting and sparring with men left her feeling defeated, especially when she didn't grasp the techniques right away. Other times, she loved it.

"Okay," Sensei continued. "You guys are tired. That's enough for today."

River went through the line and did her dojo bow. Afterward, she grabbed her bag and headed for the parking lot. Exhausted and a bit hungover, she got the feeling she was being watched. River checked her surroundings as she unlocked her Jeep and climbed inside.

For a week he watched her every move. Hiding his face with a magazine while sitting in a parked rental car, he was in awe of how amazing she looked. River always had curves, but never so voluptuous. She was still petite and tiny, but delicious in all the right places. He just wanted to eat her up.

As she pulled out of the parking lot, he followed her. He was curious to see where she landed. Driving slowly through town, in the direction of the mountain, he realized she was headed for home. His face was covered in scratches from his last brush with the coyote and the cactus in her yard. It would take him a while to summon up the courage to pursue her in the daylight hours again. His plan was to knock on her front door and let the cards fall where they may, which in his warped mind meant her falling irresistibly into his arms. He knew they were destined for each other, and that nothing could stop destiny. Besides that, he knew he was an attractive man, always popular with the ladies. He was used to getting what he wanted. On top of which, he considered himself a patient man, so he decided not to follow her home. Making a giant U-turn, he headed back to his hotel for a swim in the pool and, perhaps in a bottle of tequila. He knew that River worked the next day, and his plan was to visit her sometime within the week.

Walking through the hotel lobby, he felt little pangs of excitement just thinking about her and how great it would be to go to bed with her and wake up beside her. He whistled his favorite tune, as he inserted his key card and pushed open his hotel room door.

"OWW!" he shouted, as a beautiful, young Native American woman bumped into him from behind, slamming his elbow into the door frame.

"Excuse me. I'm sorry," she apologized, profusely.

The man stopped to hold his arm for a moment. His scowl quickly vanished when his eyes briefly met with hers. The woman's long, shiny, black hair bounced in perfect straight waves along her back, as she disappeared down the long hall.

"No sweat," he said with a seductive look that was lost on her. *Damn! Housekeeping is hot*, he thought.

"Did you get in?" Joshua asked, as Violet tramped from the hotel to the parking lot.

"Yes. You forgot to warn me he was coming! I almost got caught." Violet replied in a rage. "I was forced to climb out of a window, landing in the hotel courtyard that was secured by a large brick wall. I had to climb back through another open window to get out of there. This could've been a disaster!"

Joshua exhaled, feeling a pang of guilt.

"I got sidetracked," he said. "I ran into Nick; we got to talking."

Nick was an old friend from the reservation.

"Fuck Nick! AND FUCK YOU!" Violet roared.

"Hey! Calm down. I was trying to score some bud for the weekend. What the hell?"

Joshua picked up his pace, so as to get in front of Violet, as she stomped away from him.

"Hey," he said, grabbing her shoulders and turning her around to face him. "I'm sorry. I messed up."

Violet pouted. She wondered how Joshua could be so handsome and yet so stupid at the same time.

"Okay," she huffed. "Did you at least get your weed?"

"Yeah. Did you get any info on our mystery night stalker?"

"No," Violet said, pulling her hair back into a bun, sweat beading on her forehead. "He drinks a lot of tequila. No weird pictures or body parts. Nothing unusual in his suitcase, just a half-empty bottle of booze. And if it makes any difference, he is a *very* bad stylist."

Joshua grinned.

"I purposely bumped into him, trying to pick his wallet, but he had this long, vest-type jacket on."

"Yeah. The dude is hiding something. I can't wait to go on the res, see some familiar faces," Joshua sighed, as they headed back to his truck.

"I know," Violet agreed. "Erik will be with River all weekend, so we have a couple of days to do whatever we want."

Violet was looking forward to the break. Joshua turned the engine to the truck, and the pair took off to Atler's Ranch to see Erik and to let him know about the stalker.

CHAPTER TWENTY-FOUR
Clocking Out

The next morning, River hurried through her medication pass and then started on her charting. Everything was going perfectly. She had no complaints, no angry family members to deal with. She was feeling well rested. After the patients ate breakfast, she started moving through her usual routine. When she looked at the time, it was 9:11 a.m. Having a free minute to spare, she went into the breakroom to call Erik.

"What are you doing?" she asked.

"I've got a sick horse."

"Oh no … what do you have to do?"

"I've called the vet, but I think he's just too old," Erik replied, sounding a little frustrated.

"I'm sorry, Erik."

"Have you talked to my brother today?" he enquired.

"No. He's probably a lot busier than I am right now. He's on another unit, and my patient census is very low."

"Oh," he sighed.

"Are you ok?" she asked.

"Yes. Well, I will be."

River suddenly felt strong vibrations run through her body, pulsations caused by her ring. She gasped loudly, spasms in her back causing her to reach for a nearby chair, so to steady herself.

"What's wrong?" Erik demanded.

He could feel her uneasiness. Something wasn't right. River tried to pull herself together long enough to respond through repeated spasms.

"River!" Erik shouted.

"I ... I have to go."

River dropped the call, putting the phone down long enough to catch her breath. After a spell, she slipped her cell phone into her pocket and opened the breakroom door. She heard firecracker-like pops and violent screams. The words boomed over the intercom, "ACTIVE SHOOTER! FLOOR TWO! ACTIVE SHOOTER! FLOOR TWO!"

River panicked, as she watched family members screaming in tears and nursing staff race toward her in a flurry. Some people were trying to get onto the elevators. Some were rushing down the halls in wheelchairs. Some peered in fear out from their rooms. Chaos had erupted all around her, and she wasn't sure where to start or what to do.

"Alex," River breathed, as back spasms and panic poured through her body.

"RUN AND HIDE, RIVER!" an elderly nurse screamed, as she ran past.

Voices cried out from every direction. She could hear a patient whimpering from behind the bathroom door. Patients scrambled under their beds. Many were frozen in fear at the nurse's station, unsure of what to do and where to go. River left the nursing station area, shouting to patients, "GO TO YOUR ROOMS! BARRICADE YOUR DOORS!"

"RIVER ... HIDE!" another frantic nurse shouted, as she burrowed between the printer and overhead counter. More popping sounds could be heard on the second floor, followed by more screams. River passed another nurse using the backstairs. She was crying, as she mumbled into her cell.

"Alex," River repeated, over and over again.

She was worried about him, wondering if he was okay. Sprinting to the south end of her unit, she passed a group of people waiting to get on the elevator. As the elevator door opened, she heard more screams—louder this time. Shots were fired from a semi-automatic weapon, taking them all down, every last one. River pushed herself to run faster—harder. The shooter saw her. With his eyes fixed on her, he started for her in long, steady strides, firing his rifle in every direction. She hurried toward the back exit on the south side, punching in the key code. The words, "NO ENTRY" flashed in red. She punched the code in again and again—to no avail. The door wouldn't open. Then she remembered: All exit door codes had been changed due to maintenance problems a month earlier.

Ripping a fire extinguisher off the wall, she scurried underneath a floating desk in the hallway, pulling a chair in behind her to keep hidden. The shooter was getting close. Her body shook uncontrollably. Her eyes closed tightly. She hugged her knees against her chest. More shots were fired. A dementia patient fell to the floor. Blood glazed the carpet. River cried, covering her mouth, so as not to make a sound.

Sirens blared outside. The loud buzz of helicopters and the surrounding noise was deafening. River took a quick breath, as calm and as quietly as her trembling body would allow. The shooter was standing in front of her. He was reloading. River wasn't sure if he knew she was under the desk.

"MY MOTHER SHOULD NOT HAVE DIED IN YOUR CARE!" the shooter roared. "AN EYE FOR AN EYE!"

River dropped her head into her knees. She was helpless. Just then, her cell started to vibrate and jingle inside the pocket of her blue scrub top.

Her stomach tightened, as she braced for death. She looked up at the shooter. He was dressed in black from head to toe, including a bullet-proof vest. He bent over and grabbed her leg, ripping her out from under the desk.

"No!" she shouted, kicking and trying to resist. The gun was pointed at her head. She closed her eyes, tears streaming down her cheeks. The shooter whistled, and she opened her eyes. She saw Alex's silhouette standing behind him. Suddenly River's heartbeat slowed. It echoed through her ears. The reverberation of the sound controlled her, and she was calm.

Alex made eye contact with her. Strangely, his gaze soothed her, along with his presence. Her body instantly felt light and centered, as if she knew she was going to be okay. She sensed the barrel of the rifle pointed at her, but River couldn't pull herself away from Alex's gaze. He seemed to hold her there with him, almost in a state of paralysis or giddy hypnosis. Just as the shooter pulled the trigger, Alex shifted the man on his heels, scattering gun shots into the air. In one ruthless movement, Alex broke the shooter's neck and, while doing so, his eyes never left River. Her peace remained, as the shooter dropped with a heavy thud to the floor.

A SWAT team made their way toward them, shouting commands that echoed down the hall. Alex reached for River, helping her to her feet. She couldn't feel her feet. It was as though she was floating. Her mind was still. River followed Alex's lead, as he held her hand and walked calmly down the hall through the remaining chaos.

Later that night, River carefully watched Alex during his interview with law enforcement. He tried to explain how he broke the shooter's neck and how he (mysteriously) was the only one among the nursing staff who survived the massacre on the second floor. Alex was humble, avoiding and evading direct questions on how he had handled the assailant.

On the way out, he pushed the news cameras out of his face, protecting River from it all. Tucking her under his arm, he kept her away from microphones and the greedy media, so as not to cause a scene. River couldn't talk. She didn't want to. Her cell rang out, but she ignored it. Paramedics took a look at her, but she was firm about not going to the hospital. Alex was concerned about her. He knew she was in a state of shock. He understood she was in human form, not currently as resilient as his kind, and that bothered him. He hated to see her so vulnerable—fragile. River walked briskly to her Jeep, away from him. Alex bolted after her.

"Hey! Let me take you home, River," he insisted.

"No."

"I want to help you home. Erik wants me to take you home, too."

"No," she replied, realizing she had not clocked out. "I gotta go."

Alex stood, in a lurch, as River turned around and went back inside the building. Walking through the blood-smeared hallway, stepping over a dead body, she made her way to the time clock. It was 9:11 p.m. She punched in her I.D. number, added her fingerprint, and clocked out. Something inside of her knew; that was the last time she would ever walk through those hallways. It was the last time she would ever punch out again.

CHAPTER TWENTY-FIVE
Mother Earth

Over the next few weeks, River completely changed her life around. She found a new job. It was closer to home, and to her surprise, she was making more money. The last workplace shut down for a while because of the shooting. It didn't matter. She never wanted to go back there, not in her lifetime. The news became increasingly disturbing to her. Since the incident, her intuition seemed to have swelled exponentially. She was emboldened, in that she knew who was calling before her cell phone even rang. She could sense earthquakes, planetary alignments, along with other natural disasters before they happened. When researching her new skill, she read that trauma can cause extra-sensory abilities. She took that onboard as reason enough.

Erik and Alex tried to get her to talk about the shooting, but she told them not to mention it again. They both grew more concerned about her, but they decided not to get on her case about it. Erik visited River quite a bit when she wasn't working. They made small talk, worked in the garden and went horseback riding. He rarely left her alone, even though she seemed to be emotionally distancing herself, building walls between them. She and Erik held onto each other and kissed sometimes, but nothing more than that. Erik wanted her, but he knew every time they went down that path of wanting that led to making love, there would be risks and consequences that came along with it.

One late evening, Erik played with River's hair while they lay together on the floor. He reached for her hand and gave it a delicate kiss.

"I want you to know that if you ever need to talk to me about anything, no matter what it is, I'm here for you."

"I know. I'm fine," she reassured, as she curled her body into his and traced the curve of his lips with her finger. "Sometimes, I feel like I've known you and Alex before, like in a past life or something. I don't know what I would do without you two."

A tear trickled down her cheek.

"I don't want to live without you Erik, and I hope you will never leave me. So many people have come into my life and then left. I feel so tired," she sighed.

She was relieved to let go of the words.

"I will never leave you. I'm here to stay."

They held onto each other. Just then, a crack of thunder rolled in with a low rumbling throughout the desert sky. River sat up quickly.

"Let's go outside! The rain!"

She hurried down the steps and flung open the screen door leading to the porch.

"You are barely dressed, River!" Erik exclaimed, as he watched her twirl in the rain with nothing on but a crop top and panties.

"I DON'T CARE!" River shouted, smiling as the rain poured heavily over her hair and body, melting her curls into long strands against her neck. She tilted her head back, opened her mouth, twirled and closed her eyes.

"Come out here Erik!"

Erik just leaned on the porch and smiled at her. The water turned into large puddles of sloshy mud surrounding her feet, as she jumped in place and laughed. Erik laughed with her until a giant bolt of lightning shot across the sky. Its intensity scared her and sent her running for the porch. They both laughed at how fast she moved, and for the first time in a long time, she wasn't so uptight—full of anger, bitterness and numbing silence. Looking into Erik's eyes, she realized that he was the one, the *only* one.

"Erik," she whispered.

He leaned into her wet, tiny body and gave her a simple, sweet, kiss on her lips.

"You are so beautiful," he whispered, looking down at her soaking wet shirt. He was instantly aroused by her hard nipples peeking through. Her strong abdomen was crushed up against him. His need for her was torturing his soul. He grabbed her up into a fury of passion and began to kiss her wildly.

"Take me upstairs," she whispered into his ear.

Erik did as he was told, kissing her all the way up the steps. Placing her onto the bed, he practically tore off her shirt, throwing it into a wet ball on the floor. Before helping him pull off his shirt, River put her hand inside his jeans. She could feel him. He was hard and ready. They kissed wildly and deliciously, savoring every inch of space with love.

Erik massaged her breasts and nipples with his lips. River's thighs burst into flames. She moaned. He traced his tongue down the middle of her stomach until he reached the sacred bud of her bloom. She moved her hips in harmony with the call of the thunder outside. His name escaped her lips over and over again. Her core vibrated through his whole essence. His entire being was to plant himself firmly inside of her.

"Please now," she groaned for him.

Erik mounted her perfectly, showing off his glowing body, as he grabbed her pelvis, lifting her to take in his peaked readiness. He gently inserted himself into her tiny chamber. She ignored the pain and went even more wild for him. They moved in unison, both enlightened with euphoric emotions. The rain continued to smack against the windows. She held him tighter, wrapping her legs around his waist. They both shuddered with the arrival of heightened ecstasy and vivid awareness.

Erik sat up on his knees, pulling her on top of him. River felt some pain but pushed through, allowing him to lead her on the ride. Intense moans escaped his lips. He rocked back on the bed, holding her even tighter. His fingers lovingly glided along the sides of her face.

"I will never let you go," he whispered into her ear. Erik knew their love making was drawing supernatural attention, but in the moment, he ignored it. As for River, she had no idea he was drawing the thunder while they were in bed together, and it was he who made the storm's fury more powerful and pronounced. River, in her innocence, thought it was just Mother Earth.

Violet and Joshua watched over River's house from under a large boulder that protected them from the rain.

Did you see that? Joshua conveyed.

They were both captivated by the spectacular chakra-colored lightshow coming from inside the windows of River's house.

Yes. I saw it, Violet responded, slipping her snout under her paw.

What do you think it means? Joshua probed.

I think it means that we are in for a real shit show.

Obviously, Erik and River were having sex, and there was a

a very real possibility the "others" would intervene. Stepping out from under the large rock to shake out her fur, Violet watched as the rain slowed to a trickle. Joshua did the same, scratching his ear with his hind leg.

I think Erik will keep watch tonight. We should head back to the reservation, Joshua thought.

Yeah. River is safe with Erik, and, besides, we need to speak with 'Rising Fire,' Violet replied.

Let's go, Joshua conveyed, as he climbed up a large canyon, jumping a large trench. Violet followed swiftly behind him. They waded through puddles of water, making their way around Superstition Mountain. A waterfall cascaded down the side of the butte and a rainbow, made up of brilliant colors, highlighted the landscape. It was all because of the night's powerful rainfall. A pack of mule deer trotted past. Violet stopped in her tracks and watched the deer. Her stomach growled with hunger. In fear for their life, the mule deer darted away.

Come on Violet! We don't have time for that, Joshua barked.

Violet picked up speed until she was running beside Joshua. They valiantly jumped a large electric fence together. Running through a deserted meadow, the pair raced around saguaro cacti and barrel cacti until they crossed the highway into protected land.

A large Navajo man wearing faded overalls, two long braids and a round copper earring in his ear stood in a gravel path waiting for Violet and Joshua. He was known on the res as Rising Fire.

"It's safe for you here," he said to the two panting coyotes.

The pair walked over to Rising Fire. On the short jaunt, they both went through transference, returning to their human form. Rising Fire motioned for them to follow him. They walked quietly toward a small teepee set up in his backyard behind a mobile home.

"You will find robes in here, my friends. So, *please* put them on," he said, mostly implying that Joshua need to cover up. As asked, Joshua and Violet put on the native robes and sat down. They often visited Rising Fire on the Navajo Reservation, always feeling welcome.

"Earth is our mother, and our mother is in a time of distress and need," Rising Fire said. "The mother will grieve large pains, giving birth to destruction for humans and all life kind. From that a new planet will arise and be born. You two are watchers and protectors of those chosen to help, and you must be prepared."

Rising fire burned sage, as he walked around with a slight limp.

"Now, I have brought you a message, but do you have a message for me?"

Joshua and Violet exchanged a strange look, not knowing how to respond. They knew he wanted to hear something. Joshua took the lead.

"Our people are your people. You are descendants of us and where we come from. We cherish Earth as much as you. We will always respect the planet, both spiritually and physically," Joshua said, trying to sound as dignified as Rising Fire.

"Very old tales of my people coming from the sky—the Heavens above … another star system. We heard these tales as children and never knew what to truly believe," Rising Fire chuckled. "I dreamed my ancestors would bring me two coyote friends, and you came just like my dream."

Endearingly, Violet smiled at the elder man, gently touching his hand. Joshua and Violet both liked to visit with him, and they both knew he would soon be going home again, back to his *true* home. Rising Fire started to cough uncontrollably. Joshua grew concerned.

"Violet help him!" Joshua urged.

Violet tapped on his back. Rising Fire put his hand up to stop her.

"I'm fine … just ninety-two years young that's all," he retorted.

Violet's heart sank.

"You kids have a very special bond. You should get married."

Violet laughed out loud at Rising Fire's remark. Incensed, Joshua gave Violet a dirty look.

"Why are you laughing?" he asked.

"It's funny … that's all. Us? Married? What a joke!"

Rising Fire laughed. Riled up, Joshua stomped out of the teepee and sat on a large mound. He needed some fresh air anyway. The smoke from the purifying sage was giving him a headache. As he laid back and gazed up at the stars, he wondered how much longer they would be here. He wondered when they would be going home. Violet walked out from the teepee and sat beside Joshua.

"You shouldn't be so sensitive, Joshua," she whispered.

"I'm not. I'm just worried about how much longer we will be here and if they even care that we are gone."

"They haven't forgotten about us," Violet assured. "I promise. We are merely here to help Erik and River."

"I know," Joshua agreed. "She was always so good to us."

A handful of native teenagers rushed through the yard to greet Violet and Joshua. Joshua bumped knuckles with one of the natives. As Rising Fire ducked out of the tent, he nodded to them all and limped back to his mobile home. One of the native teens enquired about the robes, asking if Joshua and Violet had sweated it out in the teepee.

"Yeah. Our clothes were muddy from the rain. Rising Fire let us use his washer," Joshua lied.

"Come on! Let's go to my sister's house. We can get you some spare clothes there," one of the teens suggested.

Violet and Joshua followed the pack of teenagers back through the yard and across the street for some fresh clothes.

CHAPTER TWENTY-SIX
On Blue Honor

Riiver stared at her television, listening intently to the news about UFO sightings over Superstition Mountain in Apache Junction. Impressive home video recordings by various residents were being aired. Most appeared to be strong lights in the shape of triangles. The images weren't clear, but you could tell they were unidentified flying objects.

A truck skidded loudly into River's drive. She jumped to her window and saw it was Erik.

"Hey," he said, looking anxious and out of breath.

"What's wrong?" she asked.

"I just … we need to talk."

"Okay. Sit down with me," River insisted, pressing her crumpled shirt against her skirt and turning her attention to him. "What is it?"

Erik glued his eyes to the television, watching as a female reporter interviewed a local man who recorded a UFO sighting.

"Erik, what's going on?"

"Can we turn the television off?" he asked.

"Sure," River said, turning off the tube and scrunching closer to Erik. "What is it?"

"I may have to go out of town for a while. I received some bad news today," Erik exhaled, standing up and peering through the blinds in paranoia.

"What kind of news?"

"It's my parents. They need me. I can't explain it right now, but it's serious."

"What about Alex? Does he know," River probed.

"No."

"Shouldn't he know? Aren't they his parents, too?"

"Don't worry. I will be talking to Alex. It's important that you know that *if* I go, I *will* be back."

River nodded, feeling uneasy.

"Erik, I will be here waiting for you. We can keep in touch over the phone and internet…."

Erik jumped up, interrupting her. "That could be a problem."

"Why?"

"My parents live off the grid, no wi-fi."

River got quiet. She was questioning his honesty. She wondered if he was done with her. Was this his way of blowing her off? Was he *really* planning on coming back?

"Do you … want … me … to come?" she asked.

"No … not now. Not until I know for sure what's going on with them," he replied.

River became noticeably distant.

"Are you trying to break up or something?"

"No," he sighed. "And it's important that you never think that—no matter what happens."

Erik got down on bended knee, grabbing her hands. He looked deep into her eyes and said with watery eyes, "I love you."

River looked away, so she wouldn't be tempted to cry.

"I love you, too," she muttered.

River's cell rang. It was Alex.

"Alex," she sighed, deeply into the cell.

She was relieved to hear his voice.

"Hey! Is my brother there?"

"Yeah. Hold on," River replied, handing Erik the phone.

Erik took the phone and walked outside.

"You aren't answering your phone," Alex said, sounding troubled.

"Busy."

"What did you do?"

"You know?" Erik asked.

"Yes. You pissed off our parents," Alex replied.

"Maybe …"

"I think we both pissed them off," Alex admitted. "Or, maybe, it was just you."

"Alright … you're not helping, Alex."

"I'm on my way … almost there."

Alex sat on the couch next to River, as Erik tried explaining to them both why he needed to visit his parents. It was some kind of family emergency. Alex glanced over at River. She was nervously fidgeting with her skirt hem, trying hard to hide her disappointment.

"Would you like to go with me, Alex?" Erik asked, sternly.

"Hell no!"

River shot Alex a quizzical look. Attempting to shift the attention back to Erik, Alex added, "You can handle it. I've got too much to do."

"You sure? It's been a long time," Erik coaxed.

"No thanks," Alex replied sarcastically.

Erik rolled his eyes.

"I thought you weren't sure you had to go," River interjected.

"No. I'm not sure. It seems serious though."

"How serious are we talking?" Alex asked, trying to seem like an innocent party. Erik ignored the question, to which Alex gave him a slight nudge.

"Don't worry," Alex said, smiling. "If you go, I can take care of River."

"You guys are freaking me out," River said.

"Alex! Outside, please!" Erik commanded.

"What did you do, bro?" Alex asked, stepping outside.

"I … *we* … made love."

Alex tried hiding his jealousy, but the anger stabbed at his soul.

"Wow!" Alex whispered. "Stupid."

"You were going to do it," Erik snapped.

"No. I wasn't. I knew she would say no."

Erik glared at his brother.

"You would have, if I hadn't intervened!"

"It didn't happen, so it doesn't matter," Alex replied, trying not to break a whisper. "You made love to her. Okay? The parents know, so you will have to deal with it."

Alex felt a tinge of compassion for his brother. He could see the panic in Erik's face.

"Just go to them and get it over with. I've got your back. I will take care of River."

"You sure you won't come with me?" Erik asked.

"Are you crazy? River is wearing a ring we can't get off her finger. She needs protection. Why take us both away?"

Alex was becoming super annoyed at his brother's ignorance.

"Just go before they summon you. That way, you won't have to sit in the tank for a while."

"Yeah, like a prisoner," Erik retorted, anxious at the thought.

"Yep," Alex agreed. "Been there, done that."

"You promise to watch over her?" Erik asked.

"Yes."

"I have to tell her goodbye."

"I know."

"SHIT!" Erik shouted, angrily.

River watched from the couch, wondering what was really going on. She dared not interrupt the brothers. Their conversation appeared intense. Turning the television back on, she watched more footage of the local UFO sightings.

Later that afternoon, River was desperate to make love to Erik. He didn't resist. He had already drawn attention to himself the first time, and he knew this was the easiest way to turn himself in. He held River, kissing her, thinking about how he would treasure this moment since he was suddenly so unsure of his future. When he entered her, he could feel the earth shake around them. A blue-auric energy field blasted flecks of green from his heart. River didn't notice. Her eyes were shut. Her chest was open and pressed firmly against him. Their connection was real—powerful!

When River fell asleep, Erik sent a text message to Alex. It read: "I'm turning myself in. Please watch her till I get back."

To which Alex replied, "On blue honor, bro."

Erik empathically summoned Violet and Joshua. The two coyotes met him outside of River's home.

"I have to go back and turn myself in," Erik commanded, standing shirtless with worn-out jeans that showed off his fit abdomen. "Do whatever it takes to keep her protected, alive and well until I return."

How will you get back? Joshua asked.

"No matter what, I'm coming back."

Violet moved her sweet coyote body toward Erik's leg. He bent down to pet her.

"Don't worry Violet," he sighed. "I will be back soon. Looks like I will be leaving tonight."

Don't forget about us, Joshua thought, pacing.

"Never." Erik assured.

Erik returned to River, kissing her on the forehead while she slept. He then hopped into his truck and sped off, back to the ranch where he left a note for the Atler's. He apologized for leaving on such short notice, but it was a family emergency. He assured his employer that he would return as soon as possible.

As Erik sent River one last text, letting her know he was leaving, a sudden flash of light shocked his entire body, releasing prisms throughout the cabin. And then he vanished. His cell phone crashed to the floor.

Alex stared at his brother's last text. He felt a pang in his side.

"Be careful, brother," he whispered, looking out the window of his parked car, seeing a large burst of light flash over the Atler's Ranch.

Alex had planned to go home after he left River, but he was concerned for his brother, even though he was a pain in the ass, and he was always having to save him from trouble. He knew Erik was finally with his parents, so he pulled into the drive and walked into his brother's cabin. He saw the cell phone on the floor and picked it up. Alex exhaled, as he read the message meant for River: `"I had to go to my parents. I'm sorry. I will be back. Hang out with Alex as much as possible. Don't hold back."`

Alex smiled, as he pushed "Send." He put the phone in his pocket and walked back to his car.

River sat up when the text came through. Erik wasn't in her bed. She unlocked the phone and saw a new message from him. She read it with watery eyes. Lying back down, she had this rotten feeling that something else was going on and that there was a possibility he might not come back to her. Yanking the linen duvet off her body, she ran outside barefoot and walked along the side yard. Noticing a folded-up piece of paper on the ground covered in cactus needles, she picked it up, brushed it off, opened it up and read it.

BABY, I'M HERE. I'VE BEEN WANTING TO SEE YOU. I'M IN TOWN FOR A MONTH OR SO, AND I WANT YOU TO GIVE ME A CALL—740-341-3323. I LOVE YOU.

ALWAYS AND FOREVER, COTY

The color in River's face drained. Coty was here. That's who she heard that night outside her window. She darted inside the house, locking the door behind her. Taking a Louisville Slugger out of the closet, she curled up in bed with the wooden weapon and slept the rest of the night with every light in the house turned on.

CHAPTER TWENTY-SEVEN
Amariah

E rik sat in the tank, typically used for prisoners, while a fumigating light reflected from the cell walls, pulsating through his body. A male officer dressed in royal blue stood with a female doctor at the glass-paneled cell door.

Erik, good to see you. We will be giving you a shot that will fuse with your cells, cleansing you of ultra-violet light hormone, the doctor said in Pleiadian.

Erik sat still. He was a little lightheaded, still not himself.

Erik, we fumigated you with Romativarian crystal. It's a natural microbial and anti-bacterial, she explained.

"I know what Romativarian is. I discovered it." Erik mumbled.

Yes. Of course. Please look up at the ceiling and relax. You will be given a shot through the panels. As you know, the only side effects will be the sharp pains through the abdomen, and it will make you sleep.

Erik looked up at the top panel, absorbing the flashes of light that broke through the cell. Flashes of light were now dispersing through his body. Cellular mitigation had begun.

Perfect, Erik, the doctor smiled. *Thank you.*

Erik was lost in his thoughts, going back to the beginning, before he returned to Earth this last time. He saw her laughing with him, as they ran down the spaceship hallways together, darting through the most remote corridors filled with crystal encrusted tunnels. Some doors and panels were constructed of Chakra-prism glass with jeweled handles that were made on his beloved sphere—Planet Erra. Taking after his father, Erik was the ship's finest Pleiadian astronautical engineer. He became the most notable and the best. When he fell in love with her, he was willing to disobey and rebel, even if it meant throwing everything away.

The Pleiadians were vibrational empaths. They did not speak with their mouths, if they chose not to. Every time Erik closed his eyes, he could see her dressed in her blue uniform and blue, high-collar jacket. While working, they would sneak peeks at each other and smile. He groaned deeply at the thought of her. Her light was so warm and powerful. It made his kind melt with love while in her presence. When they found out she was being sent to Earth on a mission to be a Pleiadian star seed, he tried persuading the counsel to let him go in her stead, but as usual, they refused to listen.

Erik's memory of her became more vivid. He remembered her kissing him on Planet Erra and how it felt when he reached out to touch her face. So perfect, glowing and radiant with delicate Pleiadian features. Her hair, the color of golden straw with a hint of fire orange at the roots, was seldom down. She kept it pulled up tightly into a bun, high on top of her head. He loved her so much, her high cheek bones, almond-slanted eyes, and ombre-tan skin. He wasn't the only one who adored her. In fact, he had an enormous amount of competition.

Erik's thoughts transitioned to the beautiful flowers, exotic creatures and abundance of produce on Planet Erra. The animals he carried conversations with empathically were valued and held in high esteem, unlike the animals on Earth. Nothing that gave life or breath was destroyed on his planet. It was Erra law—stern and true. He remembered watching the dolphins, as she pulled a starfish from the ocean and wished it well before putting it back. They were descendants of the Orion galaxy and the Pleiades star system, and that made his kind the supreme healers—curators of all science and magic, Master of Physics in all the universe.

Erik, his mother whispered

He heard her, but he couldn't open his eyes.

ERIK, his father called.

He tried, but he couldn't get off the floor. Erik felt pinned down.

Take him to his quarters, please. Let him sleep this off, his father instructed.

Erik felt his body levitate and drift slowly backward. He was finally able to open his eyes, but his vision was hazy.

"Where are you taking me? Put me down."

While being transported in a rhodium chamber, he couldn't move his arms or legs.

"Where is she?" Erik asked.

He was feeling groggy, as he tried to move his limbs.

Who? asked one of the transporters.

"Amariah," Erik breathed.

He got no reply. His body hit the floating bed. He heard the chamber door to his quarters seal shut. Erik drifted off to sleep again, flashbacks consuming his mind in a series of sequences. Suddenly, he was watching Amariah spar against Mahendra, another star seed just like her. With her crystal-embedded sword, she defeated her opponents over and over again. No one was quite as ruthless. Mahendra came close, but only because they were sisters. Amariah taught her sister everything she knew.

Erik snuck up behind her. She turned quickly, but Erik caught hold of her sword and pulled her in for a kiss. That memory startled him out of a deep sleep. He managed to push his body toward the glass table next to his floating bed. He poured himself a glass of molecular water, infused with absorbable crystals. His pores immediately began to emanate light, and he was starting to feel better. He fell to the floor, as he tried standing. He was still unstable.

"STRATUS!" he shouted.

"Yes, sir! How can I help you?"

The robotic voice reverberated through the walls.

"Open the doors, so I can get out of here!" Erik shouted.

"I'm sorry, sir, but I have been instructed that you stay in your chambers till otherwise ordered."

The computerized voice echoed through his brain, messing with his memory of Amariah's face. Erik curled up into a fetal position on the floor and fell asleep.

The next morning, Erik showered in the natural landscape waterfall in his room. It was surrounded by plants and exotic flowers. He dressed himself in his blue uniform and waited patiently. He fell asleep on the woven, green chair. Feeling his mother, Yilene, enter the room, he awoke. Yilene was a beautiful, tall and stately woman with ombre hair, transitioning from black to brown. Her face was accented with high but delicate cheekbones, almond-slanted, green-bedazzled eyes, and naturally pink lips.

Erik, it's good to see you again, Yilene said, in empathic Pleiadian.

Mother.

How is she? Yilene enquired.

Living a hard life ... without a clue, Erik conveyed.

As always, she's working hard, Yilene replied.

It's too dangerous for her. I need to get back. She needs me.

We *need her, and you know that. She has the brightest and the most penetrable light of all the 145,000 Pleiadian star seeds now planted on Earth. She is helping to ease the transition of the upcoming planetary global shift. When she went vegan, millions of humans decided to go plant based. When she showed concern for the welfare of the environment, millions of human minds made that shift with her. Her strength is a royal-blooded masterpiece. You have not given that enough respect,* Yilene thought, clearly upset with her son, Erik, for disobeying orders and chasing after her.

Erik's actions were selfish in his mother's eyes. He put everything her people had worked to preserve in danger. Moreover, he put Earth and Amariah in jeopardy.

Amariah is your brother Alexander's responsibility. You were not to get involved. Your place is here, among us, and the ship, she conveyed.

"No!" Erik shouted. "She is **my** responsibility."

"She does not belong to you Erik," Yilene said, through pursed lips. "Her heart and mission belong to Planet Erra."

Yilene stepped toward Erik, so as to look him in the face.

"You do realize that when Earth makes the global shift, just as it does every cycle, *we* need to prepare to stop the nuclear reactors that humans have ignorantly put into position on that planet?"

"I already know this," Erik exhaled. "But you should have left me to her. She needs me."

"She can have you from here," Yilene replied, softly.

"I can't believe you sent Alexander to protect her."

"That is your brother's purpose. It is his place. It was never yours."

"He doesn't feel the way I feel about her," Erik sighed.

"You know, that is not true," Yilene offered.

"He's reckless."

"Absolutely," Yilene agreed. "It makes him dangerous to the opposition. He is the best of the best, and there are no complaints. Who do you think offered him this position?"

"Amariah."

"Yes. So, why are you questioning her choices and decisions? She was thinking of her own safety."

"I love her, Mother."

"You aren't the only one, Erik," Yilene said, sharply.

Those words pierced Erik deeply. He knew she was loved, and he knew there were many who wanted to be near her, especially on the Planet Erra. Amariah was beyond famous for everything she had offered and done in her lifetime. All the sacrifices she made were celebrated and promised to never be forgotten.

"When you had sexual relations with her, you brought on the attention of the Archon government," Yilene said. "We can't have that. They are looking for her now."

"I'm sorry. I never meant to …" Erik began.

"But you did, son," Yilene interrupted. "Now, we must fix that. Erik, you can't go back."

"Yes. I must," Erik said, swallowing hard.

"No," Yilene replied. "Do not forget, she is human … with very little Pleiadian DNA. She is not as powerful on Earth, as she would be here. Against the Archon, she is considered fragile, lacking her usual power."

"Send me back and I will handle that."

Erik looked up at his mother in desperation.

"We will discuss it with the Elders."

"Fair enough," Erik groaned. "Are we done here, Mother?"

Yilene nodded, turned and with telekinesis opened the door and left his room.

CHAPTER TWENTY-EIGHT
Disarmed

A lex lay stretched out on his back underneath the kitchen sink. He worked to replace fixtures while River sat quietly at her table, staring into space. She tried not to think about Erik, but with Alex around most of the time, it was hard to get him off her mind. He'd been gone a whole month, and she had yet to hear from him.

"Copper is all corroded," Alex mumbled underneath his breath.

River's cell phone rang. She quickly picked up in hopes it was Erik, but it was just the local courthouse.

"Hello, River Anderson?"

"Yes."

"This is Nadine down at the courthouse. I spoke to the judge, and based on your current situation, I was told you can file an order of protection with the court."

River quietly ducked outside to take the call, so that Alex wouldn't suspect anything.

"Even if he's out of Ohio jurisdiction?" she whispered.

"Yes. Unfortunately, however, you will need to hire a lawyer and present to the judge clear-cut evidence of any stalking and harassment issues—past and present."

"Okay," River sighed, wiping sweat from her cheek.

As she hung up the phone, she felt helpless. She wanted to avoid hiring a lawyer, at least for the time being. She could only hope Coty had gone back to Ohio ... leaving Arizona for good. Was it too much to ask that he leave her alone and focus his attention on another woman? River ambled back into the house and found Alex wiping his hands with a dirty dish rag. She tried shrugging off the disappointing telephone conversation, so as not to create alarm.

"Well ... you've got all new pipes in place. You can cash in these old copper ones at the local recycling center," Alex smiled, standing over his handy work.

River barely heard a word he said, as she sat down to the kitchen table and stared off into space.

"Hey!" he said. "What's going on?"

River took a deep, ragged breath. She looked numbly at Alex.

"I think my ex-boyfriend has been stalking me. He was ..." she broke off. "Here."

"What?"

Alex gave a look of surprise.

"Yeah. I heard a man's voice outside of my house the other night. He left a note."

"Why didn't you say anything?" Alex exhaled, leaning in.

"I'm embarrassed. He used to beat me. I don't want people to think I'm some kind of weak woman," she said.

Alex sat down beside her, as she continued.

"One day, he finally hit me hard enough to do some *real* damage. He put me in the hospital. I was a mess," River said, her eyes watering.

Unbeknownst to her, Alex already knew the whole story. In fact, he was there when it happened—empathically speaking. Moreover, he had been sent to Earth to protect her, to put himself between her and harm's way, to make sure the beatings never happened again. There was no way she could have known.

Erik, of course, stole the show when he commandeered the Saturn capsule ship, taking it upon himself to travel to Earth. It was a risk, but he felt compelled to get to River. His parents were swift in locating the ship and taking it back, but Erik had already disembarked and entered the picture. Alex kept in touch with their parents, apprising them of the ongoing situation. Of course, Erik had no idea he was alerting them to what was happening—at least until his return home. It wasn't that he wanted to go behind his brother's back, but rather he wasn't in a position to disclose any information. Technically, Amariah (i.e., River) was in command. His hands were tied.

Alex paid close attention to River, allowing her to fill in the holes of her story and all he had missed in regard to her turbulent past with Coty. What he really wanted to do was decimate the lowlife for hurting her.

"I need to be here with you, or you need to come home with me to Queen Creek," Alex insisted.

"No. I will be fine here."

"Fine," Alex agreed. "Then I will stay here with you."

"No, Alex! I'm fine. He may have gone back to Ohio by now."

"I don't like it," Alex replied. "I don't want you here alone. What if he decides to show up again?"

"Alex, I'm not the woman I used to be. I'm much meaner now, and I've been taking martial arts for a couple years. I will be fine. I want you to focus on your new job," River smiled. "Where are you working now?"

"I am at the hospital just around the corner from you. So, if you need anything, do not hesitate to call or text me," Alex said, relaxing his jaw. He wrapped his arm around River, pulling her in for a friendly hug.

"Thank you for fixing the sink, Alex. I owe you one."

"No," he smiled. "It was *my* pleasure."

"How about dinner next Thursday?" she asked.

"Sounds perfect!" he replied. "I will be here."

River ran into her karate class and started to stretch. With the stress building, she needed to relieve some tension, particularly in her shoulders and neck. Looking up from a butterfly stretch she noticed a beautiful, young Navajo woman approach Sensei. She watched as the young girl took a hair band out of the pocket of her tight leggings and pulled her thick, black hair high up on top of her head in a bun. Sensei introduced the new student to the class. Her name was Violet. River offered her a warm, welcoming smile. Violet appeared nervous. When she caught River's eye, she hesitated to return the smile. She was mostly worried River would recognize her.

"Let's partner up!" Sensei yelled.

Violet stepped forward awkwardly, standing at the far edge of the mat. River made her way to her, officially introducing herself.

"I'll be your partner," River said. "Have you studied Kenpo Karate before?"

"Sort of," Violet replied, blushing.

The two teamed up, and as the techniques started rolling, River realized that Violet was a quick study and extremely strong for her thin frame.

"We have a natural!" Sensei Pete yelled, commending Violet.

The class moved to practicing knife-training exercises. To River's surprise, Violet handled herself quite effectively in this arena. For having come off so awkward at the start, Violet was able to disarm River of her knife with little effort, which shocked everyone in the class. Until then, no one had ever been able to disarm River.

"I think you've definitely done this before," River breathed.

"I had a wonderful instructor once," Violet replied.

"Was your instructor a ninja?"

"You could say that she was a master of her craft," Violet grinned.

"A woman?" River chimed, rubbing her neck. "Wow! Nice."

"I'm sorry. Did I hurt you when I laid that choke hold on you?" Violet asked, apologetically.

"No. I'm fine," River lied.

Violet was a ruthless fighter, and that was duly noted for the remainder of practice.

"Maybe we can get together sometime, and you can show me all your moves," River suggested.

"Sure," Violet smiled. "I would like that."

"Are you free on Thursday? I'm having a friend over for dinner. Would you like to join us?"

"I would like that."

With that, both women exchanged phone numbers. After class, Violet and River walked out to the parking lot together. Joshua waited for Violet in his truck. The two women waved goodbye and parted ways.

"Really?" Joshua asked, annoyed.

"What?" Violet replied, climbing into the truck.

"You could've toned it down a bit in there."

Violet just shrugged it off with a knowing grin.

"She's the one who taught me everything I know!"

"Yes. I know, but she doesn't know that, and we are trying to keep a low profile."

"So, do you want me to dumb myself down for you, Joshua?"

"No," Joshua said, rolling his eyes. "Do it for her, for them, for the whole situation."

"What's the big deal? She seemed happy with it. She even invited me over next Thursday for dinner."

"Good, we can keep a closer eye on her for Erik." Joshua nodded.

Joshua and Violet trailed River from a distance, until she turned into her drive. Parking off road, the two hid the truck behind some tall brush, and then morphed into coyotes and took their usual perch.

CHAPTER TWENTY-NINE
Light Years Away

A lex took out Erik's cell phone from his back pocket and, with some hesitation, decided to send River a text. He hated seeing her so depressed. He felt a text message from "Erik" would be just what the doctor ordered. It was the right thing to do. Although, he knew that if Erik was never to return, he would be forced to fake his death or something to that effect, so as to cover his tracks.

River was climbing out of her Jeep when the text message from "Erik" came in. She gasped when she saw his name light up on her screen. The message read: "Hey! I wanted to send you a quick message and update you on everything. All is good. Just boring with the parents. I do not have good service, but I have gotten your messages. I may be here for a while. I am sorry about that."

River hurried with a response, her fingers trembling as she replied: "It's okay. I am just glad you are good. Alex is good, too. In case you were wondering. He's been very helpful lately."

Alex sensed her relief, so he sent a response. It read: "So, Alex is helpful … huh? Good. I am glad. Please continue to trust him and let him help you out."

Just as Alex was about to put away Erik's phone, another notification from River dinged.

River

"I will, and don't worry. Alex and I are great friends. I've trusted him for a very long time. I don't know what I would do without your brother right now. I miss you. I can't wait till you get back."

Alex took a deep breath, relaxing a little. He was nervous about her replies concerning him, especially since he had been bugging the shit out of her ... perhaps even getting on her nerves.

He texted her back, almost forgetting that it would be interpreted as Erik.

Alex

"I love you, River. Take care."

Alex did love her, and he wished she knew that.

Another notification sounded from River, "I love you too, Erik."

Alex tucked the cell in his back pocket, whispering, "You owe me one, brother."

Light years away, Erik paced up and down the length of his quarters aboard the Pleiadian ship, otherwise known as Pyalexis. He had been thinking long and hard about how to get back to Earth. His parents were a lot like him, strong, astronaut engineers who would not be easily persuaded. He had stolen the Saturn, taking off with two students named Violet and Joshua. He didn't care about the consequences. He still didn't care. He would spend the rest of his life on Earth if it meant staying with Amariah forever.

Erik walked to the upper bridge in his perfectly creased blue uniform. Realizing his parents had felt his approach, he wasn't surprised to find them awaiting his arrival.

Erik, his father conveyed empathically.

Erik nodded. He preferred to speak aloud vs. whisper, which was his parents' preferred language.

"I need permission to return to Earth," Erik said, wasting no time.

"Why?" his father, Talmud, asked.

"I can't stay here and watch her be destroyed."

"Amariah?" Talmud replied.

"Of course," Erik huffed. "Who else?"

That is none of your business, Talmud impressed sharply.

"Well, we can agree to disagree," Erik snapped, resolved to return to Earth regardless of whether or not he had permission.

You must stand before the Elder Counsel, Yilene interrupted.

"When?" Erik asked.

"Soon," Yilene whispered. "They are concerned that we are being impartial to the rules because you are my son."

"I can tell them it wasn't your fault," Erik said.

It may not be enough, Talmud conveyed.

"So, what happens if it's not enough?"

"Your father and I could lose control of this ship, and *we* are the reason the Pyalexis even exists. If we lose our place here, we would be heart broken."

"I won't let that happen," Erik replied. "Don't worry. I have information that will get the Elders' attention."

Talmud and Yilene exchanged a worried glance. Before another word was spoken, Erik turned his back and left the room. He marched straight to Amariah's quarters. He missed her terribly, enough to sleep in her room, surrounded by her things. For the time being, it would do. It was as close to her as he could get.

CHAPTER THIRTY
The Stars Align

"I t's a party, bitches!" Solene, a young Navajo woman, shouted obnoxiously into a crowd of people as she pranced toward a lakeside campfire. Violet found Solene to not only be slutty, but annoying. She always had to have all the attention on her—at all times!

Joshua's eyes shot straight to Solene's breasts, as did everyone else's eyes sitting around the campfire. It was obvious she was not wearing a bra underneath her tube top. Her energetic nipples popped for all to see.

"I bought tequila!" Solene hollered at a group of young girls on the reservation who admired her and wanted to be like her.

"She's such a slut," Violet whispered.

Joshua cringed.

"Stop," he replied. "She might hear you."

"Hear me? How? Not over that big mouth of hers," Violet snapped, turning away from Solene and her tuckered-out tube top. She watched as the younger guys jumped off the cliff into the lake.

Solene trailed behind a young girl carrying a couple of tequila shots meant for her and Joshua. She grabbed the shot glasses out of the girl's hands and with a small dramatic turn, squeezed in between Violet and Joshua.

"Have a shot with me," Solene purred in his ear.

"Okay … sure," he replied, taking the shot of tequila and tossing it back.

"Swim with me," Solene coaxed, gently touching the back of his neck.

"I don't know about swimming tonight," he replied, blushing.

Violet rolled her eyes, suddenly feeling sick to her stomach.

"Come on, Joshua. I want to spend time with you," Solene moaned, her heaping breasts about to burst through the bulging elastic.

Violet got bored and brushed the two of them off. She jumped up and walked to the cliff's edge. She debated whether or not to jump into the lake and swim across to the other side. She wanted nothing more than to take leave of Joshua, Solene and their nauseam. She wanted to run into the wilderness as fast as she could, turn into a coyote and never look back.

Joshua looked past Solene, watching Violet's every move. He knew that all the guys at the party were interested in her, even though she seemed clueless. He liked that about her.

"Jump in! Jump in, Violet!" the boys in the lake called out.

Violet crossed her arms with a sassy smirk on her face.

"No," she replied, her eyes bubbling with light, as her mixed emotions and energy boiled. Then, out of nowhere, she tore off her jean shorts and top, revealing her dainty, pink bra and panties. The boys' cheers echoed against the bluff.

"Yes!" two guys shouted.

Meanwhile, Solene continued to move in on Joshua, giving his thigh a light squeeze. In a puff of anger, Joshua stood up abruptly and exclaimed, "Solene, not now!"

"What? Joshua, don't do this right now."

Solene watched in disbelief as Joshua rushed over to his precious Violet. Jealousy coursed through her veins. She dulled the burn with another shot of tequila.

Violet felt Joshua's approach. She was suddenly overwhelmed with emotion, and it made her happy. She looked at Joshua for a fleeting second before arching into a backward dive into the lake. Joshua kicked off his shoes in a fury, ripping off his shirt and flew into the water after her. After four shots of tequila, he was feeling extremely bold and somewhat jealous, which took him by surprise. Swimming toward her, he reached for her legs, grabbed hold of one and friskily dragging her under water. Violet playfully splashed at him.

"Joshua …stop!" she giggled.

"Give me one good reason why I should stop?" he asked, flirtatiously.

"I just … you've had too much to drink," she replied, swimming away.

"Wait, Violet," Joshua said, sweetly grabbing at her toes. Violet couldn't help but notice his sexy smile.

"Yes …"

"I …" Joshua stopped himself, shyly looking away.

Violet smiled, a beam of light from her pupils danced with his.

"We should check on River, Joshua. It's almost midnight, and we've already stayed here too long."

Ignoring her, Joshua implored, "Grab my shoulders."

"What?"

"Just do it," he urged.

Violet grabbed onto the back of Joshua's shoulders, allowing him to gently tow her to the other side of the lake. The two ignored the wild calls coming from the party. He helped her onto the muddy embankment. Violet turned toward the party taking place on the other side of the lake. It might as well have been on the other side of the world.

"What about our clothes?" she asked.

"Since when have we ever worried about our clothes?"

"Come on!" Joshua exclaimed, running as fast as he could through the thick evergreens mixed with desert bonsai. Violet took off after him. Together they leapt over a large, dead tree, transforming into their perfect coyote forms and racing all the way to River's house.

River tossed and turned most of the night. Eventually, she forced herself to get up and look out the bay window of her bedroom.

"Oh ..." she whispered, figuring the full, Arizona moon might have had something to do with why she couldn't sleep.

River sat on the floor and watched the night sky. She thought about Erik. He was texting her more, but she found it peculiar he would never call. Leaning into the window, she rested her chin on the top of her hand. She noticed a blue ray of light sweep out from her mysterious ring. It aligned perfectly with a cluster of stars outside her window. Stunned, she stood up like a shot and began moving her ring finger around the beam of blue light. The ray remained in perfect alignment. It did not go away.

"What is this?" she whispered.

Racing downstairs, River rushed outside barefoot. She held the ring up toward the moon. The blue beam didn't shift as expected with its glow remaining true to the cluster of stars.

"Amazing."

River realized, there was more to this ring than anyone could have ever imagined. The more the ring opened up to her, the more she considered it precious and extraordinary. Off in the distance, she heard the call of coyotes. She looked around and met the eyes of the two animals she had frequently encountered. They were staring down at her from a boulder across the road. They both whined and whimpered when they noticed her noticing them. For reasons unknown, that recognition was a comfort to all three of them.

River returned to her bedroom. After taking a melatonin capsule, in hopes it would put her to sleep, she continued to watch the blue beam from her ring gleam toward the cluster of stars. Her thoughts drifted back to Erik. With one last, long sigh, and a yawn chaser, she pulled the covers up to her neck and fell fast asleep.

CHAPTER THIRTY-ONE

Wish You Were Here

"River, you've got some competition now," Sensei yelled, as everyone partnered up and performed a mock gun take-away technique. River was determined to disarm Violet, but for some reason, every time she looked at the gun, she would flashback to the active shooter situation at work. She could still hear the horrific screams in the back of her head. She tried to snap out of it. Sweat dripped down the sides of her face, pooling around her neck and chest. River battled through, repeating her training techniques over and over again. It didn't keep Violet from kicking River's feet out from under her while they were both latched onto the gun.

"Whoa, Violet! You are ruthless, girl!" Sensei proclaimed proudly.

Violet got behind River and held the gun to her spine. Suddenly inspired, River took a wild, deep breath, whipping her body around taking Violet into a strongarm with wrist lock. Violet fought to keep her grip but dropped the gun (with a loud CLANG!) to the floor.

"Nice," Sensei said, happy to see River fight back.

River was a good sport, giving Violet a firm handshake before walking to her water bottle for a drink.

"Hey! You okay?" Violet asked, concerned. "You seemed distant during practice."

"Yes. It's just really hot in here, maybe the air conditioner isn't working."

"Yeah. I'm hot, too," Violet agreed, anxiously staring at River's ring. "That is a beautiful ring. Where did you get it?"

"Family heirloom," River lied, taking a swallow of cold water.

Violet knew it was a lie. She and Joshua knew how Erik felt about the ring. They could feel his empathic thoughts whenever he was overly emotional about anything, especially when it came to River. When Violet watched her connect the ring to Orion's galaxy, she knew the ring must be intergalactic and not manmade.

"So tomorrow at seven?" Violet asked.

"Huh?"

"The dinner invitation. Is it still good?" Violet asked.

"Oh yeah—sorry! Yes. Tomorrow night. Vegan dinner … hope you don't mind."

"No problem."

Now that she was on Earth, living as a carnivore, Violet did mind. Back on Planet Erra, however, she only ate fruit and vegetables with other high-vibrational plants. They didn't partake in meat or the destruction of any living being. Lately, while her body embraced coyote, she loved duck more than anything.

"I think you will like it," River said, tying her shoes.

Violet grabbed her backpack, giving everyone a friendly wave.

"See you all later!"

River started for the parking lot. The receptionist stopped her on the way out.

"Somebody left this at the desk for you," she said, handing her a small envelope.

"Thanks."

River quickly opened it, not realizing the fear building in her body. The note read: I SEE YOU. DO NOT TRY TO HIDE FROM ME.

It wasn't signed, but River knew it was from her ex—Coty. He was still in Arizona, closer than she anticipated, and she wasn't sure how to handle it.

"Don't forget we start practicing for tournaments next week," Sensei said, tapping her on the shoulder as he walked past. River only slightly nodded, then bolted to her Jeep.

Once home, River slammed the door behind her, causing a bohemian print on her wall to crash to the floor. Locking her doors, she quickly sent a text to Erik.

River

Erik, I need to talk to you.

Sitting on her couch, she waited. An hour passed by with no reply. To which she followed up with: "I wish you were here."

Tears fell down her prominent cheek bones. She had never felt more alone.

Alex stood over the toilet in exasperation. He had done it this time. While reaching over the tank to grab a towel from the top shelf, Erik's cell phone slipped out of his top pocket and into the watery basin below. He quickly fished the phone out, but it was too late. No power.

"SHIT!"

Alex ran to the kitchen, dropping the cell phone into a plastic bag filled with dried rice. If River were to text Erik, there would be no reply and, truth be told, he was growing quite fond of her sweet endearing texts. He didn't want her worrying unnecessarily, which gave him an idea. He Googled a local flower shop and dialed the number.

"Hearts and Flowers Florist, this is April."

"Hey! Uh, I need to order some flowers for someone special," Alex inquired.

"Have you checked out our website, sir?" April replied.

"No. I don't really have time for that today. Just give me your best arrangement and make it extra special."

"Well, they are all *special* and uniquely designed, sir. What's the occasion?"

Alex sighed, "You know what? Just go with something big that says I love you."

"How about some roses?" April suggested.

"No ... something more colorful and really stands out."

"Okay," April hummed. "How much are you willing to spend?"

"I don't know, maybe twenty dollars."

There was a pregnant pause.

"We do not have anything for twenty dollars," April replied, sounding annoyed.

"Okay," Alex said. "Make it sixty dollars. Just throw what you want in it and make it look good."

"Okay."

"Sign the card, 'Thinking of you. Love Erik.'"

Alex gave April his credit card information and ended the call. He wondered why he was going out of his way for his brother. Erik could be gone for good, and at some point, River would need to accept that.

CHAPTER THIRTY-TWO
Show and Tell

"Wow! How much food did you actually make?" Alex asked, as he casually walked into River's kitchen.

"Not much really. It's just a raw-vegan lasagna with cashew cheese, heirloom tomatoes, and pine nuts," she replied.

Alex's smile dropped when he saw a glass pitcher full of dark, mossy-green liquid. He picked it up and took a whiff.

"What is this?" he asked

"Wheat grass with chlorella and spirulina. I thought it would be fun if we did little shots of it throughout dinner. You know, instead of the normal alcohol drinking games."

"I agree. Alcohol totally ruins a party," Alex teased.

"I forgot to tell you, Alex. I have a guest coming."

"Yeah?" he asked suspiciously, swiping a tomato off the chopping block. "Male or female?"

"It's not a setup or anything. I'm sure she's not your type. I just thought it would be cool to invite her over for dinner is all."

"Did you meet her at your new job?" Alex asked, grabbing more chopped vegetables and pushing them in his hungry mouth.

"No. Actually she's in my Kenpo-karate class, and let me tell you, she's amazing!"

"A master at karate?" Alex asked.

"She could be a stunt double in movies, she's so good."

"Kind of reminds me of a girl I used to know … way back when. *She* was an expert," Alex said, looking at River in a reminiscent sort of way.

"Well, don't make a pass at her … please," River pleaded.

"I won't cross the line. Besides, I'm interested in someone else."

"Really? Anyone I know?"

River suddenly felt odd.

"Not revealing any information right now," Alex replied, as River wiped down the counters and hurried to set the rustic table.

"Thank you, Alex, for being here with me. It's been a really hard and confusing year."

River looked up at Alex with a smile. He gave her a good, warm squeeze on her bare shoulders and said, "I will always be here for you."

With a wink, he added more freshly cut cucumbers to his mouth.

Violet pulled into River's driveway behind the wheel of Joshua's truck. When she saw Alex's car, it sent her into a slight panic. She wasn't sure if he would recognize her or not. They had seen each other aboard the Pyalexis many times. However, they had not seen one another since she and Joshua had grown into young adults. Even though they were not permanent residents aboard the ship, she and Joshua had frequented as student visitors since childhood. Like many other hopeful, strong, academic Pleiadians, they were selected to study at certain periods of time.

The Pyalexis was constantly on the lookout for team members who were unique to the service in some way. Violet and Joshua were considered astral shifters, and that made them priceless to the Pyalexis. They were able to transform into any animal they chose, but it depended on the planet and the planet's molecular makeup and magnetic energy. It was easier on Planet Earth. They were able to choose animals according to their environment, and this time it was a coyote.

Joshua, Violet commanded in her thoughts.

I'm here Violet ... right behind you, Joshua replied.

Violet saw Joshua in coyote form through the rear-view mirror. He was on all fours in the back of the truck, attentive to her every move.

Alex is here, she conveyed.

Yes, I see.

Do I take the risk? she asked.

Yes! Who cares? If he notices, he won't reveal it to River.

True. Okay, I'm going in. Stand by, Violet thought.

"Hi ... you made it! Thank you," River said, giving Violet a soft, warm hug. She immediately introduced her to Alex. Alex shook Violet's hand, appearing not to suspect anything. He surreptitiously looked around River's home for the flowers he had delivered. There was no sign of them anywhere. He even excused himself to go to the bathroom, running upstairs to see if they were there. Still no flowers.

"This raw food is surprisingly delicious," Violet said.

"Isn't it though?" Alex lied.

In the back of his mind, he thought that somewhere in the process of making that raw vegan lasagna, the flavor had been left out.

"Thank you. Who wants a wheatgrass shot?" River offered.

Violet and Alex looked down at their plates, as if synchronized.

"Come on! I put pineapple juice in it to give it a pleasant, tropical taste," River urged.

"Oh, what the hell! Give me a shot," Alex replied

"I will take one, too." Violet added, meekly.

Alex finished his wheatgrass shot with a theatrical sigh. Violet swirled hers around in the glass, hoping nobody would notice.

"River, have you heard anything from Erik?" Alex inquired.

Violet shot him a nasty look. Alex noticed it right away, and she withdrew her glance, hoping she hadn't given herself away.

"No. I haven't heard anything. It's been two weeks now. I was going to ask you the same question. I figure he might have met someone else or something …" River sighed.

"Don't think that, River," Violet jumped in, without thinking.

"Do you know Erik, Violet?" Alex asked suspiciously, as he stretched back in the kitchen chair with a smile.

"NO! I mean … no. I just … well, I know that when it comes to certain people and situations, it's often not always what we think."

Violet was getting nervous, so she threw the wheatgrass shot down her throat.

"I can tell you are just trying to be positive, Violet. It's just that I have made some bad choices in the past concerning men. And I know he's your brother, Alex. I'm sorry."

River cleared her throat faintly. Alex suddenly felt bad for bringing up Erik, but he was confused.

Damnit, he thought. Where were the flowers he ordered for her?

"River, I know my brother, and he's very loyal. We just need to give him some time to break away from my parents. They tend to make separating from them very hard," Alex said.

"Why? What's wrong with your parents?" Violet asked, innocently.

"They are parents. You know ... pushy, strict, and needy. Add sick into the mix, and you have a hell of a combination," Alex replied.

"Why aren't you with him?" Violet asked, testing him for reasons she couldn't quite explain. Alex gave Violet a look of severe annoyance, making Violet very uncomfortable.

"Let's go outside. I want to show you something," River interjected, quickly changing the subject.

Soon, they were all standing in the yard. River took a few steps forward, pointing her ring straight up into the night sky. A blue beam shot straight from her ring, trailing toward a cluster of stars.

"Do you see this?" River asked, excitedly.

"What the ..." Alex said in amazement, as the beam of light was centered, headed straight in the direction of his home planet.

Violet kept silent. She had seen what this ring was capable of, and if she were to offer an explanation, she would definitely draw Alex's attention. Alex grabbed River by the hand. He studied the light from the gemstones, as they bounded into the stars.

"How is this happening?" he asked.

"I don't know, but it's truly fantastic!" River replied.

"What do you think it means?" Violet asked.

"Maybe a constellation ring," River said.

"A constellation ring?" Alex questioned.

"Who knows, but obviously it's something." River said, gazing at the light show.

"Hold the ring up in the opposite direction," Alex commanded.

River turned around, holding her hand up in the reverse direction

The light moved to connect to his galaxy. Alex began to tremble. He staggered toward the porch.

"Let's go inside—too many scorpions crawling around here at night," he said, attempting to divert his reaction.

River shrugged, as they followed him back indoors.

"I need to get going, River," Violet said. "Thank you for the very healthy meal it was nice."

"Wait! I have board games," River coaxed.

"I've got this thing on the reservation tomorrow morning," Violet replied. She caught Alex giving her an intense look. It made her feel squeamish.

"You better get going then," Alex urged.

"Okay! See you at practice on Tuesday," Violet said, heading out the door. River waved, following Violet outside. Alex stopped her at the door, nudging her back into the house.

Awkward goodbye.

"I wish you could get that ring off your finger," he said, irritated. "I'd like to get a better look at it."

"I wish I could, Alex, but as you already know I can't."

"Yes. It's very strange. I don't think it's wise to show anyone else what it can do," he warned.

"What do you think it means?" she asked.

Alex sighed, "I think it will remain a mystery to us all, until we can get it off your finger."

CHAPTER THIRTY-THREE
Flowers and Thorn

Violet pulled the truck into a rocky mountain wash. As she parked the vehicle, Joshua hurried over to her, transforming from Coyote form to human. Violet reached into the back seat, grabbing a pair of Joshua's shorts and launching them out the window toward him. She caught herself staring at his naked body, suddenly becoming embarrassed and uncomfortable. The more attracted she was to him, the more out of her comfort zone it drew her.

"So …" Joshua began, pulling his shorts up and buttoning them. The muscles in his abdomen flexed. Violet couldn't help but notice he was growing more gorgeous every day, not to mention intimidating to look at.

"She showed us what the ring could do," Violet said.

"I saw that."

"The raw food was weird. Maybe if I were turning into a vegan bird instead of a carnivorous coyote, I would've enjoyed it, but …"

Joshua rolled his eyes, "Come on Violet, what's the deal? Did Alex notice who you were or what?"

"I don't know … maybe."

"Hopefully not. I don't want to start answering to him while Erik's away," Joshua said, breathing a little easier.

"Agreed."

"It's good that you and River are getting close. I'm sure she can use a friend. Plus, we can keep a closer eye on her," Joshua added.

The two walked toward their usual boulder with a bird's eye view of River's house.

"Did you show her any of your martial arts moves?" Joshua asked, giving Violet a playful punch to the arm.

"Quit, Joshua! You know she is my sensei.".

"I know … just messing with ya," Joshua teased. "I know you miss her. It has to suck being her right now. She doesn't even know she's a Blue warrior."

"Do you think her ring was given to her by our people?"

"I don't know. I just know it isn't from Earth," Joshua sighed, as they sat beside each other.

"Joshua, I'm tired," Violet yawned.

"Go ahead and sleep, I can take watch."

"Thank you," Violet replied, her eyes getting heavy.

She decided not to phase into coyote, as she nestled sweetly into Joshua's side and fell asleep. Joshua watched a falling star dart across the night sky. He thought about how peaceful everything felt in that moment. Within a few hours, he laid down next to Violet, wrapping his arms around her and pulling her in close to him. He soon fell fast asleep.

The next day, Alex rushed through his work. On a break, he anxiously bolted to his car in the parking lot to call the florist.

"Well, she never got the flowers." Alex said, coldly.

"Sir, they were delivered by a reliable delivery man," April retorted.

"Are you sure you had the right address?" Alex challenged.

April, an experienced florist, was beginning to feel incensed, as she repeated the house number to him.

"My records show they were signed for," she said.

"Signed for," Alex replied. "Signed by who?"

"The signature is illegible. It's more of a scribble. I can't make out the name. I can assure you; the flowers *were* delivered and signed for at the address you gave me."

Alex couldn't imagine what happened to the delivery. Where had the flowers gone? It bothered him for the rest of his shift. He knew River wouldn't throw them out. The girl was big on rescuing dead flowers patients had thrown away, let alone a brand-new bouquet. He had to know. He would have to ask her straight up and deal with the questions that followed. He pulled out his cell phone and sent a casual-sounding text.

Alex
"Hey!"

River
"Hey! What's up?"

Alex
"Did you get any flowers delivered to you
recently?"

River
"No, why? Did you send me some?"

Alex thought carefully about his next text. Obviously, someone had been at her house and intercepted her flowers at delivery.

<pre>
                        Alex
"No. What I meant to ask was, have you gotten any
flowers from patients lately? Are you allowed to
collect them from your new job like you did at
your last job?"
</pre>

<pre>
                        River
"I haven't. LOL If you have any, you can send them
                      my way."
</pre>

It was a dead end. Alex spent the rest of his shift running in and out of patients' rooms with a plastic bag, asking if they were done with looking at their flowers. Some patients scorned him for asking, while others surrendered their flowers without hesitation.

Meanwhile, Coty sat in his hotel room obsessed with the thought of River. He lit a cigarette and poured himself some tequila. The very thought of River having sex with another man, or being romantic with anyone but him, made him want to vomit. After all he'd done for her and everything he had put up with, it was beyond him how she could do this to him. He had even been locked up for over two years behind bars because of her. Maybe he beat her up worse than he intended, but she really had it coming. Every time he looked at the bouquet of flowers sitting on the dresser, the flowers he had confiscated, he wanted to do harm to her.

Who in the hell is Erik? he thought.

He questioned it over and over in his mind. Whoever Erik was, Coty felt certain he could never compete with him. After spending time behind bars, with nothing to do but exercise all day, his body was solid muscle. He knew he looked good. He looked at his right arm, flexing his bicep, while admiring himself in the mirror. Feeling amused at himself for being able to sneak into River's house a few times while she was at work, he picked up a pair of her panties that he had taken from her dirty laundry and, in one deep exaggerated whiff, he breathed her in.

"I can't wait to see you again … and make love to you," he said, almost angry. "I'm going to fuck the shit out of you."

He mused with an evil smile, and then jumped onto the bed. The booze was starting to take effect, and he started to whistle. Coty finished the last lick of liquor. Aiming the empty bottle at the vase of flowers, he threw it violently at the arrangement and watched as it all crashed onto the floor. He showed no reaction of any kind. Taking one long, last puff of his cigarette, he stood up and stomped it out on the carpet.

Coty knew he had to be back in Ohio soon. He planned on taking River with him, whether she liked it or not. They were soulmates, meant to be together. He wasn't about to let some motherfucker named Erik get in the way. He figured this guy was probably some low life just trying to get into her pants. River needed him. He was confident of that. Coty pulled on a fresh pair of jeans and tee shirt. He flirted with a woman he met earlier in the day. The woman invited him to meet her at the hotel pool. He walked out just in time to see her climb out of the water, wearing a tiny bikini. He was aroused, but it was River he wanted. He was in the mood for a little fun, and it couldn't wait. So, he wrapped his arm around the giggling woman, and the two headed back to her room.

CHAPTER THIRTY-FOUR
Message Undeliverable

River laid in bed feeling sad, lethargic and depressed. Her thoughts of Erik went dark, since it was clear that he was no longer trying to contact her. Calling out sick, she took a day for herself to catch up on sleep. Alex and Violet were unaware that she had decided to lay low. They both called, texted, and even stopped by, but she just wasn't up to being around anybody.

Feeling the emotions rise to her throat, River's body couldn't fight it anymore. The tears started to flow. He had run away from her. He was gone. Curling up into a fetal position, River sobbed as she held onto her pillow. Her phone vibrated, but she refused to look at it. No one needed her more than she needed this time to herself.

Her nose dripped and her head throbbed. She felt a migraine coming on strong. Feeling sorry for herself was not an easy thing for her to do. Reaching for a tissue to blow her nose, she cried even harder. River's thoughts grew reckless. There was no taming her emotions, not in the state she was in.

"Why?" she whispered, hoarsely.

Rolling out of bed, after an hour's worth of bitterness and crying, River looked at herself in the bathroom mirror. She stared in disgust. She was not herself. She walked over to the punching bag hanging in the corner, put on her gloves and laid into it with every silly emotion she had. She threw powerful punches and kicks. In emotional exhaustion and heavy sorrow, she finally put her head against the bag and cried some more. River missed Erik, but she was beginning to realize that he did not feel the same way about her. Wiping tears and sweat away with her t-shirt, she punched on the bag some more. No matter how hard or how long she went at it, the workout wasn't enough to ease her pain.

Slipping on a pair of sneakers, River took to the outdoors, forcing herself to run as fast as she could down the isolated desert road. She ran so fast and with such fierce focus, she couldn't pay attention to anything else. She just ran. *Move your legs. GO FASTER. NO MORE ERIK*, she thought.

Coty was drunk, having finished off a bottle of tequila and various shots of bourbon with the cute woman in the bikini. Soused, the woman wasn't enough of a distraction from River, so he left her alone at the hotel. He found himself stalking River's home. He drove past her house no less than ten times. He noticed her Jeep had been parked in the same spot. She hadn't gone anywhere.

Turning up the volume of the stereo and accelerating to excessive speeds, Coty rounded the large canyon corners, nearly running off the road several times. He vigorously searched for another cigarette, rummaging through the middle console, the dash and the glove compartment. He started to carelessly swerve from side to side. At first, River thought the noise outside was the beat through her ear buds, but as the sound grew louder, she turned around just in time to see a maroon vehicle zigzagging from left to right.

"What the hell?" she uttered, as the car leaned dangerously close in her direction. River leapt into a ditch full of river rock. She startled herself with her own scream.

Coty didn't even notice. He continued on his hazardous path down the road, until he found what he was looking for—a cigarette butt laying on the passenger seat with three puffs of nicotine left. He learned early on that this road was a long loop upward and around the Superstition Mountains. For whatever reason, Coty decided not to go any further, and so he made his way back down to the main highway, back to the bar where he had become something of a regular. The day was still young.

River skinned up her knees and the palms of her hands pretty good. She was thankful to be alive. Trembling, she made her way back up the river rock onto the side of the road. From there, she walked home.

Within eyeshot of her front porch, River tried running the rest of the way. She noticed Alex's vehicle in the drive. When he saw her approach, he jumped out of the truck and ran to her.

"Your leg is bleeding," he exhaled, concerned. "What happened?"

He waited for her to catch her breath.

"Some drunk asshole ran me off the road," she panted.

"What?! I knew it!"

"Knew what?" River asked, breathlessly.

"I just had this bad feeling in my gut about you all day, especially since you've been ignoring my texts," Alex replied, helping her up the steps. "Did you at least get the plates?"

"No," she said, wincing in pain. "I was too busy vaulting off the road to save my life."

"You should move in with me for a while, or at least let me stay with you."

"Come on! We've seen each other constantly since Erik left. Which reminds me, no more dead flowers for a while! I'm running out of room in my pantry to hang them out to dry," River laughed, hoping to lighten the mood.

"Not funny right now," Alex breathed.

"Aww, come on!" River smiled, touching his arm lovingly. "Do not worry so much about me. As we all know, shit happens to me *a lot*. I've learned to deal with it and eventually let it go."

Alex pursed his lips, wanting to tell her that he would never be fine with her life being in danger because of who she was, but he couldn't. He couldn't tell her anything about her true identity. He had sworn an oath. River was relieved to have Alex with her. The road incident shook her up. She took a quick shower, while Alex snooped around the house looking for clues of forced entry. He checked every door, scanning the house with his powerful Pleiadian eyes, but found nothing out of place … even though he could feel it.

Alex went outside and scanned the yard for anything unusual—still nothing. River dressed and hurried down the stairs, searching for Alex. Catching a glimpse of him through the window, she held open the screen door and watched him for a while. She wondered what he was doing.

"Everything ok?" she asked.

"Everything is fine. I just thought I saw some turquoise earlier, but it was nothing."

"Please let me know if you do," River told him.

"Have you heard from Erik?" Alex asked, even though he already knew the answer.

"No … and I think we both know he's not coming back, so please don't ask me about him again."

River plopped onto the couch and turned on the television.

"Don't be so sure about that. He could come back. He's just …"

"Stop," River scolded, shooting him a flustered look.

Alex felt it from across the room and stopped speaking. River's eyes watered. She bit her lip. She didn't want to cry anymore. Alex took a deep breath, and with a heavy sigh said, "Okay. I won't say anything more about Erik."

"Great. So, what are we watching?" River asked, channel surfing.

Alex tried relaxing, but River's safety was weighing on him. He considered contacting his brother but thought it best for River if Erik wasn't around. River winced in pain, as she drew her knee up to one side of the couch. Alex worried, as he watched her tiny figure try to adjust. He was consumed with worry, so much so that he couldn't focus on the movie she had settled on. River suddenly turned to Alex.

"An earthquake … a big earthquake is about to happen," she said.

"Why do you say that? How do you know?" he asked.

"I don't know. I just feel it, and then it happens. I get signs."

Alex knew River was getting close, and her power would soon become more intense.

"How long has this been going on?" he asked.

"A while," she sighed.

"Anyone else know?" he asked.

"Just you."

River turned the channel to the world news. They watched in surprise, as a large earthquake in Columbia had just occurred. They watched footage of swaying buildings and people scattering about. Alex sat back, wondering when the Archon would catch onto her now that she was aligning to her star seed light-bearing abilities. River didn't know it, but she was an extra-sensory extraterrestrial being. She had been chosen for this position on Earth for a vital reason. Her frequency and vibrations were different from everyone on the planet, and despite her trauma throughout life, it only made her stronger. She never disappointed his people. She was always a surprise. It made her special because in less time than the average lifespan, she could change millions of earthlings' minds, viewpoints and opinions. River had been sought after by the dark Archon for a long time. Chances were, they already found her and if they were to attack, Alex would be right by her side to protect her, just as he always had been. He watched her, as she toyed with the dainty, gold chain around her neck, twisting it around her finger. Her eyes never left the television screen.

"We should do dinner," he said. "How about vegan pizza?"

"Pizza," she hummed. "Hmmm … it has to be picked up, and I'm not in the mood to go anywhere. I'd like to forget today ever happened."

"Okay. You relax and take a break from the news. I'm going to get us some pizza. I will be back."

Alex took the remote out of her hand and changed the channel back to the movie. He stood from the couch, stretched with a feigned yawn and shook his legs. His fake yawns were looking more natural, as were many of his practiced human mannerisms. River patiently waited for Alex to leave before sending another text to Erik. It read: "Hey! Are you there?"

She waited for a minute, and then came the empty response: Message Undeliverable!

Those two words (written in red) left her feeling even worse. The exclamation point didn't help. River felt her insecurity rise inside her spirit.

"Just leave him alone," she whispered. "He's done with you and it's time to be done with him."

CHAPTER THIRTY-FIVE
Pleiadian Heritage

Joshua crinkled his forehead, as he watched Alex climb into his truck. From his usual perch outside River's house, he snapped without thinking, "What the hell is he doing with River?"

Violet appeared annoyed, asking the question that was burning inside of her, "Why are you so jealous?"

"I'm not jealous. It's just weird that he's constantly around her," Joshua replied, scraping his foot against some loose stones. Violet shrugged, hugging her knees into her bare chest, her long, dark hair falling loosely around her shoulders and concealing her naked parts.

"I figure he's doing what he's always done. He is closer to her than Erik ever was … if you ask me," Violet replied.

"He better not sleep with her."

"Honestly, Joshua, that is none of our business," she scoffed.

"You think?"

"I know," she said. "I paid more attention than you. You forget!"

"Forget what?"

"The truth about Alex and River," Violet replied, dropping her knees and exposing her beautiful, naked body. "I need some clothes. Mine are at the reservation, and I don't have any left in the truck."

Joshua tried hard not to stare, but she was lovely coming out of coyote form.

"Stay here. I'll go get you some clothes. Watch out for that weirdo who has been stalking River," Joshua said, enjoying the view of Violet leaning back into a strong arch, her nipples perked into the glistening sunlight. He stood in awe, his feelings for her growing in intensity. He had never felt this before. His insides trembled slightly, as he turned away from her and snapped himself out of it.

"Hey," Violet sighed.

"What," he said, turning back to her.

"Nothing too warm this time. Just bring me a few tops and shorts."

Joshua nodded then left. Violet sat back and watched a hawk swoop downward at a jumping jack rabbit. As the hare ran towards her on the rock, Violet's eyes mutated into a coyote, a fierce emerald green from her Pleiadian heritage. With snarling teeth and coyote form, she pounced onto the rabbit with her oval-shaped paws. She snapped at the animal with her coyote jaws and broke its neck. Violet ravenously tore into the rabbit's flesh and ate it with pure pleasure.

Moving her energy back into that of human flesh, Violet continued to lick the rabbit's warm, red blood from her hands. She rolled her tongue around the outside of her lips, enjoying the last of the salty, metallic flavor. Her eyes returned to their normal brown color, as she laid back against the rock that was surrounded by a pile of rabbit bones on the ground.

River's cell phone rang. It was an "Unknown Caller." She didn't take the call, but rather let it go to voicemail. A minute later, a voicemail notification sounded. She opened it up. It was Coty—drunk and slurring the words, "I know you don't want to talk to me, but just hear me out …"

River sat up like a shot—frozen. She was unable to listen to the rest of the voice message. She couldn't bare it, so she quickly deleted it. Her stomach turned, and her anxiety kicked in just as Alex burst through the door.

"PIZZA!" he shouted, excitedly.

Alex could see and feel that something was wrong almost instantly.

"Hey! What's going on?"

He put the two vegan pizzas down on the coffee table and sat down beside her. River fought the tears, even though it was so damn hard.

"Nothing. My knee is hurting," She lied.

"Say no more. I got pizza!"

River put on a brave face, forcing herself to eat with her most fake smile. She bit hard through the thick slices, trying to act as though there was nothing wrong, but the truth was something was happening. She knew it. Everything in her life was going very wrong.

CHAPTER THIRTY-SIX
For the Greater Good

Erik sat at a long, slate-blue, metal table in his lab, working steadily on his last project before returning to Earth. He accidentally broke the lens on his scope twice, which set him back because of repairs. Erik never gave up on scheming, not when it came to getting back to River. He wanted to see her, touch her and feel her again. He knew he would soon be standing before the Elders of the Pleiadian counsel, and with them there would be no lying. The Elders know all and see all. If they chose, they would have access to all his memories, dreams and earthly experiences. Therefore, he would have to keep his persuasion simple, real and honest. He was hoping that would be all it would take. The large sensor doors opened behind him. He slowly turned to face his mother.

"What is this?" she asked, her fingers running along a copper scope hooked to a flat-screen monitor registered to the ship.

Erik gently removed his mother's hand.

"It's something I've been working on for a while," Erik said, rocking back on the floating metal bench. "It will enhance communication for us between other worlds and dimensions."

He studied his mother's face.

Does this have to do with her? his mother asked empathically.

No.

"Let her live her life, Erik," Yilene whispered. "You are needed here, not to mention much more useful to all of us."

"I have to go back, Mother."

"You are only in the way," she uttered.

"She is in danger," Erik said, his sharp jaw tightening.

"Nothing new," Yilene replied, almost smiling. "She is our strongest light bearer."

"Not if she is taken."

"She won't be taken. She is heavily protected," Yilene assured.

"Some have been lost before."

"You seem to forget that she is stronger than most of us and has yet to disappoint us on a mission," Yilene answered. "Her energy is very valuable and precious to our people. We will not allow anything to happen to her. She *will* make it home."

Erik went back to his work grinding gemstones into dust, doing his level best to ignore his mother's request. Yilene gently touched his arm and sighed, "I know you love her, son … but do not jeopardize what we are trying to do here. Amariah's love has always been intended for the greater good of the Orion species and the safety of our nation and universe. If she knew what you were trying to do for her, I believe she would ask that you let her be. You are holding on too tight."

Erik turned to face his mother. Looking into her bedazzled, green eyes, he allowed her words to absorb. Yilene nodded in receipt of her son's quiet acknowledgement and then exited through the sensor doors, drifting softly into the halls of the vast ship. Suddenly Erik couldn't focus on his work. Gazing out into space through the thick, paneled glass, he watched a planet's atmospheric gas erupt with lightning-like imagery. In his core, he knew his mother was right.

You are dressed, Talmud conveyed empathically, as he walked into his son's quarters, donned in a crisp white and gold uniform with a high-pressed collar and gold slippers made from a locally-sourced exotic nut. Like all Pleiadians, Talmud was handsome and naturally young looking, despite his age. He was dark skinned with almost a blueish tinge to him. His hair was dark, bold and wavy, which lit up his bright blue eyes. Alex bared a striking resemblance to him, while Erik took after their mother.

"Yes. I am supposed to meet the Elders," Erik replied, weakly.

Yes, Talmud echoed empathically.

"Can you help me with this?" Erik begged.

I can't do that, not even for you, my son.

"Are you ashamed of me for what I've done?" Erik asked.

No. I understand, but I do believe you are out of line. I will meet you at platform, Talmud conveyed, walking away.

Erik brushed his crisp, blue uniform at the high-neck collar, and stared into the deep abyss of space. They were quickly nearing his home planet Erra, and he was nowhere ready to face the Elders.

CHAPTER THIRTY-SEVEN
Return to the Charge

Arriving on the blue, diamond-shaped lapis platform, Erik patiently waited as the large, blue, glass hexagonal doors opened. Exhaling, he stepped forward through the automatic traveling gate system. Yilene drifted angelically alongside him, while his father followed heavy-footed from behind. Erik was home. They had landed on Planet Erra. Rich deep colors surrounded them, reflecting from the purple and blue sky, hues of light sparkling boldly upon everything.

We are here, Yilene conveyed.

Erik turned to her with some relief, offering a slight smile. He looked briefly at his father who was meticulously dressed in Pleiadian warrior attire adorned with a gold sash that strung across his chest. It displayed twelve ornately jeweled pins of achievement. Erik was proud of his father. He was proud of both his parents. His heart filled with a gush of emotion at the thought of them. Running his fingers through his hair, Erik was gripped with nervous energy and anticipation for what was to come. He found it hard to contain.

Pleiadians are a lot like humans, only with supernatural and warrior-like capabilities. Their faces are more defined, angelic. Some, not all, are tinted with a hint of blue, while others exhibit a delicate pixy ear. Almond-shaped, Asian-like eyes are most common, but the planet, itself, brandishes the perfect mix of ancient colors and earlier culture.

The planet was busy, as usual. Everyone was going about their daily planetary duties. Erik caught a glimpse of a pair of planetary angels. They were flying through the sky with their majestic multi-colored wings. Sounds of soft, motivational music filled the atmospheric surroundings, sometimes ringing through strong and sometimes light. It was the music of the stars, naturally singing throughout space. Those on Planet Erra referred to it as multi-dimensional music. Every being could hear it at all times. This music kept the planet safe, warning those on Planet Erra of danger.

Erik waited with his parents for a transport. When the clean electro-magnetic, crystal vehicle arrived, the threesome took a seat, as Talmud took over and punched in the correct coordinates. They were on their way to the high Pleiadian Elder Council.

The vessel passed through exotic trees bearing magical, high-definition fruits and flowers. Colors never before seen on Earth were scattered everywhere, wildly abundant and blanketing the planet's floors.

Almost there, Talmud impressed empathically, as their transport entered a crystal-prism tunnel. Coming to a stop, all three exited the transport and were led into the crystal chamber room of the Elder Council. They walked inside in perfect formation and were solemnly greeted by the Elders who were seated around a gemstone encrusted roundtable with twelve seats of high authority. They were all young in appearance, but all very ancient in age and they rarely showed any emotion. They were stoic in nature in comparison to the lighthearted, whimsical Pleiadian who typically inhabited Planet Erra.

The Council flashed images of Erik. Each picture stirred a memory in his mind, things he had seen, experienced and even forgotten, including his childhood, his parents, heroic duties and rewards. Finally, Osiris, a high Elder, spoke empathically.

Erik, he conveyed. *We've been expecting you. As a fine, respected member of the noble, blue uniform, we expect you to tell us why you are here.*

"Where would you like me to begin?" Erik asked.

Go to the first place your intuition goes, another Elder suggested.

Erik closed his eyes. Naturally, his intuition went to her. Instantly, he was lost in her ever-changing, beautiful, sequined-colored eyes. Her body captivated him with its cymbal-exchanging chakra energy. His memory took him to a forest. The two of them were laying in a soft bed of beautiful flowers scented with jasmine and other truly exotic fragrances. Her ombre-hued hair speckled intensely with light. Erik admired her. His muscular, bronzed body lifted her with so little effort, as she laughed. In his own excitement, Erik kissed her. He remembered how they both carried jewel-encrusted swords. She held hers in her hand, as he helped her up onto a rock by the ocean, a body of water that covered most of planet Erra. The council stopped him abruptly and conveyed their thoughts, *You have shown us enough. Thank you for enlightening us on your reasoning. You do realize, however, that you are acting in love. You are acting out of context in respect to the regulation of Erra Star Seeds.*

Erik nodded. Choking back tears, he replied, "I just felt the need to help her."

*Your **help** is most needed on the ship. You are in danger of intruding on what she is trying to do for us,* an Elder interjected.

Erik nodded slightly, feeling the reassuring presence of his parents who stood very still, one on each side of him.

Show us more, Erik, Esther, the tenth Elder, commanded.

Erik drew a deep breath and held it, as he closed his eyes and pictured her beautiful face. He led the Elders to the bar where he rescued

River, and carried her safely away from harm. And then there was the motorcycle crash, and while he tried to suppress the image of River's ring, it was revealed to them.

STOP, all twelve Elders commanded in unison.

Where did this ring come from? Noah, the first Elder, inquired.

"We don't know. It was a gift left at her door. She can't remove it from her finger," Erik replied.

It is an ancient ring, and it comes from the Anunnaki, Noah announced. *It was given to the ancient Sabian during the building of the pyramid of Giza in 2,500 B.C. The middle gemstone will point to the pole star of the Alpha Draconis.*

What is its purpose? Yilene inquired.

It is a communication device, meant to connect the chosen wearer with those who are astronomically aligned with it. Esther added.

She's being tracked, Plya, the third Elder, said.

"Chosen? Tracked? By whom?" Erik replied, panicked.

The council paused, whispering to one another in an ancient language that Erik and his parents could not follow.

It is decided, Noah began. *Due to the foreseen danger of Amariah's mission on Earth, you will return to her and find out who gave her this ring. Your protection is seen as an added blessing to her, and she deserves that. When, and if, necessary, you will report back to us all that you know.*

Erik became unhinged with gratitude. Swelling with excitement, he grabbed his mother's hand. She gave him a smile of relief. The three left quickly, heading back to the Pyalexis. Erik's anxiety crept up on him, but he tried not to show it.

"How quick can I get back?"

"As soon as we get back," Talmud replied.

Erik relaxed, as he sat back in his seat and took in the ethereal scenes of his home planet. His heart leapt for joy at the thought of seeing Amariah again. He felt vindicated, if not bolstered by the fact that the council had unanimously agreed that she needed him to complete her mission.

Erik punched in the coordinates that would land him in the exact position he was needed on Earth—next to her. He chose to wear his blue jeans, the same ones he returned home with. In turn, he carefully placed his blue uniform back in its rightful place.

"It's time," Talmud whispered.

Erik took a purposeful step onto the aquamarine platform. He boarded the Saturn shell, a small ship in the shape of a triangle. Taking one last glance at his parents, he conveyed the words, *Thank you*.

The two looked on with pride, as they watched their son take off in the vessel at light speed. It wouldn't be long before he was back on top of Superstition Mountain.

Somewhere near the mouth of a small rock cave, Erik watched a mountain lion and her cub sniff around the Saturn vessel. Curious, the two wildcats jumped on top of it, stretching out for a little cat nap. Undisturbed by the animals, perhaps even inclined to join them, Erik reclined his seat and closed his eyes. He needed to adjust to the atmospheric change before disembarking from the vessel, so he took time to daydream. He could only hope that River would be waiting for him and just as excited to see him.

With the warmth of sunrise, Erik opened his eyes. He looked around at his desert surroundings and noticed that the mountain lions had moved on. Feeling refreshed, and a bit nervous to see his girl, he immediately went over to the Saturn door. Pressing his palm against the censor, he waited for it to open. The door didn't budge. He tried a few more times and nothing. With some concern, he tried employing his mental power, but it was too weak. The Saturn door would not release. Panic setting in, Erik tried forcing the door open with the weight of his body, but he only hurt his arm in the effort. He tried kicking the door open. That didn't help either. He was stuck.

CHAPTER THIRTY-EIGHT
Heart of Gold

River's work shift went long and hard. She was surprised at how busy it was, and yet the hours passed by so slowly. Alex texted her a few times, sending over funny photos from his own unusual workday. River didn't reply. With so little time in the day, there was just no spare moment. She figured he, of anyone, would understand, being that he was in the same profession.

"There's a fire! There's a fire!" an elderly patient screamed.

Dropping her pen and quickly locking up her computer, River ran to the patient's room in a panic. The woman was screaming from her bed, and there was no fire to be seen.

"Mrs. Stevens, what's wrong? Are you okay?" River asked.

"No! Why would you ask that?! Of course, I'm not okay! There is a fire in my room!"

Irritated, River looked around the room. She even made a concerted effort to open up the bathroom door to look inside for a fire, but there was nothing.

"Nope. There is no fire in your room, Mrs. Stevens," River said.

"Are you crazy?! The fire is over by the trash can," Mrs. Stevens shouted, hysterically.

River could see that her patient was clearly frightened and hallucinating, so she walked over to the trash can and waved her hand in front of it.

"No fire," River assured.

"Call the fire department, and they will see the fire."

River let out an exasperated sigh and marched out of the room. She walked up to a large, male nursing assistant and asked him to help her in Mrs. Stevens room. The two walked purposefully into the room together.

"Mrs. Stevens," River said. "The fire department is here, and he is going to put out the fire for you. Okay?"

The patient looked relieved as she watched the male nursing assistant proceed to "put out the fire."

Problem solved.

River rolled her eyes, as she walked out of the room. She thanked her co-worker with extreme gratitude. Within a couple of hours, River finished her medication pass, gave report, did a narcotics count and was out the door. Looking at her cell phone, she noticed a missed call from Violet. She wasted no time calling her back.

"Hey," River greeted, sounding more energetic than she felt.

"River, I've been trying to get a hold of you! Where are you?"

"I am in my Jeep. Just got off work. What's up?"

"My friend, Joshua and I would like to invite you to the reservation. We're having a cookout. I know you're a vegan, but it's kind of a big deal, a pow-wow with motivational speakers. I thought you might enjoy it."

"Wow, that sounds awesome," River yawned. "I'm really tired, but … you know what? Count me in!"

"We will pick you up at 7:30! Get ready for some fun!" Violet exclaimed.

River made her way home for a quick shower. As soon as she

pulled into the drive, something felt off. She parked and waited a beat, cautiously looking around the yard before exiting the Jeep. The air felt still—wrong. River noticed the screen to the front door was open. That wasn't unusual or even worrisome, so long as the wooden door was locked.

Moving toward the house, the thickness of the atmosphere was ominous and heavy, almost hard to breathe. River's heart pounded in her ears. Her small-motor skills slowed, as her fingers and legs became heavy. Slight spasms rattled up and down her spine. It must have been the ring on her finger—again. She swallowed hard. Her hand trembled, as she stuck her house key into the lock. Suddenly, a high-pitched frequency buzzed in her ears. She slowly turned the doorknob and pushed through.

A shadow quickly passed in front of her. A gasp escaped her throat or maybe it was a shriek, even she couldn't decipher what it was. Elongated, branch-like hands belonging to some sort of *thing* reached for her feet. She spun around, narrowly escaping its reach. Suddenly, more branch-like hands sprawled out from the walls, as if they were trying to grab onto her. River was petrified. She exhaled short bursts of screams, moving away from the shadowy tree-like creature in her living room.

"Greetings River," breathed a tall, luminous, pale figure with stark albino hair and a white pantsuit. The figure slowly walked down the stairs from the bedroom.

"What? Who are you?" River stammered.

Large, thick branches covered her mouth tightly, gently floating her body up into the air.

"Shh … do not get upset. I am not your enemy."

The figure spoke in a strangely deep, but genderless voice from a deep and hollow frequency. River couldn't tell what or who she was dealing with. She couldn't tell whether it was male or female. The figure's straight, long, white hair hung past its shoulders, and its face was adorned with dark, extra-large, sunglasses. The branches were not part of its actual body, but rather an extension of its shadow. Its branches hovered around River, gripping her enough to stabilize her four feet from the floor. Whatever it was, it was not hurting her. Even though three of its branches were wrapped firmly around her mouth, she could still move her head from side to side.

"It has been a long time, River ... or should I say, Amariah?" the figure said. "I've not seen you in so long. Of course, you have probably long forgotten about our secret alliance, considering your current mindless, human state."

River looked at the pale figure, assuming it was a male speaking to her. She was very confused. If this were a dream, why couldn't she wake herself up? The figure of a man slowly approached her in a steady drift. He touched her face with his cold, clammy hands, running his long wicked-looking fingernails along her cheek. The man licked her chin with his long serpent tongue. River tried to pull away. His eyes flickered from green to scorching yellow, and it took her breath away. She was full of fear, beads of sweat piercing her forehead.

"It's been too long, my dear Amariah. I've been waiting for you ... searching for you, and now I have found you. I can always count on you to make an appearance before the earth's big show," he said.

While she remained suspended in the air, the strange man walked tall around her living room, picking up her things and to looking at them in an interesting manner.

"I don't know why you keep choosing to come here. I guess you still have a heart of gold. The humans have treated you so shamefully. If they only knew who you truly are and who you represent. Tsk, tsk ... they are a lowly race."

The man looked into River's eyes. Her fear melted away from her body, and she instantly became relaxed, almost buzzed.

"Don't you hate it though? Coming to earth … pretending to be a human without any of your awesome powers?"

The man taunted her, as he flaunted himself dramatically about the room. The branches gently lowered her. She started to feel tired and lethargic.

"I've come to warn you," the man said. "I want you to keep the ring I've given you … keep it on your finger and never allow anyone to take it off. We made an alliance a very long time ago, and I always keep my promises. This ring is part of that alliance, and it will offer special protection for those chosen to wear it," he hissed.

River struggled to keep from closing her eyes.

"We are a team. Nobody wants to see everything on Earth completely destroyed, not even me. You are going to make sure Earth is protected, and I am going to help you. You need protection from the Archon," he said, looking into River's eyes.

He brushed her hair back with his clammy, pale hand.

"You are always so beautiful, yet so strange looking as a human."

The branches gently placed River onto the couch, melting away from her mouth and back into the walls.

"What were those things holding me?" River asked groggily, feeling drugged and confused.

"The roots of the earth, the trees," the man sighed. "They hear you. They see you. You should listen to them."

"Who are you?" River asked.

"I am a very old acquaintance of yours, and we shall be meeting again. For now, keep that ring on your finger!" he snapped.

River felt herself fading away, about to give in to sleep, when the man swiftly grabbed her by the shoulder and held her up.

"I am Kraylon. I used to be just like you, but I became a rebel. I fell to Earth when I refused to care for humans any longer. Now, I am alone on my own side and on my own terms."

River was too tired to care.

"Oh," she sweetly whispered, closing her eyes again.

"I've never lost faith in you, Amariah. I knew you cared too much. I knew you would be back to Earth, and I waited for you. I will put my hedge of protection around you, so we can stand against the Archon together."

River closed her eyes, unable to hold them open any longer.

"Good night, sweet warrior," Kraylon whispered, walking through the walls of her house and vanishing without a trace.

"River, River ... wake up," Violet said, vigorously shaking River.

River sat up and looked around her living room.

"Where is the tree man?"

"What?" Violet questioned.

"The man that was here earlier. He had long, white hair, long nails and a snake's tongue. There were these shadowy tree branches sticking out from him all over his body," River said, looking around confused and tired.

Violet was amused.

"You were dreaming because I see nothing here. Obviously, you are very tired because you are still in your work uniform. Do you still want to go with us?"

"Um ... I guess. I will have to change my clothes, so give me a few minutes," River said.

"Okay. We will be waiting in the truck," Violet assured.

River jumped off the couch and quickly ran upstairs to change. Ten minutes later, she was in the truck, sandwiched between Violet and Joshua. Violet introduced the two.

"You look so familiar to me," River said, flashing a beautiful smile.

"You may have seen me around. Apache Junction is not a large place," Joshua replied.

"True that," River laughed.

CHAPTER THIRTY-NINE
Peaceful Warriors

Erik struggled for hours to rewire the vessel just so that he could open the door. In order to do that, he had to use the ship's handheld tools containing cymbal and sound energy. As a Pleiadian engineer, Erik was reassured that his vessel was "human proof," but in that moment, he hated it. By design, human frequency cannot detect a Pleiadian ship, unless, of course, the Pleiadians want someone from Earth to detect it. In other words, when there *is* a ship "sighting," it is intentional.

Pleiadians are not only from another galaxy and planet, but they also come from another dimension. They are known as the peaceful warrior, the protective race of beings. Supremely involved in diplomatic affairs, their mission is mainly the prevention of nuclear war and destruction upon planet Earth.

Erik arranged the Mandala-shaped gold wiring into its correct sequence, but he was still unable to clear the security code that had been generated to automatically open the door. Frustrated, weak and exhausted from the heavy, molecular gasses in the capsule's atmosphere, he reached out to Alex. Pulling out a sophisticated laser in the shape of a pen, Erik mimicked his brother's high-pitched frequency through self-hypnosis and meditation. He wasn't sure if it would work, but he had to give it a shot before sending a distress signal to his parents. Asking them for help was a last resort.

While sending out frequency signals to Alex, Erik noticed various wild animals gathering around the capsule—a pair of bald eagles, eight mule deer, and some big-horned sheep. They appeared to be attracted to the beckon meant for Alex. Erik refused to give up. He didn't care whether or not he roused a bear or mountain lion, so long as he could reach his brother.

It started with a loud ringing in his ears that morning while he was taking a shower. The reverberation became so high pitched and loud that it twisted his stomach into a sickening knot. The second time it sounded, Alex grabbed hold of his ears and dropped to his knees while walking to his truck. By the third time the high-pitched frequency surged, he nearly swerved off the road. Alex shouted in agony. It suddenly occurred to him that the noise was a Pleiadian calling for help. He had no idea who it was, but he had to get to them. The frequency tore through his body, as he sped from Queen Creek to Apache Junction. He knew he was getting closer because as he rounded the Superstition Mountain, he was writhing in pain.

As the terrain roughened, Alex engaged his four-wheel drive. His truck tires spat gravel into the roadside ravines filled with Saguaro cactus and Mesquite trees. Slamming his truck into park, he turned off the engine and ripped the keys out of the ignition. The call was coming from the top of the mountain. After a short off-trail hike, he noticed a hiker walking toward him. Alex doubled over in pain, as the high-pitched frequency burned through him—again. He almost fell over into some brush chockfull of Cholla cactus. Cursing and catching his feet, he looked around for the hiker or any other eyes that might have seen him. He did not want to risk being seen while using his extra Pleiadian abilities to climb the jagged sides of the rocky mountain. The hiker coming down the trail was gone. Alex figured he had probably turned off toward the Manzanita grove, so he kept going.

The Superstition Mountain is a sacred place, even to Pleiadians. Not only did it have the power to enhance his abilities, but it also drained him of them. The mountain is enriched with gemstones and gold that creates a specific pull of magnetic energy that can almost be too powerful. Pushing through toward the mountain's peak and passing a few rattlesnakes, Alex made it the top, onto a flat stretch of land. Goosebumps raised on his arms from the chilly air. Stopping to rest against a rock wall, he clutched his ears in agony, as the frequency became louder and higher.

"You too?" a strange voice asked. "What is that sound?"

"What?" Alex asked, turning and looking directly into the face of the hiker he had seen earlier.

The man was of Asian descent. He had long, shoulder-length, black hair that was tied into a bun on the top of his head.

"You can hear this?" Alex asked, surprised.

"Yes. That's why I'm here. The sound started earlier today. I felt drawn to it," the hiker said, kneeling and wiping sweat from his forehead with a red bandana. "What do you think is going on?"

"I know as much as you do," Alex replied. "I'm going to take a wild guess and say you are a Pleiadian."

"A what?"

Alex looked confused.

"Nah, man," the hiker laughed, holding out his fist. "I'm just messing with you. I am from Planet Erra. My name is Sai."

"Alex."

The two bumped friendly fists.

"You should've seen your face, dude. For a second you thought I might not be Pleiadian like you, so funny man!"

"Not that humorous right now … *dude*," Alex said, dryly.

"What the …," Alex exhaled, looking off into the distance.

"What is it?"

"I know where the sound is coming from. I've been here before. Follow me!"

Alex took off running until he reached a nearby enclave carved into the side of the mountaintop.

"It's over here," Alex shouted, not realizing Sai was right behind him. The two came to an abrupt halt when they saw a small, triangular vessel half hidden in trees and brush. Through the metal, glass and crystal, Alex could see Erik sitting in the pilot seat. He didn't look well. He was nonresponsive, sweaty and fragile looking.

"Erik!" Alex shouted in a panic.

"Who is that?" Sai asked.

"My brother! Help me!"

Alex tried prying the door open, but his mortal strength was not enough, and his Pleiadian strength was draining. Sai gave it a go, but they were both powerless.

"Wait! Let's combine our power," Sai suggested.

Alex nodded in agreement. The two Pleiadians took a breath before telekinetically intertwining their power. The effort demanded most of their strength, but after a short time and a sudden surge of energy, the vessel door blew off. When the flap slammed against a nearby bolder, animals scattered like the wind.

"Erik!" Alex shouted. "Hey, brother! You're gonna be okay."

Sai helped Alex carry his brother out of the ship, leaning him up against the rock wall.

"What happened?" Alex asked.

"I will explain later," Erik gasped, trying to interchange his lungs to the planet's requirements.

In long, rugged breaths Erik asked, "Who is he?" "I thought you were going to tell me who he is." Alex told his brother. Erik shrugged his shoulders weakly as Sai introduced himself to Erik.

"I heard a high-pitched frequency. It kept getting louder. I just followed it man," Sai explained. "Glad you're okay though, dude. I didn't really know what the hell was going on."

"Then you are one of us ... a Pleiadian," Erik mumbled.

"Yeah, man. How did you do this anyway, dude? Pull me in to your frequency?" Sai asked, sounding stoned.

"My brother is the best engineer around. Nothing has ever been too difficult for him to figure out," Alex said, patting Erik's back with pride.

"Nice, dude ... nice," Sai replied, pulling a small cannabis bowl out of his pocket. "Wanna smoke?"

"Uh ... nah, man," Erik declined, waving it away.

Alex took a long toke from the bowl, turning his attention to Sai.

"Why are you here, Sai?" Alex asked while exhaling smoke.

"Long story, but I've been here since 1963, man," Sai said, lighting up another bowl. "I ain't never going back."

"You would rather stay on this shit-hole planet?" Alex asked. "Why?"

"Pussy, man!" Sai chuckled. "There's lots and lots of easy pussy."

Erik exchanged a foxed look with Alex. Sai sounded more human than Pleiadian.

"We better get down the mountain. It looks like bad weather is coming," Erik said, impatiently.

"Yeah, it's getting dark," Sai agreed.

Alex and Sai got on opposite sides of Erik, helping his weak form down the rough landscape.

"How is she?" Erik asked, turning to his brother.

"Who?"

"Who do you think," Erik replied sharply.

"Oh … River? She's good. You know, hanging out with other guys. Partying like a rock star," Alex kidded.

"What!?"

Erik stopped short, looking at his brother in disbelief.

"I'm kidding. I'm kidding. She's been okay. Hanging out with me and some chick named Violet," Alex reassured.

"Good. Violet … that's good," Erik whispered meekly.

"Oh … so you know this Violet character," Alex established skeptically. Alex had always felt something was off with Violet, but he couldn't put his finger on it.

"Yeah." Erik exhaled weakly.

"How?" Alex asked, inquisitively.

"How do you not know her?" Erik smiled.

"What do you mean?"

"Never mind. It doesn't matter," Erik said, shaking his head.

"This Violet girl seems hot," Sai interjected.

Annoyed, Erik rolled his eyes.

"Let's just get back," Erik said. "I need to see River."

Alex couldn't help but feel a bit disappointed.

"Maybe you should wait a day or two before you see her," Alex suggested.

"Why?"

"Well, for one, you haven't communicated with her in a long time, and two ... I had your cell phone and tried pretending to be you, but ..."

"But what?" Erik gasped.

"I dropped your phone in the toilet. Then I sent her flowers from you, but she never got them."

"Why not?" Erik asked.

"That is still a mystery."

"Go on," Erik encouraged.

"She never received them. Supposedly, the flowers were delivered to her house and signed for."

Erik thought for a moment. Realizing someone was stalking River, he shouted, "We'd better hurry. We've got to get to her now!"

CHAPTER FORTY
Full-Bloom Shroom

River was sandwiched between Violet and Joshua, sitting cross legged on a beautiful Navajo blanket. They were casually seated along a beautiful cliff overlooking the lake. River assumed the people among her were relatives of Violet and Joshua, so she didn't feel the need to ask who they were. Food was barbecued. Children were running and playing, as a few tribal leaders practiced songs together using native drums. Young adults and teenagers dove from the cliff's edge into the water below, as a non-native American, white man walked among them, burning sage from a large clam shell. The man acknowledged River, asked her to stand up so that he could move the smoke around her body. Smoke wafted up her nostrils. She started to cough. Violet pulled River away from the man because she knew him as a menace at times.

"He's a little odd," Violet whispered.

"So, what does burnt sage do?" River asked.

"It drives away bad energy, clears the air and makes it pure. He's just a little too eager to be like us, and it's not always culturally appropriate."

"Oh," River breathed, watching as all the young women flocked to Joshua on the blanket. "Isn't he your boyfriend?"

"No, not really," Violet said.

She glared at the women hanging all over Joshua, not quite sure why it bothered her.

"Oh, I thought you were together."

"He wishes," Violet sneered.

Just then, a young, good-looking native man wearing a gold bandana across his forehead moved in and stood next to Violet. River couldn't help but notice Joshua's displeased reaction. It wasn't good.

"You want some shroom tea?" the man asked.

Violet exaggerated a laughed, so as to capture Joshua's attention.

"You are so crazy, Luka," she flirted.

"Who's your friend?" Luka asked.

"Oh … sorry! River this is Luka," Violet said, shaking her long, black hair about her shoulders.

"Nice to meet you," River replied sweetly.

"You are both so pretty," Luka said with a crooked smile.

Violet giggled as she saw Joshua glance toward them with an irritated look on his face.

"Are you on shrooms already?" Violet asked.

"You want some?" Luka grinned, looking at River. "I even have some shroom brownies."

"I don't know. I'm kind of tired," River replied, not wanting to sound like a prude.

"You ever do shrooms before?"

"A long time ago, and I've done Ayahuasca," River said casually.

"No shit? I've never done Ayahuasca," Luka laughed. "I'm strictly a cannabis and shrooms kind of guy."

"Stop hitting on her Luka. She has a man," Violet joked.

"No. I don't," River said, shaking her head at Violet. "I am single, and I will have one of those brownies."

Violet's spine shot straight up.

"Are you sure River?" she asked.

"Yes. Give me one."

Luka ran to a nearby cooler. He grabbed it and carried it back to the girls. Joshua watched from afar. He never trusted Luka, and he hated the idea of his fascination with getting into Violet's pants. A young, pretty girl threw a water balloon at Joshua, hitting him in the back. Joshua scooped the girl up and jumped with her into the lake. Violet was jealous, and it became very apparent in her voice when she said, "You know what Luka? I'll take a brownie, too."

"You sure?"

"Yes," Violet snapped.

River and Violet sat down and ate their brownies, anxiously waiting for the effects to kick in. Moreover, waiting for the shroom brownies to take their minds off the men they were *obviously* in love with. An hour later, they were both feeling the strong effects of the psilocybin compound. Violet and Luka laughed uncontrollably, while River took in the extreme colors, lines, and psychedelic patterns around her.

"You want to see something?" Violet asked, looking over at River. River nodded, her mind taking her into a deeper and more elevated state.

"Come on," Violet encouraged, grabbing her hand.

River grabbed Violet's hand, as they stood to their feet. She and Luka followed Violet down the side of the cliff into a crystal-clear creek bed. The three waded barefoot on the river rock.

"Let's go on the other side of this wash!" Violet shouted, as though River and Luka weren't standing right next to her. Rounding the corner of the creek, River gasped in awe at what she saw. There were six wild horses of various colors grazing in green pasture. Luka knelt, as Violet called out to one of the horses. The horse looked in her direction and started trotting toward her.

"How do you know this horse?" Luka asked, surprised.

"She was stuck in a fence line one day," Violet replied. "I helped her out. Ever since then, I've been visiting her. I even healed her leg. She had a rather nasty gash."

"This is amazing!" River exclaimed. She was enjoying the full effects of the shrooms' psychedelic energy, as her spiritual nature was in full bloom—traveling. Every color was more vibrant than the last, and the horses suddenly looked like mystical creatures with wings. And, as for Violet, she looked like a goddess.

Violet recalled the moment she phased from coyote into a human to rescue the badly-injured horse. She gazed over at River, moved by her beautiful and kind spirit as it glowed in an aura of turquoise, blue and majestic purple.

"I feel like we are all meant to be connected. You know?" River sighed. "I feel like we all knew each other from a past life or something."

Violet smiled, and Luka followed up with warm laughter.

"We are more connected than you know," Violet whispered into River's ear.

The three sat and watched the wild horses until the herd galloped away. River, Violet and Luka stuck around, splashing in the water, like small children high on sugar. Giggling, smiling, and experiencing the side effects of the hallucinogens, they were in their own little world. Violet suddenly felt the need to connect to her coyote self, but knew she had to resist with Luka and River around. River covered herself in clay from the creek bank and was dressed down to only her panties and bra. The other two followed suit. Soon, they were all covered in clay, dancing around in their undies under the stars. Then, one by one they each jumped into the lake.

"What is going on here?!" Joshua shouted.

He appeared out of nowhere, looking angrily at Luka. River, Violet and Luka looked up in surprise. It was obvious Joshua was pissed. Feeling a charge, Violet smiled, ambled out of the water and laid back onto the ground with her hands behind her head.

"Relax, Joshua," Violet sneered.

"What have you been doing, Violet? Why do you look like that?" Joshua demanded, shifting his heated glare back to Luka.

"Chill out, dude! It's all good," Luka said, standing on the bank in front of Joshua. With a severe impact push, Joshua shoved Luka into the lake. Luka surfaced from under the water, gathered his footing and held his arm in extreme pain. He shouted, "Dude! There are rocks on the bottom!"

"Chill out, dude! It's all *good*," Joshua mocked.

"Fuck you, man," Luka winced, holding onto his scraped arm.

"River, what did you all take? What did Luka give you?"

"I just went to the place I came from, Joshua," River said, looking up from her play in the dirt. "I'm not from here. I belong somewhere else, and it's not here."

"OH MY GOD, VIOLET!" Joshua shrieked. "We are supposed to be watching out for her!"

"Why?" River asked. "I'm a grown-ass woman. I make my own choices."

Violet shook her head at Joshua, rolling her eyes in irritation. "Everything is fine, Joshua. We just took some shroom brownies," Violet explained.

"You are stupid!" Joshua exclaimed.

"Go back to your slutty-ass girlfriend!" Violet raged.

"We need to get back. It's two in the morning," Joshua exhaled. "Come on!"

"You are being so mean right now," River scoffed.

"You totally ruined the vibe, man," Luka chimed in.

"SHUT THE FUCK UP, LUKA!" Joshua growled.

"Man, fuck this! I'm out," Luka said, climbing out of the water, grabbing his clothes and running off through the trees.

"Come on, Violet," Joshua said softly, as he reached for her.

Violet ignored Joshua, reaching for River's hand instead and helping her up.

"It's okay, River. You can come with me," Violet assured.

River reluctantly stood up. Taking Violet's hand, they walked back to what was left of the gathering. Joshua followed in tow.

"We can sleep here for the night," Joshua said, pointing to a tent.

"I'm not tired," River replied.

"Try laying down," Joshua encouraged, his eyes staring into Violet's painfully.

As Violet fell asleep, Joshua longed to wrap his arms around her. He slunk out of the tent to throw more firewood onto the large firepit. It was more of a distraction than a need to keep everyone warm. He made it his mission to keep watch over the tent all night long.

Meanwhile, Erik stopped off at the Atler's Ranch to check on his cabin. He took a quick shower, threw on a fresh shirt and a pair of blue jeans and hurried back to River's house. It was three o'clock in the morning. Her Jeep was there, but she was gone. Troubled, Erik turned off the ignition and sat in the driveway, staring at the dark, empty windows of River's bedroom. He wasn't going anywhere, so he reclined the driver's seat and rested his worried, bionic-blue eyes and waited for her. When 10:00 a.m. rolled around, and still no River, Erik grew more concerned. He started his truck and headed back to his cabin, determined to find her.

CHAPTER FORTY-ONE
She's the One

River barely slept. By the time noon came around, the heat from the sun made everyone uncomfortable. It became unbearable, and soon they all scurried from the tents and started packing up. Joshua was swimming, while Violet quietly watched from afar for a while. River helped the others clean up the campsite. Alex had texted her a few times throughout the night. She didn't answer, except to say that she was okay. That seemed to be good enough for him.

The ride home was hushed. Everyone was feeling drained, anxious to get back to some sense of normalcy. River suddenly felt as though she needed to take a trip back to Ohio for a few days to see her grandmother. When Violet and Joshua dropped her off in front of her house, she solemnly walked through the front door. She felt so alone. She unpacked her overnight bag, along with some of the feelings she had stuffed away for far too long. It was time to face her fears ... time to go back.

After booking her flight for the next day, River took a long, hot shower and then crawled into bed. She was just about to settle in for the evening when a knock came from the front door. River pulled the covers over her head, doing her best to ignore it. It was probably Violet or Alex. She wasn't in the mood to be social. The knock sounded again, this time more urgently. She let out a stern sigh, threw off the covers and ran downstairs to answer the door. Again, a knock pounded, even more frantic than before.

"JUST A MINUTE!" she yelled.

Angrily, she unlocked the front door and yanked it open.

"WHAT!?" River snapped.

Frozen in shock at the sight of him, River's eyes welled up with tears. She sucked back any sign of emotion as best she could, considering she was furious with the man, but he looked more handsome than ever. His skin was bronze—glowing. She figured he must have gone somewhere tropical and sunny to have come back with such a beautiful, even tan.

"Erik," she said, softly. "Why are you here?"

He ran his fingers through his glowing, curly hair, trying to hold back his own surging emotions.

"You're mad at me, and I ..." he began.

River slammed the door in his face. Erik took a combat breath and knocked on the door again. River refused to answer.

"I know you're mad, and I am sorry ..." he said, trailing off. "I tried to get back as soon as I could, and I ..."

"You what?" River asked from the opposite side of the door. "You couldn't call or text me or your brother—Alex?!"

"I want to explain, River. It's very complicated. I'm sorry."

Erik rested his head against the door, tracing the framework with his finger.

"River, please ..."

"I don't trust you. It's over Erik. I'm just not ready to be with anyone. I thought I was, but really I'm not."

"River, please," Erik begged.

More than anything, River wanted to open the door. She wanted to run into his arms and kiss him because she was in love with him. His leaving her for so long with no communication did more damage than good, considering her trust issues. It was reminiscent of past relationships, bad relationships, something she definitely didn't need in her life.

"River open the door!" Erik shouted.

"Go away! I need my space," she said. "I'm going to Ohio for a few days, so leave me alone."

Erik's concern grew at the thought of her going to Ohio alone. "Open the door River."

River slowly ambled up the stairs.

"Go away Erik," she whispered.

Erik took a hard step backward, and using his telekinesis, he unlocked and opened the door. River watched as the door flew open. In shock, she ran up the rest of the stairs to her bedroom. Erik followed, taking long, purposeful strides up the stairs after her.

"You can't go to Ohio ... not without me," Erik insisted.

"I don't have to do anything that you tell me."

It broke his heart to see her so angry. He looked into her welling eyes, and he could see she was in pain.

"You hurt me, Erik! And now you do not get a say in what I do."

River's eyes were wild. Erik wanted her more than ever. He was aroused by her feelings for him. The more she tried to hide them, the more he ached. She began to cry, her body quivering uncontrollably. Erik swiftly moved to her side, gently helping her to sit on the edge of her bed.

"Listen ... I know this is weird, and crazy, but I am nothing but grateful that all this madness is with you," Erik said, cupping her face. "Please look at me, River."

He moved in close, slowly, to kiss her tears, as they stained her cheek. River wanted to kiss him back. There were strong urges ripping through her … stirring her roots that were bound and determined to dig in. Never had she wanted anyone more. She needed somebody, and it was definitely him. Nervous flows of suppressed sexual energy were now being exchanged between the two of them. River looked into Erik's eyes, touching his chest lightly with her fingertips. He took a short, ragged breath before lifting her up in his arms and lightly placing her closer to the middle of the bed … on her back. River grabbed onto his shoulders, a nervous breath escaping her lips.

"I want you," She whispered.

"I want you more," he replied.

Erik licked the outside of her ear with his tongue, kissing her neck with immense intensity.

"Maybe we should wait," River sighed.

Erik pulled her in closer to him and said, "No more waiting."

His lips connected with hers in a passionate, but soft frenzy. Magnetically engaged, it was a struggle to peel their clothes off as quickly as possible. River fumbled with the buttons that held her linen shirt together. Erik moved her trembling hands to her sides and unbuttoned the blouse for her. Jumping out of his faded jeans, he helped River out of her shorts, revealing her dainty, delicate, blush panties. Without hesitation, he went down on her, pulling her panties down with his teeth. River giggled with excitement, dying for him to pleasure her.

The sweet taste of her swelling passion excited him. He could feel the blood throbbing in his sweltering loins, as she wrapped her legs tightly around his head. It was magical. Erik mounted her, pulling her closely to him as his hardness throbbed for more. He knew in that very moment there was no one else in the world, or the galaxy for that matter, who could give him this much pleasure. River was the only one. Taking the lead, he entered her slowly. Just as she tightened up, River let out a slight gasp.

"Relax," he whispered.

River tried relaxing, as he eased himself further into her. Her lips found his, and suddenly she couldn't kiss him enough. She ravished his neck, face and lips wildly while he made love to her. Pressing his shoulders back a little, he pushed even deeper into her, making her need him even more. River wrapped her legs tight around Erik, pulling him in, despite the slight pain from his girth. They both moaned, while River mimicked the movement of his hips. A shout of nirvana escaped her several times, as he picked up speed, white-knuckling the edge of her bouncing bed. Erik groaned louder and louder, his insides trembled, provoking his manhood to explode inside of her. His body slowed, as he shook and jerked with release. Erik kissed River's forehead, holding her tighter than he ever had before.

"I love you," he breathed softly into her ear.

"I love you," she sighed, as they both drifted to sleep.

Erik woke at five o'clock the next morning to find River was gone. He yawned, stretched and smelled coffee lurking in the air. He quickly headed downstairs toward the kitchen, hoping to see her and to hold her, and to lure her back into bed for more of the night before, but there was no River. There was just a note stuck to the wall where she knew he would find it. It read: I had to catch an early flight to Ohio. I need to see my grandmother. Be back in a few days. Don't follow me. It's about me and her. She doesn't have much time left. Please lock up. I love you. ~River

CHAPTER FORTY-TWO
Back to Earth

rik was worried, but he knew River was right. She needed to see her grandmother, and he didn't want to get in the way of that. There came a scratching at the front door. Looking out the window, he saw two familiar coyotes. He opened the door for Violet and Joshua, who quickly phased into human form.

"She's gone," Erik said.

"We saw her leave," Joshua replied.

"You should have woken me," Erik snapped.

"We didn't know where she was going or even if you cared," Violet snapped back.

"You *still* should have woken me. You knew I was here. You saw my truck. You saw my truck, right?" Erik asked, almost sarcastically.

Violet and Joshua exchange a strange look.

"What?" Erik probed.

"How could we not know you were with her? The whole house and surrounding atmosphere were lit up like a chakra Independence Day while you two were ..." Joshua said, trailing off.

Erik's face relaxed in embarrassment.

"We hope no one else noticed. A couple of cars did drive by. Hopefully, they couldn't see what we can see," Violet said, nudging Erik.

Erik was becoming uncomfortable with the conversation. So, he changed the subject.

"Well, I need to get a cell phone today and get back to work. I suppose you both can take a few days off while she's gone."

"You won't be going after her?" Violet asked, surprised.

"No. She needs her space. Her grandmother is not going to survive the year," Erik replied.

Violet nodded and smiled.

"Did anything interesting happen while I was gone?" Erik inquired.

"Nothing we couldn't handle," Joshua said.

"Alex mentioned he had flowers delivered to River, and that they were signed from her house, but she never got them."

"We haven't seen anything unusual, not since that night the stalker showed up," Violet broached.

"Okay, so nothing new on him?" Erik asked.

"He switched hotels," Violet replied. "And then I lost his scent."

"Okay … both of you take a break. I will watch River's place for the next few days. Just keep an eye out if you're out and about."

River drove a rental car into the small town of Green Camp, Ohio. She passed the muddy river, taking in all of the rich, green landscape. There was farmland for miles, lined with tall maple and oak trees. Her plan was simple. Visit her maternal grandmother of European roots, in and out without being seen. Coty was out of prison. She didn't want him to find out she was in town. Every once in a while, River passed an Amish horse and buggy along the long road to Larue, Ohio where her grandmother lived.

Mary caught her breath when she first laid eyes on her granddaughter. Standing at the front door, her knees nearly buckled. Mary, being in her 80s, looked fragile, but still as kind and gentle as ever. River greeted her grandmother with a warm hug, and the two sat down and talked for hours.

That afternoon, River took a walk into the familiar backwoods, touching trees with her fingertips as she pushed through the small forest. The air was brisk with the smell of soil from the soybean fields having been recently harvested and dug up. River took off in a sprint, jumping logs and dodging branches until she came to an old hunting stand her uncle built. Climbing up into it, she laid back, looking up at the sky through the leaves. She marveled at every delicate detail in each leaf. River closed her eyes and opened up her soul, inviting in her favorite childhood memories, like those days spent as a teenager riding quads and playing tag with her cousins. Her boots were endlessly muddy.

As the sun started to set, she made her way back to her grandmother's porch. As she walked up the steps, a car pulled recklessly into the drive. It was a woman River knew well, an enemy from her past. She watched as the woman got out of her car.

"River!" the ravishing beauty shouted.

"Hi Angel," River replied, apprehensively.

"How are you?"

"Fine," River said. "I'm just visiting."

"Oh. So, you aren't back for good?" Angel inquired.

"No."

River shifted her weight, hoping this conversation was short.

"Well, I just stopped by to see if your grandmother was still making her famous tomato jelly. I need to send some to a friend of mine in

California."

"That's my grandma. She loves to do everything from scratch," River said, offering a counterfeit smile.

"I called her earlier, and she told me you were here," Angel said, a menacing smile ripping across her face. "I thought I should stop by and see how you were doing."

"I'm good," River replied. "Arizona is good. It's hotter in the summer where I live, but it's a dry heat."

River's smile was so forced, it literally hurt her face. And she couldn't believe she actually tossed in the "but it's a dry heat" comment. That was such a cliché thing to say, Arizonan or not.

"I can't even imagine living in such heat and with poisonous snakes and nothing but cacti to look at all day," Angel retorted, almost mockingly. "I am sort of surprised you moved to the desert instead of somewhere a little more picturesque."

"Actually, Angel, Arizona is so much more than what you think. Only the truly ignorant think it's simply a state full of cacti and snakes. It's quite beautiful and peaceful—no drama. I'm loving it."

"So, where's Coty?" Angel asked.

"Coty!" River fired back sharply. "Your guess is as good as mine. I haven't been with Coty, or even seen him, in over two years."

"Really? That's strange," Angel smiled. She tossed her wavy, black locks away from her freshly-painted face and continued.

"He went to Arizona two months ago to find you. At least that's what he told my husband and me one night at a bar. His car was packed and ready to go that night. Had you and I still been close friends, like we were in high school, I would have warned you. I just didn't think it was my place to intervene."

"That's a first," River sneered.

River's expression fell when she let Angel's snarky comment sink in. She couldn't even pretend to smile anymore.

"He's showing pictures of Arizona across his social media. You are in Apache Junction, right? Honestly, all I see is desert and cactus in his photos," Angel droned on. "Here look for yourself."

Angel scrolled through Coty's social media on her cell phone. River looked on, void of any emotion, and then something struck her. Grabbing Angel's phone, she scrolled through the posts, panic taking hold of her. There were photos of cacti, desertscapes, state parks, bar scenes, women, of course, and then she froze. It was a photograph of her house. The caption read: "Wonder if she's home? Should I knock? LOL"

It was obvious. Coty was stalking her.

"Oh my God!" River gasped.

Angel snagged her phone and replied, "Maybe you should give him a call. Let him know where you *really* are."

"What? Why? So, he can finally kill me," River said, coldly. "He left me for dead, Angel."

"Come on, River. Coty told us the truth," Angel countered. "You attacked him, and without thinking, he pushed you … and you fell down the stairs. You were drunk."

"That is not how it happened. I wasn't drunk and I was nowhere near stairs. I think you should leave, Angel."

"I believe him. I'm sorry. I just do," Angel shrugged.

Just then, Mary, who always had a strong sense of trouble, stepped out onto the front porch and shouted, "River, come inside! It's getting dark and cold! Angel, I told you on the phone I do not have any tomato jelly!"

River glared at Angel. Their eyes locked.

"Okay, Grandma. I'll be right in," River answered, taking a hard step closer to Angel. "I NEVER want to see you or Coty again. I never liked you, and somehow, you keep popping into my life, and it's starting to piss me off!"

"You are still a bitch, River. I guess, not much has changed, huh?"

River's face felt flush, hot and angry.

"No wonder Coty kicked your dumb ass," Angel continued. "That mouth of yours really got you in trouble, didn't it?"

Before Angel could get another word out of her mouth, River conservatively clocked her in the eye with only half of her true strength. Angel fell backwards. River, shocked by her lack of restraint, offered to help Angel up. As she attempted an apology, Angel grabbed hold of River's leg, yanking her down to the ground. The two rolled around on the cold, hard gravel, throwing jabs. Angel bit River on the shoulder, while simultaneously pulling her hair.

Loud gunshots rang through the evening air, startling both River and Angel, causing them to come to a halt. Mary stood on the front porch with a mean shotgun and a cold, hard, troubled look on her face.

"Get off my property, Angel," Mary barked, as she racked the slide of the shotgun. "Now! And if you want more jelly, get your mama to make it! She should be doing more than starting trouble with other women!"

River suddenly felt ashamed. She looked back at her grandmother with remorse in her eyes.

"Sorry, Mary," Angel breathed, as she scurried to her car. "Please don't tell my mama. I will go."

Angel pulled out of the driveway quicker than she pulled into it. River watched Angel leave, as she sat on the ground with small scrapes up up and down her arms.

It started out as a small giggle, then morphing into a loud cackle. Before long, Mary was in a full-blown fit of roaring laughter. Astonished, River turned to her grandmother.

"Are you okay, Grandma?"

Mary laughed uncontrollably, as she set the gun down and slowly teetered down the steps to help her granddaughter up.

"I never liked her. That girl is always coming around, asking about you for Coty. I always wanted to chase her out of my house with a shotgun. I never thought that day would come, but it looks like she finally got the hint," Mary smirked. "Want some tea?"

River raised her eyebrows, impressed by her grandmother's gumption. Mary took River's hand, helped her up and the two walked back into the house arm-in-arm, primed for some hot tea.

Later that night, River looked through some old photos she found in her grandparents' antique hutch. Like her, Mary was a registered nurse. They were more alike than she realized. River liked that.

Her phone dinged—incoming text message from a strange number. River hesitated, but curiosity got the best of her. It read: "Hey! It's Erik. I have a new phone. This is my new number. How are things in Ohio?"

Glancing at the scratches on her arm, River fired back, "Fine. Nothing happening … really. I'm leaving tomorrow."

"You aren't staying longer?" Erik asked.

"No. I need to get back."

"Is everything ok?" Erik texted.

"I am fine. Trust me. No need to worry," River lied.

"I love and miss you, River."

"I love you, too."

CHAPTER FORTY-THREE
Out of a Nightmare

iver pulled the handmade quilt around her neck. Feeling miserable, she thought about how she would handle Coty when she returned home. Closing her eyes, she listened for and clung to the flicker of the flames in the fireplace, and soon fell into a dream that began sweetly with Erik's face. He held her close. They danced in a majestic place that was surrounded by wildflowers. It was surreal. They exchanged a soft kiss. Erik grinned knowingly, giving River's hand to Alex.

Dressed in a blue uniform, Alex had a huge smile on his face. Taking River by the arm, he led her down a long aisle of people, each and every one of them happily cheering her on and congratulating her. River wasn't sure what all the fanfare was for, but it certainly made her feel loved. Suddenly, and without warning, a hard hand grabbed hold of her free arm and pulled at her, yanking her downward. She couldn't get out of the fierce grasp. Focusing through the fog, she could see it was Coty. She clutched tightly onto Alex, who, with a pulled sword, fought to keep her close. The ground shuddered and opened up beneath her. River vanished into its gape and into Coty's waiting arms.

Landing on a marsh of grass, Coty laughed as River pushed away from him, taking off into a full sprint while wearing a long, white dress. She felt heavy, and she couldn't run fast enough. Reaching the edge of a cliff overlooking a waterfall, Coty clawed and grabbed at her. Without hesitation, River jumped, screaming all the way down. Just before hitting the water, she awoke from her dream with tears in her eyes. Suddenly sitting upright, she looked at her cell phone to check the time. It was time to leave. River rolled out of bed. After packing her bag, she shared a quick cup of coffee with her grandmother. It was with a short, sweet and sad goodbye, then she headed for the Columbus Airport.

Erik helped a young twelve-year-old girl named Kaylee off her horse. Gently ruffling her hair, he smiled and said, "You are getting so much better, kiddo! Soon you will be riding like a champ!"

Kaylee smiled big and proudly ran off to her mother, who was waiting and watching by the fence line. Dusting off his gloves, Erik caught a glimpse of his brother's car pulling in. Alex and Sai got out of the car and strode towards him. Erik was not surprised to see Sai with him, but rather annoyed.

"Wuz up?" Erik asked, dusting off his rugged jeans.

"Not much, brother," Alex replied, casually leaning against the fence. "Sai and I were talking and thought you would like to hang out."

"No … not really. River might come back today. *That's* my plan."

"Great! We can all hang out at River's place tonight," Alex suggested.

"Nope, definitely not," Erik said sternly.

He didn't trust Sai, and he certainly didn't want him anywhere near River.

Alex leaned in and said, "Sai may know a little something about that ring stuck on River's finger."

"You told him about the ring?" Erik snapped, irritated. "Why?"

"It came up," Alex shrugged.

Erik coiled his arm around Alex's neck, forcing him to walk with him, as Sai leaned back on to the fence line.

"We can't trust him," Erik whispered. "I don't care if he is like us. Haven't you wondered how he mysteriously turned up and how, all of a sudden, he's your best friend?"

"Do you mean, how he turned up out of nowhere to help rescue your ass? Look, he's a good guy. Give him a chance, and if he's a threat, we will take him out—together." Alex quipped.

Erik and Alex glanced back at Sai, who was sneaking a whiff of his arm pits.

"I don't like it," Erik said gruffly. "He's very strange."

"Come on! One look at the ring is all I'm asking," Alex coaxed. "He's really intelligent."

Erik exhaled a long, deep sigh, and then kicked some dirt around with his boots.

"He used to lead expedition teams on the Sidar ship," Alex added.

"What?" Erik asked, surprised. "Him? Seriously? How?"

"I don't know. He's like you … bigger than life, but then he wanted out."

"That's hard to believe. The Sidar?" Erik asked, glancing back at Sai again.

"Yep."

"Okay, but not today. I've got to warm River up to the idea of seeing this guy," Erik said.

"Okay … but this week," Alex agreed. "Shoot me a text and let me know when."

Erik nodded, as he watched Sai remove the bandana from his head and sniff it curiously.

"Everything okay, man?" Erik asked.

"I smell garlic," Sai said, grinning. "I love garlic, man."

Erik shook his head, uncertain about Sai.

CHAPTER FORTY-FOUR
The Warning

River made it home. Leaving her luggage in the Jeep, she unlocked the front door to the house and dashed upstairs to her nice, warm bed. It felt good to be home. The drive from the airport stressed her out, so she decided to save the unpacking for morning. All she could think about was Coty and what she would do if he showed up and started trouble with her. River was miles past exhaustion. All she wanted to do was forget about him and sleep—hibernate like a bear. Her soft, pillowy bed swallowed her up whole. Closing her eyes, she let her lethargy take her, as she curled up into a fetal position and fell fast asleep.

Unbeknownst to her, Kraylon had returned. River woke up to find herself tied to the bed. Kraylon's roots held her hostage once again, his magic sourced from trees. Kraylon hovered over her with his long, white hair floating around his face. River opened her eyes, and before she could scream, Kraylon whipped out another branch to seal her mouth shut.

"No," he whispered. "You need not worry, my sweet, sweet Amariah. I am purely protecting you. Be very quiet now and don't say a word."

River trembled. She turned her head to the sound of loud, heavy footsteps coming up the staircase. She wasn't sure if it was a part of Kraylon or something else like him. In a panic, she struggled to free herself, but the roots and branches only tightened around her wrists, ankles and mouth. The more she fought it, the greater hold it had over her. Kraylon put his long fingernail to his lips.

"Shhh …" he shushed.

A man suddenly appeared in her room. His back was turned, as he looked around. He didn't seem to notice Kraylon or the fact that she was bound to her bed by tree branches. River gasped when she saw the man's face. It was Coty! She couldn't scream. She could barely breathe, as she helplessly watched Coty rifle through her drawers. He tore through her jewelry box and even stopped to smell her dirty laundry, the pink panties that were lying on the floor. He pressed his face hard into the silk drawers and took a long whiff.

The sound of a truck engine tore into the drive out front. Coty ran to the bedroom window for a peek. He quickly raced down the staircase and out the back door. River was shocked.

"Be careful of this man," Kraylon warned. He is deranged."

River nodded, as Kraylon's branches released their grip and gently tucked her back into bed.

"I will always be near," Kraylon whispered, just before vanishing.

There was a knock at the front door. River ran to look out her window. It was Erik. Relieved, she ran downstairs, threw open the door and jumped into his arms.

"Wow! You really missed me," Erik laughed, kissing her on the cheek and walking her back inside. "You're trembling. What's wrong?"

River was silent for a beat, as she clung to Erik tightly. She tried not to cry, when she spoke.

"I just missed you so much."

"I missed you, too," he replied, kissing her again and again.

Erik kicked the door closed and carried River upstairs.

CHAPTER FORTY-FIVE
Sudden Showers

R iver and Ryan teamed up for a mock-attack scenario in Kenpo karate class. They stood on the mats, ready to go at it, and all River could think about was Coty going through her dresser drawers and smelling her underwear. Sensei backed off, signaling the start of scenario. Ryan grabbed River by the shoulders, and before he had time to dig his feet into the mat, something inside of her snapped. Thrusting her knee into Ryan's groin, her elbow crushed his face as he doubled over in severe pain. River then grabbed him by the scruff of his neck, twisting him to the ground and forcing him into a chokehold. The entire class watched on with their mouths gaped. Realizing Ryan was actually choking, Sensei jumped in to break it up. Everyone stared, secretly wishing they would get the same chance to do that to Ryan.

Ryan stood up, brushed it off and shook his head in frustration when Sensei asked if he was okay.

"You are very fast," Violet whispered to River, smiling.

"Yeah, I guess."

"No … really! You are," Violet continued. "That swiftness will take you far, particularly when up against a slower opponent. So, are you doing okay?"

"Yeah. I'm okay, I just have a lot on my mind."

"Hope it's nothing serious," Violet said, noticing the hesitation in River's eyes.

"I can't really talk about it right now," River replied, wanting to end the conversation.

"I'm here if you need me. We can talk," Violet offered, stepping onto the mat to spar with Ryan.

River nodded. She wasn't ready to tell anyone about Coty breaking into her house just yet. All she wanted was to be physically and mentally prepared for him when he came back.

River went straight from her Kenpo karate into weight training. She started lifting, squatting, and running on the treadmill, all the while ignoring text messages from Erik. Afterward, River went straight home and locked her doors. With energy yet to burn, she continued her workout by pounding feverishly on her punching bag. She kept to the music, picking up her punches—harder and faster—when the music picked up. The higher the beat count, the higher her kicks and heartrate.

Erik waved his hand, telekinetically removing the lock from the front door of River's house. He stepped into the house and headed upstairs to her room. He walked in on River giving a mix of upper cuts and hard rights and lefts to the punching bag, sweat pouring down her face. Erik picked up on her energy. He got the sense it was bad. Something was wrong.

"River," Erik said.

River didn't respond. She didn't even notice he was in the room.

"Hey!" he exclaimed. "River!"

She still didn't respond. Instead, she kept punching. That's when Erik noticed her ear buds, realizing her music was blasting. He walked over and gently touched her shoulder. River jumped, screamed, and swung at his face with a hard fist, which he stopped abruptly by grabbing hold of her arm.

"Don't ever sneak up on me!" River shouted, breathlessly.

She ripped the ear buds from her ears. She was a hot mess, a pool of sweat gathering between her breasts and her hair pasted to her forehead. Erik was instantly aroused by her fierceness.

"What's going on with you?" he asked.

"Nothing. I'm just training. I want to be in better shape," she replied, jabbing the bag with a hard punch and kick. Erik grabbed her arm before she could strike the bag again.

"You are in fantastic shape," Erik smiled. "You didn't answer any of my texts or calls today."

"Would you, please, let go of my arm?"

Erik did as she asked, taking the wraps off her hands.

"I'm sorry," River continued. "I've been distracted lately."

"I can see that," Erik said. "I am just concerned; I'm not trying to annoy you."

"It's irritating," River huffed, pushing her pasted bangs away from her face. " I mean, I'm one step away from my black belt, and I let you sneak up behind me! I couldn't even defend myself."

"You need to use your senses more, be aware of your surroundings."

"You sound like a professional," River teased.

"Nah … just be open and trust your instinct. Next time someone sneaks up on you … and touches you from behind, don't waste time turning around. Instead, just elbow them in the face and back kick them in the groin—unless it's me, of course."

"I would never do that to you," River giggled. "How do you know all this stuff anyway?"

"I was taught by a very good instructor a long time ago."

River looked at him in complete surprise.

"I didn't know you were in martial arts."

"I was involved in a lot of different martial arts. Believe it or not, so was Alex. It was kind of our thing," Erik said, casually.

River realized she didn't know that much about Erik's past … let alone Alex's. This made her uncomfortable because she never even asked. Her issues had become her first priority, and she should've made more of an effort to enquire about them. Erik noticed her slight embarrassment.

"I am an engineer, and I worked for the highly-elite in government," Erik said, kicking himself for saying that much.

"You were in the military?"

"It is a lot like the military. Yes. I can't tell you everything, but I can tell you we handled a lot of big projects."

River chewed on this new information for a moment. Erik was a ranch hand/horse trainer on the surface, but underneath it all he is an engineer who is trained in martial arts and who worked for the government. This surprised her. Perhaps this was the *real* reason he took off for a few months—top secret, classified and off the record. Erik reached out to touch River. She reacted with a quick jerk, pulling away.

"Are you scared of me now?" he asked.

"No. I'm not scared of you," she sighed. "Sorry. I don't know why I did that. Do you want to know my biggest fear?"

Erik nodded.

"Becoming too dependent on you."

"I would never hurt you, River," Erik assured.

"When you left and we lost touch, I didn't know what was going on. I started to doubt you, thinking you had a wife and kids somewhere … another life."

"That is fair," Erik said. "You are right. I never talk about my past. I guess you and I are similar in that way. You rarely talk about where you come from … where you've been. You still refuse to tell me how the visit with your grandmother went."

River nodded. She knew he was right, and yet she was still not ready to talk about it … not about the fight with Angel or Coty's recent involvement in her life. Instead of opening up, she pulled out a basket full of clean clothes and started folding towels.

"There is really nothing good to say about my past. It's a lot of painful drama, and I'm just moving forward. It's better that way."

"I understand."

Erik sat on the bed and helped fold laundry.

"I promise you," he continued. "I never intentionally wanted to leave or hurt you. I really had no other choice. I had to go."

Erik reached over and took River by the arm, gently whispering, "You are so beautiful. I can't keep my eyes and hands off you."

Rubbing her back, he could feel the tension in her shoulders release. The expression on her face revealed that she may have felt some peace, too.

"You want to take a shower?" he asked.

"I could use a shower."

"Let's take one together."

River smirked, loving the idea. They quickly stripped to nothing and entered the large shower. Erik sprayed her body off and helped her wash her curly hair. In exchange, River was only too happy to wash his broad shoulders and back. She let her soapy hand slide down to his groin. She massaged him until he was aroused and groaning softly. Erik turned to face her, catching her wet lips in a kiss. With her hair clung to the back of her neck, River knelt down to pleasure him. Erik resisted at first.

"You don't have to do that, River."

River looked up at him with sparkling eyes, ignoring his protest. She grabbed his manhood, tasting it with her full lips and mouth—blowing his mind over the next several minutes.

Not again, Violet sighed in her coyote mind. Violet and Joshua watched as River's house lit up like a rainbow chakra.

They are worse than newlyweds, Joshua's mind muttered.

I don't like this. They will bring trouble on all of us, Violet measured.

The Archon will come either way, Joshua stated.

I suppose, Violet yawned, stretching her paws.

Joshua snapped his coyote jaw at a horsefly.

Forget it, Joshua. I've been after that nasty fly all night.

Violet rolled over on her back and scratched against the rocks.

We really should practice phasing into other animals, Joshua suggested.

Erik said predator of the desert, Violet reminded.

What about mountain lion? Joshua posed.

Too much attention. Everyone who sees us will want to kill us, and you know that. Human nature is brutal, Violet ruminated.

You mean, we would bring more attention than Erik and River are right now? Joshua teased.

The two coyotes watched as River's home shot out purple blasts of light like a firework's display.

Good grief, Joshua muttered. *What are they doing in there?*

Must be amazing, Violet hummed.

Joshua scooched his body next to Violet's and rested his head on his front paws, as Violet scratched her ears.

Are you attracted to Luka? he asked.

No. He is good looking, but he's just a friend.

Oh, Joshua sighed.

Why?

He's irresponsible and ignorant. I don't trust him, Joshua replied.

Don't worry. You can trust me, Violet assured, noting Joshua's obvious jealousy.

Violet sat at high alert, a familiar smell of tequila, sweat and cheap cologne wafting through her nose.

HE IS HERE, Violet barked.

The two coyotes watched in anticipation, as Coty drove slowly past River's home.

Who is he? Joshua asked.

A stalker ... I guess, Violet posed.

We need to tell Erik, Joshua urged.

Violet nudged Joshua to his hind seat.

Not yet. We will wait until they are finished doing whatever they are doing, she resolved.

CHAPTER FORTY-SIX
The Round Table

Erik walked through the door to a small Mexican diner. He was exhausted and somewhat averse to find Alex. He made his way through the tight maze of round tables and outdated booths. When Alex saw Erik, he waved him over. Erik let out an exasperated breath, as he sat down to the table. A slim, retro-styled waitress with heavy makeup took his order.

"Where's River?" Alex asked.

Clearing his throat and settling into his seat, Erik took a big drink of ice water and replied, "She's not coming. I'm having a security system installed in her house, as we speak. She wasn't too happy about me taking control of the situation."

"Not coming? She needs to be here because she is, as you know, attached to the ring," Alex reminded.

"No worries. I have a picture of the ring."

"You and I both have a picture of the ring! It's not enough," Alex exclaimed.

Sai walked out of the men's room and sat across from Erik.

"May I see?" Sai asked.

Hesitating, Erik handed the phone over to Sai. Sai scrolled through every photo of the ring without a hint of emotion on his face. After a minute or two, he laid the phone down in front of him and said, "Yes, I know this ring. You should know it, too. Your people created it."

Alex and Erik exchanged glances.

"Unfortunately," Sai continued. "It was stolen by the Anunnaki."

"The Anunnaki?" Alex asked.

"These gemstones are representative of the Orion Galaxy, the seven Sisters star system. This gold piece, in the shape of a small temple, is the Temple of Dandarah. At one time, it was a portal for us and a multi-dimensional teleport. The frequency was high enough for use on this planet to ensure our visits would be kept short. This ring was actually one of many rings created by our people to help ground our energy in case anyone was too far from the temple. It was to be used in emergencies. Eventually, all remaining rings left on the planet were claimed by the Anunnaki after we aborted mission," Sai explained.

"So, there are more rings out there," Erik replied.

"Well, yes, but not for humans to find. The Anunnaki is all about protecting the secrets of life on other planets from mainstream humans, and so any artifacts we left behind would have been quickly collected."

"I want to know who would give this ring to River," Alex insisted.

"Obviously, it is someone who knows she is here, someone who either wants to protect her or has a higher agenda," Sai replied.

"Does the ring protect her?" Erik asked, concerned.

"It will … if she needs to teleport out of a situation, but *only* if she can maintain the light body of a Pleiadian. I'm not sure, but I am thinking since she is in human form, she is not a complete light source yet," Sai concluded.

"No," Erik added.

"Could it be the Archon?" Alex asked.

"No," Sai answered emphatically. "The Archon would not protect her. It's some *thing* or someone else. If I were you, I would keep a close eye on her. River could be in more danger than you realize. This ring is interdimensional—that is to say it moves between worlds. Someone could be using her or preparing her for something she isn't ready for."

Just then, the waitress placed their food order on the table. Sai surrendered the serious attitude almost instantly.

"I love chimichangas," he said. "Man, they are so good!"

Sai didn't wait on Erik and Alex. He dug in fork first, while the brothers exchanged worried frowns.

"I'm confused," Erik began. "The Counsel Elders said these rings were not Pleiadian."

"The Elders are motivating you to investigate. They know about the rings, talismans and pendants. There were many in use in ancient times … after the flooding of Noah. They also know that we no longer have use for them, but the Anunnaki do. As a matter of fact, the Anunnaki are unable to move through dimensions without this ring. Of course, the Elders are concerned," Sai said, between obnoxious bites.

"This has gotten weird," Alex said, pushing the Spanish rice around on his plate with his fork.

Erik did the same. He had lost his appetite.

"If she could achieve at least ninety percent of her full potential as a light being, perhaps this ring could be of use to her—as in time travel and her ability to cross different dimensions. Obviously, someone knows something," Sai said, chasing chimichanga with a big gulp of water.

"Many of the rings and talismans were claimed and confiscated with the help of King Solomon," Sai continued. They were melted down and destroyed, but the Anunnaki kept hundreds for themselves."

"Someone is stalking her," Erik blurted.

"What? Who?" Alex asked, not piecing together that River had recently complained of her ex being at the house because he was currently stoned.

"I don't know … some guy—clearly human," Erik replied.

"She told you this?" Sai asked.

"No. I learned this on my own. River is very private, and I'm not sure she would ever volunteer this information," Erik explained.

"He's been to her house?" Alex asked.

"He has," Erik continued. "He has driven past, and I think he confiscated the flowers you sent."

"If he signed for and stole the flowers, he's doing more than driving by. I'll bet he's been in her house. That son of a bitch wants to die," Alex snarled.

"Calm down, Alex. We can't let this get messy," Erik said. "We will handle it. Don't you worry."

"If you don't mind me asking," Sai said. "Who *is* River? Really?"

"Someone we used to know," Erik replied.

"She must be special for you to leave the Pyalexis and go rogue for," Sai said, catching on. "Come on! What's really going on here?"

"The less you know, the better," Erik cautioned. "Don't make me leave you out of our conversations."

"I was aboard the Sidar. I led serious expeditions. Granted, I've gone rogue myself, but I still know a thing or two, and this girl is no ordinary human," Sai breathed, unraveling the mystery. "I may be able to help you more if I have the full story."

"You know about the ring and that's enough," Erik muttered. "I'm done. I have work to do."

Erik slammed his napkin down onto his plate, along with a ten-dollar bill before leaving.

"What's his deal," Sai asked in between bites.

"He's in love."

"You both love her," Sai replied.

"Let's just say, we both took an oath to protect each other, and sometimes that oath gets out of hand."

"I see," Sai nodded. "Interesting."

CHAPTER FORTY-SEVEN
Her Home Defense

Erik decided the only way to catch a stalker was to become a stalker. So, the next day he staked out the parking lot of River's workplace. Using his bionic eyes, he looked into every single vehicle, coming and going, including ambulances. He was looking for anything outside of the ordinary. He found co-workers smoking weed in one car, and more co-workers making out in another. Outside of that, there was nothing suspicious.

Erik waited for hours, until River finally walked out of the nursing facility wearing gray scrubs. He surreptitiously followed her Jeep through town to her dance class. He saw nothing unusual, but continued to patiently wait out her class, just in case. An hour passed and still nothing. River walked out of her class wearing workout attire and a sweet, sweaty glow. Erik was beginning to feel extremely vulnerable to her. She was breathtaking and, in his mind, no one could ever compare to her. Seeing that she was fine and there didn't seem to be a threat, he headed back to the Atler's Ranch. He figured he would pick up the "stalking" of the woman he loved the next day.

River ruled that if she saw Coty again, she would tell him the truth. The truth was that she had moved on and she never wanted to see him again. If he didn't like it, that was too bad. And, if he put his hands on her, she was prepared to defend herself as best she could. She could only hope Coty would understand, and that their next encounter, should there be one, would not revisit physical violence.

Every night she returned home, she stretched out and boxed, consistently practicing her self-defense moves, including the rear chokehold, the overhead attack, the front chokehold and the hair pull. Those were Coty's go-to moves. She wanted to keep those basic techniques at the forefront of her brain if he went after her.

Every little noise in the house sent her into a panic when Erik wasn't around. She would do walk throughs, making sure windows and doors were locked. She would double and triple check the new security system to make sure the cameras were working. That evening, after River finished her workout, she went outside to water the garden before it got too dark. Sometimes the hot sun would burn her tomato leaves, so she stopped watering earlier in the day. When she got to the back yard, she stopped short. She was aghast. In front of her stood hundreds of two-foot sapling trees. They were everywhere … from out of nowhere!

River stepped closer to the trees, examining them closely. She did not recognize the tree type, not from anything she had ever seen growing locally in Arizona. The thought of Kraylon popped into her mind. She knew this had something to do with him. A part of her was happy to find the trees growing in her backyard, but there was a part of her that knew it would come at a price. Shade is great! A natural ecosystem is wonderful, but what is the *actual* cost of all this? And what does it all mean?

As she bent over and touched one of the sapling's leaves, Erik crept up slowly behind her without detection. He gently grasped the back of her neck. River tucked her chin into her chest, grabbed both of Erik's hands, shifted her body to the left and thrust a swift side kick into his right thigh. Erik fell flat on his stomach with a loud thud. River stood up quickly, relieved to find it was him. Trembling and somewhat happy for the chance to practice her skills, she offered him a hand up. Erik looked into her amazing eyes. He was aroused by her show of confidence, feeling a surge of uncontrollable passion.

"That was hot," he smiled.

"Was it good for you?"

"Like you," he replied, taking her hand. "It was too good."

Erik noticed the hundreds of tree saplings surrounding them. "Who planted these?" he asked.

"I didn't."

"What?"

"Kraylon probably planted them," River whispered.

"Kraylon! When did you speak to Kraylon?!"

"You know Kraylon?" River questioned.

"Yes. I know Kraylon," Erik said, changing his tone.

He released her hand and gave her a forced half smile. He then spun her around, facing away from him, and with a force of power, he touched the back of her neck. River swiftly fell asleep. As she fell back, Erik scooped her up and carried her inside. Laying River in bed, Erik ran downstairs and quickly called Alex.

"What's going on?" Alex asked, sitting at home with Sai, smoking a bowl.

"I know who's stalking her," Erik said, his jaw clenching in disgust.

"Yeah? Who?" Alex asked, sitting up on his couch.

"Kraylon."

"What in the fuck!? Are you kidding me?" Alex barked. "I suppose you will get revenge on Kraylon after all."

Alex stood up, stoned and unsure of what these intense feelings meant. Sai watched on, also stoned.

"Looks like it," Erik said, peeking in on River as she slept.

"Does River know?"

"She has been communicating with him," Erik confirmed.

"WHAT?! Did you tell her anything about him?"

"No. I need a minute. I put her to sleep, so I can figure out the next move," Erik replied. "I've got to go. I think she's waking up."

Erik hung up the phone, as River sat up in bed.

"What happened?" she asked.

"You fainted. It's hot out there."

River leaned back against her pillows, touching her head quizzically.

"I have been doing a lot lately," she pointed out.

"As usual … a busy mind has no time to think," Erik said.

"What were we talking about before I fainted? I don't remember. I don't even remember …"

"It's not important," Erik interrupted. "You need to rest."

River nodded in agreement. Erik helped her get ready for bed. Looking into her eyes, he said, "River, promise me one thing."

"What's that?"

"No more secrets."

"Huh," she asked, confused.

"No more big secrets. If someone is trying to hurt you, stalk you, or threaten you … I need to know right away."

"Oh."

"Is something wrong?" he asked.

"No. I'm just really tired. Can we talk about this later?"

"Of course," he sighed.

"Thank you, Erik."

"Get some rest," he said, kissing her lips softly.

He laid down next to her, this woman he loved, and watched her peacefully fall asleep. So as not to crash and burn with her, Erik rolled out of bed and sat in her oversized chair in the corner of her room and watched her sleep until morning. Kraylon had always been a pain in Erik's ass, and he couldn't wait to see him again.

CHAPTER FORTY-EIGHT
Spoiling for a Fight

"**I** can't believe Kraylon's been stalking her this whole time, and he helped himself to the flowers I ordered," Alex whispered, as he and Erik waited patiently for River to arrive at the gym.

"You just can't get over those flowers, can you?" Erik asked.

"They were quite expensive, and you should be mad too! They were supposed to be from you."

"Okay. I get it," Erik submitted.

"What's going on here today anyway?" Alex asked, taking a seat on a long bleacher in the karate gym.

"Some kind of Karate recital," Erik replied. "I thought she might meet up with us before it began, but maybe it will make her too nervous."

Alex caught a glimpse of River and Violet standing in a far-off doorway. He nudged Erik and pointed at them. Both men waved at her. Joshua ran into the gym and sat beside Erik.

"Who's he?" Alex asked.

"A friend," Erik answered.

"Are you sure you can handle this?" Alex asked, playfully.

"Of course. Are you sure *you* can?"

"Just warning you. I know what she's capable of," Alex noted, measuring up Joshua from head to toe.

The gym suddenly went black, as lights hovered over the mats and karate team members during their sparring performances. Erik watched Violet perform. He was amused at her technique, and especially impressed by how she took on two men in an attack-scenario match. Erik muffled laughter, as she made one man scream out in pain. He had to admit, Violet was really good.

"Hell yeah! That's what I'm talking about!" Joshua shouted, as he jumped to his feet, giving Violet a standing ovation at the end of her match. He whistled and clapped.

River and Ryan were up next. The match was merciless and grueling, as River found herself on the ground a few times too many. Erik winced when the reality set in that this wasn't the tap-point version of karate. This was fierce and as real as it got. He was proud of River. She stood her ground, dishing out flawless, and ruthless kicks and jabs. In the middle of it all, Ryan grabbed hold of her right leg. River pushed off with her left leg, kicking his left leg out from underneath him. The move backfired, and Ryan landed with a loud crash on top of River.

"I told you, man," Alex said. "You can't handle this."

"I'm fine," Erik whispered.

"Relax your fist then, bro."

River braced for the last round. This time Ryan got the best of her, as he punched her in the head gear a few times. She didn't have a moment to adjust. Erik, Alex and Joshua tensed up, all of them pissed off. Alex attempted to move from his seat. Erik stopped him.

"Calm down," Erik exhaled. "This is not what she wants."

When River was swept onto her back for the last time, Erik stopped nervously tapping his foot and let go a sigh of relief. He couldn't take anymore. Alex, on the other hand, was ready to tear Ryan limb from limb. After River bowed to Ryan and her Sensei, she sprinted over to them.

The knot in Erik's stomach was finally loosening up a bit. He was glad it was over.

"I lost," River said, her lip busted and bleeding.

Alex was at a loss for words.

"You did a good job," Erik replied. "Against a man! A black belt, right?"

River nodded, dabbing her lip with the back of her hand.

"Do *not* be hard on yourself," Erik insisted, looking over at Alex who was staring angrily at Ryan.

"Yeah, it was great," Alex managed. "You did good River."

When it was all over and they were all headed outside, Violet kept close to Joshua.

"We should all get some beer or something," Joshua suggested.

"I'm in," Alex chimed in.

"The saloon over by the mountain is a low-key spot," Joshua said.

"So, this is why you've been training so hard at home, huh?" Erik asked, putting his arm around River.

"Yes," River lied, trying not to look him in the eye.

They all met up at the Old Time Saloon, ordering three pitchers of beer and a shot of tequila each. After one beer and one shot, Erik refused to drink anymore, especially when he noticed River drinking too much. She was already getting tipsy. When she nearly slipped out of her chair, Erik grabbed hold of her and asked her to slow down, but she ignored him. Violet reached for River's hand and pulled her out onto the dance floor.

The two danced to a 50s song playing on the jukebox.

"Let her have a little fun," Alex said, looking over at Erik. "She is so uptight. She needs this."

Joshua watched Violet like a hawk, as an elderly man stared intensely from his bar stool at her ass. River was feeling so good; she had one hell of a buzz. She was flying so high that she didn't even notice Coty sitting at the bar. He was wearing a large cowboy hat. He watched her from afar with a disgusted look on his face. Like a preying animal, he moved from table to table, so as not to get caught. He wanted to get closer to her, so he could watch her shake, twist and move with her friend. All the while, he downed tequila—hard and fast.

"We should go," Erik said, leading River off the dance floor.

"*No!*" she protested, tearing her arm from his grip. "I want to dance, and this is *SO* much fun!"

Erik felt something, a presence. With all the drunken people filling up the bar, he could feel something was off.

"Just a few more songs, Erik," Violet winked.

Erik made his way back to Joshua and Alex who were involved in a heated debate over a football game happening on a nearby television screen. Alex was heavily intoxicated. Joshua was drunk, not nearly as far gone as Alex. Erik shook his head, returning his attention back to the girls.

The girls were gone!

In a panic, Erik scanned the bar. Not seeing them anywhere, he pushed his way through a drunken crowd, looking at every face and in every corner booth. He moved quickly across the room, and just as he was about to lose it, he saw River and Violet walk into the women's restroom together. He exhaled—his heart pounding.

"Relax," Alex said, walking up from behind. "You are getting too worked up over this Kraylon thing. Kraylon would never hurt her. He used to be on our side remember?"

"*USED* to be." Erik barked. "I still don't understand why she never mentioned Kraylon until now. Apparently, he planted hundreds of trees in her backyard."

"That's not creepy," Alex said, sarcastically. "Well, what did she say to you about him? What do they talk about?"

"I put her into a deep sleep. I don't want her to know I know yet."

"Kraylon is weird, but he's always been that guy you don't want to stand next to at the party. I know he wouldn't hurt River. He's just always had this weird infatuation with her," Alex assured, gesturing to the bartender for another beer.

"Haven't you had enough Alex?" Erik asked.

"It's not a problem, I will call for a ride home."

Coty couldn't take his eyes off of River. He kept a close, scowling eye over Erik. He figured River was likely sleeping with him, and as far as he was concerned, whatever happened to Erik would be considered collateral damage.

The girls made their way back to the dance floor. Violet spun River around. Losing her footing, River got tripped up by a bar stool, and fell to the ground in a drunken fit of laughter. Coty bolted over to River, offering to help her up. Putting his hands on her, he assisted Violet in picking River up off the floor. River laughed in hysterics. She had no idea how drunk she actually was or that Coty, her violent ex-boyfriend, was touching her. Erik strutted over as fast as he could, putting himself between him and Coty.

"Thanks," he said, sharply. "I've got her."

Coty stepped out of the way, glaring at Erik. He hated seeing his hands on *his* girl. The tequila was telling him that it was a good time to let Erik have it. Coty kicked Erik in the chest with his big boot, knocking him off balance. River dropped to the floor.

"HEY!" Violet shouted, giving Coty a swift kick in the gut.

River had no idea what was going. Everything was happening so fast. The room was spinning. Joshua spotted Violet striking Coty on his carotid artery. He shouted out, attempting to get Alex's attention. Alex turned, just in time to catch a glimpse of his friends in the middle of the scuffle. Without hesitation, he jumped over the table and ran into the fray with Joshua to help Erik and the girls.

Erik backhanded Coty square in the face, pissing him off even more. The bartenders shouted from behind the bar, attempting to squash the skirmish with verbal commands, but their demands went unnoticed. Coty's low-life friends stepped in to back him up, doubling the ruckus. From there, all hell broke loose.

After taking a few punches from Alex, Coty had had enough and took off running out the back of the bar. His nose was bloodied, and his ego bruised. Erik, Joshua and Alex fought off a gang of drunken idiots who had no idea who they were up against, nor did they care. Erik turned to Alex and shouted, "FUCK! USE OUR POWER!"

"No way!" Alex shouted back. "Just beat his ass!"

With River laying on the floor in a drunken stupor, Violet kicked, punched and pushed anybody who came too near her. Meanwhile, Erik and Joshua continued throwing punches, while Alex was lifted up into the air by an enormous, muscle-bound man and thrown across two tables. Having seen it happen, Violet jumped onto the man's back and gouged at his eyes with her fingers. The man swung this thick body around, hurling Violet's tiny figure across a table. Joshua rushed to her rescue.

River, who had puked up everything but her lungs, was laying on the floor in her own vomit. Two big bouncers struggled nearby, rounding people up and kicking them outside. When the police rolled up on scene and things had quieted down, Erik scanned the bar with his eyes. He found River passed out in the middle of the floor. He ran to her side, scooped her up and took her outside to his truck. Joshua and Violet helped Alex back to his feet. The fighting had ceased, and the drunken idiots had surrendered, as they all hobbled out to the parking lot, busted up and bleeding. Alex was hurting.

"Put him in the back of the truck," Erik said.

Violet and Joshua helped Alex into the truck, just before phasing into coyotes. The two took off into the night through the vacant field. With his brother and River in tow, Erik pulled out of the parking lot and shot down the dusty, desert highway. He was anxious to get them home.

"I'm going to be sick, Erik," River warned.

"We are almost there, baby."

Erik picked up speed, as Alex bounced around in the back of the truck. He moaned loudly at every bump and turn. He rested against the truck bed, riding out the pain. They would be home soon.

CHAPTER FORTY-NINE
The Rundown

Joshua and Violet were two very drunk coyotes, as they raced through the desert. Both prairie wolves squealed in pain as their hind legs were stuck by cacti, but they kept running. When they neared River's home, Violet ran swiftly across the highway. Joshua followed. Without a moment to react, oncoming head lights flashed, brakes squealed and BOOM! Joshua was hit. The car swerved, but it never stopped.

Violet's fur stood on end, as she stopped and turned to see Joshua laying helplessly in the middle of the road. He was resting in a small pool of blood. Violet's watery eyes dripped, as she raced to his side, grabbed him by the nape of his neck with her teeth and struggled to drag him off the road.

HELP! she choked and yelped. *HELP US!*

She cried for someone, anyone to help her, forgetting she was still in coyote form. No one was around.

Joshua! Joshua! I love you, she moaned.

Joshua panted heavily. His respirations became labored, and his body remained in shock. Violet noted his body temperature dropping. In the heat of the moment, she darted for River's house. Clawing frantically at the front door, she sent Erik telepathic pleas for help. Erik never came. He wasn't responding to her.

HELP, ERIK! she yapped.

"Argh …" Alex exhaled, stirring in the truck bed. "What the fuck is going on?"

In a daze, he managed to move his body out of the truck.

Alex! Alex! Violet howled, leaping at him and begging for help.

"Whoa! Down dog. DOWN DOG!" Alex shouted, pushing at her.

Violet yelped and climbed on him even more. Nipping at his pant leg, she tried to get him to follow her.

"What the?" Alex exhaled, adjusting his eyes.

His vision was blurry, but with the assistance of his bionic eyes, he realized this was no dog. It was a coyote.

"WHOA! SHIT!" he hollered.

Help me, Alex! Please, Violet whimpered.

"Wait! I can hear you. You are talking. I knew I shouldn't have smoked that weed with Joshua," Alex muttered.

It's me. Violet!

Right before Alex's eyes, Violet merged into her naked, human form. Alex's jaw dropped. He took a moment to assess and then realized what he was seeing was real—or was it?

"Alex, I need your help. Joshua was hit by a car," Violet cried.

"You were a coyote just now, right?"

"Yes. Please follow me," Violet said, shaking.

She didn't notice Alex staring at her nakedness.

"Alex … please," she begged, grabbing his hand and pulling him.

"Okay. Lead the way," he said. "But first, take my shirt!"

Alex reached back and grabbed the collar of his white tee and pulled it over his head. Handing it to her, they ran toward the road together. Violet didn't miss a beat, as she quickly slipped into the shirt. She and Alex ran no less than half a mile down the dark road.

Erik wiped puke from River's mouth, as he helped her to her feet. She tried cozying up to the bathroom floor, but he wouldn't have it. Not on his watch. Helping her into bed, Erik slipped off her shoes, and pulled the comforter up to her chin. She was exhausted, not to mention too stubborn for her own good.

With River safe and fast asleep, Erik shot down the stairs to see to Violet. She seemed so desperate.

"Violet!" He shouted, flinging open the front door.

He couldn't help but notice the deep scratches in the wood on its front side. Something had gone terribly wrong, so Erik followed her scent. It led him to the edge of the drive. Alex was no longer in the back of his truck, and that's when he panicked. He waited a minute before jumping in his truck and tearing off down the road. He saw them almost instantly. Violet and Alex were carrying a bloody, naked man along the shoulder of the highway. Tears welled up in his eyes when he noticed Violet sobbing. It was then that he recognized who it was they were carrying.

It was Joshua.

Erik threw the truck into park and ran out to help them.

"What happened?!"

"He was hit by a car … as a coyote," Alex said.

Alex was still trying to fill in some of the blanks in this story, but obviously, he figured out that Violet and Joshua were Pleiadian-shape shifters, traveling alongside Erik on Earth.

"Let's get him in the truck," Erik exhaled, trying to stay calm. "Violet, go stay with River. Someone needs to stay here."

"But I want to go!" Violet protested.

"Violet … please," Alex insisted.

Violet took off running toward the house to be with River, while Alex and Erik screeched off toward the hospital with Joshua in tow. Erik explained as succinctly as he could why Violet and Joshua were there with him. Alex listened intently, understanding the importance of their presence.

"River will never forgive me if we lose Joshua," Erik whispered.

Realizing the gravity of the situation, Alex put his hand on Erik's shoulder and said, "Step on it, brother."

CHAPTER FIFTY
Three Ring Circus

"How is he?" Violet asked, trembling. With tears streaming down her prominent cheekbones, she was almost afraid to ask. River squeezed Violet's hand compassionately.

"He's stable," Erik replied. "Believe it or not, the alcohol actually helped him. He's doing better,"

"I need to see him," Violet said, choking out the words.

"I will take you but listen … do not answer any questions to hospital staff, under any circumstance. We, um … Alex and I took care of his story. We needed to make sure we were here, in case he accidentally turned into a coyote. For now, it's handled. The police weren't called, and if we don't raise any suspicion, they won't need to be." Erik said, getting super serious.

"Okay," Violet replied, nodding.

As soon as Violet walked in to see Joshua, she choked back loud sobs. River stayed outside of the room, wearing her darkest sunglasses and feeling worse than she had ever felt. She plopped down onto the nearest waiting room chair. Erik sat down beside her, looking rather morose, himself.

"How do you feel?" he asked.

"Like crap."

"I figured as much."

"How did this happen? How did Joshua get hit by a car?" River inquired.

"He was drunk, running around like a fool after I took you home last night. Someone hit him."

"I don't get why he would be on the road. We were all so drunk last night," River noted, laying her head on Erik's shoulder. "I wish it would never have happened."

Her tribal, fringe purse hit the floor.

"Drinking isn't for everyone," Erik said.

Violet came out of Joshua's room. She sat down beside Erik.

"Are you okay?" he asked, putting his arm around her.

"Yes. They are taking cactus needles out of his ankles right now. They asked that I step out of the room. You both can go. I'm going to stay the night. I can't remember a night without Joshua by my side, not since I was a toddler. We've always been together. I'm just so glad he's going to be okay. I don't know what I would do without him," Violet whispered, tears running wild and free now.

"Are you sure, Violet? I can stay with you if you want me too," River replied.

"No. He's on the mend—a few broken ribs and a collapsed lung. He's going to need me to take care of him for a while."

Violet wrapped her arms around River, taking advantage of a long, much-needed hug—with an extra thirty seconds for the road. Erik squeezed Violet and said, "I will see you and Joshua later. Take all the time you need."

River nodded in agreement, as Erik grabbed her hand and walked her out to her Jeep.

"Do you remember much about last night?" he asked.

"No. I don't, and please don't make me."

Erik smiled, "So you don't remember the bar fight?"

"Please, Erik … I feel bad enough as it is," River groaned, leaning into him.

"I'm only asking because there was a man there who tried to help you up when you fell. I thought maybe you knew him. He was so enraged when I told him that I had you that he kicked me."

River grimaced, "I guess it was just a drunk jerk. I wouldn't know any man at that bar, Erik."

"Do you think you can make it home okay?" he asked.

"I think so. Getting here was fun. I wanted to vomit at the slightest turn. I'm just really tired. I need water and sleep."

"Call me when you wake up," Erik said.

The two shared a big hug and a short kiss.

"I will," River whispered.

Erik followed her home in his truck, honking affectionately as she pulled into her driveway. He drove onward, headed back to the ranch.

River sat in the warm shower, letting the water run through her hair and over her body with it's healing effects. Hugging her knees, she thought about what she could remember from the fiasco the night before. She checked her cell when she got out, but didn't respond to any of the messages that awaited her. As she was about to crawl into bed, there was a loud knock at the front door.

"Seriously?" she said. "*No* …"

River walked to her bedroom window. There was a black

Mercedes Benz in the driveway. She slipped into a tropical robe and answered the door. It was definitely not Coty. He could never afford a car like that. River peeped through the sliver of open door, as she hadn't unlocked chain.

"Yes. Can I help you?" River asked, squinting with sensitive eyes.

A beautiful woman peered back at her through Chanel sunglasses. She was a tall, pale blonde with a bob-framed face.

"Hello. Are you River?" the woman asked with a strong European accent.

"Yes."

River kept the door locked, as she waited for an explanation of her existence on her porch. The woman's full, red lips turned to the man behind her and said, "Charles, the paper."

Charles was dressed in a black suit. He was much taller than the woman. The woman yanked the paper out of Charles' hand, holding it to the open crack in the door.

"River, I am Charlotte. This man behind me is Charles. You and I need to talk," the woman said.

River looked closely at the paper but couldn't see it very well.

"Do you have this ring?" Charlotte asked.

River stared at the paper. Knowing she had a mysterious ring stuck on her finger, she opened the door. In that exact moment, a sharp spasm shot through River. Touching the paper ever-so slightly, she realized that this was, indeed, the ring.

"Is it stolen or something?" River asked.

"Something like that. I see you have it on your finger," Charlotte noted, eyeing the ring on River's hand. "It belongs to my family. It is sort of an heirloom."

River took a deep breath, nervously biting her lip. She unlocked the door chain and invited them in. Charlotte and Charles were extremely tall, both blonde with pale skin. River wondered if they were brother and sister. She offered them a seat on her couch. Charlotte nosily scanned her home, making River feel uncomfortable.

"Nice place; it's very bohemian meets farm girl ... I guess," Charlotte said, shrugging her shoulders and sounding a tad disapproving.

River smiled faintly. Considering Charlotte looked to be quite wealthy, she figured that wasn't a compliment. Charlotte kept a black Prada bag tucked into her side. Together, with the heels, probably cost her more than River's monthly mortgage payment.

"How did you know I had the ring?" River asked.

"First of all," Charlotte began. "Let me assure you that you are not in any trouble, so long as we get this ring back."

Charlotte marveled River's ring. It was beginning to creep River out. She could hear her cell buzzing nonstop in her bedroom.

"I'm sorry," Charlotte politely inquired. "Do you need to get that?"

"Well, maybe I ... um ... let me just grab my cell and put some fresh clothes on really quick. I had a rough night."

"Okay, dear. We will wait."

"Excuse me," River said.

She ran up the stairs, two at a time, threw on a ragged pair of jeans and the first clean tank top within reach. She quickly grabbed her cell and messaged Erik.

She wrote: "Some people are here about my ring, Erik. They said it was stolen from them."

After hitting send and silencing the cell, River shoved the phone in her back pocket and ran back down the stairs, ignoring Charlotte's scrutinizing expression at the sight of her ripped jeans.

"Charlotte, can I see the paper again please? The print of the ring?" River asked politely.

Charlotte handed the paper to Charles, who then handed the paper to River.

"Yes. This looks like my ring."

"THIS is most definitely not your ring. This is an artifact that belongs to me and my family," Charlotte stated, sternly.

River looked more intently at the print.

"Wait a minute! The ring in your photo has a different color gemstone than the ring I am wearing."

Charlotte became discernably irritated.

"That's quite alright because the gemstone could have been replaced over the years. It's still our ring," she noted.

"How do I know for sure it's *your* ring?" River challenged.

Charlotte started to sweat, becoming even more pale than she already was.

"Are you okay?" River asked with genuine concern.

"Look … I do not want this to get out of hand. However, I do, obviously, need to get more to the point. I want *my* ring back. It does not belong to you, and I will not leave this house until I get it," Charlotte broached.

Charles stood up slowly, crossing his arms in an almost threatening manner. River suddenly felt uncomfortable, aware the situation could quickly become dangerous.

"I actually don't have a problem giving you the ring. I do, however, have a problem getting it off my finger."

River held her breath, watching Charles very closely.

"Let me get a closer look," Charlotte said, moving toward River.

River noticed Charlotte's gait was slightly odd. She figured it was because she was so tall and gangly. Charlotte's hands were ice cold to the touch, and River responded by pulling her hand back slightly.

"You have beautiful, tiny fingers, like a child's hand," Charlotte complimented.

She caressed River's fingers in a strange manner while looking even more closely at the ring. River could have sworn she heard a hissing noise coming from Charlotte's throat. In response, she tried pulling her hand away, but it was caught in the web of Charlotte's long fingers.

Just then, the front door opened in a fury. Erik appeared out of nowhere with anger pouring from his eyes.

"GET YOUR VILE HANDS OFF HER!" he ordered.

Charlotte removed her hands immediately.

"River get away from her," he said. "Get beside me!"

Charlotte grabbed River's arm, showing off her jagged, razor-like teeth. River shrieked. Charles clamped down on River's other arm, eyeballing Erik.

"I WANT THE RING!" Charlotte hissed, viciously.

Erik grabbed hold of Charlotte's throat, sending a surge of energy through her nervous system—electrocuting her.

"Pleiadian monster!" Charlotte choked.

Charles went for Erik's throat but hesitated when Erik tightened his grip on Charlotte's neck, forcing Charles to back away.

"Why do you want the ring?" Erik asked, angrily.

"It belongs to us. In the wrong hands, it could be dangerous to our existence on this planet," Charlotte said through strangled breath.

"How did you know it was here?" Erik asked.

"She's been signaling us," Charles interjected. "The ring gives off distress signals with location tracking. We thought it was one of our own."

Just then a large, roaring engine pulled into the driveway. Within seconds, Alex was standing at the door.

"Okay. What's going on here?" Alex asked, cautiously advancing.

Charlotte released River's arm, in hopes Erik would let her go. His grip was so tight around her neck, Charlotte's feet were not touching the ground. Erik was relieved that she had released River, but he did not let Charlotte go.

Incensed, Charles reached into his suit pocket. Erik could see with his bionic eye what he was reaching for.

"Don't even think about it, buddy. I can kill her, and I will without a second thought," Erik warned.

He wrenched Charlotte's neck, knocking her Chanel sunglasses off her head and onto the floor, revealing her red, fiery eyes. River screamed.

"No one has to get hurt," Charles said. "We just want the ring."

"I can't take the ring off my finger," River cried, breathlessly.

"THEN … WE CUT OFF YOUR FINGER!" Charlotte hissed.

Alex moved toward River, tucking her into his side.

"THEN I WILL BE FORCED TO KILL YOU BOTH," Erik said through clenched teeth, matching Charlotte's might.

River cringed, as Charlotte flickered her red eyes at her.

"No one touches her," Alex said, putting himself between River and harm's way.

Erik's body began to vibrate, and Alex knew what that meant. He was losing control of his power.

"Is this real?" River whispered.

"Yes." Alex affirmed.

"Who gave you this ring?" Charles asked, looking at River.

"Kraylon," River replied.

Charlotte's emotions erupted.

"KRAYLON! THAT TRAITOR!" she shouted, then suddenly backing down when she realized Kraylon could be nearby.

"Where is Kraylon?" Charles asked.

"I don't know. He shows up unannounced. He told me the ring was to protect me," River said, turning to Erik. "This feels like it could be a dream."

Erik and Alex both shook their heads.

"Protect you?! That's absurd!" Charlotte hissed. "By giving it to you, he put you in more danger. YOU ARE NOT ONE OF US!"

"No," Alex replied with a malicious grin. "But she is one of us, and I do believe our people created this ring. It was a gift that was specifically given to her. It would be *very* impolite to take it away."

Charlotte looked to Charles.

"Kraylon has gotten out of control. He's gone too far," she said.

Jerking herself out from Erik's loosening hold, Charlotte turned to River and crept slowly toward her, and hissed, "Who exactly are you anyway? What are you? Why would Kraylon do anything for you?"

River wasn't sure how to answer. She could see herself trembling inside the fiery reflection of Charlotte's red eyes.

"I don't know. I thought it was a dream at first, but he came to me a second time. I still wasn't sure, but I think his coming created new trees in my backyard."

"Why would he plant trees in your backyard?" Alex asked.

River shrugged and said, "He sort of has these tree-branch-like limbs that are connected to him, so I thought he was responsible."

"HE IS A GHOUL!" Charlotte hissed.

"Kraylon has been stuck on this planet for hundreds of years. He's no longer just Anunnaki. He's become something more fierce and powerful than us."

"I will give you this ring, just as soon as we can get it off her finger. However, you need to leave her alone until then," Erik bargained.

"Who is this girl to you, and why are you protecting her?" Charlotte asked, dismissing Erik's demand.

"What is she talking about?" River asked.

"I've gone rogue. I needed a break. She is just someone I met along the way."

It suddenly occurred to River that Erik must be playing it off because of his top-secret government job from the past.

"I will allow you to take the ring off her finger, but there will be a time limit. This is not because I am afraid of you," Charlotte uttered. "I just do not want to see Kraylon again. He is a monster."

River was surprised at Charlotte's remark, considering it was she who appeared to be the *real* monster.

"Why he wants you, I will never know. Humans can't cross through upper dimensions, not like we can," Charlotte continued, glaring at River.

"I see," Charlotte whispered. "An Arizona starseed. So that's what we have here? I suppose a starseed can cross over, but then what? Where would she go? How will she carry on without her previous memories? Kraylon uses no caution with her, she could easily end up lost. You would never see her again. I guess since you just met her in passing, it would mean nothing to lose her."

River was officially confused. She wasn't sure if this was CIA drama or something deeper.

"Look, Charlotte … you will get your ring, so just leave," Alex said, staring her down.

"Let's have a word, Charlotte," Erik exhaled, intensely.

"Okay. Let's take it up in my Benz," Charlotte agreed, motioning for help from Charles.

"Quickly, Charles! Help me down these stairs. The air is dry and stifling."

Alex followed Erik out to the Mercedes, as River watched from the door. She rifled through a drawer and took out a tablet full of paper, along with a pen. She wrote down some of the information she heard in this crazy conversation or bad dream—whichever it was. She noted words, such as Anunnaki.

Twenty minutes passed, and Erik finally walked back into the house without his brother.

"Okay, River," he said. "Let's talk."

"Where's Alex?"

"I figured you and I could get through this little Q and A together," Erik smiled, totally smitten.

"I get it," River sighed. "You were in a government job, the CIA perhaps, and somehow I got caught up in the middle of all this mess. This woman, Charlotte, must be a member of the opposite side of things. I'm guessing and … "

Erik stopped her, pressing his finger against River's soft lips.

"Shhh … just kiss me."

River closed her eyes and leaned in for a kiss—the sweetest kiss. Erik put his hand on the back of her neck and, once again, used his power to wipe her memory of what had just taken place. She fell fast asleep without so much as a whisper.

Alex returned, as Erik was placing River gently onto the couch.

"Are we ready?" Alex asked.

"Yes."

"Good. Let's get that damn ring off her finger," Alex replied, kneeling down beside River.

"Not so fast gentleman."

Erik and Alex turned to find Kraylon standing in the doorway. He was dressed quite dapper, despite being so pale and clammy. He wore a wide-brimmed, white fedora with a matching white suit and white dress shoes.

"Kraylon? Is that really you?" Alex asked, shocked by Kraylon's appearance. "What happened to you?"

Kraylon scowled and said, "The ring stays on her finger, or she will die."

"She won't die, Kraylon. We both know you are using this ring to link yourself to her," Alex said, standing.

"Yes. Perhaps that is true, but as you can see. The planet is wonderfully on the verge of its routine cycle of shift. What if. Your beloved starseed doesn't pull through? What if she isn't carried home properly?" Kraylon posed.

"That's why I'm here, Kraylon. Your help isn't needed. In fact, you are just drawing unneeded attention to her!" Erik exclaimed.

"And you aren't?" Kraylon snapped back. "Seems to me some fireworks have been sparking from your end as well."

"Seriously, Kraylon. What happened to you?" Alex asked. "What is the green stuff growing around your wrists and neck? Is that algae?"

"I'm very connected to Earth now, and to keep my power, I draw from the planet in exchange for its appreciation and protection."

"It's creepy," Alex said, clearing his throat.

"I have helped Amariah many times during her stay here, and you two should acknowledge that. Sometimes from afar, but not this time. She needs me," Kraylon protested.

"You still haven't gotten over her. You tried marrying her as a Viking in one of her lifetimes. You weren't good for her then, and you aren't good for her now," Erik said.

"Regardless of how you feel about it, I truly loved Amariah … River. And I know if she remembered me, she would still love me, too."

Erik pulled a jewelry cutting saw from his pocket. Turning it on, he looked over at Alex and whispered, "Hold her hand up for me, Alex."

"STOP!" Kraylon shouted, using his power to render the tool useless. "I can help you protect River, and with the power of this ring, I can make sure she is pulled directly into any dimension at the appropriate time."

"The Anunnaki want the ring back, Kraylon," Alex chimed in.

"Nonsense. They know I gave her the ring. I highly doubt they are willing to fight me for it."

"I can't take that chance, Kraylon," Erik said.

"Take the damn ring off her finger, Kraylon!" Alex demanded.

"No."

"Even if I could arrange for your return to Planet Erra?" Alex asked.

Kraylon's eyes filled with wanderlust. As he reflected on the planet, he whispered, "Aww ... I long to return to Erra—such a beautiful place. But I was banned."

"We could get you back there, if you'll remove this ring," Alex insisted.

"Alexander, you were always my favorite Pleiadian," Kraylon crooned.

Erik rolled his eyes.

"Fine. We have a deal," Kraylon continued. "You talk with your parents, the Elder Counsel and, if you can get me back to Erra, I will release River from the ring."

Alex nodded in agreement, "Sure. It won't be a problem."

Kraylon gazed at River for a long, loving (albeit creepy) moment before he released the ring from River's finger. Using his power, he floated the ring through the air, slipping it onto his pinkie finger.

"You have thirty days to get permission for my return to Erra or the ring goes back on River's finger."

Kraylon turned, fell through the door and vanished in dramatic fashion.

"What was that?" Alex asked. "And Charlotte and Charles? They couldn't come up with better names than those?"

Erik smacked Alex upside the back of his head and said, "Why did you tell him he could return to Erra? There's no way they will let him return."

"No. Of course not," Alex agreed. "He's a criminal, and I'm not exactly sure what else he is with all that green shit all over him, but I got the ring off, didn't I?"

CHAPTER FIFTY-ONE
Broken

Life, particularly the last week, had been a blur. River was beginning to think that because she kept falling asleep abruptly and waking up with zero memories of the day's events, she had some sort of condition—Narcolepsy or some other health issue. It was starting to worry her, and so she made an appointment with a doctor. After a thorough checkup and labs drawn, she was given a clean bill of health. Her doctor simply advised, "You need more water and rest."

The most surprising issue was losing her ring. While River was happy to have it off her finger, she wasn't happy about losing such a treasure. She laid awake at night wondering what could have happened to it. So much for the much-needed rest, especially with her busy schedule—Kenpo karate, dance class, work, and Alex constantly dropping by with Sai, his stoner friend.

The company prompted River to prepare bigger meals in the evening because she knew they would randomly show up. Sai was very laid back, and a little on the strung-out side, but she could tell he was extremely intelligent. River was intuitively gifted, especially when it came to picking up on someone's personality. Sai seemed harmless, but she knew he was hiding something, not just from her but from the world. She knew better than to say anything, so she kept her intuitions to herself.

Erik, on the other hand, did not like Sai coming around with Alex. He made sure to end his lessons early enough every day, so to be at River's house by the time Alex and Sai showed up. River ignored Erik's concerns because Sai was knowledgeable on the planet's current crisis. Like her, he was aware of the number of natural disasters adding up. For River, that constituted stimulating conversation.

River was an activist, fueled with a passion that no one could contain. The trees in her back yard continued growing vigorously through the weeks, and soon they were taller than Erik. Every day she would look out her kitchen window in simple pleasure, smiling and praising them. River loved trees. Because he loved her, and he loved to see her smile, Erik hooked up another water hose to a sprinkler, so they would thrive in the unbearable heat of the Arizona desert.

It was a Tuesday afternoon. A blissful breeze blew in through the windows from the west. Inspired, River lugged her sewing machine out of the closet and put to good use some heavy-duty cream linen fabric she had been saving for the right project and made some curtains. Listening to Indian flutes on Pandora, she pushed her little sewing machine beyond its limits. It began to make a clanging sound each time the needle pierced through the fabric.

"Oh no," she whispered.

Trying to dismantle the machine, so to fix the problem only overwhelmed her, especially since she couldn't put it back together again. Before she knew it, her hair was disheveled, and she had black grease all over her fingertips. And, of course, the tickle on her nose left a streak of grease across her face. Coty watched her from outside the kitchen window.

She had never looked more beautiful, which caused him great anxiety.

He almost had her in the bar the other night. It made him hard just thinking about it. She was obviously too drunk to notice he was there. What Coty needed, more than anything, was to tell her how much he still loved her and that he wanted her to come back home to Ohio. Ohio was her home, not Arizona. River needed to be reasoned with. She wasn't thinking straight, nor was she making smart decisions. Coty considered it his duty to take control of the situation and the woman he loved more than anything.

Coty flinched at the unexpected sound of a car pulling into the driveway. He ran beyond the bushes, taking the long way back to his car, which was parked along a dirt path near the highway. Completely unaware of his surroundings, Coty narrowly escaped stepping on a small, Western diamondback rattlesnake. He shrieked at the sight of it, kicking it into the air with his boot. Jumping into his car, he sped off down the road.

Meanwhile, Erik and Violet helped Joshua out of the truck. They led him towards River's porch when all of a sudden Violet stopped. Inhaling deep whiffs of the surrounding air, she asked, "Do you smell that?"

Joshua shook his head and replied, "I can't smell anything right now. I can barely inhale with my ribs hurting the way they do."

"What is it?" Erik asked.

"It's him," Violet said.

"Him who?"

"River's stalker. He's been here," Violet said, helping Joshua onto the porch.

Erik instantly let go of Joshua and started scanning the property. There wasn't a trace of the stalker, but Erik did not yield. Violet knocked on River's door and waited. Moments later, River peered through the door looking a little ruffled, giving Erik and Violet pause.

"Are you ..." Violet began.

"Don't ask," River laughed, wiping grease from her hands with a kitchen towel. "So good to see you, Violet! I've missed you. Karate isn't the same without you there."

River and Violet helped Joshua to the couch. He winced as he leaned back into the cushions. Erik stayed outside, checking things out.

"How are you, Joshua?" River asked.

"I'm okay. I just can't do anything too fast, like burp, cough, and breathe. But other than that ..." Joshua replied, sarcastically.

River ambled into the kitchen and began rifling through her herbal supplements and vitamin supply. Yanking a bottle of pills from her cabinet, she returned to her guests.

"It's a potent mineral supplement that will heal your bones up quickly," River said, handing him the bottle.

"Thank you," Joshua whispered, favoring his sore ribs.

"What did the doctor tell you?" River asked.

"Nothing really. There's not much he can do about the broken ribs. I just need to take it easy."

"I'm just glad you're alive," Violet interjected.

"Yeah. You've said that a million times," Joshua grumbled.

Violet rolled her eyes—exasperated. Feeling angry, she stood up with tears in her eyes and stormed out of the house.

"What's going on with her?" Erik asked, walking inside.

"She's getting on my nerves, controlling my every move."

"She loves you, Joshua," Erik said, stating the obvious.

"She's like a broken record, man! I need a break," Joshua said.

"Are you saying you wouldn't be acting the same way if it were her who got hurt?" River asked.

"I suppose. River can you just keep her busy for an hour? I just want to close my eyes without her voice in my head." Joshua pleaded.

"Yeah, sure," River replied, standing up.

As she went to find Violet, Erik stopped her.

"You have black streaks on your face," he said, smiling.

"Oh!" River clucked. "My sewing machine is acting up again."

She pointed to the machine parts scattered about the kitchen table

"I'll take a look at it."

Erik gave River a gentle hug and watched her walk outside onto the back porch.

River found Violet sitting at the bottom of the back-stoop steps. She looked out into the desert sky. The sun had begun its decent. She inhaled a deep breath and asked, "Violet, what do you think of all these trees cropping up?"

"Amazing."

Violet barely finished speaking when she began to sob. River rushed to her side and gave her a hug.

"Calm down," she whispered. "It's going to be okay, Violet."

"I'm exhausted! I just want him to get better and pay attention to what I and the doctors are saying," Violet said, choking back tears.

"He almost lost his life, but he didn't," River reassured. "He's so lucky to have you by his side."

Violet took a long, calming breath, wiping tears from her eyes. She was comforted by River's warm energy and light. She could feel its intensity.

"Joshua and I have been together since we were very young. The thought of him being taken away … terrifies me."

"I get it. Just allow yourself to feel. It's okay."

Violet trembled, as River touched her arm. She couldn't help but notice that River was not the same. Erik stepped out the back door and asked, "Is everything okay?"

"Yes," River replied. "Just girl talk."

"I need to speak to Violet when you are done," Erik requested.

Violet wiped her eyes with her sleeve, responding coolly, "Okay. Now is fine."

River got the hint when both Violet and Erik gave her the "this is just between us" look.

"Alright ... I will see if Joshua needs anything," River said, walking back into the house.

Erik looked behind him, waiting for the door to close.

"I know you are worried about Joshua, but do you think you can help me keep a lookout for this stalker tonight?" Erik asked.

"Yeah," Violet replied, nodding. "I can help you, but tonight isn't good. Joshua needs me. He can barely get out of bed. Erik, he's not healing well. Being here on this planet is not to his advantage. It has me worried."

Joshua staggered out of the house, holding onto his side.

"I can do it."

"No Joshua!" Violet exclaimed.

"It's no big deal. It's just watching out for the guy, Violet. Although, I'm still not able to manifest into Coyote. I've tried, hoping it could speed up my healing."

"Okay. Look ... never mind. I will just stay with her as much as I can over the next couple of days and see if I can catch this weirdo myself. I am sorry for asking. I know it's rough for both of you right now."

Annoyed, Joshua shook his head and hobbled back into the

house.

"Sorry Violet," Erik whispered.

"I love River as much as you do, Erik. She's always been there for us. It's just not a good time—not yet. And with Joshua unable to transition into a Coyote … I am concerned," Violet said, feeling vulnerable.

Suddenly Joshua roared in pain. Violet rushed inside to be by his side. She cried, "Are you ok?"

"Yes," He winced.

"Where does it hurt the most?" River asked.

"I'm okay. I am fine. Don't worry."

"I have your pain medication in my purse," Violet said, unzipping her purse.

"STOP VIOLET!" Joshua demanded.

Violet was stunned. Throwing her hands up in the air, she backed off and ventured off into the kitchen.

"She just wants to help you, Joshua," River said.

"I'm okay. I'm just frustrated because I can't transform my body, and I can't protect anyone right now." Joshua slipped, forgetting who he was talking to.

"What do you mean by transform? And who do you have to protect?" River asked. "I've seen Violet in action. The girl can handle herself pretty well, I'd say."

"Sorry," Joshua apologized, realizing his fumble. "I didn't mean any of that. It's the medication talking. I have definitely had enough."

"It's okay. You both need some rest. Why don't you two hang out here tonight. I have an extra bedroom. You can stay relax and watch movies together."

"Yes! Great idea!" Erik exclaimed.

From the kitchen, Violet gave Erik a funny look, followed by a long sigh in agreement. It was for the best.

"And don't you worry, Joshua," River added lightheartedly. "Violet and I are perfectly capable of protecting *you,* if anything were to happen."

Later that night Erik and River made their way upstairs. They climbed into bed together and made love. Afterward, he protectively held her close as she fell asleep in his arms. He couldn't sleep. He was restless. The thought of River's stalker gnawed at him. Running his fingers through his hair, he knew he wouldn't sleep.

So, he gently rolled River over onto her side of the bed and threw back the covers. He moved toward the bedroom windows, scanning the property again and again. River stirred. She saw Erik standing near the window, the moonlight glowing on his masculine physique. She asked, "What's wrong? Is everything okay?"

"Nothing," he whispered. "I thought I heard something. Go back to sleep. Everything's okay."

"Alright."

River pulled the comforter up to her neck and dozed off. Erik walked downstairs wearing only a faded pair of work jeans. He quietly peeked in on Violet and Joshua. They were lying together on the full-size bed with oceans of space between them. Erik closed the door behind him and walked outside barefoot. He listened to the desert's night sounds.

Nothing seemed to settle the sour feeling he had in his gut, knowing this guy was hanging around and watching her every move. Erik needed to catch this man—fast! Walking around the outside of the house, he scanned more of the property. There was nothing out of the ordinary. Erik sat on the front porch. Old memories took hold of him, and it seemed to be the only thing to quiet his mind.

The very first time he kissed her lips, they were on board his parents' ship, standing in the entrance to his room. He and Amariah spent lifetimes getting to know one another, taking turns existing as starseeds on Earth. It was tough, since neither one ever really knew who and what they were to each other (or how much they meant) during that time. It wasn't until they returned home from a human's death that their purpose (and love for one another) came into focus.

Then, of course, there was Alex. He would often get in the way, but Erik always ignored him. While Alex had a necessary and indispensable presence in Amariah's life, he persistently pursued her on a more personal level. He wanted her for himself.

Amariah was on Earth because she was so much more than an ordinary starseed. She was an evolutionist, and her presence, alone, had the power to change how millions of people thought and behaved. Amariah was a celebrity on Erik's planet, known throughout many galaxies, dimensions and other worlds.

He had been there for every assignment that Amariah had been deployed to, and it always sent his mind reeling, but this time was different. He felt in his heart that he *had* to be there for her go round, lest he take the chance of losing her to Earth's uncertainty and magnetosphere developments brought on by its approaching planetary routine that happens every 5,000 years or so.

Of course, it had to be Amariah that was deployed to Earth for this assignment, but Erik would not take the risk of losing her. There was, and would be, a chance she wouldn't make it out, at least not as the Amariah he knew and loved.

Headlights lit up the brush, as a car rounded slowly up the road. It snapped Erik right out his reminiscing. He knew it had to be him, the stalker. This put Erik on full alert. Before it reached River's place, the car came to a complete stop. Erik jumped to his feet and took off in a dead sprint toward the vehicle. The driver, surprised to see another man standing on River's property, punched the gas and sped away, narrowly missing Erik.

Erik chased after the car for a few minutes down the old road, but a cactus needle stuck deep into his bare foot and hindered his hunt. It was Coty in the car. He fumed, as he watched Erik from his rearview mirror. He was also a little terrified at how fast the man could run. It made him a little jealous.

Erik? What's wrong? Violet asked, while in her coyote form.

She sniffed around and conveyed with a slight sneeze, *It was him again. He came back. Boy! He never goes a day without tequila and cheap cologne.*

"Yes," Erik replied, catching his breath. "It was him. We need to catch him before he hurts River. Something tells me he is going to try."

Violet nodded, her shimmery coat glistening under the moonlight. She knew Erik was right. Something had to be done and without police involvement. They would only let him out, and that wasn't good enough. The stalker could never be a threat to River again. Violet and Erik's eyes met. Her concern compounded his. They both knew and understood what they had to do.

"If her eye is injured, injure his; if her tooth is knocked out, knock out his, and so on—hand for hand, foot for foot, burn for burn, wound for wound, lash for lash."
-Exodus 22:24

CHAPTER FIFTY-TWO
Jungle Cat

A voice called out, "River, River!" She tried responding, but she couldn't answer. It was as if she were voiceless. "Come with us," the voice begged. River tried opening her eyes to see who was calling out to her, but she couldn't. She couldn't see anything. Was she asleep? No. She couldn't be. It felt too real to be a dream.

"River, come with us."

There were more voices, each of them light with a silent echo, but River couldn't open her eyes to see who it was. There was only darkness.

"River ..." one of the voices sang out, elongating her name. Finally, she was able to answer, but not with her mouth. Her body was frozen, heavy with sleep paralysis. She couldn't move. It was only with her spirit that she was able to open her eyes and sit up. It was as if her spirit separated from her, leaving her physical body behind. River's spirit stood next to her sleeping body. That was when she realized she was a spirit body.

"River ..." the voice sang, stretching the vowels for all they were worth.

River was suddenly down the staircase and within an instant she was standing outside. Erik's muscular bronze body flexed and glistened in the moonlight. As she heard him talking, River drifted closer to him and saw that he was having a conversation with a coyote. River recognized the coyote. It was the same coyote that hung around her every so often. River bent over to pet the animal's fur, but her hands blew through it. She could not feel anything.

"Yes," Erik said to the coyote. "It was him. We need to catch him before he hurts River. Something tells me he is going to try."

River stepped back. She couldn't imagine what he was talking about. She asked, "Who will hurt me, Erik?"

Erik couldn't hear her. River stood in front of his face and shouted, "ERIK!"

Erik didn't even blink. She heard the voices calling for her again, and she followed them into the backyard. River looked up at the fast-growing trees, as they opened up and created a protective tunnel for her to walk through. Stepping into the tree tunnel and walking through, she was startled as it closed up behind her. The spirit of the forest moved her, and she realized these were never just regular trees. They were so much more than that.

When she realized she was in a jungle, she called out, "Kraylon? Are you here?"

A large rodent jumped onto her leg, ran up its length and traveled to her neck. River let out a horrifying scream.

"NO SCREAMING! HUSH!" a voice roared, demanding silence.

"Huh? Who are you?" River asked.

"I'm behind you."

A large tree reached out, grabbing her by the waist with its branch and snatching her off the ground. River tried to get out of its grip, but it was no use.

"Put me down!" River shouted.

In an instant, River was thrown to the ground. She landed in a mushy, marsh of wet moving grass. Regaining her bearings, she stood up and planted her feet. She noticed the mud caked to her legs. Wherever she was, it was no dream.

A low growl startled her from a large tropical bush across the way. River turned urgently and ran, but the trees closed up, blocking her path. The growls continued. It was unsettling, and it put her into a full-blown panic. There was no obvious way for her to escape. She must have been sent there to die.

A pair of glowing, green eyes emerged from the bushes, and out of the darkness came a large, black jaguar. It stealthily strutted toward her, and as it did, it spoke, "You have come, dear friend. I have waited a very long time to see you again."

River started to slowly back away, breathing heavily and feeling her heartrate pick up deep inside her chest. The jaguar unexpectedly turned into a beautiful woman who lit up the jungle with her green, goddess aura. She was tall with long, golden reddish-brown hair. Her dark skin was almost the same color of the jaguar's black fur. Her tiny, grass-green top was woven with rubies, sapphires and crystals. It was matched with a gold, tribal-cut bottom. A necklace hung just above her full bosom. It was made of watermelon tourmaline and tanzanite strung with gold. She was the most beautiful and exotic woman River had ever seen in her life.

"Where am I?" River asked.

"You are in the Amazon. You have slipped into another dimension. Close your eyes, listen and immerse yourself in my world," the woman said, her accent was thick and unplaceable.

River closed her eyes and tried to tune into this world. She could not only hear the roars of jungle cats, the chatter of monkeys, the chirps of birds and insects and a waterfall, but she could feel and suddenly smell them, too. Everything came to life as soon as she opened her eyes, the beauty of the rain forest started to move with excitement around. Nothing was still.

"Who are you?" River asked, afraid, but not as much as before.

"I am Tequita, and you know me. Well, you knew me very well. You will not remember me yet, but you will again. You and I share a very rich history together. We have helped each other in the past and throughout many of our lifetimes. One day I left you, ascending into something much more powerful. I now remain here in a dimension on the 'New Earth.' I take care of this new Earth and the old Earth. I have made it my purpose, and it oddly has fulfilled me."

Tequita purred, as she walked slowly around River touching her shoulders and hair.

"Why am I here?" River asked meekly.

"You are ready. It is the appointed time. You will help me ease Earth's transition, as it goes through its normal planetary cycle. Together, we will transform and wake up humanity and wildlife on the planet. You are always so raw and beautiful in any form. You harvest a very natural light from your soul, and it is transmitted through you to the world, but you probably don't remember that; do you? You always glow wildly, so much more than the others."

River wasn't following Tequita very well. She thought the conversation was a bit strange. She asked, "How can I help you?"

"You will know what to do when the time presents itself, but for now, you need to spiritually wake up to who you truly are. When you do, the Archon will be an opponent we will overcome," Tequita whispered, grabbing River's hand and pulling her in closer.

She placed River's hand over her heart. A light green mega aura emanated, and River gasped.

"Remember me," Tequita said, her exotic voice echoing.

River was swept into the recesses of her mind. Two Egyptian women were running during a war. They were helping each other get away from something terrible. When safely hidden, they both hugged one another, speaking in an ancient dialect.

Tequita let go of River's hand, and River was quickly taken out of that lost memory. She said to River, "That was you and me. At the time, they killed our husbands and our children. Even though we were on a mission and not exactly human, it still hurts, and that haunting memory still has the ability to destroy our light while we are here. That was lifetimes ago, but one of the most painful human experiences I ever had as a starseed. We had many missions together on this planet, River."

Tequita was obviously disturbed by what they had seen together. Tequita held River's hand and walked her to the edge of a tropical waterfall.

"I have given you a message today and have shown you a great secret. Now you must be released back to your current world," Tequita said, squeezing River's hand lovingly. "Until next time my friend."

"But how do I get back?" River asked.

"Don't be afraid," Tequita whispered, before pushing her, almost savagely, from the edge of the large waterfall.

"NOOOOO!" River screamed, as she fell over the roaring waterfall toward the pool of crystal-clear rushing water. Plunging into the cool, deep pool, she felt herself falling deeper, as the current pulled her under. River pulled herself out of the water and struggled to move her wet body onto dry land. She was no longer in the Amazon jungle, but in her own back yard, staring at the back porch of her home in the Arizona desert.

Climbing the steps back to her bedroom, she watched herself sleep.

Erik held her physical body tightly to his. After a moment, River's spirit funneled through a filtered light back into her flesh. Finally, she was able to open her eyes and sit up. With the memory of all that had just transpired, she shot out of bed and ran out to her growing forest of trees. She stood staring at them, as the sun started to set. She realized there was no Amazon Forest, just desert trees. River couldn't tell if what she saw was real or just a dream. It felt so real. Erik woke up and reached for River, but she wasn't there. He climbed out of bed and searched for her. He found her barely clothed in her backyard, staring out at her trees.

"What's going on?" he asked, putting his arm around her.

"I have to tell you something," River replied.

CHAPTER FIFTY-THREE
Astral Projection

Later that day, Erik sat next to River on the bed, listening intently to every detail about her experience the night before. He knew of Tequita. She was a Pleiadian legend. While he had never met her personally, he knew River's experience must have been real.

"Do you think I'm crazy?" River whispered.

"No. You aren't crazy."

Erik sat upright, as River put on some clothes.

"Did Tequita say anything else?" he inquired.

"Something about fighting the Archon."

Erik's stomach and chest tightened.

"Have you ever heard of that, Erik? The Archon?"

Just then, there came a quiet knock on the bedroom door. River quickly pulled her shirt over her head and invited Violet in.

"Joshua and I are leaving. There's an event at the reservation, and Joshua doesn't want to miss it," Violet said, looking young and beautiful, albeit tired. "Okay. Give me a hug."

In the middle of a warm hug, River asked, "Have you ever heard of the word Archon, Violet?"

Shrugging, Violet shot a surprised look over at Erik.

"No. Never heard of it," she replied.

"Well, I better be going! I will see you both later."

And with that, Violet promptly left the room.

River Googled the word Archon on her phone. Unsatisfied with the ambiguous results, she sighed, "It could just mean a ruler. Not much of a definition."

"That could be it," Erik said, uncomfortable with the subject.

"What's wrong, Erik?"

"I have a lot on my mind," he replied. "I have some horse shows coming up, and it's just very competitive for my students."

"Oh, horse shows."

"Yeah," he sighed. "Competitions and kids, it's grueling. I need to use my free time today to pull some of that together."

"I understand, but I am curious about one thing though," River inquired, raising an eyebrow.

"What's that?" Erik asked.

"What do you think about me leaving my body?"

Erik reached for his boots and forcefully shoved his feet in.

"I think you had an experience, an OBE. It's not uncommon to have an out of body, astral-projection type of thing."

"Okay," River shrugged. "I can't wait to tell Alex and Sai. They would be *very* interested to hear about it."

"Or, maybe, you could keep it a secret for now ... please," Erik advocated.

"Not really feeling that," River smirked.

"Why not?"

"I want more feedback, and I get the feeling you can't handle this subject ... for whatever reason. They can."

"That's not it, River." Erik replied, exasperated.

"Then what is it?"

"I am just worried about you is all," Erik said, tucking a long, loose curl behind her ear.

"So, you do think I'm crazy?"

"No, not at all. You are beautiful, intelligent and of sound mind."

"Then, why don't you want me to tell them?"

"Never mind. You are right. Tell them," Erik said, grabbing her tiny frame and passionately kissing her on the lips. It was a sweet mixture of surrender and "I'll see you later." With that, he hurried out the door.

Violet and Joshua visited a friend's house on the reservation. It was a chance to relax, but mostly Joshua was looking forward to smoking weed for his pain.

"I've tried CBD oil, but it doesn't help as much as I thought it would. The pain is terrible," Joshua said in between drags.

"You could take the pain pills the doctor prescribed," Violet said.

Ashton Pipkins, a muscular Navajo native chimed in, "No. He shouldn't take pain pills or any of that crap. That's how my sister got hooked on pills then heroine. It killed her."

"He's in a lot of pain though." Violet remarked.

Everyone took a hit from the small glass pipe.

"You both are younger than me. Trust me when I tell you, prescription drugs are poisonous, and they are always approved with barely enough testing. We are the fucking lab rats!" Ashton exclaimed.

"Yeah," Joshua interjected. "Look at all the lawsuit commercials on television. You see them all the time man."

In his best lawyer-like voice, Joshua added, "If you or a loved one took this drug and suffered from acute paranoia, stomach bleeding, rectal bleeding, head trauma, suicidal thoughts or you just plain almost fucking died, call this lawsuit company at 1-800-BUL-SHIT!"

Joshua leaned back, smiling, as if entertained by his own humor. Ashton looked at him through glossy, (stoned!) eyes, and after the ten seconds it took him to register Joshua's joke, started to laugh hysterically.

"I just got that shit, man! That's crazy and so true," Ashton said.

"Nah, man! That shit ain't funny. It's really messed up when you think about it," Joshua said.

"Yeah. That's deep." Ashton nodded.

Violet rolled her eyes, making herself useful and cleaning up Ashton's place. Picking up pizza boxes, beer bottles, and emptying the trash gave her some peace of mind. She only stopped long enough to glance over at Joshua who had fallen asleep on the couch. Moving the hair out of her eyes, she secretly admired his physique for a long, hungry moment. Exhaling, she went back to cleaning Ashton's dirty home.

CHAPTER FIFTY-FOUR

The Devil

Coty packed supplies, including rope, duct tape, scissors, and a concoction made up of drugs and alcohol to do the trick. He even packed a knife, wondering if, perhaps, that was a bit too much. He picked the knife out of his bag and looked at the craftmanship on the handle. If nothing else, it will scare her. He wouldn't use it for anything more than that.

There was a loud knock at the door. Coty hurriedly hid the knife in the bag. He was still a felon, and he wasn't supposed to carry a knife that big, according to his parole officer.

"Yes?" he asked, looking through a small crack in the door.

There was a small Mexican housekeeper standing before him. With a heavy accent, she asked, "Towels?"

"No thanks! And no more interruptions tonight. You hear me?"

The woman moved her cart in a hurry down the hotel hallway. Shutting the door, Coty grabbed his bag, poured some tequila down his parched throat and headed out for a little more to drink.

Impatiently, River waited for Alex and Sai to arrive, but it was getting late. Surfing hundreds of television channels over and over again wasn't satisfying her, so she texted Alex.

River

"What's going on? Are you coming or should I go to bed?"

River waited. Seven minutes passed before he finally answered.

Alex

"I will be a little late. I'm helping Erik with a wounded horse."

River

"Oh no! Tell him I'm sorry. Do you need any help?"

Alex

"No. We have it handled."

Trying to get comfortable, River laid back on the couch. She tried not to fall asleep, but her eyes grew heavy and soon the remote control slipped from her hand and fell to the floor.

Alex and Sai helped get the wounded horse onto the trailer, so that Erik could get his favorite horse to a 24-hour veterinarian in Maricopa County.

"I'm sure it's more than arthritis, but I don't really know. He just collapsed out of nowhere. When I got him up, he couldn't stand for long periods today," Erik explained. "So, listen … while I have both of you here, I wanted to tell you what happened to River last night."

Erik explained, in full detail, the out-of-body experience River had with Tequita. Alex waited for Erik to finish, and after a moment of silence, he said, "I thought Tequita was just a tall tale they used to tell us as kids. No one could ever confirm or deny whether she was an actual Pleiadian warrior."

"No," Erik replied. "She's real. River met her in a few of her human lives on Earth, although she never talked too much about her."

"So, what now?" Alex asked.

"What else did Tequita say about the Archon?" Sai asked, concerned.

"Only that she would help River in a fight," Erik added. "Why?"

"Just thought she might have revealed a timeline for this supposed fight is all," Sai said.

"No. I'm sure that will be a big surprise, like everything else in this crazy universe we were sworn into." Alex told Sai.

"Don't tell River I mentioned any of this to you. I know you are both going over there, so act like you don't know anything about it. And, Alex, don't give out too much information about us," Erik warned.

"I won't. Chill out, brother! I know I can't do that," Alex replied.

"You tried to sleep with her though."

"What does that have to do with anything?" Alex asked, annoyed. "I told you it was just because I knew you were somewhere lurking around. It was to pull you out of the dark."

Sai shook his head and said, "Come on! Let's go."

"Would you stop bringing that up, please?" Alex pled.

"Don't try it again!"

Coty was feeling pretty damn good after a few shots of bourbon. He had a few women hitting on him, but all he could think about was River. He was prepared to get her back and take her home to Ohio, even if that meant taking her by force. It didn't matter to him whether or not she wanted to go. Coty knew that once she saw him, she would fall in love with him again and everything he had ever done to her would be water under the bridge.

Feeling confident, he decided to head straight to River's place, hoping no one would be there to screw up his plan. He turned on some R&B tunes from the 90's, put his ear buds in and relaxed on the ride. Soon, he found himself masturbating at the thought of River and the explosive fairytale he had conjured up in his mind. He purposely tossed in a waitress he met the other night. The three of them were in bed together, and he was ready to do some nasty forbidden things to them.

When he finished, Coty wiped his hands on a dirty shirt he had balled up in the backseat. He swallowed some warm tequila from a bottle on the floor and took off around the bend. It was time. This was it—now or never. He was convinced of it, as he spit a loogie out the window.

Parking off the road, under some large oleander bushes, he picked up his duffle bag of supplies and made his move. Creeping slowly through sage brush and across an open desert field, Coty watched for night predators, ducking out of sight for passing cars.

Once he reached River's back porch, he adjusted his jeans, brushed back his hair and reached his fist out to knock on the back door. Suddenly, he heard a car pull slowly into her driveway.

Two car doors slammed shut, and Coty took two hard steps backwards into the guise of night. He heard a loud knock at River's front door.

"Shit!" Coty growled, deciding to wait it out.

"River! Come on, girl," Alex barked, as he rapped at her front door. "We're here. Come on! It's chilly out."

River stirred awake, quickly opening the door for Alex and Sai. Coty listened in from a nearby window. He had to stifle a chuckle, as she talked about an out-of-body experience and some other stuff that made him scoff. River was always a bit different. She was filled with wacky notions that he often had to snap her out of and put her in her place.

"It was really crazy!" River said, excitedly. "I knew you two would appreciate it ... and get it."

"Well, naturally, I believe that something really cool happened to you," Sai said. "Did Tequita tell you anything else about the Archon?"

"Nothing really, only that she would help me fight them. I don't even know what that means or what an Archon is. Why would I have to worry about something like that? Do you know what it is Sai?"

"It's like the Devil and his army," Sai replied.

Alex nudged Said roughly, but Sai ignored him.

"The Devil?" River asked.

"Pretty much sums it up," Sai said. "Ancient rulers of this world or so they believe. Fighting them has gone on as long as Earth has been around. You have a very strong and energetic light, River. You attract trouble. They don't like you."

"That is what Tequita said! She talked about my light," River replied in amazement.

Eavesdropping outside, Coty whispered, "Fucking nut jobs!"

"Do you really believe in the Archon?" River asked.

"Most definitely," Sai replied. "It's real!"

Alex sighed heavily, as he leaned up against the wall.

"We should go. I have to work in the morning," Alex interrupted, super irritated with Sai.

He knew River needed to know the truth, but the timing wasn't right. The less she knew, the better. Otherwise, Erik would be on his ass. Starseeds must wake up to their call naturally and organically or not at all. This could be disruptive to the sequence of everything.

"Yeah … okay. Let's get moving then," Sai said, standing, stretching and yawning obnoxiously.

"I'm glad you stopped by. Do you know if Erik will?" River asked.

"Not sure. He's taking a horse to the vet right now," Alex replied.

"I will send him a text."

"You do that," Alex said, grabbing River and hugging her warmly. "Now give me a hug, girl."

Alex's muscular arms flexed around her body. River wondered why she never noticed how strong his arms were before.

Sai walked out the front door, making his way around to the backyard. He felt a presence, and he smelled something peculiar.

Walking through the garden and around the bushes, Sai thought he smelled cologne. The wind was picking up speed. A dust storm was nearing. Coty laid low as Sai walked past. Although he was lit, he did his best not to make the slightest sound.

"Sai," Alex called out, impatiently. "What are you doing? Come on. The dust storms coming. Let's hit the road."

Alex jumped in his muscle car and started the engine. Sai paused for a moment, turning to scan behind him before jumping into the passenger seat. Sai wasn't comfortable leaving, but he complied.

CHAPTER FIFTY-FIVE
Showdown

River locked the door behind the boys and texted Erik goodnight, as she lay back on the couch. A rattle at the back door startled her. She quickly turned down the volume of the television, her cell gripped tightly in her hand. She cautiously peeked out the back kitchen window. Not seeing anything outside, she brushed it off and headed back toward the couch.

Suddenly, there was a loud knock at the back door. River's heart leapt. She went to the front of the house to see if there was a car parked in the driveway—nothing. Feeling afraid, she dialed Erik.

"Hey baby," he answered.

"Erik, I'm scared." River whispered.

"Why?"

Erik was hoping Alex and Sai hadn't opened their big mouths about the Archon.

"I keep hearing knocking at the back door."

Erik's stomach tightened. He was almost back in Pinal County, but not quite to Apache Junction. He had just dropped the horse off at the vet and was no less than forty minutes away from her house.

"River, I want you to make sure all your windows and doors are locked up tight. Make sure the alarm system is on, too. If you see anyone in the camera connected to the alarm or someone knocks again, call 911.

Do what I say … okay?"

"Yes."

"Keep your phone in your hand. Do not open your door for anyone you don't know. I am coming as fast as I can."

Erik zoomed around cars on the freeway, pushing 85 mph.

"Stay on the phone with me." River begged.

"I will, baby."

"Tell me about the horse."

Alex and Sai were in town when Alex couldn't bite his tongue any longer. He turned to him and said, "Really, dude? You talked to her about Archon? Erik's going to get all over me for that."

"She needs to know."

Sai was still uneasy about leaving River at home alone, knowing something or someone was lurking around.

"Could River be dating anyone else?" Sai asked.

"No way! She's exclusive to Erik, for now anyways," Alex replied.

"I smelled something strange in her yard. It was different."

"What?! Tonight?"

"Yes. I think they were out back before we got there. Could still be there," Sai continued.

"Why in the hell would you wait until now to tell me this?!"

"I need you to take me home first," Sai said.

"Huh?"

"Don't worry! She will be fine. Take me home for a minute, and we will drive back to check on her."

Alex stepped on the gas, attempting to call River.

No answer.

He tried calling Erik. It went straight to voice mail.

"Right here! My house!" Sai shouted.

Alex executed a harsh gangster turn into the driveway.

"Hurry up!" Alex demanded.

Sai ran inside.

River felt more at ease with Erik on the phone. She turned on the stovetop to heat up some water for chamomile tea. Sitting to the kitchen table, she waited for the water to boil. The dust storm forced trees to bend and debris to hit the house. River thought it was probably what she heard at the back door. Perhaps a branch was being tossed around in the wind.

Erik told her a joke and she laughed lightly, even though it wasn't very funny. In the midst of her laughter, the back door was violently kicked in, and the home security system failed to alert. A scream ripped through River's throat, causing Erik to jump in his seat and nearly swerve off the road.

There he was. It was Coty, standing in the doorway wearing a weathered sweatshirt and dark jeans. He was carrying a large knife.

"COTY! OH MY GOD!" River screamed.

Coty moved his right hand. River's eyes were drawn to the blade of the knife. It was shiny and large. The mere sight of him holding it sent chills down her spine.

"River! River! Answer me!" Erik shouted.

River held tightly to her cell, not wanting to let it go. However, knew it was what she had to do.

"Erik," she said, trying to sound calm. "I have to go. No matter what happens to me tonight, know that I love you and Alex."

River tried keeping her fear to herself while Erik yelled for her not to hang up the phone. Sliding the phone into her back pocket, she was ready. This would be the fight of her life, but it was what she was preparing herself for all this time.

"You won't be satisfied until you kill me," she said.

Her hands trembled, as she stared him down.

"I don't want to kill you. I never would've hurt you before if you would just do what you're told."

"My boyfriend is on his way. I suggest you leave."

Pissed off, Coty rushed River. He grabbed her throat with his big, calloused hand, pressing the knife hard to her neck.

"Shut your dumb, fucking-ass mouth!"

Tears ran down River's cheeks, as scenarios raced through her panicked mind. She tried to imagine a way out of this situation. All of her martial arts techniques became a messy, muddle in her head. She knew that without them, he was stronger.

River didn't want to die, not this way. Coty grabbed the back of her hair, pulling her closer to him. The overpowering stench of his cheap cologne mixed with the alcohol on his breath made her nauseous. The very thought of putting herself back through a sadistic, abusive, slave relationship with this man again made bile rise into her throat. She would rather die, and she would do so fighting.

"You and I were made for each other! You have no fucking boyfriend other than me!" Coty growled.

River watched the knife, as it pushed harder into her neck. She tried not to make any sudden moves, lest he lose control and slice her. He was drunk and that meant danger.

"Coty, please, put the knife down. I will do whatever you want me to do. You don't need the knife."

"What I want is my life back! The life *you* took away! I want you back!"

He choked back tears. River knew he was not thinking rational. The knife cut into her throat deep enough to trigger a trickle of blood. River panicked. She knew she had to do something, or he would kill her in his drunkenness. With the blade cutting into her carotid, her nostrils flared, as she tried to remain calm.

"We had some great times together! Denying that is bullshit!" he shouted in her ear, spraying her face with spit.

The knife pressed deeper into her throat. River's cell phone continually vibrated in her back pocket. She wished she could answer and tell Erik she loved him one last time. She needed to hear Erik's voice one last time and Alex's, too.

"Fuck this guy! Give me your phone!"

Coty tilted her slightly, attempting to take her phone out of her back pocket. That's when River saw her chance. Grabbing the arm with the knife, she pushed it away from her, delivering a swift, hard kick into his scrotum. Coty bent over in agony. River reacted, thrusting her right elbow into his eye. His head flung back. The knife was still in his grip. Before she could make a run for it, Coty lunged forward. River turned and palm heeled him in the nose. The knife came forward, and she kicked him as hard as she could in the scrotum a second time. River took hold of his arm and threw him against the wall. Targeting a pressure point in that same arm, the knife finally fell out of his hand. Coty's nose was bleeding, and his eye was swelling. However, she wasn't about to stop. River kicked the knife through the broken doorway. She heard it fall down the concrete steps outside. Perspiring, and full of fear and adrenaline, River waited for Coty to stand up. She wasn't about to run. This was River's biggest fear. He was her biggest threat. The man tried to kill her once before, and he had shown up to try and hurt her again. Coty tried to destroy her. The only difference, this time she was prepared to fight back! It was time to take her life and power back. Nobody would steal it from her ever again!

"Stand up Coty!" River shouted.

Her teeth and fists were clenched. She didn't even notice, but she was no longer trembling. And if she was, it was all rage. Coty moaned and struggled to stand.

"What did you do to my nose? You hurt me!" he shouted, staring at his bloody hands.

"STAND THE FUCK UP!" River demanded.

"I am standing, you bitch! I'm not bent over anymore! Are you planning on kicking my ass?" he laughed.

"If I don't have to kill you first," River replied.

"Let's go!" Coty exclaimed. "You want to fight like a man? Bitch, I will fight you like a man!"

Coty ran for River, and River ran right back at him. She wasn't about to back down.

CHAPTER FIFTY-SIX
The Sidar

Erik heard River's screams over the phone. His heart pounded hard in his chest. He flew at top speed down the freeway, as he heard her shout, "COTY! OH MY GOD!"

Erik was in flight mode. Nothing could stop him from getting to River.

"Pick up!" Erik exclaimed through gritted teeth, as he called Alex.

"Yeah!" Alex answered.

"Get over to River's! Her ex, Coty, is the stalker! Something is going on. He's there!"

Alex was startled by his brother's tone. His instinct was always to protect his family. Alex slammed on the horn in an attempt to hurry Sai, and just as he was about to pull out of the drive without him, Sai came darting out. To his surprise, Sai was dressed in black from head toe—black trench coat, black sunglasses and a black duffel bag. His jet-black hair, which is usually twisted up into a man bun on the top of his head, was loose and long, free flowing over his shoulders. Alex was at a loss for words, mouthing to himself, "What the fuck?"

Sai jumped into the passenger seat. He was no longer Sai the stoner, a bohemian idiot. He was a completely different person.

"Let's go! I know River's in trouble!" Sai shouted.

Alex couldn't help but notice Sai's stoner accent was gone.

"Dude, what is happening?" Alex asked in disbelief.

"Do you really want to do this right now or do you want to save River?" Sai asked in a very even tone.

Alex punched the gas, and they were off, leaving black rubber on the road.

Erik made it to Apache Junction in record time. As he was getting off the freeway on the Ironwood exit, his rear truck tire went flat. Pulling safely onto the side of the main road, he locked the door and took off on foot. Once out of human view, he took flight with his Pleiadian power, using his energy light to fuel him. Erik tried calling Violet with his empathic abilities, trying to tune in to her location.

Violet was making food for Joshua in Ashton's kitchen while the guys played cards. Violet jolted to a stop. She felt Erik's call in her veins and dropped her spatula to the floor.

What is it? Joshua asked, empathically.

River is in serious danger, Violet replied.

Ashton looked at Violet, then he looked at Joshua.

"This is another one of those telepathic things you two do, right?" Ashton asked. Ignoring him, Violet and Joshua continued communicating with each other.

I will go with you, Joshua said.

No. You are too weak.

Then go, Violet, but don't get hurt. Joshua conveyed.

Violet looked deep into Joshua's eyes, as she nodded. And then, in the blink of an eye, she was out the front door, manifesting large coyote, which caught her completely off guard. Violet leapt from the porch into the dark, desert night. After rounding a cactus, jumping a fence and bursting through a creek, she was gone.

Alex said nothing to Sai, but instead kept glancing over at him anxiously while driving. He wasn't sure what was happening, but it was profoundly odd.

"Watch the road," Sai said, low, and dignified.

"You know, you look a lot like the movie Men in Black right now," Alex joked, taking a rough and wild turn.

"Just drive," Sai replied, sternly.

River and Coty ran toward each other at full speed. Coty threw a wide, right punch, leaving himself exposed. River ducked backwards, catching his arm. Moving slightly out of the way, she threw him forward with full force. Coty landed on a small, glass table, shattering it into a million pieces. River turned quickly in an effort to escape Coty, but he scrambled through the broken glass and grabbed hold of one of her legs. Viciously, Coty pulled River to the ground, her cheek landing in the broken glass. Dragging her toward him, he threw himself on top of her, pressing all of his weight onto her body.

River tried gouging his eyes, but he grabbed her arms and held her down. As his long tongue made its way to her lips, River shouted, "NO!"

She struggled and screamed, but she couldn't break free. Coty laughed, pressing his mouth hard against hers. Hating the thought of him touching her, she bit his lip until she tasted blood. Coty cringed in agony. Deranged, he laughed and licked at her with a long, lizard-like tongue that she had never seen before. River screamed, but he muffled her mouth with his hand, tickling his tongue along the side of her neck and face.

Wrapping her legs around him, she thrust her hips upward to push him away from her. Coty repositioned himself to counter the move. River's fighting was making him hard. Using the weight of his body, he manipulated her hips, forcefully pressing her down onto the floor. River felt powerless. As he tore at her shorts, she closed her eyes, mentally preparing herself for him to rape her. Tears streaming down her bloodied cheek, she fought to free her arms.

Violet stormed through the back door in full, large-coyote flight, blasting over Coty and quickly turning around to face him. Blood thirsty, she snarled, wanting to rip his heart out. She had never felt that before. Coty squirmed, but still did not let go of River. Violet lunged at Coty, digging her iron jaw into his ear and ripping it off. Coty shouted in agony, his blood splattering across the floor.

Grabbing hold of what little was left of his lobe, Coty rolled off of River. Violet lumbered hauntingly toward him, ready for the kill.

"GET AWAY MUTT!" Coty shouted, scooting away from her, slipping and sliding in his own blood.

River stepped out of Coty's reach, taking a traditional Kenpo Karate fighting stance. Violet tried nudging River out of the way with her snout, but she was immovable. Violet sidestepped and leapt at Coty with a nasty growl. He lifted his big boot and kicked her as hard as he could, knocking her out the back door.

"NO!" River screamed.

Coty sprang at River, grabbing her by the hair and dragging her down the concrete steps into the backyard. River felt the painful scrape of each step dig into her back. Violet scrambled to her feet and raced toward him. Coty raised his knife, shouting, "Get away or I will kill you, like I did the last coyote I encountered on the road the other night!"

Violet shuddered, her coat quivering. It was him, the man who almost killed Joshua with his car. If she wasn't angry before, she really had reason to rip this guy's throat out now. Violet hurtled herself at Coty with everything she had. With her teeth bared, she lunged into the air. Just then, Erik rounded the corner, and in one fluid motion, he pushed Violet out of the way of the knife that was aimed for her heart. Erik jump kicked his boot into Coty's sternum, sending him forcefully into a tree. Grabbing Coty by the arm, knife still in hand, it was an instant grapple for control. River watched in terror.

"Coty, stop! Coty!" River shouted.

Her left eye was swollen shut and bleeding. From her one good eye, River saw movement in the distance, not far beyond Erik and Coty. It looked like two large figures walking rapidly toward her from the front of the house.

Alex melted when he saw River. Clearly, she had been beaten and bruised, but she was on her feet with a few of her curls glued to her face from the blood. Alex snapped. A deep, heedful roar rose from within him, as he jumped into the fray. Throwing Coty off his brother, Alex put him three feet deep into the ground.

Alex's eyes glowed an emerald green. River gasped at the sight. She stood in awe as she watched Alex reach down and grab Coty, lifting him up over his head—no less than twelve feet in the air.

"I'm going to bury you!" Alex growled.

Out of nowhere, Sai appeared and touched Alex on the shoulder. He eased in with a troubled expression and whispered, "Stop. Get a hold of yourself. You will draw attention, causing an earthquake, if you do what I think you are about to do."

Alex knew Sai was right. So, he took back his power and let Coty

339

fall to the ground, only a little less hard than he had planned.

"I will handle him, Alex," Sai said.

River could barely digest the events as they unfolded in front of her. It even took her a moment to realize the large coyote standing next to her. River looked over at Sai, wondering why he was dressed all in black. She wondered what he was up to, as he rolled up his sleeves, revealing a black watch. Sai reached deep into his duffel bag and took out a long, strange-looking tube. He attached one end of it to his watch, aiming the other end at Coty. Sprawled out on the ground, Coty struggled to find his feet. He was in no hurry to rebound into another fight. River walked over to Erik. He looked at her and said, "River, go inside."

"No," she replied, stubbornly.

"You are all crazy!" Coty shouted. "Especially you, River! *You* trying to fight *me*!"

River shuddered. He was right. Why would she try to fight him?
Bad idea.

"That is quite enough," Sai said.

Adjusting the large, watch contraption and taking aim, he pushed a button that emitted a green light from the lasers inside. Coty was immediately sealed in a bright beamed cone.

"What's going on?" River asked, frantically.

"He isn't who you think he is, River," Sai said.

Coty stood up and pounded on the vortex surrounding him, revealing his long, serpent-like tongue.

"What? He's part of the Archon?" Alex asked in awe.

"Most definitely!" Sai exclaimed.

"Sai," River began.

Ignoring her, Sai walked toward the green-vortex cylinder cell.

"Who are you?" Sai asked.

Coty said nothing.

"Okay. I'll force you to answer."

Sai pressed a code into his watch, seizing Coty's nerves with wired Black Obsidian crystals.

"NO! NOO! NOOO! OKAY! STOP!" Coty begged.

"I'm Nordit," Coty said coldly. "I am a part of the Archon. I was sent to kill her a long time ago, but it didn't work out. The human was weak."

"Show yourself!" Sai demanded.

"That is against Archon law!" Nordit roared.

"I don't give a damn about your Archon law," Alex muttered.

"Oh, you will, Alex," Nordit raged. "You all will. They are coming for you … all of you, and we, the ARCHON, CAN NEVER BE STOPPED!"

He tried beating down the walls built up around him. Sai had enough. It was time for this monster to go. Pressing a button on his watch, Sai forced Nordit to reveal his true form. As the mutation began to take place, right before her eyes, River gasped in disbelief. She couldn't believe what she was seeing. It was Coty's upper body, a strong, muscular build, but the lower body belonged to something inhuman. She watched as Coty's two legs turn into eight large, white tentacles covered in brown spots. As the tentacles moved about the cylinder barricade, River lost her stomach and vomited at the sight. Erik took hold of her hand, also in awe of Nordit's tentacles as they slithered around the light cell.

"What now?" Alex asked. If it were up to him, he would blast the creature into a million pieces.

"He will be sent to the Pleiades for incarceration," Sai answered.

Nordit pressed his tentacles up against the cell, staring helplessly at all of them.

"Where?" River asked. "I'm sorry did you say the Pleaides?"

River tasted bile rising up in her throat. Sai quickly pushed another button on his watch, and Coty shot into the sky. He disappeared into the stars. It was as if space had swallowed him up, never to be seen on Earth again. Because of an injury, Violet manifested back into human form. Embarrassed, she stood naked in front of them.

"This isn't real. I must be dead," River muttered. "Coty killed me."

"Oh, it's real," Alex said, pointing to Sai. "And this weird, sly cat has some explaining to do."

"I have no problem with that," Sai said. "We are all on the same side. So, we may as well work as a team. If you will follow me inside, perhaps we can get your friend, Violet, some clothes."

They all followed Sai into River's house. Violet ran upstairs to find clothes. River, out of sorts, slumped into the first chair she saw, attempting to wrap her brain around what had just happened. She couldn't get over how Violet, someone she thought she knew well, had gone from being a large coyote to a human. She kept mulling it over in her mind, still not convinced she wasn't dead. Soon everyone was sitting around her, amidst bits of broken glass and blood. The mood was somber, as they waited for Sai's explanation.

"Let's talk," Sai said, clearing his throat. "The Archon has a political agenda that always concerns their weakest hit, which is Earth and the Pleaides. They want to destroy as many light bearers as possible, especially the regional and geographical lamp stands, like Amariah … umm, err … River. For ages, Sidar has mounted exploratory missions to overtake and keep watch of the Archon. And, yes, I still lead most of those special assignments. As you are well aware, River is always a top priority for our government."

Erik, Alex and Violet nodded in agreement. River was becoming more and more numb, blank and confused.

"River, alone, can change a platform of a million human mind sets in a single season. Someone with her kind of power must always be protected. Losing her would be a devastating backslide for the future of our world. We at Sidar protect light bearers, like her."

"How long have the Archon tracked River?" Erik asked.

"Since birth, and they have been using everyone within her reach to get to her."

"How long have you been assigned to River?" asked Alex.

"From birth," Sai smiled. "She's bumped into me from time to time throughout her life. I was always able to reprogram her mindset, but she doesn't remember."

"You were the paramedic, weren't you?" River gulped, suddenly recalling faint images. "The paramedic who helped me after Coty, or whatever that thing was out there, broke my back. I remember you. Something about you was different."

"Yes, River. I was with you. My guess is the morphine you received must have interfered with my power. That can happen from time to time," Sai replied.

"I remember seeing you change from one person into another, and you kept telling me that I would be okay. At first, I thought I saw you change from one person to another because of the morphine, but I didn't receive morphine until I got into the emergency room. I figured you were an angel," River recalled. "I also remember you telling me I had to rise above it, move on. You said what happened to me would make my light brighter,"

"Uh … yes," Sai nodded. "I suppose that was me, and for reasons unknown to me, you were able to see through my programming that day. Hmm … I will have to look into that some more. Perhaps, persistent trauma throughout one's life will foil my ability."

"Okay. Well, you can research that later. Let's get back to the Archon," Alex interjected.

"The Archon will come," Sai replied. "There will be thousands, and we will have to fight them. They are preventing the shift and mass awakening, *but* we intend to force them into their underworld dimension for a thousand years or more. Eventually, they always find a way out, but they aren't as wise as us, so it takes a while. Unfortunately, by and large, there is a lunatic who accidentally lets them out."

"How do we assemble an army big enough to battle the Archon?" Violet asked.

"We build one," Sai said, matter of fact.

Sai commanded everyone take leave for the night. River was relieved. Surprisingly, she didn't ask any more questions. She was too tired and was only able to process what had taken place that night. She wanted to know more, but it could wait until morning, after she cleaned up and got a good night's rest. Coty was out of her hair, and Erik was back by her side. That's all that mattered.

As they crawled into bed, having washed away the blood, sweat, tears and broken glass, Erik held onto her and played with her hair until she fell asleep. He wanted nothing more than for her to relax. River had a lot to absorb. Conversation could wait. She was with him, safe—finally.

"Let me get this straight," Alex said, smoking a bowl with Sai. "You really don't believe I am Sidar material?"

"Absolutely not," Sai answered.

"I'm every bit as important and worthy as you are."

"You? On Sidar with me? That would be a challenge," Sai huffed.

"Shit," Alex muttered.

The two broke out into a fit of laughter.

Violet, manifested into a normal-sized coyote, ran back to the reservation. She jumped the wooden fence leading to Ashton's house, and before she made it to the door, Joshua was waiting on the porch. Slowly, she returned to human form and walked toward him. He limped in her direction. Violet's stomach was bruised from where Coty had kicked her, but she didn't care. She ran straight into Joshua's arms.

The night sky was glowing with its full moon and glittering stars. It was perfectly beautiful and inspiring, considering everything that had happened that night. Joshua grabbed Violet's behind, bringing her in closer to him. The two held each other tight, and Joshua finally made his move. Lifting Violet's chin up with his forefinger, he went in for the kiss. It was long and sweet. Pulling away, he took her hand and whispered, "Come."

Leading Violet into Ashton's spare bedroom, he sat on the edge of the bed and admired Violet's naked body, as she stood in the moonlight pouring in from the window. Violet bent over and gave him another long, wet kiss, comforted by the fact that they had found themselves together, raw … in bare skin, in love and in making love.

CHAPTER FIFTY-SEVEN
The Morning After

"So, let me get this straight. You are an alien from outer space, and, like you, I am an alien, only I am implanted into a human body?" River asked.

She nervously paced the length of her living room while Alex installed a brand-new backdoor and Erik investigated the broken security system.

"We prefer the term ultra-intelligent or extrasensory beings to the word alien," Alex replied, exaggeratingly.

"Or 'dimensional' works," Eric added. "Pleiadian is good, too."

"Is this my body? Or did the same thing happen to me as it did to Coty? Am I ruining this experience for someone else?" River asked.

"Coty was a completely different circumstance. He allowed a takeover, and it probably happened easily because he was an addict and alcoholic," Alex assured.

"This is your body, your mind, your heart and your beautiful soul. You were sent here from our world to have the human experience from birth … to fulfill a mission," Erik said.

"I don't understand my mission."

Alex sighed. They had been over all of this with her before, but she had forgotten. And now they were another five hours into the same exact explanation. Erik stood up, gently leading River to the couch.

"Where we come from, you are a leader, not to mention very accomplished at many things. For now, all you have to do is what you are already doing—living, breathing, sleeping. Your very existence is healing, and it is reflected on other humans. Earth is going through a planetary cycle and that happens every so many thousands of years. We need you here to help ease the transition, and you aren't alone. There are thousands here with you, doing the same thing. You are one of the many leaders. On a subconscious level, you already know this, as do the others. However, on a human level you don't see it," Erik explained.

"Why is Archon after me?"

"Why is Archon after anybody? They are disgusting, fallen Pleiadians who are irrational and who want to fight us all," Alex interjected, looking at River's photographs displayed along the wall.

"They want to extinguish your light, and they don't want you to achieve your purpose here," Erik added.

"Your superpower is your light, River. It's as simple as that," Alex encouraged.

River sighed, "What about Sai? Where does he fit in?"

"He wants what we want, and that is your protection," Erik replied.

River was clearly overwhelmed, not to mention bruised, swollen, and upset. Erik gave her a couple of kisses, one on the lips and another on the crown of her head. He whispered into her curls, "When this is all over, and you return home, this will all make sense. I promise."

"Will I have a human death, or do I go back like Coty?"

"Good question," Alex smirked. "If my brother had it his way, you wouldn't even be here right now."

"I don't know," Erik said. "This time around, during the cycle, it is different for everyone. None of us truly know for sure."

"Okay." River said, gently touching her black eye.

"Does your eye hurt?" Erik asked.

"No … not really. It's numb."

Alex took over mending the back door, tightening the last few screws.

"The door is done," he said, opening and closing it a few times to make sure the hinges, along with the new framework were solid.

"There is something I've been wondering. This whole fight with the Archon, it sounds more serious this time. Where is the location of this alleged event?" Alex asked, looking to Erik.

"Sounds like a question for Sai," Erik replied.

"Yeah. He's very secretive on the subject. We've already talked, and he's pretty serious about Sidar. Neither one of us has a chance of qualifying for that holier-than-thou ship," Alex declared. "Well, I've got to go. I'm working the night shift tonight,"

Alex gave River a quick hug and took off, leaving her with Erik.

"Do you want something to eat? I can cook some rice," she offered.

"Nope," Erik smiled, appreciating her offer. "You sit down and relax. I've got dinner. How about some vegan sushi?"

"What? Really?"

"Oh, yeah! Since we are letting all the secrets out, I may as well tell you that we are holistic naturopaths on our planet. We love fruits and vegetables. In fact, many of our practices were handed down to Earth. You know, martial arts, energy healing, sound healing, aromatherapy," Erik replied while rummaging through her kitchen drawers.

River watched him with her legs propped up on the coffee table. She was trying to relax, but it just wasn't happening.

"What do we look like on another planet?" she asked.

"Well, for the most part, Alex and I are the same. We emanate color and light from our soul. We are multi-colored. They call us a light-body being. We change color, according to our mood."

"People look human though?"

"Some, not all. Our DNA changed throughout history, but everyone looks how they should. There isn't racism or judgement based on shape, color or form on our planet. We are more concerned for the evolvement of other species … of Earth and the betterment of all."

"So, you are basically a saint?"

"No … not exactly. We still have some issues and drama, but if anyone has ever been a 'saint,' it's you," Erik smiled. "Thoughts on Earth are different. It's the planet of experimental trial and error established in free will. Unfortunately, it's a bit dangerous here, compared to other planets. Do you have a sushi roller?"

"Bottom drawer," River replied, picking up her cell phone and scrolling through social media. "What do you think will happen to Coty?"

Erik thought about it for a moment, realizing he needed to use caution with his answer. Grabbing the sushi roller, he said, "He will go on trial before the high counsel."

"Then what?" River asked, trying to act like it didn't bother her.

"River, that wasn't Coty. It was Nordit, a fallen being. Coty checked out a long time ago. Nordit was on a mission to kill you."

"I don't understand what you mean by fallen being."

"Pleiadian soldiers who rebel against the establishment fall to Earth and become a part of the Archon government. They get lured in, under the false pretense they will have power and control. However, once they get here, they become a dark, sadistic energy. Some are trapped, never to be saved again."

"His lower body was an octopus," River whispered.

"Do you have any Nashoyu?" Erik asked, rolling the sushi and cutting it into pieces.

"Yes."

River stood up to find the ingredient for him.

"No. Sit. I can find it."

Erik created a pretty array of colorful sushi, topped on a handmade wooden platter. He placed the food in front of her and then sat down beside her.

"Yes. Coty was part squid. That means, he was like Violet and Joshua at one time. When he lived on Erra, it is likely he lived in the sea. We have many oceans there—by the way. It is a tropical paradise."

River nodded, as she took a big bite out of the sushi. She sighed in contentment and with a mouthful whispered, "Thank you! This is amazing."

"Anything for you," Erik said, smiling. "You are amazing!"

Erik leaned in and gave her a quick kiss on the forehead.

"It is just all very frightening for me. Last night was just too much," River admitted before taking another big bite.

Erik grabbed hold of River's chair and pulled her closer to him. He wrapped his arms around her and looked into her eyes.

"I promise to protect you. That's why I am here. Alex has your back, too. As a matter of fact, there is more you should know about Alex, but he needs to be the one to tell you."

"I can't handle any more information today," River said, swallowing. "But I'm sure I will want to hear more soon. I'm tired now. Can you just lay down with me … and hold me?"

"Of course," Erik smiled. "Let's go upstairs."

Erik and River curled up together on the bed. They touched, kissed and made love.

Violet watched River's house from the usual perch. The colorful chakra outbursts started off like small sparks of embers at first, swelling into a large rainbow formed over the house. Violet yawned, shook her coyote head and stretched out her legs and paws. It was time to get back to Joshua. Violet took off running out of the small rock cave, making her way back to the reservation. River had Erik. She was safe, but Joshua needed her. She needed to monitor him, especially around Ashton, lest he do something stupid. She ran faster through the Tonto National Park, pushing through a great wall of dust-monsoon season.

CHAPTER FIFTY-EIGHT

Dream Warrior

High-alert warnings came through on River and Erik's cell phones for dust, rain, and flash flooding. Erik ran outside to make sure the truck and Jeep windows were rolled up. River closed up all the open windows inside the house. The two met back at the sofa and cuddled together, as the rain started coming down. River drifted off to sleep.

In her dream, she could hear the loud beating of tribal drums. The rhythmic harmony stirred her, the pounding growing louder and louder. Each beat of the drum vibrating inside of her.

River suddenly found herself outside of her sleeping body. Once more, she was staring down at herself, only this time she had no fear. Looking at Erik, who was still sitting on the couch, skimming through television channels, she ran her hand in front of his face, but he didn't see her. The drumbeats were growing louder still, and she knew it was time to meet with Tequita.

Walking outside, the ground felt different. It was more like a moving Earth sponge. Her bare feet glided toward the trees. It was raining, but for some reason River couldn't feel the moisture. Everything felt different in her spirit body. It amazed her that she could feel the ground, but not the rain.

"The ground is my connection," she breathed.

As River neared the trees in her backyard, they magnified in size, inviting her in by clearing a pathway for her to walk. As she stepped inside, everything fell silent. She was surrounded by all of nature—trees, leaves and branches. She stood silent and still, waiting. When nothing happened, River closed her eyes and put her head down. After a moment, she lifted her head and opened her eyes. It was if a light switch turned on.

Everything around her was alive. The sound of a roaring jungle stirred into motion with colorful birds, rushing water, insects, flowers, vines and monkeys. River, herself, stirred to life. She walked among the wildlife and vegetation. Something amazing was happening—outside and inside of her. She could feel it, taste it, smell it. The change was happening, and she knew what that meant.

An exotic figure, shimmering with gold, stepped out from the overgrown flora. She was barefoot, and she was not alone. It was Tequita followed by a few other exotic-looking females and two rather large, muscular men with dark skin. They were all donning warpaint streaked across their faces. Their bodies were also covered in gold shimmer.

"Meet our warrior sisters and brothers, River," Tequita said. "They know you well … from long ago."

Each warrior stepped forward, stating their name. River couldn't remember or pronounce any of their names, except for one, a male warrior named Abra. River stood mesmerized, captivated by them all. Each warrior wielded a sword with a handle wrought with gemstones that glistened.

"They will teach you more than you already know about protecting yourself while in battle, and each member of my team will present you with a gift," Tequita said, gazing into River's eyes without any real emotion. "You have natural instincts within you, but you must be reconditioned."

Tequita's pupils turned a vibrant green that danced like the Milky Way on fire. River nodded. She understood.

"When I call you from your sleep, River, you must come, and you must be ready to train."

"Okay," River replied.

"Take her to the clearing and show her everything," Tequita said. "Practice, but do not give her your essence yet."

River followed the warriors as they walked to the edge of a waterfall. Looking around, she realized there was nowhere to go, but downward into the pool below. To leap was the only way to cross over to the clearing. One after the other, four of the warriors jumped, flying high over the 200-foot waterfall, landing lightly on the flattened path of greenery and exotic wildflowers. Abra did not jump. He stayed behind with River. When he reached for her hand, she backed away, refusing.

"Oh, no! I can't jump like you."

"Wait! You must!" Abra replied.

"I'm not like you. I'm human. I could die."

"You will not die here. You must hold onto my hand," Abra said.

River's hand trembled, as she cautiously took Abra's hand. Their fingers locked.

"There is a part of you that remembers that nothing is as it seems, and you and I are a part of each other," Abra said.

River took a deep breath. He pulled her closer to the cliff's edge.

"You were always the risktaker," Abra whispered into her ear.

River didn't believe him, but she wanted to. In a flash, Abra pulled her into him, and they flew off the cliff into a back-flip motion, landing a somersault while in midair. River closed her eyes and shrieked. Her heart raced, and her belly flip flopped.

She clung to Abra, as they landed quietly and safely in the clearing across the falls. River excitedly jumped for joy. Abra laughed at her exhilaration.

"Next time you will do it yourself," Abra smiled.

River wasn't so confident.

River sat down and observed various warrior techniques, mostly martial arts play. Each warrior demonstrated several moves. River was asked to practice them upon request. Every now and then, she would be tripped, kicked or pushed to test her skills. River felt no pain. And there was a strange sound coming out of her mouth every time she landed on the ground. It was different, sounding a lot like someone she may have known a long time ago.

"You are still so reserved and somewhat shy," a beautiful female warrior named Astrayak remarked.

River looked up at her, as the woman made her way around the other warriors to have a seat beside her.

"You remember me?" River asked.

"Of course. We all do. You are well known in the immortal world. I can only tell you that one day you will see what we all see, and until that time, it is best you find the key to unlock your own secrets."

River picked at the grass, nodding. Turning her attention to Abra, who was practicing another technique with his sword, she smiled. He was making comical faces while showing off his skills. He had all the warriors laughing, including River. Suddenly, they all stood up in unison with fluorescent, glowing green eyes. They looked over at River.

"It's time to go back, River," Abra said.

River stood to her feet, wondering how she would get back this time. A black Jaguar appeared from out of the jungle, running fiercely toward her. River backed away, and with a loud scream, she ran. River jumped into the water below the falls. Her body was quickly swept up and pulled under by the rapid current. After some time, she surfaced, inhaling a big gulp of air. She noticed she was no longer in the jungle, but standing in a large, mud puddle behind her house.

River grabbed at the ground, pulling herself out of the thick muck. Eventually, she found her footing and found herself standing in the rain. She felt nothing but could see the monsoon storm all around her. River's hair and body appeared to be wet, but she couldn't feel the moisture. She could only feel the mud stuck between her toes. Walking toward the front porch, she exhaled, taking one last look at the rain behind her.

Opening the door and stepping inside her house, River was suddenly dry from head to toe, no proof of the rain or mud or monsoon. Erik was gently nudging her, preparing to pick her up and carry her upstairs. River watched him, as he held her in his arms. Swiftly, she merged her spirit body into her physical one, just in time to be carried upstairs to bed by the man she loved.

CHAPTER FIFTY-NINE
Human Interest

Every Thursday, River would become extremely tired and routinely have her out-of-body experience with Tequita and the other warriors. The only two warriors she could name were Abra and Astrayak. When she would try to pronounce the others' names, they would all break into a fit of laughter.

The circle of warriors taught River how to outsmart on-coming attackers, and by the third month, she was effectively fighting with a sword, although she never had one of her own. When she questioned using a sword in battle against the Archon, Abra quieted her, assuring her that the sword was the most precious weapon of the spirit. River kept the out-of-body experiences and trainings with Tequita and the warriors to herself. For whatever reason, she didn't even talk to Erik about them. What he did not know, would not worry him.

River kept up with her regularly-scheduled Kenpo karate classes, incorporating some of her newly-taught, warrior techniques. While sparring with Ryan, she jumped into the air, quickly turned and ripped the plastic knife from her opponent, then gave him a swift back kick to the chest. It caused quite a stir. The entire class stood with their mouths open in amazement. Some gasped and others were heard cheering. Sensei was just a tiny bit concerned. He questioned her, asking if she had been studying karate at a new Dojo. He definitely wouldn't have liked that. River smiled and said, "I picked it up off YouTube."

It was no secret River spent a lot of time studying YouTube tutorials, but seeing Ryan lying flat on his back on the mat, gasping for air, he wasn't convinced there was a YouTube tutorial that could teach that kind of kickass. Violet watched River in amusement. This was the master who had taught her and Joshua everything they know. Violet smiled, knowing that River was returning to her original being. She waited for River after class.

"YouTube tutorials, huh?!" Violet laughed lightheartedly.

"Something like that. How is Joshua doing?"

"He's doing great! He told me to tell you hi."

The two walked together out to River's Jeep.

"Is he able to … turn yet?" River asked, somewhat embarrassed because she wasn't sure of the appropriate term.

"No. He's been trying, but nothing seems to help," Violet replied.

"What is it called when you change from one form to another?" River asked.

"Well, the Navajos call us Skinwalkers, but we aren't the legendary 'Skinwalkers' they talk of. We are on the other side, the good side."

"Oh, so, there are some that are not good?" River asked.

"Yes. I thought Erik went over this with you. Many of the Pleiadian rebels shift, but, unlike Joshua and I, they do not carry complete DNA of the creature they transform into."

"It's so much to take in," River sighed. "I'm still learning. I'm sorry if my questions make you a little uncomfortable."

"I'm not uncomfortable," Violet shrugged. "I want you to know. I wish you could remember me and Joshua. We took your classes aboard the ship. We've studied under you since we were very young. That's why we chose to help Erik keep you safe. We love you."

Violet's eyes filled with tears.

"I don't remember, but I will one day. I love you, too, Violet."

River grabbed her friend and gave her a big hug. Violet took a hard step backward, just as soon as River let her go.

"Whoa! You are getting so strong!"

"Yeah. I've been working out more," River replied.

Violet rubbed the soreness out of her arm, wondering where this extra strength was *really* coming from.

"I've gotta go! Text me if you need anything. I'm going to make Erik dinner tonight," River said, jumping into her Jeep.

She waved, threw the Jeep in reverse and took off. Violet waved, noticing a bruise already forming on her arm.

"What in the hell?" she said.

The whole thing was puzzling.

That night, Violet planned to help Joshua transition. They had tried many times in recent days to manifest coyote together but failed. Joshua was stuck in human form. As frustrating as it was, Violet was feeling good about it. She had taken River's advice some time ago, putting Joshua on a nutritional supplement regime to nourish him back to health. Every so often, she had even gotten him to drink wheatgrass. That, for both of them, was a pretty big deal since they had established a carnivorous diet as coyotes.

Violet drove their battered truck back to the reservation. She was tuned into a classic rock station. Her beautiful long, dark hair glistened in the sun, and her beaded, turquoise earrings dangled gracefully against her neck. Spotting Joshua and Ashton at a nearby park, tossing a football around, Violet pulled in to see them.

"You must be feeling really good today," Violet said, joyfully.

"Yeah. A little bit," Joshua replied, tossing the football to Ashton

"So, are you two going to get married or what?" Ashton asked, sarcastically.

Violet looked away. She hadn't realized she was holding Joshua with her eyes for so long.

"Shut up Ashton!" Joshua exclaimed.

He threw the football long and hard at him.

"Hey Joshua! Are we still going to the Canyon Ridge tonight? You know, to see if you can … " Violet began.

"No, Violet! I really just want to let that go for a while. There are too many hikers and campers this season we have to be careful."

Feeling a bit defeated, Violet sat down on the bench of a wooden picnic table. She started playing with a seed from a Mexican guaje tree. Joshua sat down beside her. Some young ladies caught Ashton's attention, and he walked over to talk to them.

"Why are you so down? What's going on?" Joshua asked.

"I'm just a little bummed we aren't together, like we used to be. Our coyote runs were always the greatest, and now it just scares me that everything could be changed forever."

"Shhh," Joshua shushed. "No way! You and I are inseparable. We've been best friends and soul companions since birth. We were meant to be. I would never leave you. I can't even picture my life without you in it."

Joshua nervously fidgeted with the wood grain of the table. Violet wiped away a tear, as she watched the sun go down over the mountains.

"I miss our home," she whispered.

Joshua nodded in agreement.

"I miss our beautiful oceans … how clean they are. I miss swimming with the dolphins," Violet continued.

"You know what I miss? I miss playing in the rainforest. I miss how pure it tasted and felt when the rain hit our bodies," Joshua replied.

"Oh yeah."

"Look, Violet … when my body is ready, I will manifest back to coyote, but it just isn't ready yet. For now, let's just forget about it. I can still hang out with you. I can even patrol with you. I will just be in human form while you are coyote. The only real change is that we will have to take the truck over to River's house from now on."

"No … no, Joshua. I don't want you to do that. I just want you to get better. I want you to rest," Violet protested.

"I don't like you patrolling by yourself all night long," Joshua said. "I worry about you, Violet. That thing with Coty could have gone really wrong, really fast."

Joshua's expression melted into sadness at the thought that he could have lost her.

"Soon. I promise. I will be 100 percent again," he assured.

Looking over at Ashton, who was flirting with the girls, Joshua shouted, "Hey Ashton! Throw me that damn ball!"

Joshua stood to his feet and walked in Ashton's direction. Annoyed, Ashton waved him away, as he attempted to get a girl's phone number.

CHAPTER SIXTY
Of the Essence

R iver was busy at work, wishing she was no longer a nurse. Once again, everything was going wrong, and no one, not even her, was taking accountability. She barely spoke to anyone unless it was absolutely necessary. River rushed up and down hallways, looking for supplies, restocking, answering call lights, passing medication, charting and wishing for a break. When her shift ended, her replacement texted that she would be late. It was just as well since she had fallen behind on charting.

Without warning, a CNA came charging out of a patient's room to tell her that Miss Davitt had stopped breathing. River's adrenaline shot through the roof, as she turned her attention to the task at hand. She double checked the patient's chart for full-code status, shouting, "Call 911!"

Grabbing the crash cart, she raced into the room. Everyone worked frantically, pulling the 34-year-old patient onto the floor and placing the Ambu-Bag mouthpiece over her face. River immediately began chest compressions until medics arrived, all the while knowing that the patient had passed on.

After the time of death was pronounced by EMS, River stayed behind to help the CNA return Miss Davitt's body to the bed, so that she could bathe and prepare it for the family's arrival. As the two women worked together, River pulled the body toward her, onto its side, so that the

CNA could wash underneath. As she leaned in to hold the body in place, the dead woman opened her eyes and, in a horrifying voice, breathed the word, "ARCHON!"

River screamed, jumping back at the same time.

"What is it?" the stout CNA asked.

River pointed at the patient. The CNA proceeded to walk over to River's side of the bed. Her eyes followed River's finger, but she saw nothing.

"Are you okay, River?" she asked, confused.

"I'm fine," River said, her chest heaving. "Her eyes just opened and shut."

"Oh yeah. I've seen that happen," the CNA added.

River nodded, walking out of the room. Trembling, she finished her charting and, without haste, returned home.

River never thought she would be so happy to see Alex. Running into the house, she gave him the biggest hug, even before Erik.

"I really miss working with you," River sighed.

"Okay. What happened?" Alex replied, frowning.

River replayed her frantic day in grave detail. When she got to the part about Miss Davitt coding, the CPR and the lips of a dead woman speaking the word Archon, Alex and Erik exchanged a concerned glance.

"Did you know this woman?" Alex asked

"No. We only received her a few weeks ago. She was a stage four cancer patient."

River took off her shoes and ran upstairs to change out of her scrubs.

"What do you think?" Alex asked, whispering to his brother.

"I don't know," Erik replied. "Are you sensing how strong her energy is right now?"

"Yes. It's very powerful. I could feel it when her Jeep hit the driveway."

"Yeah. Me, too," Erik sighed. "Something doesn't feel right."

"What do you mean?" Alex asked, digging through a pantry looking for snacks.

"It feels intense, leaning on the aggressive. I can't explain it."

"I know what you mean," Alex added, throwing a handful of granola into his mouth "Maybe it's the transformation process. You know, her gifts and all that."

Erik rolled his eyes, wondering how his brother could eat as much as he does.

"You could be right … I suppose."

Alex sat to the kitchen table with dill Pickles and crunchy peanut butter. He combined the two elements and began powering them down. Erik watched in total dismay.

"That's so gross, dude." Erik said.

"What?"

Erik shook his head and left the room to go find River. Alex shouted, "Dude, I weightlift! I need a lot of food!"

Erik found River laying on the bed, wearing nothing but a pair of panties and a cream-colored, silk crop top. She was sound asleep in the fetal position. Erik was worried that she was abnormally tired. It wasn't like her. However, he had to take into account her job and the past year.

That, alone, was enough to exhaust anyone. Bending over, he kissed River sweetly on the cheek, gently caressing her hair and then headed back downstairs to keep his brother company.

Both men dismissed River's current energy "crisis" as a heightening Pleiadian gift. The two settled on a classic, action-adventure movie with fresh popcorn. Erik felt grateful for his new bond with Alex. As stubborn as he was, he knew, had it not been for River, it never would have happened. They would never have become so close. He watched Alex laugh at the least funniest movie scene. In that moment, he felt the most love and compassion for his brother.

While napping, River was pulled away into the supernatural, Amazon dimension with Tequita. While sparring with her new friends, Tequita stopped them. Loud drums beat fiercely in the distance, from every direction. River looked around, only to find herself totally alone. There was only the sound of tribal drums, reverberating intrusively throughout her body. The pounding and beating echoed in her brain. She could literally feel the rhythm palpitating inside her chest. Tequita came forth with the others, her emerald-green eyes dazzling, piercing River's soul.

"What's happening?" River stammered.

"Kneel down, River … Amariah," Tequita said.

River was confused, but she knew that command was meant for her. So, she dropped to her knees, looking somewhat fearful.

"You are no longer the leopard without spots," Tequita said. "You will now show your truth, and your spots will come forth."

River looked to Abra, the warrior to whom she had grown close. He nodded slowly, assuring her everything would be okay.

"Give her your essence," Tequita commanded. "Her truth will emerge and be brought forth with the sword of light."

Suddenly, all the warriors were facing River, and then, one by one, they encircled her, touching the crown of her head, each with a steady hand and fluorescent-glowing eyes. There was a large explosion of light, particles of gold dust absorbing into her skin and skull. River couldn't move, but she was comforted by a warmth that was saturating into each and every cell in her body. She could feel the light moving at lightning speed inside of her.

Something tugged at her jaw, leaving her mouth gaping. She felt so much joy, as her neck opened up. She wanted to be fed more light. She wanted to receive it all. Just then, bees flew into her mouth, hundreds of them. She could hear and feel them buzzing. Her skin lit up. Like a sparkling diamond, it flickered. Within moments, the bees left her body, flying from her mouth. All that was left was honey dripping from her lips. When they finished giving her their essence, River sat peacefully, not wanting to move from the spot she received their gifts.

Opening her eyes, they were all gone. River called out to them.

"Tequita?! Abra?!"

No one answered. No one came. A big, beautiful butterfly showed up from out of nowhere, landing on her shoulder. River reached out her fingers, and then there were five butterflies.

"How will I get back?" she asked.

Again, no answer. River cringed at the thought of another wild animal chasing her to the water's edge as a way of sending her home. This time, she chose to do it herself. Climbing to the top of the waterfall, she stood at the cliff's edge, looking down into the 200-foot drop. There was no fear, only courage and confidence. She knew she could do it this time, and she knew why. River was sent here on a mission, and she was focused on completing it. The planet depended on her. No one could stop her.

River closed her eyes. Something was happening. She heard someone crying. Turning to her right, she saw a beautiful female who looked a lot like her. The girl was afraid of something or someone. River reached out to her, but her hand went right through the holographic girl.

"You will be okay," River breathed. "All you have to do is jump. You will land on your feet. Everything will be fine. You will be safe."

The girl still appeared terrified of something, but River could not see who or what was scaring her. She reached out her hand and said "I want you to hear me. Please … hear me. I want you to feel me. Please … feel me."

Suddenly, as if she heard her pleas, the girl looked around and found River's eyes.

"I can hear you," the girl said.

"Grab my hand!" River exclaimed.

The girl grabbed River's hand. The two bonded together.

"We're going to jump together," River said. "You don't have to be afraid."

Exhaling, River reached one arm up into the air, bringing the young girl close to her with the other. The two jumped toward the water, free falling—fast and feet first. Rotating her hips, she tucked into a couple of quick backflips before hitting the water. When she landed, River opened her eyes, but she couldn't see the girl. The girl was gone. River found herself swimming amongst exotic fish. They were everywhere and, in every color, hues she had never seen before. When she reached the shore,

River climbed out of the water, feeling pretty good about herself. It seemed much easier than the last time. She stood strong and sturdy, like the sun that shone on the horizon. Her life was never going to be the same, and she knew it.

River walked by Alex. He was fast asleep on the couch. She crept upstairs to her bedroom where she found Erik lying next to her in bed. He was holding her. She looked down at her physical body. She was taken at how delicate, weak and fragile she looked in human form. With a strong determined voice, she said, "YOU AND I ARE TO BECOME ONE, AND OUR SOUL WILL BE FILLED WITH LIGHT AND POWER!"

River fell backwards into her physical body, choosing to sleep in with the man she loved.

CHAPTER SIXTY-ONE
The Pleiadian Princess

The next morning, Erik slipped out of bed, leaving River to sleep in. She needed the rest. He made his way downstairs to the kitchen to make her breakfast. As he rustled together the makings of a vegan omelet, the house began to rumble. The thunder and rattle took Erik by surprise. He opened the backdoor to investigate and discovered large trees pushing up from the earth's soil, covering over an acre of desert land. Everywhere he looked, new trees were sprouting up, maturing at a rapid speed. His jaw dropped in absolute amazement at the newly green forest in River's back yard. Gone was the barren, rocky desert. In its place a green, vibrant oasis.

Erik pulled his cell phone out of his back pocket and snapped a picture of it and sent it over to Alex. In a text, he wrote: "Get Sai, and get over here now!"

Erik walked through the long path of trees, the songs of birds filling the air. He was not comfortable with this new development. From behind he heard footsteps approaching. He turned to find River standing barefoot, scantily dressed, wearing only a loose, off-the-shoulder top and a pair of panties. Her eyes were wild with excitement, as she clasped both her hands together.

"Don't you love it?!" She asked. "It's amazing! This is home!"

She held her arms out wide in gratitude. Her eyes were simmering fluorescent green. It startled Erik. He took note of how her energy had grown stronger and more powerful. River had changed. His enthusiasm did not match hers.

"I can feel the earth all throughout my body, Erik. The Universe gifted me with trees, and God is going to help us defeat the Archon."

Erik looked at her intently.

"What are you talking about? Who gifted you?" he asked.

"I was blessed by Tequita and the five warriors. I've never felt so together or so ready to help humans and the earth. I know I have what it takes now!"

Erik looked away, drawing in a deep, rich breath. And he thought his biggest problem that morning would be making a vegan omelet.

"I don't understand this," Erik said, sounding concerned.

"You weren't meant to," River said.

"What do you mean?" he asked.

River walked toward him with the force of an angelic warrior. She smiled and said, "You were not meant to fight the Archon, Erik. You involved yourself when you shouldn't have. You will not be fighting by my side."

"What?" Erik asked. "That is absurd. There will be no fight that includes you without me next to you."

Erik's phone dinged, a text message from Alex that read: OMW.

"I will advise you not to get in my way, Erik."

"What has gotten into you?" Erik asked.

"Tequita and the warriors," she commanded. "They have blessed me. They gave me strength, and I intend to protect this planet, and nothing you can do will stop me."

"I only want to protect you!" he shouted.

"No, Erik. You came for selfish reasons, to remove me from my position. You don't care about the consequences of your desire."

River's voice was different, more defiant and somewhat dignified. Erik was in shock. He realized she was acting very much like her Pleiadian self, and for some reason that made him very uneasy.

"Tell me, Erik, what do your parents think about you deporting yourself, going rogue on your duties to their ship to save me?"

Erik shifted his weight, digging his hands into his jean pockets. Staring intently at the trees, he had no idea how to respond.

"We both know that what you did put this whole operation in jeopardy, so from now on you will stay out of my way," River said, coldly.

Sai and Alex appeared behind River. She felt their presence miles before they got to her.

"Sai, thank you for everything you've done for me," she said.

River turned to face them. Sai appeared puzzled at first. Her appearance had changed. She was not the same, and her eyes kept flashing a brilliant Pleiadian green. Sai realized River was no longer human, not completely. She was Amariah, the Pleiadian Princess, someone whom he and all of Sidar had sworn to protect no matter what.

"Of course, Princess," Sai said, bowing his head.

River turned to Alex and said, "Alex, my dearest, most honorable friend."

"Welcome back, Amariah," Alex said.

Alex was in awe, but not in shock. In fact, he felt nothing but love, respect and admiration for her in that very moment.

"Call me River. I am still River … for now."

"Of course," Alex replied, smiling. "Understood."

Alex leaned into Erik. With an onery smile, he patted his brother on the back and whispered, "She's back! Good luck, brother."

"Knock it off," Erik said.

The three men watched River walk away. They were mesmerized by her new presence. River was something else, and they could all feel it.

"Now what?" Alex asked.

Sai rubbed the back of his own neck, taking a better look at the massive overgrowth of new trees.

"We just keep doing what we are doing. Just know though, this means the time is near," Sai said.

"Now that she knows who she truly is, we have a problem. It's a game changer. This will be a little harder," Erik said.

"You mean, your role in her life could change?" Alex asked. "You were able to play the protective boyfriend while she was human, but you and I both know she is not quite her human self anymore. So, those roles we've both been playing along with may no longer apply."

"The princess has always been the one in charge. I mostly meant that we may not have a say in what she wants or needs anymore," Erik said, sullenly.

"So, we don't take charge. We let her lead," Alex agreed.

"I agree with that, for now," Sai chimed in.

Alex watched his brother carefully, as Erik touched a trunk of a large tree and brushed at the bark.

"We need to help build a bigger army against the Archon," Erik said.

"Not your problem," Sai replied. "The army is built and currently being reinforced with some very special young starseeds, some who are more like her."

"Really? Where?" Erik asked, surprised.

"Another group coming from Ohio," Sai continued. "They are the same as River. Ohio is a major portal for us into higher dimensions. Many are born there, but not all make it. They will come to us."

"When?" Erik asked.

"Soon. Only they can meet us in battle. They are currently in another dimension of place and time on this planet. Not in our current time space or even born yet," Sai replied.

"Michael's team," Alex said.

"Yes. Michael's operation," Sai explained. "And this, Alex, is your operation."

Alex nodded in agreement.

"I was going to explain that to River, but I didn't," Erik added.

"If she doesn't know, she will soon enough," Alex said. "However, I'm not going to push any more information on her than I need to."

"Another storm is coming," Sai said.

The trees started to move and thrash violently, as the wind picked up. River opened up the back door. Stepping out, she was wearing a tight black crop, zip jacket with tight black pants with her hair pulled back into a fierce chignon. Her physical shape was changing before their eyes. Her cheek bones were more prominent. Her lips were poutier, and her new ripped abs were showing through.

"I have a lot to do today, so what's the plan?" River asked. "Come on boys. Figure it out. I won't be babysitting, and you won't be babysitting me any longer. There is a lot of training I need to do."

Erik was still in shock and a little broken because he knew this could change everything for him. Alex, on the other hand, loved it. He smiled big, loving her new self-esteem. He missed that. They all three walked inside, recognizing who was in charge. Erik didn't care. He wouldn't allow her to face the Archon without him.

CHAPTER SIXTY-TWO
The Shift

"Joshua did you hear that?" Violet whispered. Violet shook Joshua, but he only turned over. Violet heard a large crash coming from the kitchen. *It could be Ashton*, she thought. Realizing Joshua wasn't going to wake up and check it out, Violet crept slowly out of bed and quietly made her way into the kitchen.

Broken glass covered the floor. The kitchen door leading to the outside was wide open. It rained most of the evening, and all that was left was mud and the occasional drizzle. Violet walked down three steps, scanning the yard with her super-bionic eyes. Her heart shuddered when she saw Ashton being punched in the face over and over again. A large man held Ashton's arms from behind, as another large man clobbered him from the front.

Violet bolted across the mud, her toes sinking into the earth, as she rushed to save their friend. She jumped into the air, delivering a perfect back kick into the chest of the man hitting Ashton. The man fell back into mud, spattering the muck in everyone's face. The man holding Ashton, let loose his grip and went after Violet. She stationed herself firmly in a fighting stance, blocking every punch that came at her. The man caught her off guard, kicking her front leg out from under her. Both men had her by the arms, dragging her toward their car.

"Let me go!" Violet shrieked, as she tried fighting her way out of their grasp. The men had no mercy on her. One of them grabbed her by the hair, ripping out a big handful.

Joshua woke up in a panic after sensing Violet's urgent telepathic cry for help. Meanwhile, Ashton rolled onto his stomach. With two swollen, black eyes and a severely battered face, he tried to get up to help Violet. He could see Joshua running toward him. Ashton, worried Joshua was going to topple over him, held up his hand. Joshua leapt over him, and in a flash, landed on the other side of him in the form of the largest mountain lion he had ever seen.

Joshua growled at the two men. He protracted his claws before lashing at the one holding Violet by the hair. The man screamed out in pain, falling back onto the ground, blood pooling in the large scratches tatted across his face. Joshua moved toward the other large man, but that man had already released Violet. He was running to his car. Joshua chased after him. Knocking him to the ground, Joshua flipped the man over, ready to rip out his throat.

"No Joshua!" Violet shouted. "Don't do it!"

Joshua stopped and roared violently in the man's frightened face. The man urinated on himself, as he shook uncontrollably.

"Let him go, Joshua." Violet insisted.

Joshua moved his manifested mountain lion off of the man and walked toward Violet.

"Skinwalkers," Ashton whispered, just before passing out.

Joshua transformed back to his human form, left naked.

"Are you okay?" he asked, caressing Violet's hair.

"Yes. I'm fine, but Ashton is hurt."

"Yes. Let's get him inside," Joshua said.

"Should we take him to the hospital?" Violet asked. "Should we call the police?"

"No," Joshua said. "Honestly, who knows what Ashton did to these guys. He could owe them money. I don't think they will mess with him again."

"Okay," Violet answered, as they helped Ashton into the house.

Ashton hobbled between them, regaining full consciousness.

"Who were those jokers?" Joshua asked.

"I owe them money," Ashton replied.

"Shit! You almost got Violet killed," Joshua said, irritated.

Ashton lost his balance, falling backwards onto the recliner behind him. Violet and Joshua left him there, as they returned to their bedroom.

"You transitioned," she whispered.

"Yeah."

The two hugged before indulging into a slow, romantic kiss. Violet pulled him onto the bed … on top of her. Rolling him over, she tasted his neck, mouth and face with her lips. Joshua gently pulled her hair back from her face, as she slipped out of her clothes. Kneeling over top him, she helped him inside of her.

"What about Ashton?" he asked.

"We will get him some ice later," Violet whispered.

They made love twice until the early morning hours.

Over the passing weeks, Erik became frustrated with River. She was no longer the same sweet human. She had become her strict Pleiadian self, a master warrior at her craft and the woman who separates emotions from missions. It was as if River no longer felt love and warmth for him, not like before. She had shrugged him off. All she cared about anymore was preparing for the battle with the Archon Forces, and every time she left on her journey to visit Tequita, she returned more fierce, more intelligent and knowing. This angered Erik. He was losing control, being taken out of the loop. It bothered him to think of her going toward the Archon without him. He couldn't allow that to happen. Alex, Violet and Joshua noticed the growing tension. It was uncomfortable for all of them. Sai, on the other hand, felt Erik was an unnecessary distraction that she didn't need. He considered Erik's attitude selfish.

While River, Violet, Sai and Alex practiced weapons in the backyard, Erik paced up and down for more than an hour. He couldn't take it anymore. He had to speak his mind.

"I hope you and Tequita know that you are not going without me to face the Archon."

River sighed, somewhat annoyed.

"I want you to go back home, Erik," River replied. "And I don't mean the ranch. I mean back to your parent's ship."

"Why? How could you say that?" Erik asked, hurt.

"You will only get in my way, like you are now."

"Maybe we should go," Alex said, looking at Sai.

Sai nodded, and he and Alex quietly excused themselves. Violet and Joshua had already slipped away, avoiding an awkward situation.

"How much do you remember about us?" Erik asked.

"Everything, and more comes back to me every day."

"Do you remember how I always promised to protect you?" Erik asked. "Always keep you safe?"

River nodded, and said, "When it comes to my missions, I have many protectors. Everyone is sworn to protect me."

"Without me around, there is never enough protectors," Erik said. "What do you think would've happened if I wasn't at the bar the night you were almost raped?"

"That was you?" River muttered. "Of course, it was you. Regardless, you know the rules. Never interrupt a mission."

"Normally, I wouldn't, but I needed to make sure you came home this time. This war involves the black-hole abyss and extra dimensions. You could easily be lost or taken away from me."

River's eyes flashed green, as she looked at Erik. She cleared her throat and said, "Kraylon is here."

"Yes. I am," Kraylon said. "Thank you for noticing, River. Where is Alex? He and I made a deal?"

"He just left. Kraylon, what can I do for you?" River asked.

"First of all, welcome back to your memories, Amariah," Kraylon hissed, latching onto her arms with his long, pale, white fingers in excitement.

Kraylon raised his finger at Erik when he tried moving toward him and said, "Don't you dare touch me or try to do anything stupid, Erik."

Kraylon turned his attention back to River.

"I will be waiting for you, helping you on the other side, River."

"What?" Erik asked.

"Erik, you knew Kraylon was a big part of this," River said.

"Why are you so surprised?" Kraylon asked, flamboyantly.

"Whatever," Erik muttered. "How do I become a part of this?"

"Tequita, she is the only one with the key," Kraylon responded.

"How do I contact her?" Erik asked.

"Perhaps, River could send off a message for you," Kraylon said, grinning mischievously.

Erik cringed. River wasn't going to help him, and he already knew that.

"Or, maybe, the high council will consider it. However, if the princess says no, and you are nothing more than a distraction ..." Kraylon purred.

"I am not a distraction!" Erik shouted.

"Hmmm ... maybe, but some would disagree," Kraylon said.

"Kraylon, you have to help me get in," Erik begged.

"Don't help him," River commanded.

Kraylon threw his hands up in the air and huffed, "I can't deal with this drama today. Please tell Alex he needs to pay up on his agreement in order to open my restrictions to Planet Erra. I will be in touch."

With that, Kraylon vanished into the wind.

CHAPTER SIXTY-THREE
Going Viral

River zipped into the local gas station, parking her jeep at the furthest pump. Pulling out a credit card, she selected regular unleaded and then proceeded to pay for and pump the gas.

"Hey!" a muscular man said, startling her from behind.

River turned in the man's direction, unsure what he wanted.

"Can you move your Jeep, so I can get my truck and trailer in here for gas? I'm in a hurry."

River looked him up and down, from head to toe, sizing him up pretty quickly.

"No. You can wait until I'm done," she snapped.

"What did you say?" the man asked, angrily.

River looked at the man more closely, finding him very odd.

"I said, I am already pumping my gas ... SO, NO YOU CAN WAIT!"

She was losing patience with this guy. She got the sense the situation was about to escalate, so she tried steadying her trembling hands and mentally prepare herself. The man shook his head as he turned to walk away. But then the man stopped cold in his tracks. He turned and walked toward her and screamed, "FUCK YOU, BITCH!"

And without warning, the man spit in her face.

The man drew attention from other customers pumping gas, as he continued to shout lewd profanities at her. River calmly finished fueling the Jeep up. She wiped away the man's saliva from her chin. Turning to him she shouted, "NO. FUCK YOU!"

The man lunged at her with a left hook. River ducked, narrowly missing the man's fist. She quickly stood up and responded with a swift kick to the man's dick. As he fell forward, she cocked her elbow and jammed it in the back of his neck. For added love, she delivered one last kick to the rear, sending the crown of his head into the brick wall holding pumps. The man toppled over like a lead balloon.

River straightened her spine. Looking around, she noticed she had an audience. Some had captured her response to that asshole on their cell phones. This sent River into a panic, as she quickly jumped into her Jeep and sped off.

Erik sat amongst the trees behind River's home, trying to use his power to communicate with Tequita. It wasn't getting him anywhere. He couldn't contact her.

"Tequita, please answer me," He whispered.

Birds chirped endlessly among the large trees. Alex watched from a far, trying not to disturb his brother. He was confused. He had no idea what Erik was doing.

Erik adjusted his legs in three different yoga sitting poses. He closed his eyes each time, pausing a few minutes. Erik, who was in serious concentration mode, began to float off the ground. Not noticing that his body was moving, he kept his eyes closed and started to chant. Alex watched with his jaw hanging as Erik propelled at full speed into the forest, vanishing amongst the trees.

"What do you mean he just took off flying into the forest, Alex?" River asked.

"Just what I said. He was sitting cross-legged on the ground, meditating and chanting, and his body lifted up and sped through the air. I looked for him but couldn't find him anywhere."

"He can't do this," River said.

"Do what?"

"Constantly get in the way, thinking he can save me," River replied.

"That's a little rough," Alex said. "Take it easy on him."

"No," River said, slamming the rustic table with her kitchen chair.

"Did you even think that maybe I am worried about him, too? *You* probably think I'm being ungrateful and selfish, but I'm not. I love him. I don't want him hurt."

River didn't want to cry. She pushed back the tears, telling herself THE NEW RIVER DOESN'T CRY.

"Well, I have to admit, you've done one hell of a job saving your own ass, River," Alex said, coming to his brother's defense. "Hell, if Erik and I hadn't come to your rescue on multiple occasions, you would be dead by now. You are a danger magnet on this planet."

River said nothing.

"We protect our own. You are family to us. It's what we do, and sometimes we may both do something that isn't strictly by the book. Just lighten up on my brother," Alex added.

River walked out the backdoor, as Sai walked in, having only caught the last part of the conversation.

"Leave her, Sai," Alex said. "She will be alright. I hate to say it, but maybe I liked earthling River better."

"Did you?" asked Sai.

"She was sweeter," Alex laughed.

"How long have you been in love with her, Alex?" Sai asked.

"What?"

"Anyone who knows you three, knows the whole story. You were after her long before Erik."

"How does anyone know this story?" Alex asked, surprised.

"I am from the Sidar ship. We know everything, and we see everything."

"Well, it's a false narrative—not true," Alex insisted.

"Tell yourself whatever you need to, but it will not change what you already know inside of you, and that's the truth."

Alex groaned, leaning over and pressing his forehead to the table.

"I know," Alex sighed.

Sai patted his friend on the shoulder, as he broke out a bowl and sat beside Alex. The two men smoked a little weed in quiet contemplation.

Erik felt his body moving at the speed of lightning. He opened his eyes and watched himself swiftly pass through a forest of trees and shrubbery, straight into the opening mouth of a portal of another dimension. Erik found himself in the jungle. He willed himself to slow down to a halt, so that he could put his feet firmly on the ground. Looking around, he saw the rushing waterfalls scrumptiously pouring into a pooling river 200 feet below. Inhaling a deep breath, Erik tasted the pristine air. It was pure, and it instantly gave him more vibrant energy. Then came the sound of an exotic accent from behind.

"Why have you come?"

Erik turned to find Tequita in all her beauty, along with all five tribal warriors dressed in war paint and armed with spears. All were fit, dark, beautiful and clearly Pleiadian—slanted-green eyes, high-pointed ears, and blue auras.

"I am looking for you. Tequita, I presume."

Erik noticed the warriors were cautious and ready for anything.

"You are Erik?" she asked.

"Yes. I want to volunteer my services to you and to those fighting the Archon battle."

"You are worried River can't protect herself?" Tequita asked.

"Please let me stand beside you, as added precaution," he pleaded.

"She will have Alex," Tequita said.

"Alex and I are brothers. We have only her best interest in mind."

Erik knelt down on one knee, vowing, "I would die for her and Alex, if needed."

"She doesn't want you involved," Tequita said.

"I know."

"Do you know why?" Tequita asked.

"Because she thinks I am a distraction."

"Perhaps, but sometimes, when trying to protect others, we do so blindly because we love them."

"I don't understand," Erik replied.

"River can see and feel things now that others cannot. It is a part of her gift. You must ask yourself, what does she see? Sometimes, we just need to let things be, or they will never go any farther," Tequita whispered.

"I'm not sure I follow you," Erik replied, still confused.

"I will allow you to cross over at the appointed time, I do know your intentions are pure."

Erik nodded, and sighed, "Thank you."

"Anything else?"

"No," Erik breathed.

"Then you may go. You must return from the edge of the waterfall," Tequita added, gesturing toward the falls.

She and the warriors walked into the distance until they became a blur within the shrubs. Erik ran toward the falls and jumped without hesitation—feet first. He swam through the lagoon, until he reached the edge of the forest floor. He made his way back through the trees until he reached River's home.

The first set of eyes he saw were Alex's. Alex was relieved to see his brother. He had waited for Erik's return for the better part of the evening. Erik and Alex took a seat on the porch steps. They talked about Tequita. Alex listened for the most part. He understood exactly why his brother needed to be there. A part of him wanted Erik to be there on the battlefield against the Archon, especially after seeing the clips of River kicking some guy's ass at a gas station. It was all over social media. He decided to keep River's viral sensationalism to himself. Erik had enough to think about, but he was concerned about what or who could approach her next, putting her in harm's way without anyone around to back her. Alex felt River's power was in their numbers.

CHAPTER SIXTY-FOUR
The Descent

River endured embarrassment following the gas station incident, having gone viral. It seemed the whole world was talking about her. After just 24 hours of all the rhetoric, good and bad, she unplugged from social media. Erik casually mentioned it over coffee one morning, but she just put her hand up and stated firmly, "NO!"

Sai paid a visit to River's attacker from the gas station. As soon as the man opened his front door, Sai turned the guy around and lifted him by the back of his neck and said, "If you ever spit or put your hands on another woman in your whack-ass life again, I will hunt you down."

Sai let the man fall to the floor with a large thud, leaving the man in a brain fog of confusion and deep concern.

Joshua and Violet had begun to manifest together on a regular basis. Violet loved how quick Joshua could change from coyote to mountain lion, as they ran through the Superstition Mountains. They couldn't seem to get enough of each other. Violet admitted to herself, on more than one occasion, that she was in love with Joshua.

Meanwhile, River was becoming increasingly strong and powerful, but also mysteriously agitated. She was more aware of her surroundings at all times, and that often made her raw with paranoia about every little sound. She stayed away from crowded spaces. She didn't even want to venture out to the grocery store. The need for peace and quiet became of the utmost necessity. Alex willingly took over the duty of grocery shopping and errand running. He didn't mind doing it.

River casually slumped into an oversized chair, her mind ever ready and calculating. Her fingernails were long, painted red to match her red lipstick. The bold changes happening outwardly coordinated with the changes happening inwardly.

Alex roared into the driveway on his motorcycle. Her heart secretly leapt, as she stirred from her position in the chair. Suddenly, Alex was in the doorway with a massive smile on his face. River stared into his eyes, feeling a faint memory from long ago, but didn't fully recognize.

"What do you want to do today?" Alex asked, excited.

River turned to look at the news on the television. In a simple expression, Alex got the hint that meant only one thing. Nothing.

"No more television. No social media. No cell phone. We are getting out of the house today," Alex said, ignoring her protests.

He pulled her to her feet and said, "Let's get on the bike."

River would've normally vehemently opposed the idea, considering Amy's death, but the new River understood that it was all a part of life, and sometimes shit just happens. It is all a part of the divine interaction. Walking out, River grabbed a helmet and climbed behind Alex, wrapping her arms around him and taking in the fresh scent of pine, sandalwood, amber and cedar. Down the road they shot, merging onto the highway and heading into the desert landscapes.

The connection was deepening between her and Alex. She didn't question it. She just existed alongside him. Every time Alex touched her, she found she wanted more. However, she remained reserved, resisting the urge for more. Alex pulled the bike off to the side of the road and parked near a canyon's edge.

"It's a beautiful place," Alex said.

"Absolutely," River agreed.

Alex grabbed her as she lost her footing on some loose rocks. She slipped closer to the edge. Pulling her into his chest, River's heart pounded. She wasn't sure if it was because she almost fell to her death or because she was so close to Alex.

"Be careful," he whispered.

He held her close to him … tightly. River nodded, shaking out a ragged, nervous breath. Alex led her into a slow dance, as the sun started its descent. He turned her around and pulled her back in close to him, continuing to dance with her slowly.

"Everything is changing," she whispered.

"I know. Just enjoy the ride," Alex sighed. "I only have your best interest in mind. You are very important to me."

River looked up at this man. For a moment she was lost. Alex pulled away gently and said, "You ready to ride back?"

He didn't want to take her back just yet, but he knew she didn't need any more confusion in her life. River didn't want to leave, but the words never flowed from her mouth.

"Come on let's go," Alex coaxed.

He lifted River up and spun her around one last time before they got back on the bike.

When they pulled back into the drive at River's place, they found

Charlotte, Charles and Erik talking with one another. Charlotte's long legs noticeably tensed up as she made her way down the steps toward River. Cupping River's face with her long, creepy fingers, she caressed her cheek ever so slightly with her nails.

"I came for my ring, but I see Kraylon may have already come for it. Do you think you could set up a meeting with him for me?" Charlotte asked.

"I will tell him you would like to see him," River said, Alex keeping close to River as a precaution.

"Excellent. Thank you," Charlotte said.

She was about to leave, but stopped and turned to River one last time and said, "I hope you will forgive me for our last meeting. I didn't realize who you were. I understand now, and I wish you the best in saving all of us who remain here."

River nodded without a word, displaying hardly any emotion. River, Erik and Alex watched as the strange Anunnaki couple took leave. The reality of the situation was hitting home. The time was near.

CHAPTER SIXTY-FIVE
Pleiadian Knights

Violet and Joshua ran urgently through the desert in coyote form. They were feeling Erik's empathic call.

This way! Joshua shouted empathically as they rounded a corner that would take them on a shortcut to Erik's cabin. Shots echoed in the canyon. Violet leapt over a rock. Losing her footing, she tumbled and rolled down a small steep. Joshua stopped in fear. He thought she had been shot.

"Fucking coyotes!" an old man on a horse shouted before aiming his rifle at the two wild animals again.

Shit! Violet, faster! Joshua conveyed.

The two ran quickly, jumping a wire fence as more shots whirled past their bodies.

Good thing he's a bad aim, Violet thought.

Just keep going! Joshua shouted.

Erik took another swig of whiskey, kicking the stool next to him. He finished half a bottle of the strongest bourbon he could find in his cabin. He was quite drunk and frustrated. With nothing better to do, he decided to go to bed. He was worried for River, and he knew soon they would have to face the demons who plagued the planet.

A knock came at his front door, but he ignored it. The knock became more persistent.

"GO AWAY!" he growled.

Erik moved a little, showing off his shirtless, muscular build as he sprawled across the bed. The knock came harder and louder.

"NO!" he shouted, drunk.

Erik buried his head into his pillow, thrusting his leg under the covers as he tried to get comfortable. He was hoping to pass out. There was a loud crack and then a thump as the front door burst open, nearly off its hinges. Erik sat up in shock and said, "What the?!"

Adjusting his eyes, he watched as a large, stout man dressed in jeans, a t-shirt and a cowboy hat approached. The man was carrying a large bag. Another man dressed similarly followed in from behind. Erik could barely stand, but he tried.

"Thomas? What are you doing here?" Erik asked.

"You're drunk," Thomas said, moving back slightly after getting a whiff of very bad whiskey. "Where's Amariah?"

"You mean River," Erik said, walking unsteadily back to his table and pouring another shot of whiskey. "She's at home. She doesn't like my company so much right now."

Thomas looked behind him, motioning with his head.

"Lars will help you back to bed, but we need to see her."

"Everybody wants to see her, but why are you here?" Erik asked.

Lars tried helping Erik to bed, but Erik shrugged him off and grumbled, "You may as well wait till morning. You can stay here if you want, but fix my fucking door first."

Erik threw himself on the bed and soon was fast asleep.

Violet and Joshua walked into the cabin naked.

"Lars?" Violet asked, excitedly.

Lars gave her a big hug.

"You need some clothes?" Lars joked.

"We keep a stash here," Violet smiled, as she went straight to Erik's closet.

"I see Erik hasn't changed much," Thomas said.

"No. He's still very attached to her," Joshua replied.

Thomas and Lars looked a little uncomfortable, as Joshua stood naked in front of them with his hands on his hips.

"Joshua," Violet whispered. "Clothes!"

"Oh, yeah! Sorry. Just a habit." Joshua laughed, pulling on a pair of jeans that Violet had found for him.

"How are things going on the Pyalexis?" Violet asked.

"Boring," Thomas replied. "We've been pulled here. We have word the Archon is preparing."

"Take us to River," Lars commanded.

"Sure. Come on!" Violet exclaimed.

They all piled into a 1960's muscle car that belonged to Lars and were on their way to River's.

"Okay. She's not answering," Lars said. "Let's take the door off."

"WHOA!" Violet said. "Slow down, fellas. No need to take her door off. She is in there, but she's waiting for Alex. She just got off the phone."

"Why?" Thomas asked.

"Alex told her if she had anymore weird nighttime visitors, she should call him or Erik," Joshua said. "Just to be on the safe side, especially after her ex broke in."

"So, has Alex taken the reigns? Because Erik looks a bit broken," Thomas asked.

"Alex was always her favorite high-ranking officer in the field," Lars smiled.

"Yes. True!" Thomas agreed, before letting loose an atrocious belch.

"We all fought many wars together," Lars said, adjusting his large stature and pulling a couple of custom knives from his pocket. "Just a few of my finest hand-crafted—crystal tips, agate filled with metal edges. The Archon hates crystal."

Joshua took a step backwards because Thomas and Lars were known for being a bit on the mentally-unstable side. They had spent too much time on Earth, and, unfortunately, there are always negative side effects to that.

Alex recklessly pulled into the driveway. He and Sai shot out of the car and walked toward River's front porch. Alex stood in shock when he recognized Thomas and Lars. After giving them a hug, his expression turned solemn and serious.

"You're here, so that means it is time," Alex said.

"Yep, old buddy! It is time," Thomas replied.

"Pleiadian knights!" Sai exclaimed.

Thomas and Lars didn't do well with newcomers, so they stood still and made no expression to Sai's comment.

"Who are you?" Lars asked.

"I am Sai, an officer of Sidar."

"Sidar ... huh? What's that about?" Thomas asked.

"Not sure what you mean," Sai replied.

"Just wondering what's that about," Thomas said.

There was an awkward silence.

"So, are we coming in?" Lars asked.

Alex texted River, asking her to open the front door. When she saw Thomas and Lars, she didn't recognize them fully. After a few hours of talking and Sai smoking weed, River decided it was time to get down to the business at hand.

"So, are you two telling me that you are here to assist me in battle?" she asked, looking at Thomas and Lars.

"Yes, ma'am! The battle will be in a dimension we know very well. It's pretty much like being on another planet. There is a portal access for us and ships, if needed," Lars explained.

"Thomas and Lars are two of your bravest knights," Alex said. "They will do anything and everything that is required of them in battle."

"My knights?" River asked, surprised.

"You are a leader to our military," Alex advised. "I thought you remembered that."

"Not really ... no," River sighed. "I didn't realize that it would all be to this extent."

"Well, you have an army, and I am here to go over strategic co-ordinates and plans with you," Thomas replied.

"An army?" River whispered.

"Yes," Sai said. "You are a leader of the most elite and highly capable. As is Michael."

"Who is Michael?" River questioned.

"You will see," Sai said. "You also should know Alex is your right-hand guard. He does everything. Michael is on your left."

Alex shot Sai a look of disapproval. He didn't want to overwhelm her.

"What?" River asked, turning to Alex.

"He's your heavy hitter. He's never let you down," Lars said, drawing a sword out of his bag and admiring it.

"The Archon is ready to make a move," Thomas said.

"How will they get here?" River asked.

"Through the thinnest side of the realm, which is now located in your backyard," Lars explained.

"Seriously?" River asked in shock.

"Yes," Thomas and Lars replied in unison.

"Where is Erik?" River asked.

"He's drunk as a skunk," Lars said.

"Really? That is strange," River muttered.

"Don't over think it. He's just worried about you," Alex said.

"Yeah," Lars agreed nonchalantly. "Because of the presence of the Blackhole Abyss. It's a place you could get lost in during battle, but don't worry! You will probably remember once you transition over."

"Blackhole Abyss?" River asked.

"Okay. Let's all calm down," Alex reassured. "That's enough information for tonight. Let's all get some rest, and we will come back to this later."

River watched the stars from the front porch while Thomas and Lars setup a tent in the yard. Violet and Joshua manifested coyote and took off into the night. Sai pushed through the television channels while Alex commented and watched. The only thing River could think about were the words "army," "leader," "Archon," "spaceships" and "Blackhole Abyss." It was enough to keep her from sleeping over the next few days, and at the same time she could feel in her bones that this was her life. It was who she truly was. She knew it was all true.

CHAPTER SIXTY-SIX
Battle Ready

The next two weeks were even more strange for River. Erik was oddly distant and drinking a bit more. Thomas and Lars were constantly roaming around, looking like wilderness hillbillies dressed in outback garb, hunting for food. River tried telling them there was no need to kill wild game when there was a grocery store just down the road. She convinced them to go into town with her one day. Thomas insisted on wearing multiple weapons strapped to his body. Store security grew suspicious and stopped them in the middle of frozen foods. Lars used Pleiadian energy to control the situation by freezing the security officer and sliding him across the grocery store floor with a flood of light. The trio quickly left the store, but not before Thomas zapped and short-wired all the store security cameras. River was humiliated, to say the least.

Thomas and Lars were already camping in her yard, along with Violet and Joshua. Privacy had become an issue. Thomas insisted on using regular work buckets for a toilet. Alex was working less, so he could be around more. Mostly, he just seemed to be on edge. His mind was stuck on the battle with the Archon. He did a lot of pacing up and down hallways and working out with Erik. Both men were mentally checked out. Sai stayed close, but refused to move into River's house. He didn't want to burden her. When he did visit, it was mostly just to chat with Alex and smoke weed.

River decided not to go back to Kenpo Karate class or any other class, for that matter. That was a very hard decision, considering she was pursuing a black belt. Unfortunately, she had become too strong for the rest of her classmates, and she didn't want to cause any more suspicion. She felt it best to stay away, so she threw herself into work—nurse by day and warrior by night, sparring with Thomas and Lars, mostly with swords.

"Are you thinking of Erik?" Alex asked out of the blue.

"Kind of. I am worried about his drinking," River sighed.

"He will be fine," Alex reassured. "Don't worry. This is just his way of numbing his thoughts. It's not who he really is."

River nodded, but she wasn't so sure. Erik was usually very sensible. Lately, he drank whiskey like it was going out of style and seemed lost in thought.

Erik sat beneath the trees in the backyard and took another shot of bourbon. His mind was reeling in respect to River and her protection. He was beginning to wonder if he was really just in her way. He tried think about other things, but he couldn't let it go.

Sai's vehicle pulled into the drive. Getting out of the car, he made his way toward Erik, ignoring everyone else around him.

"Yeah … so, I will just cut to the chase," Sai said. "It seems Coty, River's ex, escaped Sidar custody."

"What? How?" Erik asked, sitting to attention.

"Inside job."

"So, now what?" Erik probed.

"Just play it by ear. We are unsure if he will even return."

"Don't tell River," Erik replied.

"You sure?"

"Yes," Erik said. "There's no reason to right now. It will only complicate matters."

"Why are you so intense right now Alex?" River asked.

"What do you mean?" Alex replied.

"You've been pacing and fidgeting for weeks."

Alex looked out the window and said, "I'm fine. Just a lot of weird energy right now, and it's building up in the atmosphere."

"Do you want to watch a movie or something?" she asked.

"No," he responded. "I definitely can't sit through a movie."

"Should I be concerned?" River asked.

"I won't lie to you anymore," Alex said, straight up. "Yes, you should be concerned."

He stepped in close to River. Brushing some of the hair from her face, he whispered, "But no matter what, I got you."

Just then, Thomas and Lars barged into the house. They were dressed in highly-unusual clothing and strapped with even more gear.

"What are you two up to?" River asked, annoyed.

When it came to those two, she felt like she was babysitting a couple of ten-year-olds.

"Setting traps," Lars replied.

"Traps?!" River gasped.

She was starting to freak out.

"Relax. They are not for animals," Thomas assured.

"What are they for?!"

"For any Archon that may pretend to be human," Thomas smiled.

"Oh …" River replied.

She shot Alex a concerned expression and then shook her head behind Thomas and Lars' back. Alex squeezed River's shoulder lightly and said, "I'm going to run a few errands. Is there anything you need?"

"No."

Alex walked out the door. River collapsed on the couch, closing her eyes. She was going to attempt a nap, even though everyone around her was moving about and making so much noise that it was almost impossible to rest. She tried to drown out the sounds, but Thomas and Lars were setting up the loudest laser beam traps. They sounded like firecrackers every time they tested them. River decided to go find Erik, who was sitting outside next to Sai. She willed herself to engage in conversation.

"Erik, are you okay?" she asked.

"I'm okay. How about you?"

"It's really noisy around here—no privacy," she said.

Sai and Erik both chuckled.

"Thomas and Lars are very unique individuals," Sai smiled. "Some say they have been to Earth one too many times, and that's why they are the way they are. They volunteer as often as they can and because they are so skilled, fearless and experienced, they pretty much get whatever they want."

"Oh," River sighed, laying back onto the ground and watching the trees sway in the breeze above her.

Suddenly the ground rippled and rumbled, abruptly shifting beneath them.

"What? Is it an earthquake?" River panicked.

"I don't know," Sai said. "I don't think so."

"Hey, you guys! Better come over here!" Thomas screamed.

Sai, Erik and River found their feet and ran over to the far side of the trees. River gasped, her heart catching in her throat. Tequita was in the form of a black jaguar, her five warriors standing behind her with swords drawn. Astrayak and Abra were looking at her with serious, mighty expressions. River was unable to catch her breath. Tequita restlessly pounced back and forth, roaring so loudly it made everyone jump.

"It is time, River. You must come," Astrayak commanded.

"Tequita," River murmured.

Tequita stopped moving long enough to flash her beautiful, emerald eyes at her. Erik turned to River. He was nervous for her and for himself. They both felt each other's anxiety rising.

"Come," Astrayak commanded.

They all moved forward with caution into the forest. River suddenly stopped and shouted, "WAIT! WHAT ABOUT ALEX?!"

"There's no time, River," Abra said.

Tequita roared again and then leapt into the forest. The trees opened up for her. Everyone followed at a slow jog behind Tequita. Sai grabbed River, throwing her onto his back as they passed through a triangular energy field of light. A shower of gold dust fell to the forest floor, as a curtain of swirling, bold colors filtered in front of them. River noticed everyone was moving so fast. She could see faint traces of their body images lagging and that was it. Within a moment they were thrust through a portal door that carried them all into the next dimension. They landed feet first onto a deserted wasteland, void of vegetation and trees. There were dark, jagged mountains as far as the eye could see, but nothing green existed. They were not on New Earth or in the Amazon Jungle.

There were thousands of soldiers and warriors dressed in blue and gold fitted uniforms. Tequita had morphed into human form, but she was not in her usual goddess tribal garb. Her hair was pulled back tight, and she wore the same uniform as everyone else. River suddenly remembered something. This world was more alive and more real to her than any other, even the one she had just come from.

The one thing she noticed was that everyone had the same emerald, almond-shaped eyes and ears that came up to a point. It reminded her of an elf or a fairy from a classic bedtime story. Sai put River down. She got a look at herself, wearing a blue, fitted uniform. As she moved around, she noticed the fabric was absolutely great and she could hardly feel that it was on her body. Sucking in a big breath of air, she smelled the barren desert around her, and she wondered why there was not one living creature around.

"Where are we?" she asked.

"Planet Surya. It was ravaged by war and left desolate. Many who survived the war left for Earth thousands of years ago. We now use this planet for such times as now," Tequita explained, as four round, circular spaceships flew in and hovered high above them. "Your parents are here, Erik."

"I know," Erik whispered.

"This is a large army," River said, inhaling.

Erik could feel she was frightened. He wrapped his arm around her, pulling her in close to him and giving her a quick kiss. River turned around to find Thomas and Lars. They were no longer the crazy-looking men she had become accustomed to seeing. They were suddenly impeccably dressed in uniform, not to mention much younger, brighter and much more handsome. Thomas was amused by her astonishment.

"Yes. Well, we all have a role to play on Earth, River," Thomas laughed.

"Come, River," Tequita said, pulling River away from Erik. "I want you to meet a group of people who you have helped in the spirit world and who have helped you in spiritual battle, or should I say interdimensional confrontation? One thing though; they are not dwelling in your world on Earth in the same timeframe. They are from another time, one farther in the future from you."

River nodded and walked with her to a group of young adults. River stared at the young girl who looked quite similar to her. She recognized her right away. It was the young girl she helped jump from the Amazon falls. The girl seemed a little surprised to see River, as well.

"This is Tia, Fern, Nicki, Rob, Michael, Ben, Brandon, Crystal, Talon and Aaron," Tequita said, introducing them.

"I remember you, Tia," River said to the young, beautiful girl.

"I remember you, too. Thank you," Tia said.

River noticed Tia's sword. It was beautiful, almost unrealistically made. Nicki reached out to shake River's hand and said, "The name is Nicki. It's nice to finally meet you. I've heard so much about you from Michael."

"Michael?" River asked.

"Right here, River," Michael said, stepping forward. "We know each other very well. Long time, no see, my friend."

River whipped her head around to find a large man with huge elaborate wings. He, too, was carrying a large sword. Standing behind him were more troops with wings. They were in uniform, not the same as hers.

"An Angel?" she asked.

"You could say that," Michael grinned, his bronzed body and hair were almost too bright to lay eyes on.

"You and Alex … is Alex like you?" River asked.

River was interrupted by the sound of growling and the swirling of dirt. A wall of dust was picking up around the mountain. The dirt and the noise became louder and louder, almost deafening.

"What is this?" River asked, muffling her ears.

"The Archon is here," Erik said.

He fought the urge to run away with River, to board his parents ship—the Pyalexis. Erik gritted his teeth, knowing she had to be there. And he knew that he had to stand with her. River's energetic field was crucially needed in this battle.

River tried hiding her fear, but she was suddenly unsure of herself and what she was bringing to this battle. The sounds of the Archon became louder. It sounded like a multitude of chainsaws. It took her breath away, as she watched the troops coming over the mountain in strange-looking, recycled vehicles and upcycled aircraft carriers. Some were running on foot. River wasn't sure what to make of them with their deformed, half-human, half-animal faces and human bodies. Some were in alien form, large part human, part bird. Creatures soaring through the air, spitting green fire. There was no vegetation, so nothing burned. Every now and then a dragonesque-type creature showed up. River gasped at the sight of these ghastly and dangerous creatures. She was frozen in place.

"You will know what to do," Tequita said. "You are a leader. These are your troops. They wait for you."

River shook her head in protest. Michael grabbed her from behind, lifting her up and telling her to open her mouth. When River did as he commanded, she heard the buzzing of bees. They flew into her mouth by the hundreds, illuminating her tiny physique. Michael held her in the air, balancing her with his sword. When the bees disappeared inside of River, she closed her mouth and held them within in her. She could taste the honey dripping creamily and sweetly from her lips.

Michael lowered his sword. River planted her feet back onto the ground. After a few minutes, River was fully recovered, fully blessed and never so ready to do battle in her entire set of past lives. She kept her head down while she adjusted her stance. The Pleiadian Army waited and watched in silence. When she lifted her head, it was suddenly known. Everything about her had shifted. Flashing her emerald-green eyes of fire, River grinned. She was ready for battle.

CHAPTER SIXTY-SEVEN
Treacherous Ground

Alex had a bad feeling as he pulled into River's driveway. He had been feeling it all day, and it was growing stronger with every hour. As he walked through the house, he called out, "Anybody here?"

Stepping outside, Alex noticed there was no one around. A voice startled him from behind. He turned to find Violet and Joshua.

"It's just us," Violet said.

"What's going on?" Alex asked.

Violet could sense his anxiety and fear right away.

"They left," Joshua replied.

"Where have they gone?" Alex probed.

Violet pointed to the trees.

"We tracked their scent over an hour ago," Joshua added. "We could only get halfway into the forest. It wouldn't let us in any further than that."

Alex panicked. Realizing they all had crossed over to battle, he said, "There has to be a way in."

"We couldn't find it, but we can try again," Violet said.

"Okay, then let's get moving!" Alex commanded.

They ran to all sides of the forest and moved to the center from each side, but nothing opened up for them. Alex could feel the energy from the portal on the other side. He just couldn't penetrate it. Suddenly, all three of them could hear tribal drums. The pulsating rhythm grew louder and more intense. Alex, Violet and Joshua faithfully followed the sounds through the forest, and this time the trees opened up for them.

They stood before a swirling chakra of prism lights. This was it. Without hesitation, all three jumped into the triangle. They were swallowed into the portal entrance, traveling at the speed of light and landing in the midst of an ongoing war. War cries echoed all around them. Violet was instantly thrown into battle, alongside Joshua. He had manifested into a great lion, ripping the head off an Archon beast who had threatened Violet's existence. Violet manifested into a giant bird—ancient, beautiful and colorful. She took off in flight to find Erik and River.

In search of River, Alex ran at full speed, propelling himself from one clifftop to another. In passing, he saw his best friend, Michael, struggling to fight off a large, jagged-tooth beast with a sword. Michael was strong and powerful, but Alex stopped to help him out. He stealthily moved in from behind, pushing his light-filled fist through the beast's chest, as it dangerously stood over Michael. With one quick thrust, he savagely ripped the creature's heart out. Michael nodded in gratitude, as the beast collapsed at his feet. Alex lifted his chin, and quickly moved onward, as fast as his Pleiadian body would allow.

River fought fearlessly, quickly discovering that her whole arm could manifest into a sword. Tia and Crystal, from Michael's team, landed nearby, and the three helped each other out in the fight. They did not allow any Archon beast to live. Once it had attacked, it was as good as dead.

Erik was struggling. While faithfully watching over River, he was fighting off two to three Archon beasts at a time, and even though Erik was among the best warriors, it was taking its toll on him. His energy was quickly depleting. The Pyalexis ship, his mother ship, drew near to him. His concerned parents called out to him, begging him to come aboard. Enemy bombs blew up, throwing fire and shrapnel. Like rocket destroyers, they left behind wounded Angels and Pleiadian soldiers along the deserted battle ground. Alex swept over the perilous ruins, taking tight, tactically-sound turns, so to escape the surrounding danger.

River happened to catch Erik, as he struggled to fight off an ugly monster. It wasn't until she got closer to him that she realized it was Nordit (alias, Coty). Shocked, but not nearly as taken aback as she once would have been, she ran to Erik's side to help him defeat this terrible monster. She could see Nordit's tentacles had pierced into Erik's ribcage.

Nordit was mostly human, but for all intents and purposes, he was some sort of eight-limbed mollusk, violently releasing an electrical charge from his tentacles into Erik. This *thing* was torturing the man she loved. River screamed, manifesting her arm into a large, bejeweled sword. She stabbed Nordit through his backside. She could feel the warmth of his blood and guts, as he wriggled and wrought in pain. Yanking her arm out of this horrible creature, she felt a sense of restoration as it fatefully fell to the ground.

"Are you okay, Erik?" she asked, kneeling down beside him.

Erik slouched over, trying to recover. Before he could answer, Thomas and Lars backed into them, fighting off multiple beasts. River jumped in to help with Tia and Crystal by her side. Tia's sword was huge, powerful and full of ancient energy that stopped most of the beasts in their tracks. Some would even stop to think before they would go in for the kill. Some did not. Those brave enough, would soon regret their decision, usually as they fell into a pool of their own blood. Tia was fierce, hungry, highly admired and protected by her peers. Throughout the massacre, Tia wondered how it all would end. She heard those around her shouting, "STAND GUARD! STAY FOCUSED!"

River noticed that Ben and Rob had never left her side, even though they struggled to keep up with her. Distracted, she was grabbed from behind, thrown to a lower part of the cliff's edge. She grabbed onto a big boulder, bracing herself from a fatal fall. Loose rocks spit out from under her feet. River was losing her grip.

Ben, who was fighting alongside Tia, swung his sword, slicing off part of the wing of a dragonesque-flying beast. As the creature's clipped wing dropped from the sky, he noticed River was in trouble. Ben leapt onto the cliff's edge, gliding downward and catching her just in the nick of time, as she lost her grip from the rock. He scooped her up and set her down onto safe ground.

Ben wasted no time, jumping back into the fray to help Tia fight off yet another large monster. Spaceships roared past, firing missiles at the enemy. The Pyalexis was just the backup they needed. River was relieved to see the ship. A mountain in the distance shot off a brilliant array of light. River watched from afar, knowing what she had to do. She had to get to that mountain!

Taking flight, she moved onward with a power she never could have contained on Earth. Erik saw her and followed along behind, but he was injured, and his body was unable to move at normal speed. He could hear his parents empathically calling out for him, but all he could think about was River and keeping her safe. Therefore, Erik pressed on, fighting dark creatures along the way. Thomas and Lars kept close to his side, knowing he was weak. They helped keep the beasts from getting the best of him.

Meanwhile, Sai was communicating with Sidar. As the Sidar ship showed up, it dropped powerful, laser-like explosives on the enemy. It was enough to create a distraction. Sai was overcome with joy when he spotted Alex. He knew if anyone could get River to her destination, while keeping her safe, it was him.

Alex was fast. He literally flew like a flash of light to catch up to River. He had spotted her from afar, persevering until he reached her. Many tried to attack him along the way, but as soon as Thomas, Lars, and Erik saw Alex, they did what they had to do to keep the dark Archon away from him. The fight was wearing on Erik, but he wanted to help his brother get to River.

Tia fought alongside River, helping her battle monstrous beasts. As they climbed up the jagged mountainside, they both realized it was their destiny to be there. The light coming from the mountain was pulsating, and as they neared the opening, they both looked up and saw the Blackhole Abyss in the sky. It swirled with color just waiting to suck in the souls of the wounded and the dead Archon. Once they reached the top of the mountain, they followed the light and moved inside the cave.

"What is this?" Tia asked.

"Believe it or not, it's us. It's our light. It contains all the light of a Starseed," River replied.

"Where?"

"Just below," River smiled.

"Okay! Let's go!" Tia shouted.

The two jumped onto their backs and slid down the waterfall on a smooth slab of rock into a pool of murky water. Wading through the pool, they both noticed they were getting closer to the pulsating light. Just then, something massive grabbed a hold of Tia and sucked her under the water. Tia screamed, as River manifested her arm to sword and looked around for the young warrior. Tia's head popped up, just long enough to get a short gulp of air before being dragged back down into the water. It was a large anaconda-like snake, wrapped around Tia, crushing her bones.

Without hesitation, River cut into the beast multiple times with her sword. The snake screamed in agony, but still wouldn't release Tia. Alex heard River and jumped down the watery slide, meeting her in the pool of water. Ben was right behind him, and they both attacked the snake until it met its death.

Ben grabbed onto an unconscious Tia and carried her out of the water. River went to Tia, but Alex grabbed her and shouted, "No time! GO! GO! GO!"

River scurried to a cave containing a large, pyramid crystal that beamed with oscillating lights. She marveled at it for a moment, in awe of its beauty, but Alex commanded her to touch it so they could end this war once and for all. Even though she didn't fully understand, she knew she had to do it. River placed her hands over the crystal triangle. She could feel its magnetic draw. She clamped onto it. The sky suddenly grew dark, as the blackhole in the sky picked up speed and lifeless souls were being pulled into it like a vacuum.

Alex held onto River tightly, making sure she didn't lose connection with the crystal. A loud, forceful, sucking wind powered all around them, but the crystal would not let her go. It kept her magnetized. After a solid seven minutes, the vacuum suction around them stopped, and the crystal released River. The sky went back to its normal color. River and

Alex made their way out of the cave. They saw Ben and Tia standing outside, both smiling in victory. All four made their way back to the others.

River activated the light seeds who were asleep on Earth. The true awakening had begun. She listened intently, as Alex explained it to her on the journey back. This was all a part of a cycle the Pleiadians had been engaged in for thousands of years. Only this time, it had become more crucial, as the Archon fallen increased their army.

When they returned to where the battle had begun, medics from various ships were picking up the injured Pleiadians. Everything was busy, and River noticed the blackhole was no longer in the sky. Excited, she ran to Tequita, Lars, Thomas and Sai. She was met with their unhappy, sorrowful expressions. In that moment, she looked for him.

"Where is he? Where is Erik?" River asked in a panic.

She couldn't see him anywhere. Erik's parents rounded the corner. They were dressed in full uniform. In an instant, River knew exactly who they were. They knelt down and bowed before her. It felt like a large dagger had been thrust into her heart, as they empathically showed her and Alex what had happened to Erik. In an attempt to protect her, he had been wounded in battle, and even though Thomas, Lars, Sai and Kraylon tried to keep Erik from being sucked into the blackhole, it was of no use. Erik's light had drained from his body. He was one of the fallen.

River blacked out the images Erik's parents had shown her. She turned to Kraylon and screamed, "NOOOOO! WHY?!"

Kraylon wrapped his arms around her, attempting to console her, but there was no consoling her. River fell to her knees, consumed by the tragedy of losing Erik. It was too much. Alex and Sai picked her up and moved her aboard his parents' ship, as hundreds of soldiers watched in helplessness. River was given a light-molecule breeder. It brought her back to reality. She was aware of her surroundings, as she tried to stop the tears from falling.

Opening the closet, River put on a fresh uniform. She pulled her hair back into a chignon. Looking into the mirror, she noticed her hair and skin color were different. Her features were of her people. Sucking up her emotions, River went over to the window and commanded, "Stratus, I want to see out the window."

"Yes, Princess Amariah," the ship's computer board replied.

The window blinds rolled up, and River looked out into space. The stars, planets and cosmic images were all so familiar to her. She commanded her door to be opened, and she walked to the conference room to meet with Alex and his parents. All three were noticeably distressed.

"Send me back," River said.

"Why? You've accomplished what you were sent to do. It is done," Alex said.

"I am going to find Erik."

"No! Absolutely not!" Alex commanded, as Yilene burst into tears.

"You have no command over me, Alex. Send me back to Earth immediately. I will take a Saturn shell. I know I can find him."

No one could argue with her. She was a leader. She was royalty and Amariah was her true name.

"Right away," Alex muttered, storming out of the room.

Violet and Joshua watched on, as River boarded the small Saturn ship. They secretly hoped River would find Erik. Alex climbed into the seat beside her, and the two took off at light speed from the Pyalexis with only one destination in mind—Earth, the co-ordinates pointing to Apache Junction, Arizona. Landing on Superstition Mountain, Alex walked with River every step of the way. Neither one said a word, as they walked a handful of miles back to her home. Stepping foot into her yard, they both noticed there was no forest to be found—no trees. Alex wiped away a tear, knowing what he had to do for River in order for her to continue. It bothered him, but as he watched her return to that of a frail human being and he listened as her heart returned to its normal human rhythm, he knew what he had to do. In order for her to move on from this and for her to forget him and Erik, he would have to erase it all.

"I will start streaming coordinates. I know I can find Erik, Alex. Don't worry, I'm intelligent enough to figure this out," River said.

Alex knew it would be impossible to retrieve Erik from an interdimensional blackhole.

"I know you will, and when you do, everything will be back to normal. We will all be happy," Alex whispered, hugging River.

A stream of tears trailed down his cheek. Alex grabbed her by the back of her neck, making her forget everything she had recently gone through. As River passed out, he whispered, "I will wait for you when this is over. You move on with your human life, and I will be waiting for you on the other side. I love you."

Alex kissed her and then carried her inside. He watched her sleep for a while, but by the time she woke up, he was gone. River remembered nothing—not Alex. Not Erik. Not even her deceased friend Amy.

Groggy, she realized it was time for a change, perhaps a new job or a new location. She wasn't sure why. All she knew was this place wasn't working for her anymore. As for Alex, he boarded his parents' ship and broke down in his room. He cried for the loss of his brother Erik and for River. However, he knew that even though he was struggling with it, what he did was for the best. River needed to move on. He was comforted as the Pyalexis picked up speed and careened across the galaxy, Earth vanishing in the distance.